MUD

on the

STARS

The Library of Alabama Classics,
reprint editions of works important
to the history, literature, and culture of
Alabama, is dedicated to the memory of
Rucker Agee,
whose pioneering work in the fields
of Alabama history and historical geography
continues to be the standard of
scholarly achievement.

MUD

on the

STARS

William Bradford Huie

With an Introduction By Donald R. Noble

The University of Alabama Press
Tuscaloosa and London

Introduction copyright © 1996
The University of Alabama Press
Tuscaloosa, Alabama 35487–0380
All rights reserved
Manufactured in the United States of America

The Library of Alabama Classics paperbound reprint edition is a
facsimile of the edition published by L. B. Fischer Publishing
Corporation, New York, copyright 1942. Copyright renewed
1969 by William Bradford Huie.

∞

The paper on which this book is printed meets the minimum
requirements of American National Standard for Information
Science–Permanence of Paper for Printed Library Materials,
ANSI Z39.48-1984.

Library of Congress Cataloging-in-Publication Data

Huie, William Bradford, 1910–1986.
    Mud on the stars / William Bradford Huie ; with an intro-
duction by Donald R. Noble.
        p.   cm. — (The library of Alabama classics)
    ISBN 0-8173-0872-5 (paper : alk. paper)
    I. Title.   II. Series.
PS3515.U32M83   1996
813'.52—dc20   96-23433

British Library Cataloguing-in-Publication Data available

Cover photograph: William Bradford Huie, c. 1930s. (Courtesy of
Bachrach, Inc., Photographers, Watertown, Massachusetts. Used
by permission.)

"Where there is no vision, the people perish"
PROVERBS 29:18

William Bradford Huie, June 1984 (photograph by Leon Kennamer [a friend], courtesy of Leon Studio, Guntersville, Alabama)

Introduction

Donald R. Noble

IN 1928, WHILE STILL AN UNDERGRADUATE at The University
of Alabama, William Bradford Huie sold his first story to
True Story Magazine, a McFadden publication. Huie continued to write and sell stories through the rest of the afflu-
ent twenties, after his graduation in 1930, through the Great
Depression, through the war years and the cold war years
and the civil rights years and through half of the eighties. He
was working on several different books at the time of his
death on November 20, 1986.

Huie was a professional writer in every sense of the word
professional. He wrote for money to earn a living. He wrote
every day, usually seven days a week, customarily rising at
five A.M. to begin. He wrote fiction and nonfiction. He wrote
stories that interested him or touched him personally in some
political, intellectual, or emotional way, and he wrote stories
that he knew would interest others: in other words, stories
that would sell.

It is fair to say that Huie was never not writing, and the
results were remarkable. He published hundreds of magazine articles, in all the major magazines of the day. Huie,
over some fifty-eight years, published twenty-one books; fourteen of these became best sellers, including such classics as
The Americanization of Emily, *The Revolt of Mamie Stover*,
and *The Execution of Private Slovik*, and seven were made
into Hollywood films. *Mud on the Stars*, his first novel, published in 1942, was a huge success and in fact was made into

the movie *Wild River*, directed by Elia Kazan and starring Montgomery Clift and Lee Remick. Huie later told interviewers, "It sold for $123,000, and I thought that was a fortune. I didn't think I would ever be broke or need money again."*

In conversation, Huie liked to tell people that his first story, the racy little tale sold to *True*, had been written in the "*Sister Carrie* formula" and that most of the rest of his books were too.† This often-repeated casual remark reveals some useful truths. Huie's comment was intended to inform people that he wrote risque, controversial books. The part of the *Sister Carrie* formula with which Huie wanted to associate himself was the story of the girl who, arriving in the big town, in Carrie's case Chicago, becomes the girlfriend or mistress of increasingly sophisticated men and in the end moves to the even bigger town, New York City, where she enjoys fame and fortune as a musical comedy actress. When Theodore Dreiser's *Sister Carrie* was published, first in 1900 and then after legal battles in 1907, it was this sexually sensational element on which reviewers, preachers, and readers focused. Carrie demonstrates a dubious and utilitarian morality, and instead of winding up alcoholic, heartbroken, and dying in childbirth, preferably in the gutter as the heroine of a nineteenth-century cautionary novel should, Carrie gets away with it, beats the system, and achieves the American dream of respectability and prosperity.

Carrie's story is very much the model for Huie's *The Revolt of Mamie Stover* and several other Huie works. The sinful, sensational, and controversial dominate. But Huie spoke truer than he knew, for the *Sister Carrie* recipe, without a dash of naughtiness, is also the formula for Benjamin Franklin's *Autobiography* and the formula for numerous novels by Horatio Alger. In these books, as in *Mud on the Stars*, the protagonist, burdened with a cheap suitcase full of naïveté, moves from the country or small town to the big city and

---

*From interview with Martha Hunt Huie, Memphis, Tennessee, August 11, 1995.
†Ibid.

there *learns.* The title of *Mud on the Stars* could well be *The Education of Peter Garth Lafavor*, as the titles of many Huie books could be *The Education of Someone or Other.*

The education of the inexperienced youth is after all the quintessential American story, and a strong case can be made for Huie as a quintessentially American writer, thoroughly steeped in the traditional value system of rugged individualism, self-reliance, plain dealing, and independence of mind and spirit. Nevertheless, he was fully involved in the issues of his day, steadily learning, changing, and struggling to understand them, whether the issue in question was the coming of the "socialistic" New Deal to the Tennessee Valley, the Civil Rights movement of the 1960s, the sexual revolution, or the problem of international control over the atomic arsenal of the United States as the cold war grew into a larger and larger terror. A biography of Huie should perhaps be titled *The Education of William Bradford Huie.*

Mud on the Stars could be titled that, too. Despite the three-page disclaimer in the first person "To the Reader" at the beginning of the book, *Mud* is a highly autobiographical novel, as even reviewers in 1942, who knew nothing about Huie's life, sensed. This is not a problem, however; we know that the author, if talented, will include only the details that matter, omit the truly irrelevant, and bend the story of his life to fit his fictional needs. Huie does just this.

William Bradford Huie was born on November 13, 1910, to John Bradford Huie and Margaret Lois (Brindley) Huie in Hartselle, Morgan County, Alabama. It suits Huie's fictional purposes to have *Mud*'s Peter Garth Lafavor born three years later in 1913. Where Huie was first a farm boy, and then after his father became a railroad agent, a town boy, raised in a middle-class family, Lafavor is the scion of the fictional Garth Island. Huie's protagonist is the eighth generation of Garths descended from Peter Garth, who had been deeded more than three thousand acres, two thousand on Garth Island in the middle of the Tennessee River and more than a thousand for his services in the fight for freedom in South Carolina during the American Revolution.

Lafavor is not raised in what one would call luxury. Life on

Garth's Island is close to the bone, with the land providing a livelihood in whole or part for twenty "Garth families" and at least fifty sharecropper families. Life there is nearly feudal, certainly paternalistic, but secure. Success is measured by blacks and whites alike in such terms as whether the black families eat biscuit or cornbread for breakfast and whether Peter is sent to school in new or mended pants.

Most important, however, is that Lafavor sees it all as *right*. The protagonist of *Mud* is utterly convinced that life on the land is virtuous, that life in America is fair, that to the swift go the spoils, and that all things should continue as they have been. Peter Garth Lafavor expounds these very ideas in his valedictory address at Morgan County High School in May of 1929, just as Huie had done as valedictorian in 1927. Drawing on his own boyhood, Huie, in the first third of the novel, gives the reader a detailed account of rural life and race relations in the Tennessee Valley in the early years of this century.

Peter Garth Lafavor, like William Bradford Huie, moves on to The University of Alabama, in what is to many readers the most absorbing section of the novel.

At the university, Lafavor's experiences are typical. He is hazed as a freshman; he joins a fraternity; he travels on riotous "football specials" to away games; he loses his virginity in a local brothel. But some of his more unusual experiences would not have been possible before 1925, when The University of Alabama football team traveled to the Rose Bowl in Pasadena and won not only the national championship but also national attention as a university. The administration decided to capitalize on this fame and advertised the school in the metropolitan New York City newspapers. The university could boast of the championship football team, low out-of-state tuition rates, mild winters, and no "quotas," and it was quotas that were keeping many Jewish students in the Northeast out of some of the more prestigious schools. Jewish students came, four hundred in 1926 and eight hundred in 1927. By 1930, spurred on by the stock-market crash of 1929 and the subsequent depression, one third of the student body of The University of Alabama was

Jewish. Huie's description of the southern boys' reactions to this "exodus" is priceless. In the novel, Lafavor and his Alabama pals linger outside the Jewish dormitories to hear accents they have never heard and smell odors they have never known. But it is the assimilated Alabama Jews of Birmingham and Montgomery who are the most discomfited. In their efforts to distinguish themselves from the Yankee newcomers, they educate the Alabama boys into the difference between German Jews and Eastern Jews, established families and those they call "kikes." What a scene of cultural confusion it must have been! Sixty years later it is not unusual for a professor to ask a Jewish student from Newark how he came to choose The University of Alabama and hear in response: "My family has always gone to school here."

Among the fictional Jews in *Mud on the Stars*, however, there is one who rattles and reshapes the mind of Peter Garth Lafavor, Harry Lerner from Brooklyn. Harry and his ideological comrade Adeline Reed of Chicago are Communists, and although they never convert Lafavor to the Communist faith, they are powerful influences on his development. Lerner and Reed, as much as any people or any experience, help Lafavor to see the inherent injustice in the sharecropper system and the racism that is all around Lafavor but largely invisible to him. For example, unconscious racism is evident in the story Lafavor tells of his companion and retainer, Raccoon Charlie, who found another black man, Hawk Burton, "on his nest," that is, in bed with his wife. Charlie shoots Hawk to death, but the sheriff at Decatur doesn't act on it because both Hawk and Charlie have followed the unwritten social rules. Nobody, including Lafavor, seems to notice the implication here: that black lives were not really worth worrying about or going to court over.

Another aspect of Lafavor's ongoing education is revealed in an incident regarding his family. Lafavor is something of a spoiled child. His family has sacrificed more than he knows to send him to the university. Nevertheless, he does not take his family entirely for granted. Indeed, his powerful family loyalty is revealed in one particularly poignant scene. As Alabamians know, the state mental hospital, Bryce Hospital, is located adjacent to the university. This is the source of some confusion and much merriment, but no merriment exists when Lafavor goes with his psychology class to Bryce to be shown Case No. 4864, a patient suffering from both chronic alcoholism and chronic syphilis and now enduring the delusion that he is under constant attack from giant potato bugs. The class is seated, the patient is brought, and Lafavor realizes it is his grandfather, who has been taken to Bryce by his family without Lafavor's knowledge. Lafavor bravely acknowledges the old man, takes him by the hand, and leads him back to his cell. The reader is moved and pleased that the boy rises to the occasion.

One realizes in reading *Mud on the Stars* that Huie's strength, his most effective creative unit, is the long scene, the chapter, the vignette. Readers of *Mud* will perhaps be a little disappointed that the whole narrative is not more tightly woven. It is picaresque and somewhat disjointed. But in *Mud on the Stars* as in his other novels and in his books of nonfiction, it is the individual episodes that are often striking and memorable.

Huie had the ability not only to tell a powerful story in a limited space but also to arrange these incidents in *Mud on the Stars* so that they build on one another and reverberate. For instance, he first relates his version of the trial of the Scottsboro boys and then the story of Roosevelt Wilson.

In Huie's opinion, the Scottsboro boys were guilty. They *had* raped the two white women on the freight train, and the fact that the women were ignorant and itinerant was irrelevant; they were still unwilling victims. Through Peter Lafavor, Huie expresses his disgust with the propaganda generated by the American left, which claimed that the Scottsboro boys were tortured, kept in rat-infested dungeons, and starved, none of which was true.

The execution of Roosevelt Wilson, on the other hand, presents for Huie a clear-cut case of American racism. Wilson was a Negro found guilty of the rape of a white woman, although it was clear to everyone, including judge, jury, and press, that he was innocent. The woman had agreed to have sex with him in exchange for a ring and then claimed rape.

Roosevelt Wilson went to the electric chair because he was black, not because he was guilty.

Reading these two stories side by side in *Mud*, one sees Huie's methods most clearly. Each story has its lesson to teach; each reflects and illuminates the other.

The rest of *Mud on the Stars* from the time of Lafavor's leaving the university is organized mainly as a series of novellas. Lafavor takes a job as a reporter with the *Birmingham Press*; Huie went to work for the *Post*. As a reporter, Lafavor, like Huie, spends a great deal of his time covering the violent labor struggles at the mines and mills of the Birmingham area. The moral ambiguities here are not easy to sort out. As they are described by Huie, the steel companies, mining companies, banks, and power companies are dictatorial and greedy.

The big companies hire an army of Pinkertons to fight and break the unions. This private army is heavily armed and ruthless. Huie also describes, however, the methods used by the unions to recruit members and keep the dues coming in. Recalcitrant workers have their homes dynamited or are shot dead in their own yards or gardens. Throughout the novel, indeed throughout his career, Huie the journalist and Huie the novelist both know that every story has two (or more) sides, and in fairness, they must all be told.

Through the second half of *Mud on the Stars*, Lafavor continues his journalistic career until the national political movement to the left is intolerable to him. President Roosevelt's attempt to pack the Supreme Court, the rise of what Lafavor sees as communism in Alabama, and finally, the appointment of Hugo Black to the Supreme Court are more than he can stand. In disgust, Lafavor quits his job at the *Post* and begins his own right-wing weekly newspaper, the *Deep South Defender*, dedicated to preserving "Alabama as it was." (p. 234). In 1936 William Bradford Huie was the founder first of the right-wing *Alabama Magazine* and later of the *Cullman Banner*. (Huie left both these journals behind him and from 1938 to 1940 lived in California and worked as a free-lance writer.)

On a November afternoon in 1935, Lafavor marries his childhood sweetheart, Cherry Lanson, in Hartselle, Alabama.

Huie in fact married Ruth Puckett of Hartselle on October 27, 1935. They had been sweethearts since 1920 when Huie was double promoted from the third to the fifth grade, met Ruth, and fell in love. The Huies were married until Ruth's death in 1973.

Lafavor's move to the political right in the middle thirties is followed by the last, and in many ways the most important, act of the novel: Lafavor's conversion to the New Deal. Garth Island and indeed most of the family land is flooded by the Tennessee Valley Authority Project. The family fights this bitterly. To Lafavor and others, the Roosevelt administration seems to represent the rise of American communism and the end of the traditional American way of life. But *Mud on the Stars* is a novel of education, and Lafavor, who like Huie graduates Phi Beta Kappa from the university, is a highly educable individual. He comes to understand the injustices of the old way and the advantages of the new and finally goes to work *for* the same TVA that flooded his home place. His education/evolution is complete. The Lafavor who fought to maintain the quasi-feudal system of Garth's Island and who fought so ferociously to have the Alabama Legislature pass the Anti-Sedition Act, has become a man who believes in the power of government to provide the greatest good to the greatest number, and he is willing to fight and die to preserve this *new* American way of life.

As the reader is told at the front of the novel and reminded at the close, Peter Garth Lafavor is in the army, ready to be sent overseas to the Pacific theater. It is New Year's Eve, 1941. Peter Garth Lafavor's story ends there; Huie's story continues. William Bradford Huie was in New York City in 1941 and 1942, working as associate editor of the *American Mercury*, H. L. Mencken's old magazine. While at the *Mercury*, Huie published as nonfiction magazine articles many of the set pieces that would go into the novel *Mud on the Stars*, most effectively of all "The South Kills Another Negro," the story of Roosevelt Wilson's execution. It was typical of Huie, as a professional writer, to try to sell everything more than once, a kind of wringing dry of each piece. Also while at the *American Mercury* in 1941, Huie made the acquaintance of Zora Neale Hurston, the black anthropologist and fiction writer. Hurston had submitted several pieces that were not yet polished enough for publication. After Huie reworked the pieces, they were published with Hurston's byline. The friendship between Hurston and Huie endured for many years and was the reason Huie later got involved with the Ruby McCollum case in Florida.

At the *Mercury*, Huie became acquainted with a retired army colonel, Hugh J. Knerr, who was writing articles about the need for a greatly increased role for the Army Air Corps, as it was then called. Knerr, who was an expert consultant for the Sperry Gyroscope Company, was writing scathing pieces accusing the army and especially the navy of resisting the expansion of land-based air power. He and Huie collaborated on *The Fight for Air Power* and were to be coauthors. According to Huie, Knerr, who had been denied restoration to active duty a number of times, was put back on active duty so that he could be ordered not to publish this book. The book was of course published—by a German refugee publisher, L. B. Fischer, the same company that published *Mud on the Stars*—and there are white stripes on the dust jacket that indicate where Knerr's name was to have been. *The Fight for Air Power* launched Huie's nonfiction career, and in many ways the two serve as indicators of the directions his writing career would take. Both are "controversial," both "take on" the establishment and tell the stories of the dissenters, the ones who believe changes should be made, and both point out how those in power have many selfish reasons for wanting the status quo undisturbed.

The Fight for Air Power is part history, part polemic, part prediction: a typical pattern for Huie's nonfiction work. Huie sketches in the history of the debate, accuses the admirals and army generals of territoriality at the expense of American preparedness, explains how the attack on Pearl Harbor could have been prevented, and predicts that land-based air power will be *the* military tool of the future. As in much of his nonfiction, Huie is convincing and arousing—talents that were to be recognized by the military and put to their uses.

In 1943, married but childless—the Huies were to have

no children—Huie was sure to be drafted and so joined the United States Navy. He received a commission as a public relations officer in the Naval Civil Engineers Corps' Construction Battalions, the Seabees. He worked directly under Vice Admiral Ben Moreell and in 1945 published *Can Do! The Story of the Seabees.* This book, still readable and enjoyable today, tells the story of the Seabees who landed with the marines at Guadalcanal and Wake Island, Sicily and Salerno. Seabees had traditionally been civilian battalions, experienced civil engineers, carpenters, and so forth. They were put on a military basis in World War II and made a major contribution by building roads and airfields while under enemy fire, thereby incurring many casualties and winning the deep respect of many, even the U.S. Marines, in the Pacific campaign. Huie's book is laced with personal anecdotes, interviews, and photos.

As D-Day in Normandy approached, the Seabees were to be called upon to aid in the landing, mainly in the areas of underwater demolition and the clearing of obstacles on the Omaha and Utah beaches. Huie's second book about the Seabees tells of their contributions at Normandy, Iwo Jima, and Guam and the Pacific landings and battles in the latter half of the war in the Pacific.

By the time *From Omaha to Okinawa* was published in 1945, Huie had been discharged from the navy and was a civilian foreign-war correspondent assigned to the U.S. Navy in the Pacific.

As a civilian, Huie was free to write exactly as he chose, but there is no exposé here; the Seabees could hardly be praised enough. Nevertheless, Huie later said that it rankled navy brass that he did not have to clear his manuscript with them and that he got his royalties, which he had not with *Can Do!*

After the end of the war in the Pacific, Huie went back to the *American Mercury* and also returned to his old concerns with air power and inter-service rivalry. The navy brass was much less pleased with his next book, as the title *The Case Against the Admirals* must suggest. The subtitle adds information: *Why We Must Have a Unified Command.* During

U.S. Navy Photograph of William Bradford Huie in Correspondent's Uniform, 1945 (Courtesy of Martha Hunt Huie)

the war Huie had seen what appeared to him to be wasteful and dangerous competition and duplication in the efforts of the services. He remained convinced that the best way to achieve efficiency and rationality, especially as it pertained to land-based air power, was through the then hotly debated unified command.

The Case Against the Admirals put Huie in the national spotlight, where he was to remain for much of the next twenty-five years. His charges against the admirals and generals were sensational and controversial, with suggestions that money and even lives had been lost unnecessarily. The controversy launched him into his first nationwide lecture tour. Huie lectured thirty, forty, or more times a year for the next twenty years, earning very healthy fees for his talks and, of course, promoting sales of his most recent books.

Huie's military experiences in Europe and in the Pacific gave him material for more than just these four nonfiction books. Huie's two most successful novels would also be set during World War II and were, like his first novel *Mud on the Stars*, to varying and provocative degrees, autobiographical.

While in the Pacific as a war correspondent, Huie traveled extensively, from Washington, D.C., to Guam to Iwo Jima to Okinawa. As was often the case, his path took him many times to Hawaii, especially to Honolulu. There he noticed the book, *Honolulu Harlot*, by Jean O'Hara. Huie read O'Hara's memoir with great interest. O'Hara was furious with the hypocrisy of the Honolulu elite. They profited from prostitution, in conspiracy with the Honolulu madams and the Honolulu Police Department. The exploitative system lasted until the influx of thousands of military personnel disrupted this small, tightly controlled system.

Huie met O'Hara and spent about four weeks with her, researching the brothels and "the life" in Honolulu. Huie obtained permission to use O'Hara's material, and upon his return to the States, began work on his next and most successful book, *The Revolt of Mamie Stover*, published in 1951.

Mamie Stover was a *truly* controversial and racy book, and it *was* written in something of the *Sister Carrie* formula. Mamie was a poor, abused young woman from Leesburg, Mississippi, more or less forced into prostitution in Honolulu. Conditions there were as feudal as on Garth Island. Under a set of rules known as the Thirteen Articles, prostitutes were not allowed to own land or automobiles, have bank accounts, patronize first-class restaurants, live in certain parts of town, swim on Waikiki beaches, or even telephone the mainland. Mamie "revolts." She not only sets up a kind of sexual assembly line inside the brothel but also secretly saves her earnings, buys property, and becomes a

xviii

wealthy and respectable woman. The protagonist and narrator of the novel, Lieutenant-Commander James Monroe Madison, is Mamie's friend. (Madison, Huie's fictional alter-ego, is also the protagonist/narrator of *The Americanization of Emily* and becomes Emily's lover in the novel.)

The Revolt of Mamie Stover is a titillating comedy. The novel sold more than five million copies in several languages, and in 1956, Twentieth-Century Fox made it into a film starring Jane Russell. *Mud on the Stars* had been a best seller; *Mamie* was a bonanza.

Huie had spent much of the war in England as a public relations officer for Admiral Moreell. Besides writing *Can Do!* Huie was a "dogsbody," a go-fer and aide to senior naval officers. As D-Day approached, these officers became increasingly anxious over whether the U.S. Navy, which would provide the armada with transport across the Channel but not actually go ashore to fight in France, would receive adequate recognition. A scheme was hatched to highlight the contribution of the naval bombardment, particularly of the underwater demolition teams, by sending a crew to film them while at work, under fire. The title of the film was to be *The Navy in Normandy*. Huie would tell afterwards that he was not merely *on* Omaha Beach on D-Day, the sixth of June, 1944, but that he was perhaps the *first* American ashore on D-Day, with a film crew, to make a record of the frogmen blowing up beach obstacles and to film the LSTs filled with navy pilots, landing and disgorging the soldiers.

Huie's story was that his own LST was swamped, most of the men and all of the equipment lost, and that he spent the first several hours of D-Day crouched behind beach bulwarks hiding from German fire. As readers of *The Americanization of Emily* (1959) or viewers of the film—the screenplay for which was written by Paddy Chayefsky and which starred James Garner, Julie Andrews, and Melvin Douglas—know, Huie's experiences are recreated in the climactic scenes of that fine story.

Emily is not a documentary, however, but rather a tragi- or "dark" comedy, filled with irony, often sarcasm, bordering on absurdity. The admiral's scheme for the film is depicted as mad; he has suffered a nervous breakdown. The American officers in England are overpaid, oversexed, overfed, and in fact constitute something of an army of occupation to the war-exhausted British. Emily and her family have endured the Blitz; she has lost her brother and her fiancé. The British have suffered shortages and rationing and have not seen fresh fruit in several years; the Americans fly in steak, chocolate, nylons, and bananas from America. The "Americanization" of Emily is in a benign way the seduction of Emily from wartime austerity to American luxuries. Huie saw both sides to the story of the Americans' being "over there."

These two wartime novels were written over a period of thirteen years, during which time Huie was preternaturally busy. He traveled the country as a lecturer, speaking in at least thirty different cities per year. In that same period, Huie bought the magazine the *American Mercury* and made himself editor-in-chief. He published his own stories and articles in a steady stream, indeed a torrent; in addition, from 1950 to 1953, he was the co-host/interviewer on the television show *Chronoscope*, a forerunner of public affairs programs such as *Meet the Press, Face the Nation*, and so on.

In 1954, Huie achieved enormous success with another controversial nonfiction book, *The Execution of Private Slovik*. As the public now knows, Private Eddie Slovik was the only American soldier to be executed for cowardice and desertion in the face of the enemy in the Second World War. In fact he was the first American soldier so executed since the American Civil War. It was such an extraordinary event that the authorization for his execution went all the way to General Eisenhower. Slovik's death by firing squad was particularly problematic because he had already declared himself and demonstrated himself to be unfit for any military duty, never mind combat. He had been drafted late in the war, after having been classified "unfit," and was a none-too-bright young man with bad nerves. He was also a self-confessed coward.

As is painfully clear in his sometimes poignant letters to his wife, the uneducated, inarticulate Slovik never seemed to grasp the seriousness of his position. He thought he would be put in the Fort Leavenworth Stockade for a few months, but officials in the army, worried about desertions, needed to make an example of him after the scare of the Battle of the Bulge. In many ways, *The Execution of Private Slovik* marks the beginning of a new phase in Huie's career, of Huie as voice for the voiceless, the explainer—not necessarily the advocate—of the little guy's position and point of view.

In *The Execution of Private Slovik*, Eddie Slovik is never made into a hero; that would be dishonest. But Huie makes clear that he was a scapegoat and a victim of the army's bureaucracy and nervousness.

When this novel was dramatized for television in 1974, starring Martin Sheen as Slovik and Ned Beatty as his chaplain, it ran for two nights and was watched by more viewers than any made-for-television movie until that time.

In 1954 Huie was literally called upon to be the voice for the voiceless. A black woman, Ruby McCollum, had been arrested in Suwannee County, Florida, for the shooting murder of the town's beloved white physician, C. LeRoy Adams. Contrary to all laws, local, state, and federal, McCollum was being held incommunicado. Zora Neale Hurston, then working for the *Courier*, a black newspaper in Pittsburgh, was denied access to McCollum, as had been every black journalist who had tried to see her. Hurston, whom Huie had helped and befriended several years earlier back at the *American Mercury*, called Huie.

Hurston thought that perhaps a white journalist could gain access to Ruby McCollum while a black writer could not. Huie went to Florida reluctantly, but when he also was denied access, he became determined to pursue the story. He so incurred the wrath of the local judge that Huie was arrested and convicted of contempt of court. It was soon widely known that Ruby McCollum and C. LeRoy Adams had been longtime lovers, had even had a child together, and that the judge, Hal W. Adams (no relation), and the rest of the local white power structure simply wanted to deny McCollum her constitutional rights in order to save the doctor's good name. The Florida State Supreme Court upheld Huie's conviction for contempt, but he was finally pardoned by the Governor of Florida. *Ruby McCollum: Woman in the Suwannee Jail* was published in 1956. Ruby McCollum herself was declared legally insane and spent many years in the Florida State Mental Hospital in Chattahoochee, Florida.

Although the book was not legally banned in the state of Florida, it was not sold there, because Huie's publishers wished to avoid the lawsuits that were threatened if it were distributed there.

The Ruby McCollum case was not a financial success for Huie. His expenses in investigating the matter and then his legal fees and fines were greater than his royalties. In fact, the case so distressed Huie that it affected his health and generated some medical bills as well. But there was something about this case and the Slovik case that goaded Huie into a line of work he would pursue for the next ten or so years. He was resensitized to the race issue in America, and he developed a powerful drive to tell the stories of individuals who had been abused by the system, lost in it, or ignored by it. This "obsession" of Huie's resulted in book after book. He published *The Hero of Iwo Jima* in 1960, following the career of Ira Hayes, the Pima Indian marine present at the flag-raising at Iwo Jima who later slid into alcoholism and despair. He published *The Hiroshima Pilot* in 1964, but in writing it he learned that the claims of the man, Major Claude Weatherly, who said he was emotionally destroyed by having dropped the atom bomb, were false, and Huie said so. This revelation did not endear Huie to the increasingly powerful "peace lobby."

Huie's interest in telling the stories of the disenfranchised and voiceless dovetailed perfectly with the events boiling around him, namely, continuing racial violence and the Civil Rights movement. Ruby McCollum was certainly one such small story of racial injustice, but the Emmett Till case was a watershed event. Historians now understand the importance of the Till case, as they did not at the time. David Halberstam, in his book, *The Fifties*, suggests that the murder of Till, a teenager from Chicago who *may* have whistled at a white woman in Money, Mississippi, and who told some other teenagers that he had a white girlfriend back in Chicago, may have been the real catalyst for the Civil Rights movement,

xxii

more important even than the Montgomery Bus Boycott or any other single event for attracting national coverage by the press.[‡] Till was snatched from his family's home, murdered, and his body thrown into the river, weighted down by a large cotton-gin fan. When the body was found and taken to Chicago, Till's mother insisted on an open casket at the funeral, so all America, on newsreels and television, could see what racists had done to her boy. This resulted in a national outcry, but the murderers were acquitted by an all-white jury. Now no one would ever know exactly what happened. But Huie, determined to get at the truth, met with the murderers in Mississippi, paid them each thousands of dollars, and got the facts from them. Huie in effect invented checkbook journalism, a commonplace now but unheard of then. Since the murderers were immune by reason of "double jeopardy," presumably they told Huie the truth. When criticized for giving money to killers, Huie would reply, "I'm not in the law-enforcement business. I'm in the truth business." He simply felt no other way existed to get the story and present the truth. The resulting magazine stories and the book, *Wolf Whistle and Other Stories* (1959), added to the horror Americans had felt on seeing the funeral films, and the Civil Rights movement received enormous support.

Huie, who had moved back to Hartselle, Alabama, in 1957 to live permanently, became active in the movement, but in a typically independent way. He was not a joiner of committees or organizations and in fact declared on many occasions that he was not a liberal, as he defined the word. In *Ruby*, Huie had announced, "I don't think any more of the rights of Negroes than I do of white men" (249). Huie was a *reporter* who wanted to cover the most important stories of the day, and he had a passion for fair play—the level playing field of which Peter Garth Lafavor speaks so eloquently in *Mud on the Stars*.

It was only natural then that Huie would go to Philadelphia, Mississippi, in 1964 to report on the murders of the

[‡]David Halberstam, *The Fifties* (New York: Villard Book, 1993), 436–37.

three civil rights workers, Mickey Schwerner, James Chaney, and Andy Goodman. Huie was a stringer for the *New York Herald Tribune* through these years, and his work on the Civil Rights movement appears there first and then in book form as *Three Lives for Mississippi* (1965), still the authoritative account of the great tragedy of that Freedom Summer.

Other reporters went to Mississippi, investigated, filed their stories, and left. Huie, based in Alabama, stayed, interviewed tirelessly, and then reworked his material into lasting, permanent form, so that the curious can go to the library shelf and get the whole story.

In 1967, Huie published his novel of racial violence, *The Klansman*, set in an Alabama town much like Hartselle. In spite of the even-handed depiction of the sheriff and many of the townspeople as decent folk, the novel caused an uproar in North Alabama, especially among Klan members. In July 1968 the KKK burned a cross on the Huie lawn in a much-reported event, and Huie's public appeal to Governor Albert Brewer, for the same State Police protection former governor George Wallace was receiving as a presidential candidate, was refused, setting off another round of controversy. Huie the writer was once again Huie the public figure.

Huie was often interviewee as well as interviewer, but never so often as in relation to his book on James Earl Ray, *He Slew the Dreamer: My Search, with James Earl Ray, for the Truth About the Murder of Martin Luther King* (1970). This material first appeared as three articles in *Look* magazine.

Huie infuriated many with this title, even though he concludes that Ray did in fact kill King and that Ray acted alone. Some thought it was wrong to "glorify" Ray by writing his story at all. *Many* felt it was wrong to pay James Earl Ray some $35,000 for his story. This too, the criminal's profiting from his crime, has become an issue in American journalism and law; again, as with checkbook journalism, Huie might be credited with starting it. During the writing of the Ray book, Huie was arrested again, this time for ignoring the judge's order against pretrial publicity. These charges were later dismissed.

He Slew the Dreamer can be considered the last of Huie's
xxiv

major appearances on the public stage. In 1975 he published a novel, *In the Hours of Night*, based loosely on the life of James Vincent Forrestal, World War II secretary of the navy and later secretary of defense, which concerned the international control of atomic weapons. *In the Hours of Night* was the first volume of what was to have been a trilogy, with the second volume set in Vietnam and the third dealing with the Watergate conspiracy. Huie wrote several more volumes of nonfiction, such as *It's Me O Lord!* (1979) and *A New Life to Live: Jimmy Putnam's Story* (1977), but his day was largely over. In 1974, the movie version of *The Klansman* was released and, in spite of starring Lee Marvin, Richard Burton, and O. J. Simpson, was a major disappointment. Ruth Huie died in 1973 after a long, painful, and expensive illness, and Huie married Martha Hunt Robertson on July 16, 1977. Huie's own health declined in the 1980s, and he died in his native Alabama in 1986, with all twenty-one of his books out of print. In his last months, however, he was writing his autobiography, alternately entitled *Report from Buck's Pocket* and *Recollections of a Loner*. These memoirs, still unpublished, are his last look at the most important years of his life, his boyhood in Hartselle, his time at The University of Alabama, and his years as a young newspaperman. Huie's instincts in his last days had not failed him. Just as Mark Twain was at his best when writing about the antebellum South and the Mississippi River Valley, Huie was at his strongest when writing about the events of his youth in Alabama—the events dealt with so powerfully in *Mud on the Stars*.

Mud on the Stars

To the Reader

THIS IS THE STORY of one soldier in the New American Army and of what he did and thought during the years from 1929 to 1942. I have thought of it as an historical novel of the Present.

You will want to know whether or not it is an autobiography. It is not. I am an Alabamian, born in the Tennessee Valley, educated at the University of Alabama, and I once worked as a newspaperman in Birmingham. I have written about a people and a section of America which I know. Most of the action is real. But the main characters and all persons mentioned herein, except the well-known ones like Mr. Roosevelt, Hugo Black, John Lewis, Tallulah Bankhead, and Aimee Semple McPherson, are fictitious. I have worked with the material of my experience, but in no case have I intended to imply any resemblance between a character in this book and any real person I have known.

You will want to know whether I have thought of Garth Lafavor as a "typical American soldier." I have not. After spending many hours around the Army camps, I am convinced that there is no typical soldier. This country is much too big and too complex to produce one man who can be called typical. However, you can find Garth Lafavor in the ranks of the New American Army if you search for him. I have met him. He is there, still a bit shell-shocked from the debunking blitzkrieg, still confused by all the terrible forces which have beat down upon him, and still fighting within himself for a new faith and a new belief in the nobility of Man.

In writing this narrative I have had but a single purpose. I have wanted to show how one young American has reacted to the national experience since 1929. I have sacrificed everything in an effort to keep the story honest and real. I hope you will find it free of tricks and fabrications. It is young men like Garth Lafavor who must kill the berserk brute, and who must build the new and better world. You will want to know his beliefs, his fears, his hopes, and his dreams. I have believed that you would want him presented to you as he is, and not as you would like him to be.

In presenting Garth Lafavor as he is, I have had to risk offending those who will resent some of his statements and beliefs, and the statements and beliefs of some of those he met along his way. You will find something about Jews in this story, and you may accuse me of being indiscreet in mentioning Jews at such a difficult time. Yet I find it impossible to present Garth Lafavor honestly without showing his reaction to the Jews he met. Jews, unhappily and unjustly, are one of the things this war is about. Jews will have to be considered in the new world which Garth Lafavor must help to build, and I believe you'll want to know what to expect from him. If you find him guilty of using generalities and half-truths in his reasoning, please remember that this is a human frailty common to most of us. I can only ask you to accept my statement of good faith and honest intention.

I have risked handling many hot irons in this story, not because of any desire to be sensational. You will note that I have neglected opportunities to be dramatic and sensational. I have handled these hot irons because I am afraid of the developing tendency to take the Short View of this war. I don't want to see this war fought for the simple objective of defeating Adolf Hitler. Hitler is an effect and not a cause. He is only the most pernicious of the outward manifestations of a Trend. I have never been to Germany, yet I have met a dozen Hitlers. Living in Alabama and in California and in New York, I believe I have met all the forces which have been working in Europe. The trend which produced a big Hitler in Europe and some smaller Hitlers in America is the result of our having lost our faith in God and our belief in the nobility of Man. We have come to doubt that men are noble, and unless they are noble, why should they pretend to the right of self-govern ment? I have met people in America who believe that men are little nest-fouling, nose-picking creatures for whom the lash is a proper weapon of Government.

I want us to beat Hitler, but if we become smug and self-righteous in the process, the fight will have been in vain. If we pretend that the Enemy is only in Europe or Asia and not also within our own borders and within our own selves, we shall fall short of the larger victory. This is a war in which we must conquer our own tendency to despise Man; in which we must regain respect for ourselves; and in which we must return to the belief that man can be a noble creature, created in God's own image, who of a right ought to be free and independent.

By fighting for the long, hard objective in this war, I believe we can win the world and win our own souls; but if we are content with a lesser objective, we may gain a temporary victory and still lose our own souls.

WILLIAM BRADFORD HUIE

I wish to express my appreciation to the publisher of *The American Mercury* for the right to include in this narrative such portions as have previously appeared in that publication.   W. B. H.

To the Roosevelt generation of Americans;

to the modern children of confusion; to the

fellows who, at the end of an era of cynicism,

were forced suddenly to stand in their tracks

and die for the proposition that men are

noble creatures, worthy to be free, this story

is dedicated.

IT'S NEW YEAR'S EVE. In three hours it will be Auld Lang Syne and 1942. We are likkering up in a honkytonk. The beetle organ, all lit up like a passionate gargoyle, is giving out with Remember Pearl Harbor. We are singing:

> Let's re-mem-ber Pearl Har-bor
> As we sail a-gainst the foe,
> Just re-mem-ber Pearl Har-bor
> As we did the A-la-mo . . .

What-the-hell have we got to remember about Pearl Harbor except that a clever enemy caught us with our pants down? Can't we arouse ourselves without using a blood-scent? But it's a lively drinking tune.

> We will al-ways re-mem-ber
> How they died for lib-ber-tee . . .

We are dancing. Crazy, jitterbug dancing by the guys from Up North, and close, hot, breast-feeling dancing by us Southerners. We've got women. Damn good women for soldiers on New Year's Eve. Cajun women and lint-headed women. Sticky, sweaty, sinuous, writhing women. You just grab a-holt, honey, and

hold on. They don't charge for it. They do it because
they love it. We've got likker and women and music
and moonlight. Big Louisiana moons and soft Spanish
moss and pine needles. And we've got to drink and
"make Mary," for in four hours we'll be pulling out
for 'Frisco.

It's strange how things happen. I never thought I was
the kind of guy who'd join armies. I hate armies. I hate
the whole process by which armies are built. I hate the
idea of one man being forced to keep step with ten thousand others. I guess I'm afraid of armies, too. I'm afraid
of what they'll do to me inside. I'm afraid it may be true
that to destroy a brute you must become a brute. Yet
here I am. Pvt. Peter Garth Lafavor of the New American Army. Great-grandson of the Old South. Phi Beta
Kappa. Beta Rho. One-time editor of the *Deep South
Defender*. A gentleman who has bathed twice in a single day, perfumed his arm pits with essence of tumble-
weed, and slept in silk pajamas. A scholar who once
wrote a thesis on "The Effect of Senecan Stoicism on
the Elizabethan Dramatists." A subscriber to *Esquire*
and the *American Mercury* and the *New York Times*.

Yet here I am. Pvt. Peter Garth Lafavor. Dressed in
the same Boy Scout suit that I "used influence" to
avoid wearing when I was in college. Being ordered
around by officious clodhoppers who require me to
grunt like a boar when I yank my bayonet out of a
dummy's belly. In an army you have to do more than
learn how to ventilate a man's guts. You also have to
learn to enjoy the act of ventilation, and you must
grunt to show your savage satisfaction.

All the things a civil man likes to do in private I now
have to do before a pushing, wise-cracking, waiting-in-
line audience. Even when I go to a brothel an MP is
there to herd me into line and ply me with the latest
Boy Scout advice, so I only go when I'm very drunk.
I wonder if I'll be allowed the luxury of dying in pri-

vate? If I get my bullet in Australia or India, I suppose there'll be a dozen fellows to watch me gag in the dirt.

War is a filthy, brutal business to me. There is nothing about it that thrills me. I have only one reaction toward it. It was inevitable. We are in it. So let's get on with the goddam thing and get it over. Let's don't waste any time on parading and band playing and flag-waving and trying to whip up our emotions. There is a berserk brute in the world trying to take advantage of our confusion and cross-purposes to enslave us. Before there can be any hope, the brute, in all his forms, must be killed. We must meet him on desert sands and in jungle mud. We must kill and be killed. We must strew guts and have our own guts strewn. We must hope that some day either we or those who come after us can build a proper world. But our job now is not to build the new world. Our job is to kill the brute.

Sure, I could have waited and gotten a soft commission in public relations. But, hell, if I come through this war I've got to live with myself, haven't I? And what this Army needs is more fighters and fewer press agents. Sure, I could have "used influence" again and done my fighting with benefit of a cushion and a water closet. But here I am. Pvt. Peter Garth Lafavor. Just another American guy whom the war caught up with. Just another guy who enjoys comfort and privacy in his own little world but who suddenly found a brute standing on his door step. Just another guy who, while he was hating and fighting some things he didn't like here in America, suddenly had to wheel around and confront the brute which was creeping upon us. Just another guy who suffers from confusion and cynicism inside, but who now must choke it all down until the world is safe for peaceful disagreement again.

And since I have chosen to share the blood and mud in this struggle, I am sick of those people who regard our winning as the inevitable result of a long process of sacrifice and attrition. I'm sick of those guys who

3

compose fine phrases about how slaves win the battles, but the free men eventually win the wars. I'm not so sure about that. The slaves have been doing all right so far. I want the free men to begin winning battles, and quickly. I want to make the world and America and a spot back in the Tennessee Valley safe for future generations, but I'd also like to make them safe for myself. I'd like to live on that spot back there in the valley in peace and dignity, so I want us free men to stir off our stumps and get on with the job of winning, and not leave the winning to a "slow but inevitable process."

There is an even more important reason why I want to get on with the winning. Like most Americans, I, too, am fighting on two fronts. I am prepared to fight the brute wherever I contact him, but I must also fight within myself for the new faith which we, somehow, must find and hold.

The war caught me sadly short of faith. By struggling, I feel that I have laid hold of faith, and by continuing to struggle I hope to hold it and make it a part of me. But I have made all the common mistakes and a few uncommon ones. I suffer from the cynicism born of my own experience and of our national experience. While I fight the brute on one front, I shall have to fight doubt and cynicism on the other front. The result on the faith front may be contingent on the result on the brute front.

Down here in Louisiana you have plenty of time to think. You lie out on your shelter-half under the stars. You feel the oppressive stillness of a swamp around you. You look up at the skies, and by fighting hard, you can see the Answer spinning like a star through its nebula. The stars are bright and clean, and you are glad you found the courage to join the battle against the brute. You know what you must do and why you must do it. You feel strong and sure and resolute. Then the Answer fades again into the white, gaseous mass.

4

Mud collects on the stars. The ground feels hard and you toss about nervously. You feel yourself saying: What-the-hell? Then comes: Why-the-hell? Then, in a moment, the old one: Am I my brother's keeper?

You think of all the things you hate and fear in America. You think of some Red bastard who's going to stay at home and try to take what you've got while you are gone. You think of people in high places who use their influence to help their friends get commissions to save humanity. You think of Old Senator Pusselgut hiding in an artificial fog of patriotism while he votes himself a fat pension. You think of labor unions striking in a shipyard over "jurisdiction"; of a Great Industrialist saving democracy at a four hundred percent profit; of farmers squawking for "parity and more parity"; and of all the little American pressure groups tugging away like dogs over a bone while you sleep between two cotton rows. Your belly-knot of cynicism rises, and you flop over and mutter: "Goddam!"

But you must hold on, fight like hell against that belly-knot, and pray for the clean, clear stars to come back out. For the chips are down now. It's dying-time again. Dying is easy. After you've been attacked, you or any man can die boldly for the record, even in a barroom brawl. But to endure armies and the whole sordid process of brutalizing yourself in order to conquer a brute, you need faith and a vision studded with bright stars. You need faith in God and faith in man and faith in yourself. You need to believe that men are grand and noble creatures, and that you are a part of a grand and noble movement toward a grand and noble end.

There is a shortage of weapons in the New American Army, but there is an even more tragic shortage of faith. The genius of industry, in time, will supply us with weapons; but it remains to be seen whether a genius will rise who will help us find and hold on to our faith.

We of the New American Army are like crustaceous animals. Our beings are circumscribed by shells. Shells which have grown harder and tighter and thicker with each passing year. Shells composed, not of calcium compounds, but of this cynicism and suspicion and lack of faith. Shells which we have developed to protect ourselves from the flying debris of blasted bastions. And shells which are the result of our own indiscretions.

I am twenty-eight now. I have had time to learn about shells—how one is formed, how it can gall your back, how it can restrict your view, and how you are inclined to crawl up under it when danger threatens.

But I have also had time to learn that faith and hope and an effort to understand can soften the hardest shell in the world.

1929

"THE GOOD LIVERS"

On a May morning in 1929 my shell had not yet begun to form. I was sitting on the stage in the auditorium of Morgan County High School in Hartselle, Alabama. Back of the stage hung the American flag presented to the school by *The Literary Digest* for using that publication in our current events class. From the walls the dusty countenances of Washington and Lincoln and Lee gazed austerely down. Before me sat a crowd of soap-scrubbed, god-fearin', prayin' 'n' propagatin' Tennessee Valley folks. There were dirt farmers and their wives and their uncounted broods in boiled overalls and starched gingham with flour smeared on their faces to take off the soap-sheen. Some had come in wagons with grown-ups a-settin' in cane-bottomed chairs and the young-uns a-settin' on quilts and a-fightin' to see which-uns could hang their feet out the hind-gate. Their boy or girl who had walked six or eight miles a day to school was a-graduatin' in town. There, too, were the town folks, one to twenty years removed from the farms, parents of the better dressed graduates-to-be, differing from the dirt farmers only in the texture of the soap they used or in the texture of their clothes. With me on the stage

7

sat my thirty-seven classmates of the graduating class.

We were a crowd of six hundred Scots-Irish folks, not one of whom had ever seen an orchid or heard a symphony. Not one of us had ever seen a fur coat or a copy of *Vogue* or a tile bath. Not one of us had ever seen an atheist, and few of us had ever seen a Catholic. Outside of the teachers and a lawyer and a doctor, not one of us had ever seen a college or a library, and not one of us had a remote idea what the best-selling book of the day was. We were the mud-bound multitude of the South. We were the people who explore the dust and never know there are stars in the sky. The people whose hearts scrape daily against the jagged rocks of reality. Who live close to mud and sweat and dung and all the soul-shriveling slimes of life. We were the people whose women's bellies are over-teeming with progeny which the Good Lord has willed. We were the people whose men struggle against patched patches on the seats of their britches, and whose women struggle against having to make their chemises out of flour sacks. We were the people who are often duped by leaders who despise us.

And yet we were the people who believed in the majesty of man. We were the people who believed a United States senator was great and honest because he was a senator. We were the people who sang of Zion and who hipped and hollered and wept when the band played "Dixie" and "The Star-Spangled Banner." And we were the people who supplied the greatest percentage of volunteers for democracy's army in 1917.

It was a proud day for these people; and it was an uncommonly proud day for the Garths. For I was the son of Mary Garth Lafavor, and I was graduating with the highest average in the twenty-year history of the school. I was going to make a speech. The mayor was going to present me with a medal and a ten-dollar gold piece. So from Garth's Island and from up and down river the Garths and our kin-folks had come to

8

share this proud occasion. They all sat together—forty or more of them in their starched and mended bests—all clustered around Old Mis' Ella and Mary Garth Lafavor. Great-uncle Watts Garth was wearing his wedding suit, the one he stood up in thirty years ago when he got back from the Spanish-American War. It was the only suit he owned except his overalls and jumpers. Great-uncle Crazy Tom Garth was wearing one of Grandfather Crawford Garth's old coats. They were all proud of me—proud because they know'd I was a-goin' to amount to something.

This uncommon pride extending beyond the immediate family may puzzle you. But you must realize that we Garths still clung to a conception almost dead in America. We considered ourselves a Family. All the others considered me not merely the son of John and Mary Garth Lafavor, but a son of The Family. That my name was Lafavor meant nothing; for when the Garth women married they remained Garths, and they reared their children to think of themselves as Garths.

I wish you could have been sitting on the stage with me that morning where you could have looked into the faces of those four generations of Garths. You would have seen a one-hundred-sixty-year-old American family still struggling to remain an entity; still fighting to fill the gullies in its eroded fields and to cover with a tattered cloak of family dignity its eroded characters. As if by a magnet your eyes would have been drawn to two faces. For Old Mis' Ella Garth and Mary Garth Lafavor were the drive-wheels of a family which since Appomattox had depended much on its women for both motive power and stability. The Garth men since Appomattox had been a mercurial lot, given to drinking, wenching, and fighting. But the women were of a stern stuff. Old Mis' Ella was eighty-nine and calico empress of the clan. She was my great-grandmother and in her fierce old eyes still burned that blue flame before which raiding Yankees and marauding Tories had quailed on another day. All the Garth women had that eye-flame. Mary Lafavor was Old Mis' Ella's grand-daughter and natural heir. Though uneducated and of the soil, she was one of those little, round-faced, high-breasted, ambitious women who drive hardest those whom they love most.

Around these two you could have picked out the Garth women by the eye-flame and the dominated, submissive husbands seated next to them. You would have noted the Garth men by their sensual, sun-and-windburned faces, and by an air which at first you might have mistaken for arrogance but which, on closer examination, you would have recognized as but the prideful self-assurance of men who live by and close to the land.

These were my people. We were the "good livers" of the Tennessee Valley. We were not aristocrats. We had no money. We had come from no English dukes or Scottish earls. We were of peasant stock. Irish and Scottish, with a pinch of French picked up in the Carolinas. But we were a proud and fiercely independent people by virtue of our land and our history. We were the sons of a Scots-Irish peasant, one Peter Garth, who came to South Carolina in 1765 and dreamed and sweated and prayed and propagated and fought a war to win land for himself; and who came to Alabama in 1785 to claim as his reward, for having fought in the Revolution, those two thousand good acres on Garth's Island and a thousand more good acres in the bottom-lands alongside it.

I was a Lord of Creation as I sat on the stage waiting to deliver my climactic speech. Sixteen, with a childhood made bookish in Morgan County by Horatio Alger, *Youth's Companion,* and *The Literary Digest,* I suppose I already had the too-mature gray eyes of the lad who has carried the burden of ambition from infancy. Since my father was French, I was smaller than

10

the Garths usually are at my age, but I had the strong Garth teeth and high cheeks, and my hair—now graying—was even then tinged in the temples. I had on a new pair of "English" shoes with pointed toes and a $27.50 tan suit which Hartselle's largest store had sent off for. So you can well imagine that I was exuding self-confidence.

When the exercises had run down to the line of the printed program marked: "Valedictory. . . . Ever Onward. . . . By Peter Garth Lafavor," the superintendent's introduction was brief. "This year," he said, "we are particularly proud of our Valedictorian. He is a member of the oldest family in the county. His ancestors settled at Garth's Island in 1785. Each school day for four years he has ridden horseback the sixteen miles from the Island to this school and back. He is graduating with the highest average in the history of our school. So I take pleasure in presenting Garth Lafavor, who will deliver the valedictory."

I knew the whole county was looking at me. I could see the Garths lean forward in their seats as I strode up to the speaker's stand. I cleared my throat and began:

"Mr. Superintendent, parents, friends, and undergraduates, we of the class of 1929 at Morgan County High School believe that we are the most fortunate generation of young men and women ever to breathe the free air of America. Ours is the rich heritage of all the ages. So at the outset we want to thank you, our parents, for what you have contributed to make this moment possible for us. Today we can tell you that we appreciate your sacrifices, and ten years from today we believe our lives will have justified them. For today is a day of opportunity. This nation was built as a byproduct of the energies expended by young men tugging at their own bootstraps. And today, more than at any time in human history, we can be whatever we want to be; we can have whatever we have the strength and the courage and the will to have."

11

Sirs, I was off. Gray heads born twenty to forty years too soon for that day's lush opportunities began nodding in assent. As I pranced up and down that platform, I Lincolned and Jeffersoned. I captained souls and mastered fates. I drew the opportunity canvas so broad that even in Alabama I dared recall that the current occupant of the White House had once pitched hay on an Iowa farm.

"There was a time," I exclaimed, "when young Americans had to seek out and make jobs for themselves. Wars had to be fought, new lands had to be conquered and new frontiers defended before work could be begun. But today, war, like smallpox, is disappearing from the face of the earth, and ready-made jobs are waiting for every one of us who wants to start work. Every business, every profession is seeking the energy and ambition of youth."

I plunged into my picture of the American way of life.

"The American way of life is to me like a great cross-country race. At intervals we young men from the high schools and colleges leap from the starting lines. Spaced along this great race-course are all the prizes for which men strive. The farther and faster you run, the richer the prizes become. The weak are outstripped by the strong, but there is enough reward scattered along the way even for the losers. Division of the winnings is neither necessary nor desirable. Except for taxes to provide for protection and maintenance of the course, every man is entitled to keep all he can fairly win. And this is as it should be."

I pointed to that big flag and every eye turned to it. I almost choked down with emotion as I described what Old Glory meant to me and to my classmates.

"That flag," I said, "flies as our eternal assurance of equal justice and equal opportunity in the Great Race. We shall never fail to look to it when we despair. For its stars and its stripes guarantee to every American

12

youth the right to stand in the mud and lift his face to the everlasting stars—and to achieve those stars if he can."

I'll never forget those faces looking up at me. Those poor, ignorant people believed every word I said. My mother was crying and my voice was so husky as I closed that the last of Emerson's words from "The American Scholar" were drowned in the applause:

" 'Give me insight into Today, and you may have the antique and future worlds.' "

You'd think that would be at least a lifetime ago, wouldn't you? Yet it was only twelve years ago. I'm not an old man dictating my memoirs. I'm twenty-eight—still young enough to join armies and go on crusades.

When the applause and nodding had ceased, Mayor Jim Beasley, who was also president of the Bank of Hartselle, advanced to the stage. "Friends," he said, "for several years now I have been worrying about who we could get to make our Fourth of July speeches when old Colonel Tompkins passes on. After today I think you'll agree we don't have to worry any more. Garth Lafavor has shown us that he'll be ready to take up where the old Colonel leaves off. So, on behalf of the city and the Bank of Hartselle, I want to present this gold medal and this ten-dollar gold piece to our outstanding scholar of the year. And I want to predict here and now that he'll be President of the United States."

What is this element in the human stuff which gives to each new generation of Americans such colossal talent for self-delusion? How is it that in every one of a million schoolrooms one little man can stand each year and solemnly declare himself to be a Master of Fate and an Architect of Destiny?

There I stood that morning, talking to the only kind of folks I knew in the world. My folks. The Yellow-Dog Democrats who voted solidly against Al Smith because he was a Catholic. The folks who deny that

13

Negroes have souls. The folks who worshipped Bryan
for fighting Darrow and the God-haters. And the folks
who, had they ever seen a New York Jew, would have
readily consigned him to the category slightly below a
"good niggah." And yet I spouted loftily about "equal
justice and equal opportunity." I couldn't talk about
the flag without tears coming to my eyes. The high
school debate that year had been about the soldiers'
bonus. I had eloquently opposed it as "an insult to the
manhood of America." What else could I have done
when all the Garths who fought in the Confederate
armies went to their graves without accepting a dime
of the pensions offered them? They would have starved
first.

I wonder why some Voice of Reality could not have
whispered from the walls that morning and said to me:
"Keep your chin down, son. You don't know what-the-
hell you're talking about. Don't be a damn fool. You
live in one little scooped-out valley that's a pin-point
on the world's surface. You think opportunity is spread
out before you, but they'll be calling you the 'Lost
Generation' in three years. You and your folks are
already an Economic Problem. You, too, will be forced
to fight a war. The most terrible war of all wars. You'll
be confused. You'll be commanded to defend a goal,
and you won't know which goal to defend. So keep
your chin down and don't be a damn fool."

But no voice challenged me; and, of course, I
wouldn't have paid any attention if one had. For I
was Peter Garth Lafavor, the smart-aleck hope of the
old Garths in May, 1929. We had been keeping cool
with a little man in a big hat who believed that the
best governed people were the least governed people.
The Great Engineer had announced that poverty had
been forever banished from these American shores. A
gangling young fellow called Lucky Lindy was still the
national hero. And when I walked out of the school
building with my mother and Old Mis' Ella on my

arms, I had never heard of Franklin Roosevelt. Nor did I know the name of the cartoon character who at that moment was probably sitting in a Munich beer cellar drawing maps of a New Ordered World.

2

The night after my speech I drove the eight miles from Garth's Island back to Hartselle to see my girl. She was Cherry Lanson. I couldn't remember the day when Cherry hadn't been part of my hopes and dreams. We were the same age; she was nine days older than I. And since we had been ten or eleven or whatever age it is that boys first begin having girls, Cherry Lanson had been my girl. To prove it there were carvings on many a tree where class picnics had been held and scrawlings on many a blackboard and back fence.

It seemed as if every great experience in my life until then had been shared by Cherry. The first time I ever played winkum at a party I winked first at Cherry. The first girl's hand I ever covertly held was Cherry's. And since the Garths were not a lip-kissing family, the only lips I had ever kissed were Cherry's.

We were fourteen when we first kissed, backstage one night practising a play. We had discussed its possibility for weeks while our hand clasps grew tighter and bolder. And on this night we both seemed to know it would happen. My breath was short as I spoke my lines and watched for the moment when Cherry and I would both be offstage and alone behind the scenery. When at last the moment came, I confessed I lacked courage for the final movement; Cherry set a precedent by helping me. She coyly held a red silk handkerchief with a black lace border over her lips, and I generated the audacity to place my lips against hers with the silk between. We could never agree who moved the handkerchief. But it was moved, and the gods must have stood at attention in Paradise while we clasped each other. For it was, indeed, a Tremendous Thing.

"Look, Garth," she whispered, "it's fifteen minutes till nine. We'll always remember the time, won't we?"

"Sure we will, Cherry."

"And if we're together you'll always kiss me at fifteen till nine every night, and if we aren't we'll think of one another."

"Yes, Cherry."

"And I'll always keep the handkerchief, and we'll give it to our children."

After that Cherry and I went out for all the school plays, because the practice nights provided luscious opportunities for backstage clinging. We suddenly became devout attendants of the Epworth League at the First Methodist Church. By going early to the Sunday night meetings we could steal many hot and precious moments in the shadowed church passageways.

As I reflect upon it now, I can't remember that Cherry and I were interested in anything else except our experiments with the delicious sensations resulting from the contiguity of young bodies. Women mature early in the Tennessee Valley. They expect to be wedded and bedded before they are eighteen. So while Cherry was a very proper little black-headed, black-eyed person, restraint was not one of her virtues.

My first lurid concupiscent dream was of Cherry's breasts pressed hot and naked against me. I was frightened and ashamed. I wondered if I should go to a doctor, and in desperation I sought counsel in that invaluable adjunct to the Great American Educational System—the boys' toilet. There I learned, in vernacular terms, that I had become a man and that I was now fully equipped to take Sally Shays, of the Senior class, for a long walk through the pine thickets.

It was the dream which stirred my first desire to feel Cherry's breasts with my hands. Through our clothing I had sensed their challenging softness when we kissed,

16

but until the dream I had hardly dared imagine I could ever properly touch them with my hands. The day Cherry was sixteen and we had our first formal date at her home, the chance for such a bold step was near. We could sit in her parlor before an open fire until ten o'clock, and after two years of furtive clasping back of school stairs and in church prayer rooms, Cherry and I were ready to take full advantage of such a comfortable occasion. Cherry was wearing one of those jackets which allows a hand to slip easily up under it, and I was certain she had worn it deliberately. Never before had our sensibilities been so convulsed as when my hand first made burning contact with the round handfullness of Cherry's breast. There is only one human action more thrillingly devastating. And we were little short of this. For soon our progressive experiments in sexual attraction had proceeded to where each session culminated in an emotional cataclysm which left Cherry's virtue intact but left me exhausted.

It was to this point that our affair had evolved when Cherry and I sat together on the stage and she listened with pride to the valedictory. So you can understand that I was exultantly happy as I drove the clattering old family Buick toward Cherry's house.

The top was down and the moon was shining. The kind of moon which shines brightest for happy people in river valleys. Cotton grows fastest when the moon shines longest, and the one hundred-forty-fourth crop of Garth cotton was growing in the moonlight. Cherry and I drove back out the East Road from Hartselle with my right hand lying in her lap; she was holding it with both hers.

Cherry said: "Garth, can you realize we aren't children any more?"

"Yes, Cherry, I think I can," I replied. "Graduating from high school is a serious thing. It's a mile-stone in our lives."

17

"Mamma married before she graduated," Cherry reflected, "and your mother did, too, didn't she?"

"She must have. She was just eighteen when I was born."

A tiny waft of fear swept across Cherry's voice.

"Garth, you know they say these days are the happiest days of our lives. That we'll always look back to them and wish we could return to them. You don't think we'll ever be that way, do you?"

I chuckled, condescendingly.

"Why gosh no, Cherry. We'd be foolish to believe that. We'll always have something better to look forward to. With the world like it is today, each year will always be happier for us than the years before it."

Along the road the green young cotton stalks were six inches high in the better fields, but in the anemic bumblebee patches they could scarcely push their heads above the clods. No wonder the Negroes said that a bumblebee could sit on the ground and lazily sip the nectar from the blooms on such cotton. Already, at eight o'clock, most of the unpainted shotgun houses were dark, for it was cotton chopping time and all hands would be up at four to sharpen their hoes and be in the fields at sunup.

We saw a lamplight framed in the window of the foot-washin' Baptist Church at Gum Springs. Old Soul-Savin' Ben Tapwood, the preacher, liked to go there alone nights and play the organ. Since the church was almost surrounded by a graveyard and the limbs of two big whiteoaks brushed the windows as the wind blew through, there were few intrusions on the old Soul-Saver's eerie recitals.

Cherry shuddered and snuggled closer to me as we passed the Morgan County Poor Farm, with the forbidding old porehouse sprawling up there in the sycamore shadows. She almost whispered: "Garth, did you hear that awful story about what happened up there?"

I was annoyed that she had mentioned it. "Cherry,

18

you mustn't think of such unpleasant things. Those creatures aren't really people. They are more like beasts." I instinctively put my arm around her to protect her from even the knowledge of such sordid goings-on.

Everybody had heard the story. An idiot girl up there had had a baby by Jess Harper, the drunken overseer. Jess had sent a colored midwife to smother it at birth, but the idiot girl had leaped from her bed, snatched the baby away from the woman, and run into the woods with it. Now they were both going to live, and I had heard my father deplore that where there had been only one idiot for the county to support there would now be two.

"That sorry Jess Harper!" Mother had exclaimed. "The county's got to run him off and get somebody decent up there to look after those people."

"Aw, what can the county do?" Father had replied. "Who else would have the job except somebody like old Jess?"

But now Cherry and I were coming into the bottomlands and so into the Garth acres. The air seemed to grow fresher. The moon seemed to shine brighter. The cotton seemed a little taller and a little greener. And the cropper houses seemed to nestle more contentedly in their shadows. I drove up to the Point, above Garth's Landing, where we could look down on the river and over to the Island. It was half a mile across from the Landing to the Island, and to go over you would ring the bell and Les Winters would bring the ferry.

Here was the three-thousand-acre world of the Garths. Here a Scots-Irish peasant named Peter Garth had seen his wildest dreams of land and liberty and freedom come true. Here Peter Garth, a successful revolutionary, had claimed his reward from a grateful new Government which he, Peter Garth, had fought to create. Here he had begotten sons and daughters to maintain and protect his new world where Garths could be free. And here seven generations of Peter Garth's sons had lived in simplicity, close to God and close to the land. And every son of Peter Garth had stood always ready to grab his gun and die for the maintenance and protection of the Garth World.

Over there on Garth's Island was the birthplace and the burying ground of the Garths. Over there on the island were the two thousand richest acres in the Tennessee Valley, while the other thousand acres lay in the bottomlands alongside. A mile wide and three miles long, the Island lay east-and-west in the center of the mile-wide river, and the river broke around it and held it in yellow arms of equal strength. Down-river were Decatur and the great dam at Muscle Shoals, and up-river were Scottsboro and Chattanooga.

"It's beautiful, isn't it?" Cherry said when I had stopped the car. "It's all so big and quiet, and with the lights twinkling in the houses, the Island looks like a big, tremendous ship floating on the river."

I squirmed to a relaxed position. "Yes, it is big, Cherry. And powerful, too. It belongs to the Garths and the Garths belong to it. You know Old Mis' Ella brings every Garth son up here on his twelfth birthday and tells him the history of the Garth world. She tells him that he is a part of this land, and that part of this land is his, and that he's got to keep it and add a little more land to it."

"I can see your house over there," Cherry said. "There's a light in the window. Your mother's waiting up for you."

"Yeah, she always does. Funny, isn't it? It's all right for a mother to wait up for girls, but it seems funny for Mother to wait up for me when I'm a boy."

I looked at Cherry for a long moment, and I thought of the little red silk handkerchief with the black lace border. To me Cherry was always a symphony in black and red. The blacks were in her hair, which cascaded

20

to her shoulders, and in her big, soft eyes with their long, curling lashes. One red was in her cheeks, but the deeper, darker, more sensual red was in her lips. There was an arrogant red hat perched over one ear, and she wore a black jacket over her red dress. She was mine. Angelic virtue to be worshipped under the sun; a Pandora's box of tingling sensations and surprises under the moon.

"Gosh, I love you, Cherry!" I said as she folded into my arms.

I have heard wise people pontificate against teen-age love, and I suppose they are generally right. But somehow they never sound convincing to me. For Cherry Lanson and I loved each other with a hot and full and noble love, the kind which grows more elusive with the sophisticated years. I wonder if some day our wiser descendants may not return to encouraging rather than discouraging young love; and won't it be ironical if they return to subsidizing young marriage with dowries for the bride and family land grants for the groom?

That night, with the moon shining above us and the Garth acres spread out below us, Cherry and I burned in each other's arms and dreamed of the world I would build. You notice I say "I" instead of "we." It's because of a difference between Cherry and me. I wanted a New World unlike the Garth world. I wanted knowledge and position and wealth. I wanted to go Out There Somewhere where my kind of world was. I wanted to conquer it and build it as I wanted it, then bring it to Cherry and lay it at her feet neatly sensual in those black pumps with red buckles. And Cherry wanted me to have this New World—but only because I wanted it.

"Garth," she said, "you know I'm not smart like you are. While you have been studying your books, I've never studied about anything but you. You have a lot of dreams and ambitions, but I have just one. I want to be Mrs. Garth Lafavor. I want to love you and

21

sleep with you and live with you and die with you. And I want you to always love me."

"I want that, too, Cherry," I told her. "But in order for us to love each other, in order for us to build a really BIG life for ourselves, I have to accomplish all those things I want to accomplish. If I ever quit going forward, I'm afraid I wouldn't be a very nice person to be around."

Cherry thought for a moment. "Let me tell you this, Garth, then we'll never discuss it again. You want to go to the university. You want to study law and you want to know big people and you want us to go places. Your mother wants you to do these things, too. If you're sure it's what you want, then I want you to do it. I'll wait for you and love you and do all I can to help you. But . . ." She hesitated, then went on. "But if I had my way you wouldn't do this at all. You'd go to college for two years. That's enough. Then you'd take a trip, maybe to New York. Then you'd come back and we'd be married the day I'm nineteen. My mother and your mother were married before they were nineteen."

"But Cherry . . ." I tried to interrupt.

"Wait a minute. Then we'd build a house in Hartselle or over there on the Island. We could be so happy, Garth. Just think of all your people who have been happy in little new houses over there on the Island. You could work with your father and grandfather at the lumber mills or on the farm. And you could read and write and study and we could continue to grow up together."

I kissed her and smiled.

"I love you for that, Cherry," I said. "But you don't know what you are saying. Life can't be that simple for us. Life is good here, but the people are ignorant and have no ambition. There's no money here, and it takes money to really live now. You want us to go out in the world where the people are clever and interesting. There's a Big Race going on out there,

22

and you want me to run fast in that race. You want me to get things for you and for us that will make us somebody in the world. We can't just rot here on the Island. Let's you and I run for the big stakes, and you can always be as proud of me as you were this morning."

She was sitting up on her knees in the seat. "But, Garth, how long will it take?"

"Well, four or five years in college, and then not more than a year to get started."

"Six years! We'll be twenty-two, Garth. We'll be old people!" A fear I couldn't tolerate was coming into her black eyes. I pulled her to me.

"We'll make up for lost time," I said. Then we clung to each other for two hours, indulging everything physical except the sacred *summum bonum* which we were saving for our marriage.

"We'll both wait and learn that together, too, won't we Garth?" Cherry said.

"Yes, darling." I meant it, too. The ideal was one man and one woman, so that's how it would be with me. I wouldn't be exploring any pine thickets with Sally Shays. And, by Heaven, I'd be setting some new records in the Great Race.

That was May 27, 1929.

3

I want you to know Morgan County as it was in 1929. For the Garths had helped to build it. Before its boundaries were marked out, the Garths had plowed its bottomlands. There was hardly a cornerstone which did not bear a Garth name. There was not a monument to war dead on which the Garths did not lead all the rest. I was a product of its way of life. My gods dwelt there. My conceptions and my hopes and my dreams had sprung from what I had known there.

In the summer of 1929, while the mills of Wall Street ground out new millionaires, life in Morgan

County flowed as complacently along toward nothing-
ness as the waters of the Tennessee River, forming its
northern boundary, flowed toward the Mississippi. Of
the county's forty thousand population, about ten
thousand lived in Decatur, the county seat; about a
thousand lived in Hartselle, where the county high
school was located; and the remainder lived on farms
ranging from thirty to three thousand acres. Except
for scattered dollar-a-day lumbering there was no industry, and Hartselle, near the center of the county,
and Decatur, on the river, competed for the farm
trade which was the county's life-blood. Each town
strove to elect county officials who would improve the
roads into one town and neglect the roads to the other;
and rival bankers stuffed their vaults with farm mortgages and reached out for more.

Government—local, state, or national—had done
little to interfere with the blessings of *laissez-faire*.
Outside Decatur and Hartselle there were no high
schools, and there was no public transportation to
schools. In a few rural elementary schools teachers
with "normal certificates" held forth for four months
a year for thirty dollars a month. Hartselle and Decatur
provided elementary training for perhaps three hundred Negro children out of a total Negro population
of twelve thousand.

In 1925, when I was twelve years old, my mother
bore her last child. I was in a welter of indecision
about the facts of life; for while I had been an interested participant, I had remained the sceptic in those
whispered councils in the boys' toilets. Even when
my cousins had illustrated their newly discovered
scientific truths with diagrams, my idealistic mind had
continued to rebel. But the night my sister was born
all doubts were burned from my brain in a night-long
agony I shall never forget.

Soon after supper that night my eight-year-old

brother, Gene, and I had been sent to our upstairs bedroom with the explanation that Mother was ill but would be all right in the morning. Gene was badly frightened and I was doing my miserable best to quiet him.

"Garth, you don't suppose Mother will die, do you?" Gene asked. He was sitting on the side of the bed, pulling off his shoes and stockings. His blue eyes were wet and his lips were quivering.

"Oh, no, Gene," I swallowed and assured him. "Doctor Persons is here. And there's Aunt Lula to help."

"But she looks so awful. She doesn't look like Mother."

We both had hung our black stockings over the foot of the bed when Gene suggested: "Bud, don't you think we both ought to say our prayers tonight?"

For two years I had been neglecting this chore by pretending to say my prayers in bed, but Gene still knelt before Mother and said his prayers aloud. And whatever my verbal contentions, I still knew that prayers were more effective when you were on your knees.

"Yeah, I guess we should tonight," I agreed. So in our brown domestic nightshirts and bare feet we knelt at the bedside. Gene asked: "Shall I say mine first, Bud?" I nodded. And in the unrestrained words of an eight-year-old and in the more stilted phrases of a twelve-year-old, we asked God to make Mother well.

We tried to go to sleep, but not a sound downstairs escaped us. Our fright turned into terror when we heard the first low, pitiful wail. We knew it was Mother and we knew she was dying. Nothing short of the approach of death could make her cry like that. Sobbing in gasps Gene clung to me. I clutched the bed clothing, too horrified to cry out. If Mother were not dying what power could torture her like that? Now she was screaming at intervals. Unnatural screams. Closer and closer together came the screams until the wailing had ceased and there was only one long, hideous gasp-punctuated scream.

It must have lasted two hours. I quit hoping for her to live. I wanted Mother to die. One moment I was on my knees praying for death to come quickly, and the next moment I was in bed with Gene, sobbing and cursing God for his cruelty. When at last I heard the baby cry and voices indicating the danger was past, I was too exhausted and hurt to be happy. It was true! All the filthy theories of the toilet tribunal were true! My mother could never be the same again. How could one smile or caress or hope or encourage after such a ghastly ordeal?

Yet next morning, when Gene and I went in to see her, Mary Lafavor was smiling radiantly. She stroked Gene's golden hair, patted my hand, and inquired anxiously if the apples and milk had been put in my lunch.

I didn't want to go to school that day. I was ashamed and afraid. I was ashamed to face the toilet tribunal which would be waiting for my confession of previous ignorance. I was ashamed to have Cherry ask me about the baby, for even then I knew Cherry would know everything. Women always know so much more about the realities than men do. Several times on my way to school I stopped my horse and turned toward the woods. I wanted to go down by the river and lie on the pine needles and think. I wanted to get away from all those creatures made in God's own image. But the smartest boy in the class can't play hookey. He has to face to the front. During the morning I kept my face in my book and didn't look at Cherry. At considerable discomfort I avoided the tribunal at the first recess, but when noon came I could avoid them no longer. Tight-lipped, head down and without comment, I walked in, confessed my obstinate ignorance, and confirmed all the tribunal's theories. And when the teacher openly inquired if the report of the new sister were true, I blushingly admitted the truth and added that her name was Leslie.

Years later I learned that Doctor Persons had not examined Mother prior to the night of delivery. Proper pre-natal care would have eliminated much of her suffering, and hospitalization would have eliminated much more of it. But in America's Golden Age of 1929 pre-natal care and hospitalization had not come to Morgan County mothers. Not even to "good livers" like Mary Lafavor.

Maxim Gorky once ascribed his ability to portray life so realistically to the fact that he had never known the convenience of a water closet. He considered the water closet a softening influence which removes men too far from reality. If Gorky were correct, there was no reason why the people of Morgan County should have lost touch with reality in 1929. Outside Decatur there were less than a dozen homes equipped with running water, and none of these was on Garth's Island. Ten years later a Government survey disclosed that eighty-five per cent of the rural homes had no toilet facilities at all.

I wish I could identify Morgan County for you as the birthplace of some important people. But, so far as I know, it has never produced a person of any prominence outside the county. The two important people who came nearest to coming from Morgan County were Joe Wheeler and Tallulah Bankhead. Old Fightin' Joe was a friend and hero to the Garths. His home was in Lawrence County, twenty miles down-river from Garth's Island. The Bankheads are from Walker County which comes near to adjoining Morgan, and in 1929 Tallulah was a legendary creature— an *actress!*—whom women discussed in whispers. The friends of the Bankhead politicians were always insist-

27

ing that Jawn and Mister Will shouldn't be blamed for the one black sheep.

No one I knew except the World War soldiers had ever been to New York, and I remember the vulgar display which an old money-lender made of his yard-long railroad ticket when he decided to squander two hundred dollars on a tour of the West. The only national mention made of Morgan County prior to 1929 was contained in the Government report which showed it to have supplied the highest percentage of volunteers for the Army in 1917.

Only two things of importance had happened in the county since the World War. One was the building of the Government dam at nearby Muscle Shoals and the other was the strike at the Louisville and Nashville Railroad shops at Decatur in 1922. Both had reacted to the disadvantage of the county. One had inspired distrust of Government; the other, contempt for labor unions.

Congress had authorized construction of the dam during the war as a military project. Its vast generators were to supply electricity for manufacturing nitrates for explosives. Work proceeded furiously and even though the war ended in the midst of it, the fever held on. Farmers in a radius of a hundred miles abandoned their crops to earn fabulous wages ranging up to fifteen dollars a day. Newspapers like the *Decatur Tribune* heralded a new era for the valley. Nitrogen was to be captured from the air and converted into cheap fertilizer for the tired lands. Industry, using the cheap, river-generated electricity, would rush to pump new blood into the desiccated arteries of the river country.

The day came when the dam and nitrate plants were finished, when the bands played "Dixie," and the orators foresaw a "Ruhr of America." A newspaperman interviewed Grandfather Crawford Garth and wrote a story about "this proud old family which still owns

28

the original three thousand acres which the Government gave to an ancestor for having fought in the Revolution." The story said in part:

"Crawford Garth is as much a part of the Tennessee River as the rocks over which it has poured here at Muscle Shoals for a million years. He was born on Garth's Island in the middle of it. Year after year the Garths have watched the river take part of their crops and draw off the richness from their soils. Now the Government has harnessed the river and is going to make the river give it all back. The Government is going to make the river restore the rich loam to the lands, new strength to the valley's muscles and a new abundance to the Garth way of life."

But the industries didn't come. The cheap nitrogenous fertilizers didn't come. The great dam was a white elephant hopelessly entangled in red tape. The *Decatur Tribune,* alongside its advertisements by the Alabama Power Company and the fertilizer companies, explained to the people that the dam could not be operated except perhaps to sell power to the power company; that the people should not expect fertilizer to be made by this cheap process since such action "would upset the delicate balance of the national fertilizer market." Power, no matter how cheaply produced, could not be sold below "a fixed and recognized standard of prices." And the big dam and nitrate plants could best serve the people by standing in lubricated idleness until explosives were needed to make the world safe for democracy again.

So while the prices of power and fertilizer remained "fixed," the proud people of Morgan County continued to plow their sallow acres and sell their cotton at prices fixed only by the grim law of supply and demand. And even this natural law was being rigged against them. For to "fix" the prices of manufactured goods, the Government of the Great Land of the Free was steadily raising its tariffs and thus making it ever more difficult for people in other lands to exchange goods for Alabama cotton.

The people had worshipped the dam as a Great White Idol which was to bring new life. Now they cursed it as a monument to false hope and Government inefficiency. They liked to drive down the broad, Government-built boulevards, now lined with towering jimson weeds, and curse the Government for such waste. And those whose business it is to provide answers for social riddles came from afar to consider the spectacle of a great natural resource, harnessed and ready to produce mountains of cheap fertilizer, wasting away in the midst of anemic farmlands from which a decaying people could no longer draw sustenance.

Hope returned briefly in 1921 when it appeared that the entire project might be leased to Henry Ford. The valley folks stood in the streets and waited for press reports on the proceedings in Washington. They stood bare-headed in the rain while Old Soul-Savin' Ben Tapwood prayed for Henry Ford. But when the power lobby prevailed and Congress nullified the deal, darkness settled like fog over the valley.

I had seen this happen. The Garths had seen it happen. And yet on the day when a passenger train pulled into Hartselle announcing with its black flags that the President of the United States was dead, we pulled off our hats and bowed our heads and shed a silent tear for a man we had never seen.

"He musta been a great man," my grandfather observed sorrowfully.

"Yeah," my father added, "it makes you sad when the President dies, even if he was a Republican."

Later on, we realized that we had wept at the death of a member of the "Ohio gang."

In 1922 the only payroll pouring into Morgan County came from the L & N Railroad. Two thousand men were employed at the company's Decatur shops. It was around these shops that Decatur had been

30

built. But in that year the long and bitter strike developed. The company recruited scab labor and the Governor called out the National Guard unit at Hartselle to protect it. I went with my father and grandfather to the train to see the troopers off. It was my first contact with the National Guard but not my last. A crowd had gathered to marvel at the machine guns and sabers. The crowd, including Father and Grandfather, was overwhelmingly for the company, and there were shouts of encouragement to the militiamen.

"Teach them damn strikers to appreciate a good job when they've got it," Grandfather yelled, and the crowd roared its approval.

Capt. Daniel E. Bingham, World War hero now in politics, made a short speech from the train platform. He said: "Law and order have been disturbed in Morgan County. And since the National Guard was created for just such emergencies, the Governor has ordered us to Decatur to restore peace and see that American citizens can work without being molested by lawless elements. You may rest assured we will do our duty."

There were predictions the train would never reach Decatur. It would be bombed. And the next day we heard excited descriptions of the scene at the shops when the Guardsmen had taken over. The strikers—men, women and children—had massed at the main gate to try to prevent operation. But Captain Bingham had made another fighting speech. He leveled six machine guns at the crowd and gave them an ultimatum to disperse in five minutes. Dramatically he counted off the seconds while his boys restrained itching trigger fingers. At the last moment the grumbling strikers shuffled off; but no one doubted that "the Cap'n would'a massacreed 'em" if they hadn't complied with his order.

Two weeks later I went with Father and Mother to view the scene at the shops. I saw the machine gunners dozing behind their weapons. And I saw for the first

31

time something I was to see many times in the future. Ragged, hungry children with clammy, chalk-white faces waiting in line for soup. Despite her dislike for strikers, Mother wanted to help feed them. But Father explained that the strikers were only parading them to excite public sympathy.

"Can you imagine a father who would refuse to work while his children starved like that?" he asked. And the question seemed to require no answer.

At first a faction in the county had supported the union, but gradually most of the people came to accept as true the newspaper charges that the union and Old Somebody who was a Socialist and who was directing the strike from some Northern stronghold were the cause of all the trouble.

The result was general disaster. The union lost the strike and the county lost the shops. For the railroad, either because of resentment at early support of the strike by certain city officials in Decatur or else because of technical improvements, decided it could run its trains all the way from Birmingham to Nashville without having them serviced.

So in 1929, at the height of the Golden Age, Decatur became a shell of the past; and Morgan County had only its sinned-against cotton to trade for the mechanical delights created by General Motors and General Electric.

4

Yet for some intriguing reason I looked out upon this land which had so little, this languid and bigoted world of the Tennessee which was the despair of the economist and the joke-butt of the sophisticated, this county where neither the *Atlantic Monthly* nor *Harper's Bazaar* had a single subscriber, and I had the monumental effrontery to call my life good. As I drove a truck that summer of 1929 hauling Garth logs to the Hartselle mills, I was conscious of no doubts or fears

32

but only of an increasing curiosity about this best of all possible worlds in which I lived.

I saw no "social problems" around me. I knew that we Garths, because we owned land, had more than most folks in the valley, and I knew that somewhere there were people who had much more than we had. But I thought this was proper. I read about the Rockefellers and the Astors and the Vanderbilts and the Fords, but I felt no resentment toward them. I was glad they could amass great fortunes. They were proper winners. They were proof that I, too, could win. I didn't want a great fortune like they had; but it was good to live in a land where a man could compete for either gold or laurel leaves and find no limits to what he could win.

Curiously, I remember that my first tinge of resentment toward great wealth was toward the Astors. It was long before I read Henry George. I read somewhere that the Astors had their millions because some ancestor had had the good fortune to own a large slice of Manhattan Island, and succeeding generations had had only to watch their millions pile up. They hadn't won prizes in the Great Race at all. I contrasted some Astor with Henry Ford, who had won his prize in the thick of the race, and I'm afraid some Astor became my first villain and Mr. Ford one of my first heroes.

I fervently believed that America was a land of equal opportunity. I didn't interpret this to mean that I had the same opportunities as Nelson Rockefeller or that a young Negro cropper on the Garth farm had the same opportunities as I. But I did believe that each of us had a corresponding opportunity to acquire those things which might bring him a supreme sense of achievement. The young Negro might want a cabin and a field of his own, a new banjo, fancy clothes and a Model T in which to parade before his women. I might want a larger home and field, a boat, a larger car and another variety of acclaim. Nelson Rockefeller might want

33

fame as a philanthropist or as a solver of international problems. To me it seemed that all three of us had an equal opportunity to obtain those prizes. There was room for all of us to run in the great race, and there were rewards commensurate with our striving.

Around me I was conscious of no "money" classes! There was no absentee landlordism. There was no leisure class, for there was no "money wealth." While other men in New York or Miami diced away ten thousand dollars in an evening, there wasn't a man in Morgan County who could have written a check for ten thousand dollars without impairing his land. Everybody worked. The more successful were "good livers," and the Trash were those families whose men refused to work and whose women had to take in a-washin' or whore around or be helped by the churches. It was inconceivable that any able man *willing* to work could have failed to provide the necessities for himself and his family.

The Garths, with about four thousand acres and sixty families of hands and croppers, were the largest landholders. If you had inquired about the wealthiest man in Morgan County, you would have been directed to Uncle Watts Garth. He, with Old Mis' Ella as his whip, managed most of the farm. Yet in his battered hat, faded overalls and rubber boots, you would have taken him for a cropper. He had the same lack of formal education, chewed the same brand of tobacco, wore the same kind of overalls, used the same cuss words, drank from the same jugs, sang the same songs, danced to the same fiddling, and went to the woods with the same wenches as the croppers did. Except, of course, he didn't drink after a "nigger." The only real difference was that he had the responsibility of dealing with the banks and dividing the meat and the meal and the flour and the sorghum.

Grandfather Crawford Garth shared with Uncle Watts responsibility for management of the Garth homeplace, but for a variety of reasons Uncle Watts was supposed to be "better off." Grandfather had been more reckless. His daughters had been more expensive. He had drunk more whiskey and spent more money on his women. But while Grandfather was stern and aloof and was called "The Cap'n," he could make a pair o' crap-shootin' mules pull better'n any hand on the place. And my father, who helped run the store and the gin and the lumber business, never hesitated to grab a pair of plow-handles when a hand fell out. There may have been places in the South in 1929 where landowners sat under magnolias and sipped juleps and dallied with their mistresses while their "niggers" toiled under the sun, but there was nothing like that in Morgan County.

Politically, we Garths were Yaller Dawg Democrats. When we thought of a Republican we thought of a bloated, cigar-smokin' carpetbagger drinking likker with a gang o' niggers and lettin' the niggers drink first. In the scale of living things, the lowest thing to us was a "yaller dawg." So we readily declared that we'd vote for a yaller dawg before we'd vote for a Damyankee Republican. But, of course, when a Republican became President of the United States our attitude toward that one Republican would change. He had become a Great and Noble Man. Nobody except a Great and Noble Man could possibly be President of the United States.

Yet politics was something we argued over but did nothing about. The state capital was a far-off place and nobody could remember who the legislators were. The Honorable Ed Almon represented Alabama's Tennessee Valley District in Congress for twenty years and during his entire service he received less than a hundred letters a year from constituents.

My idea of a statesman was Cotton Tom Heflin. Every two or three years he would come to the county for a Saturday speech at Hartselle. He'd eat dinner at my grandfather's, then we'd all go with the great man

35

to town where standing room would be hard to find. Grandfather and Uncle Watts would sit on the portico with him, and my cousins and I would worm up to the steps where we could look up at him. In his long, black coat and embroidered white vest, he would raise his arms over the crowd. From somewhere deep in the tympanous caverns of his belly his voice would start rumbling up to an eruption. He'd "thank Gawd" that he had been spared to return to give an account of his stewardship to "these, my people." He would then plunge into his inexhaustible repertoire of stories with the crowd always roaring for more.

"Tell the one about Old Aunt Annie and the lookin' glass, Tawm," someone would shout if Tom ever indicated he was about to discuss anything so dull as stewardship. Or another constituent would holler: "Tell us how you hoss-whupped that black bastard from Illinois, Tawm." And he'd be off on this perennial favorite of how he drove the Representative from a Chicago district out of the Congressional dining room.

In the end Tawm would reach his arms toward the heavens and gravely intone: "And now my dear people of the g-r-e-a-t county of Morgan, I have once again given you an account of my stewardship. I have once again eaten fried chicken with my old and true friends, Crawford and Watts Garth. So with your prayers adding strength to my muscles, I go now to continue fighting the good fight for you. Until I return may Gawd's richest blessings abide with you all."

Religion? We Garths were deep-water Baptists. The firing was hot and heavy between us and the Methodists, but by 1929 a few of us had turned heretics by grudgingly admitting that Methodists, too, could probably get to Heaven. There were no Catholics, so we hated Catholics. At singings you could hear that the nuns were concubines of the priests and that the Knights of Columbus were plotting to "slay the un-

36

born child" of the Protestants. We generally confused the Pope with the devil.

I had had a normal religious "experience." Mother had raised me to say my prayers, believe in God, and go to church at Gum Springs. When I was nine or ten the preachers told mother I was a "good listener" at the sermons, and each summer the evangelists turned the heat on me to be saved. The evangelists always came to our house to eat and spend the night during the protracted meetin's, and it seemed I was being a poor sport not to let one of them save me. A preacher and his revival were judged by the number saved. Saving young-uns was like shooting fish for a hot evangelist, so they didn't count like hard-hearted grown-ups. But they counted some. The best way to save young-uns was in groups, and to get volume every evangelist knew the old trick of stampeding a whole Sunday School class of young-uns to the altar. Three evangelists had already told me how much it would please the Lord if I would get together three or four of my cousins and all come forward and be saved together. But somehow I wasn't impressed by the group method of salvation. If I were to be saved, I'd prefer to be saved alone.

Finally, when I was twelve, I found an evangelist I liked better than the rest. The poor fellow didn't shout so loud about hell-fire-and-damnation; he was saving pitifully few souls, and there were whispered criticisms that the Holy Ghost wasn't in him. He had choruses of "Just As I Am" sung over and over while he stood pleading in the aisles, but he just couldn't shake us loose. I felt sorry for him, so one morning during the fifth chorus when he hadn't bagged a single soul, I moved out of my seat and marched down the aisle. Just a single young-un. Not much for him to show for a morning's preaching. But he seemed to appreciate it and welcomed me warmly into the Kingdom. Then all the congregation marched around to shake the new convert's hand. I saw Mother crying, so

37

I began crying, too. I never could decide why I cried, for it embarrassed me, but by 1929 I had almost forgotten the event. I went to church on Sunday, sang "Jordan's Stormy Banks" in a tenor more enthusiastic than musical, tried hard to believe what the preachers said, and kept what doubts I had to myself in deference to my mother.

I could never understand the Garth attitude toward Prohibition. We were all Prohibitionists and Morgan County was politically the driest spot in America. Yet the Garths and our Negroes had been making cawn whiskey for a hundred years, and we had openly and unhesitatingly stepped up production when the nation embraced the Volstead Act. The Garth boat, arriving in Decatur, always had a goodly shipment of Garth's Island Cawn aboard, and Uncle Watts boasted that he used whiskey profits to pay the taxes. The likker jug around a Garth house was as open and ordinary as the water bucket, and we couldn't conceive of its being any Government's damn business if a man took a tug. We were blindly patriotic and religious and law-abiding, yet we could never take Prohibition seriously; we supported the law at the polls only because it kept Kentucky whiskey out of the valley and safeguarded the substantial home market for the local moonshiners.

Only a few cantankerous fools have ever voted against Prohibition in Morgan County, and I am happy to report that in a revolutionary world the county today is still bone-dry, and its individualists are still fighting Government likker store competition and mass-produced stump water from Kentucky.

As for morals in the sexual sense, we Garths were exponents of the double standard. The Garth women were notoriously virtuous. From 1785 to 1929 there had not been a divorce in the Garth family. Garth women had borne no bastards and there were only a few births before expiration of the nine-month period of respectability for brides. Somewhere back in the

38

nineteenth century two Garth women had "gone off," and there were nasty suppositions as to what they had done, but no definite knowledge blotted the lily-white escutcheon. The Garth men were just as notorious for their wenching, and their wives accepted their profligacy as but another of a good woman's burdens. When a wench flounced her petticoat in front of a Garth, be she maid, wife, or widow, he stopped his plow or laid down his axe and took her straightway to the woods. It was a reaction as inexorable as the tides, and so it was accepted.

Only I, the student and idealist among the Garths, regarded sexual relations as something sacred and proposed to bring even my own chastity to the marriage bed.

5

It was late in July that summer when I went fishing with Raccoon Charley and Dan. It's the time in the Tennessee Valley when crops have been laid by and the dirt has been scraped off the plows and nobody works much till gather'n' time. It's the time when cotton has begun to boll and, like a pregnant animal, needs only to be left alone with its fruits. In small towns like Hartselle, one clerk is left in the stores; and he dozes back on the sugar sacks while the others lie on creek banks and watch a cork float on low waters seldom rippled by an errant breeze. It's the time when we have our 'tracted meetin's, our watermelon cuttin's, our all-day singin's and foot-washin's, and our fish-frys. At night, "niggers" go to dances and white folks go to meetin' and both groups chant wild, weird music and leap and shout and writhe and slap their thighs until rivers of sweat roll down their saturated bodies and young bucks run out the back door to the woods with their gals and writhe in sweat on a mat o' pine needles, then brush themselves and duck their heads in the rock-cold waters of the spring.

It's the time when "money food" like coffee and flour is scarcest, and when poor landowners like the Garths are hardest put to get money from the bankers to carry the croppers and hands until gather'n' time. It's the time when tempers are hottest and the big city papers despair of the Southern crime problem. When meetin's are broken up by young bucks a-fightin' each other on the church grounds and a-cuttin' each other with hawkbill knives. When heads are shot off with buckshot from double-barreled shotguns and jaws are broken by the impact of horny-hard knuckles. It's the time when "niggers" are lynched for attacking white women, and when tall, gaunt old white men take their "nigger wenches" in the back of their stores on the sugar sacks or on the shucks in their corncribs. It's the time when cows go dry and have to be driven to the bulls. When wells are low and whole families come down with the fever and lie for weeks on quilt pallets. When young-uns get runnin' sores and there's no money for iodine. It's the time when fat women rub raw galls on the insides of their fat legs and the sweat dripping from their flour-sack drawers makes the galls burn like hell-fire.

It was July in the Garth country.

Raccoon Charley and Dan had been planning the fishing trip for a month. You'd have liked those two. They were gay-hearted Garth Negroes of the fourth and fifth generation who worked on the truck with me. Raccoon Charley was perhaps fifty, though except for the white hair which gave him his name, he appeared ageless. Lithe as a catamount, his face was like good, well-worn leather, and his long, powerful hands could pick five hundred pounds of cotton a day. To Charley the white and black branches of the Garth family were one and the same—meaning no disrespect—and who am I to deny that his blood line had been bolstered with white Garth blood back through the generations?

40

Dan was his grinning yellow son, born the same day I was born.

"Man, look at dat old rivah!" Dan was pointing to the water appearing through the trees as the truck bumped and dodged stumps and neared the river bank. "Mistah Garth, we sho' am gonna ketch a passel o' dem big cats."

"What do you think, Charley?" I asked. "Does the water look right to you?"

"Sho' does, Mistah Garth. Jest as low and peaceful lak. Ef dat little breeze jest won't rise no higher, we'se gonna ketch a boatload."

At the sandy river bank the three of us piled out and began work on the trot-line, with Dan and me cutting and spacing the small lines and the Old Raccoon carefully adjusting the hooks and baiting them with the big minnows and crawfish. In trot-line fishing we use a great-line about two hundred feet long, and from this line we hang fifty three-foot lines at four-foot intervals. When the hooks and bait have been fixed on the fifty small lines, we anchor one end of the great-line at the bank and then, with the boat, we sink the great-line its full length out into the river. Back on the bank we sprawl in the sand, smoke, drink likker and spin yarns. When the spirit of either hunger or curiosity moves us, we run the line, remove the great, wriggling catfish, and toast thick slices to go with coffee and cawn pone. Then we return to sleeping and drinking and yarn-spinning, while the moonlight sifts down through the willows and the silence is broken by a bullfrog bellow from the far bank or a catfish lashing the water with his tail.

Only men who have good digestions and robust appetites and free-and-easy bowel actions and who find the life process simple and good within itself can enjoy this type of fishing. The Garths, black and white, had enjoyed it for better'n a hundred years. I enjoyed it in 1929.

We set the trot-line a mile down-river from the Island, and by the time the waning moon had come up over the high east point of the Island we had already eaten our first tremendous batch of golden-brown toasted catfish with crusty cawn pone and black coffee. For two hours before the feast we had whetted our already ravenous appetites with nips from the jug, and after we had run the line, the Old Raccoon had again proved himself the county's most skilled artist with a catfish and frying pan. Dan and I lay on our backs in the sand. Raccoon Charley sat leaning against a sycamore and when he sucked his pipe the glow illuminated his face like a censer before the face of an ancient copper idol.

"Ya know, Mistah Garth," Charley said, "dey says as how times is gittin' mighty hard ovah crost de rivah. I hears some o' dem niggahs is havin' to eat cawn pone fo' breakfus' dat aint nevah had to eat it befo'."

"Yeah, I heard about that, Charley," I answered. "It's too bad. But I think cotton'll be higher this fall, and Grandfather believes lumber'll go up, too."

"De Cap'n does believe dat? Well, ef de Cap'n believes it, dem prices'll go up."

Charley drew on his pipe, then observed further: "But hell, Mistah Garth, ah tells Dan heah and de res o' my folks dat, hell, we ain't got nuthin' to worry about. No mattah how bad times gits, de Cap'n and Old Mis' Ella an' Mistah Watts has allus give us biskit fo' breakfus'. And yore pappy and you, too, in yore time will do de same. Garth niggahs ain't had to eat no cawn pone fo' breakfus' since de Yankees cum, an' ah don't believe de day'll ever cum when we does."

I looked at the Old Raccoon and smiled in the darkness. "No, Charley," I assured him, "I'm sure you won't ever have to eat corn pone for bréakfast."

Only an old-family Southerner could have grasped the Raccoon's full meaning. Biscuit for breakfast is a social and economic self-measurement among croppers

42

and hands. Those who always have biscuit for breakfast regard themselves as successful persons of dignity. They pity and look down on the unfortunates who have to go back to corn pone during hard times. The first breakfast at which corn pone is eaten is a sad ceremonial at which the partaking family, by partaking, admit they have been deserted by their Cap'ns and have sunk to the lowest level of human subsistence. A Garth Negro or white cropper would relish corn pone for dinner or supper, but to have had to eat it for breakfast would have broken his spirit and made him feel that he had been cast into the outer darkness by the Cap'n.

Corn pone for breakfast among croppers is like a patch on the seat of the britches for a man, or drawers made of flour sacks for a woman among the landowning whites.

I thought of the night I came home from school with a tiny,three-cornered jag in the seat of my pants. While I fidgeted uneasily at studying, Mother had worked an hour until nothing short of a microscopic examination would have revealed where the hole had been. She held the pants up to the light.

"They're as good as new now, aren't they, Garth?" She was trying to convince herself as well as me. "No one can ever tell where they've been patched, for the patch is underneath and doesn't show on the outside."

"Yes, Mother, they're fine," I managed. But I was sorely troubled when I went upstairs to bed. I hung up the pants and examined them from a dozen angles. No, the mend didn't show, but I'd still be conscious of it. What if Cherry should notice? If only the patch were anywhere else but on the seat!

Next morning, with a heavy heart, I was pulling on the pants when Mother called.

"Oh, Garth!"

"Yes, Mother," My heart was leaping. I knew what she would tell me.

"I've been thinking, and I believe I'll give those school pants of yours to Dan. They're all right for you to wear, but Dan really needs a pair. So just wear your Sunday ones today and you can get a new pair of school pants at the store this afternoon."

I was like a child reprieved from a whipping, and Mother looked relieved when I went down for breakfast. And Dan got the finest pair of pants he had ever worn.

The women were the same way about flour-sack underthings. Had Mary Lafavor ever been forced to make her undergarments out of flour-sacking like croppers, she could never again have held up her head. When drawers are made of flour-sacking they take many washings and boilings before the flour-brand names fade out. And though a woman's dress may be spotless and freshly ironed, she is always conscious of "Grandma's Wonder" or "Mo-Biscuit" or "Angel Food" burned across her buttocks in scarlet letters; and when she hangs her washing on the line she knows she advertises her poverty to all the world.

You take a Southern white man who has ever worn a patch on his pants, or a Southern woman who has ever worn a pair of flour-sack drawers, and you'll find that they can't ever forget it. Though they gain the wealth of the Indies and acquire the poise of a Chesterfield, they know down deep inside that they are shams and that they can never be anything to themselves but ragged-assed and flour-sack-drawered Southern trash. In other sections of America perhaps the patch can be surmounted, but never in the South.

The moon was sailing high over the island when Dan raised up on his elbow. "Hell, pappy," he said, "when Mistah Garth comes back from collich, biskit fo' breakfus' ain't gonna be nuthin'. We'se all gonna have sto' clo'se and T Models. Ain't we, Mistah Garth?"

Before I could parry this suggestion Raccoon Charley cut in.

44

"Now der's jest whut's troublin' dis wicked world today, Mistah Garth. Folks jest wants too damn much. Why Lawd God in de mawnin', when ah wuz a young scamp ef ah had a new pair o' jeans an' de Cap'n lemme ride a mule to meetin' a' Sunday ah wuz happy as a daid pig in de sunshine. But look at it now. Niggahs an' white folks, too. Dey'se allus wantin' some-pin dey ain't got. Nevah satisfied with whut dey got. Niggahs want a T Model to eat up deir money. White folks gotta have one o' dem 'straight some-odds! Den dere's phoneygraffs an' dem new-fangled raddios."

"Yeah, Charley, we've made a lot of progress," I said. "I guess people have to have those things now to be happy."

"Dey calls it progress. But, sweet Jesus, ah kin 'member when ef ah had me a banjer an' a jug o' likker an' a gal to go to de woods with, ah didn't give a damn fo' hell. But jest look at dat Dan now! Ah tells yo', Mistah Garth, de whole trouble is dat folks jest wants too damn much."

"But pappy," Dan put in, "dey didn't have no pitcher shows when you wuz a-comin' up."

"Shet yo' mouf, boy. Yo' needs to be mo' thankful fo' whut you'se got an' whut we'se allus had."

I lay half asleep in the warm sand and listened to Charley and Dan carry on time's oldest argument. I heard Charley outline all the things Dan should be thankful for rather than wanting more. Charley's greatest source of pride was that he had never asked the Cap'n for money and been turned down. Cou'se he could 'member times when he had asked fo' a dollah an' got only a quatah, but he laughed and his white teeth gleamed in the moonlight as he explained how he had learned to get aroun' de Cap'n on this point. When he needed only a quatah he allus asked fo' a dollah.

Other things for which the Old Raccoon was grateful included the lil' extra he had always had for Christmas, the remedies he had never lacked for his ailments, a roof which never leaked, shoes during the winter, and a good church in which to hold his meetin's.

To look at Charley there in the moonlight you would never think of him as a murderer, yet only two years ago I had seem him murder a man as coldly as I would have killed a moccasin. And a year before that I had seen my first mob hell-bent on lynching him.

Charley's house on the Island stood three hundred yards from our house, and back of Charley's house the land rolled down for perhaps two hundred yards to a small creek. Beyond the creek was a hill thicketed with young pine. One late afternoon as I walked down the path toward Charley's house, I saw him go in the front door. At once a terrific commotion broke out inside. A young buck, Hawk Burton, with the fear of God in his face and struggling to pull on his overalls came falling out the back steps and plunging down the hill toward the creek. Behind him came Charley firing an old lever-action 30-30 rifle. As fast as he could run and manipulate the lever he was shooting at the wildly fleeing Hawk. The overall straps now in place over his shoulders, Hawk took a long leap to clear the creek and was heading up the hill into the thicket. Once inside the thicket he would be away.

Charley stopped short and went to one knee. Coolly, he sighted along the barrel, and I knew this time he wouldn't miss. I had seen him shoot bounding rabbits from the same position. The rifle cracked and Hawk fell as though poled with an axe.

"Ah got him, Mistah Garth," Charley said proudly as he raised up and saw me.

"Is he dead, Charley?" I asked.

"He shore is. No use a-goin' to look. Ah bow'd him rat smack through de back o' his black haid."

"What'd you shoot him for?"

"Why Lawd God, Mistah Garth, ah caught de black sonuvabitch plop on mah nest!"

46

Charley's young wife, badly disheveled, was standing in the back door with two of his young crop o' young-uns.

"Git in that house, woman!" he ordered.

Grandfather called the High Sheriff at Decatur and reported that Charley had "shot a bird off his nest," and the case was closed. Too bad, too. Hawk was a good worker. He should have been more careful.

A strange thing to me was that Charley wasn't particularly incensed at his wife. She was blameless, for nothing better was expected of her. Nor was Charley mad at Hawk when he killed him. He had known for weeks that Hawk was "tanglin' with his old lady." Hawk had boasted of it even to Charley. A contest had developed to see whether the "husband" could catch the interloper "on the nest." Charley had won the contest, had slain his game, and so he properly exulted as a winner. It was all according to the rules. Charley went blithely on begetting sons of his wife and other men's wives, and his wife continued just as blithely having his sons and other men's sons. But you were fair game when a husband caught you "on the nest."

The mob incident had come near to culminating the Raccoon's career at the end of a sea-grass rope.

Father and Grandfather bought cross-ties from the farmers, stacked the ties on the river bank, then barged them down to Decatur to be sold to the railroad. In buying the ties it was necessary for them to be measured and graded, and this procedure gave me one of my first jobs. On Saturdays I would inspect the ties as they were brought in and pay for them with a store due-bill while Charley stood by to do the measuring and stacking.

One Saturday a hill farmer, packing several shots o' cawn under his belt, brought in a sorry batch of rough-hewn ties. He had a dozen ties on his wagon, and had they all been first class they would have brought him twelve dollars. But the axe work was so sloppy I had to cut down on the grades and refuse to buy two of them at all.

The farmer was furious. "Ya mean atter I hewed them ties an' hauled 'em ten miles ya ain't gonna buy 'em a'tall?" he roared.

"I'm sorry, Mr. Lunsford," I replied. "We'd like to buy them. But these two have been cut so thin we can't sell them."

"Why ya little lyin' bastard, they ain't too thin! And ef ya say they air, I'll smack yore ears off!"

He was moving toward me but he got no further. Like a jungle cat Charley leaped on him. Down in the dirt they went, and with those meat-axe fists Charley would soon have pounded him to death. I grabbed Charley around the neck, tugging and yelling for him to let go. He finally turned loose, and the battered Mr. Lunsford struggled to his wagon and drove away.

Charley was trembling. "Ya oughta lef' me at him, Mistah Garth. Ah'd a chawed him up lak a circle saw."

I was scared to death, and with Charley I ran to the gin yard where Grandfather had his office. It was a two-room blockhouse affair built of heavy timbers. Several men were sitting around the stove when I burst in and explained what had happened.

Crawford Garth at sixty-eight was a tall, fierce old man who wore big black hats, drank gallons of cawn likker, and looked far over your head when he talked. The most reckless of Old Mis' Ella's three sons, his exploits were legendary. Everybody knew of that night forty years ago when he had camped on the river bank with a log gang waiting for rising water to float twenty thousand dollars' worth of cedar logs to Decatur. With the gang drunk and the river rising, he had gone off to spend the night with a red-headed wench. Next morning the logs were gone—scattered fifty miles down-river and most of them lost. He rode with Joe Wheeler's cavalry in Cuba, and the youngest of his three sorry

48

legitimate sons had been killed in the Argonne. Of the husbands of his six daughters, honest, hard-working John Lafavor was his favorite.

He unlocked the door to the room back of his office where there were whiskey jugs and a couch.

"Get in there, both of you," he ordered. "Don't make no noise when they come."

In the back room Charley and I wiped the dust off one pane in the tiny window and waited. Down at the Crossroads the report that a nigger had beat up a white man ran through the Saturday afternoon tipplers like fire in a sage field. In an hour Charley's victim had gathered a howling, likkered-up mob that asked no further explanation than that he had been assaulted by a nigger. Charley and I could see them coming. About half of them had shotguns and the rest were armed with axes and boom poles.

"There's fifty a' more of 'em, Crawford," a voice yelled to Grandfather. "They're likkered an' plenty worked up. Ya better give 'em the nigger."

My teeth were chattering. But Charley was only excited. Like a young-un waiting to see a circus parade pass by. The idea that the mob—even if it numbered ten thousand—could ever pass the Old Cap'n didn't occur to him.

When the mob leaders were thirty steps away, Crawford Garth picked up his automatic shotgun and stepped out. He said nothing, but the mob halted. He stood leaning against a post, the gun swinging in the crook of his arm.

"Crawford," a snuff-dipping hillsider hollered, "one o' yore niggers has beat hell out'a Sim Lunsford here. Ya know ya don't tolerate nuthin' like that. Now ya got him in there an' we mean to have him. We're gonna string the black sonuvabitch up to this persimmon tree an' cut him up."

Crawford Garth spat and said firmly: "Sim, step out there where I can see ya."

49

It was an order and Sim Lunsford shuffled out.

"Ya low down filthy bastard!" Grandfather was sneering. "Ya cussed mah grandson up here while ago. A boy fourteen years old. Ya're goddam lucky I wasn't there, or I'd a shot ya like I would'a blacksnake."

Sim Lunsford retreated hastily into the crowd, but there were yells of protest. "Now, Crawford, that don't give no damn nigger no right to hit no white man. An' by God we're a-comin' in to get him."

The guns and boom poles were waving and those in the back were inching the leaders forward. "Ya ain't comin' nowhere," Grandfather snapped. "Ya're gettin'. I'm givin' ya exactly two minutes to clear off mah land. And if ya don't start movin' there's gonna be some buckshot holes in some bellies."

There was a supercharged moment to see who had won. Yells of "rush him" came from the back of the crowd, and I was sure somebody would take a pot-shot. But Grandfather just watched them, the gun still dangling from the crook of his arm like he was rabbit-hunting.

Charley was grinning. "Look at de Old Cap'n give it to dem trash. De Cap'n ain't afraid o' dat many wild-cats."

After a few minutes of loud cussing and bickering, the mob broke up. We sneaked Charley down to the ferry and back to the Island. Grandfather told him to lie low for a few days to make sure Mr. Lunsford and his pals did no bushwhacking.

Raccoon Charley had now laid down his pipe.

"Come on, Mistah Garth. Le's run dat line and take off some mo' o' dem big cats."

6

It was late in August when I went to say goodby to Old Mis' Ella.

She was nearing her ninetieth birthday, but if the years had dulled her prejudices they had scarcely affected her vigor. In full possession of her faculties, she still read the *Atlanta Constitution* every day. Each Monday morning she still stood at the smokehouse doors while the meat for the week was doled out to the croppers and hands. Until she was seventy-five she had served as administrator for the entire estate, signing all the mortgages and notes. She liked to sit by the fire or out under her bush arbor, smoke her pipe and run on for hours about either the past or the present.

As I strode across the big pasture which separated our house from the old Big House, I could see her standing on the porch looking out toward the Landing. She was leaning on her walking stick, for her leg had been fractured twenty years before in a fall through a box which had crumpled under her great weight. The occasion had been an Old Soldiers' reunion at Hartselle and the speaker had been that silver-tongued darling of Alabama, Richmond Pearson Hobson. The band struck up "Dixie" as Hobson entered, and Old Mis' Ella leaped up on a box to lead a rebel yell that shook the tabernacle. The box crashed, but she insisted on hearing Hobson describe the charge up the Ridge with Pickett before allowing the fracture to be set.

"Well, Mis' Ella," I greeted her, "you're looking as fat and sassy as ever. Guess you're gonna live to be a hundred in spite o' hell and high water."

She laughed at my reverent irreverence and put her arm around my shoulders. "Yeah, Bud, the chances are pretty good if I can just keep away from these damn doctors. Every time Watts brings one over here he makes me sick."

"You're probably so dang contrary you won't do what the doctor tells you." I laughed.

"Well, mebbe so. Come in, Bud. I'm glad to see you. I wanted you to come over before you went off."

I was glad she led me past the parlor and on into her

own room. For her room was the Inner Shrine of the Garths. In it were the precious memorabilia of eight generations of men who had fought to gain and then to maintain three thousand acres as a foundation stone. Here was the conch shell on which Peter Garth sounded signals in the Revolution. Here was the original deed by which a grateful Congress of the United States of America granted three thousand acres to Peter Garth for his "unselfish and heroic service" in the Revolution. Here were the old family Bible and brown newspapers announcing the Louisiana Purchase, Alabama's admission into the Union, Fort Sumter's Fall, Appomattox, the sinking of the Maine, and the Armistice with Germany. Here were letters from General Marion, from Andrew Jackson, from Jeff Davis, and from Theodore Roosevelt.

As a child I sat in this room and listened to stories which left me afraid to go for a drink of water alone lest I be dirked by some lurking scalawag. On the walls hung the fading pictures of the seven Garths who fell between Shiloh and Gettysburg. Over the fireplace was the largest and proudest of these. It was Old Mis' Ella's husband, my great-grandfather, the young captain of the Fourth Alabama whose blood turned the river red at Chickamauga. Heavy with her third son who was later to be "Crazy Tom," Mis' Ella went up the river to bring back his body. The Negroes attributed the seven good crops which followed to the fertilizing blood which the river brought down from Chickamauga and spread over the bottomlands.

Three days after Mis' Ella buried her husband, the Yankee raiders came pouring across the river to burn the houses and the crops and steal the horses. They strung the Boss Slave to a tree, then lowered him before he died, then pulled him up and lowered him again, threatening each time to leave him hanging unless he told where the gold was buried. The old Negro, who had buried the treasure under the feed trough in the big barn, was determined to carry the secret to his death when Mis' Ella intervened. With the house in flames and with her standing among the soldiers clutching the deed and the conch shell, she stopped the hanging by screaming:

"Cut him down, you thieving Yankee bastards, and I'll tell you where the gold is!"

Here in Mis' Ella's room in August, 1929, sitting in a cane-bottomed rocking chair and listening to her talk, the Revolution and Appomattox and all the glorious Garth battle for our way of life was very near and very dear to me.

She lighted her pipe and leaned back in her chair.

"Well, Bud, I guess you'll be going away pretty soon, won't you?"

"Yes, Mis' Ella. I'm leaving next Monday."

"I'm glad you're goin', Bud. The Garth boys have never been scholars. Out of all my grandsons and great-grandsons, you're the only one who's ever tried to educate yo'self. The rest have been too busy working and fighting and drinking likker. The Bible and the blue-back speller are about all they've read. When you finish college you'll be the first in the family."

"But wait, Mis' Ella," I joked. "I haven't finished yet."

"You will. Mary'll see to that. And I want you to go to the top. I want you to learn what's goin' on in the world. Our people are gonna need somebody to tell'em what to do. They've gone stark, starin' crazy about money."

This was her *Delenda est Carthago*. "But, Grandmother," I said, "that's just because of all our progress and inventions. We have to have more money to live today."

"We think we do anyhow, Bud, we're like the Israelites and the golden calf. We're worshippin' money and losing sight of what really counts. The family's worse'n the croppers. Nobody wants to plant nothing except

53

what 'they can turn into money. Everybody's got to have money for a new automobile or a new radio or a new this or a new that."

"But we should have these things, shouldn't we?"

"Bud, we should have 'em—if we can produce 'em on the land. Look out that window and see what you see. You see the land and the river. Well, Bud, that's all in God's world we've got. And for a hundred and forty-four years it's been enough. The land produces food to eat and clothes to wear and houses to live in, and the river carries some of the things we produce to market where we can exchange them for things we need and can't produce."

The answer was simple and obvious to me. "That's right, Grandmother. Since we need more money for these things we can't produce, we've got to produce bigger crops so we can have more surplus to exchange."

Her eyes snapped. "Yeah, that sounds good, Bud. But let me tell you something about that surplus. What we can sell off the land is worth just so much and no more. Now take an automobile. We say everybody ought to have one. But somebody has to work to produce that automobile, and we've got to swap something we've produced for it. So we sell some timber to buy the new automobile. Then we plant more cotton on the cleared land. And a million folks like us is doing the same thing. So pretty soon the automobile is worn out, our timber's gone, and the new cotton we're raising is worth four cents a pound."

I smiled condescendingly and moved to end the argument. I didn't know just how to answer her. But I was certain that in some of my books or in some professor's lecture I would find the answer. In 1929 it was absurd to suppose that the economic aspirations of a family or a nation had to be governed by the relative value of its farm produce.

We talked for two hours about many things, and when I was nearly ready to leave, I said: "Grand-

54

mother, I'm going off to college now. I'm the first of the Garths to go. If you had one piece of advice to give me, what would it be?"

She was pleased. She thought for several minutes, looking up at the pictures and out the window toward the river.

"Well, Bud, when I was your age we were getting ready to fight a war. I remember the night before Jud, up there, left to join the regiment. We got the two children around us and prayed. We knew in our hearts the South was right. We knew that God was with us and that our cause was worth going through the back door of hell for. And I remember the night I drove back from Chickamauga with him. I looked up at the stars and my heart was breaking. I wanted to whisper: 'Jud, was it worth it?' But I didn't dare. I couldn't afford to doubt, for I had to carry on and feed the children and the niggahs, and the old folks. In the years that followed we went through hell, and then we gradually got back on our feet. And some smart people wrote that we hadn't been right at all, just damn fools. They asked me to believe that, too, and to go out there and tell Jud.

"Well, about thirty years later Joe Wheeler rode over to see me one day. He sat right where you are sitting now, Bud, and I said to him: 'Joe, I hear you're goin' off down to Cuba to do some more fighting. What are we goin' to be fighting for this time?'

"Joe Wheeler was a great man, Bud. He talked for an hour about how America was becoming the greatest nation in the world, now that the stains of the old war were washing away. He said the old war had been necessary to sort'a mould us together. And now a great nation like ours couldn't tolerate things like was happening down in Cuba.

"As he talked I got 'most as mad at the Spaniards as I had been at the Yankees, and when he left I told him to go lick hell out of 'em, and the souls of the young bucks

55

who rode with him against the Yankees would be a-ridin' agin. Crawford and Watts went down to Cuba with him and ate horse meat and saw men die like flies. We all got mad and we hipped and we hollered. And the result was the same. In a few years they were telling us what damn fools we had been to let a fool like Hearst march us off into war."

She filled her pipe again and lighted it.

"In twenty years it came again. And I was an old, old woman. But I hipped and I hollered with the rest of 'em. And when the boys of the family came over to see me before they left, I told 'em I was proud of 'em and their granddaddies would'a been proud of 'em. Right before this fireplace I got down on my knees and I prayed for 'em, and I knew in my heart we were right and God was with us. I cussed the slackers like I had cussed the Tory-Devils." (*Southerners who did not support the Civil War were known as Tory-Devils.*) "When the wire came that Joe had been killed in France I rode over to see Molly. I could see in her eyes the same question that had been in mine the night Jud and me rode back from Chickamauga. But I wouldn't let her ask it. I told her it was God's will and that the boy had died for something great. I believed it, too.

"You're old enough to know what happened after that one. We had all been fools again, they said. Just driven crazy by a bunch o' selfish shysters. Looks pretty discouraging, don't it, Bud? Looks like we ought to start losing confidence in ourselves. Sometimes I look up at Jud and I'm glad he died at Chickamauga. That minnie ball caught him at the top o' the charge and he never even knew the battle was lost. If he had lived, those filthy Yankee bastards would'a broke his heart during Reconstruction. I guess those who die are the fortunate ones. They don't have to listen to the proof that they were damn fools."

It was the first time she had ever talked to me like

56

this. I couldn't imagine what her conclusions would be.

"But here's what I'm comin' to, Bud," she said. "In spite of all the smart folks, I've never let myself doubt that Jud and me was right. I know we were right. This part of the world was ours. Our folks had fought and died for it, and it was no goddam Yankee's business what we did down here. I lived and Jud died for what we thought was right, and that made it right for us. If you ever admit the things you've fought for are wrong, what is there left to life? So, Bud, the first thing for you to do is get you some things to believe in. Get you some things to love and some things to hate. Then love 'em and hate 'em with all your soul. Twenty years later you'll be told you were a fool, but don't ever believe it. Go right on fightin' for what seems right for you and for those who depend on you. Don't ever have any patience with the folks who hang on the backin' straps.

"And, Bud, when you get through college, I won't be here. But don't go off somewhere else. Come back here and live and tell the folks what's right and take care of those who've always looked to the Garths. Be proud you're a Garth. For whatever they say about us and our kind, we're still the salt o' the earth. Come hell or high water, we'll still be eatin' and dreamin' and fightin' and making a place for ourselves and ours when all the puny, whining trash of the earth are starvin' to death."

The sun was going down when I walked back across the big pasture. Looking back, I could see Old Mis' Ella Garth standing on the porch, leaning on her stick and waving to me.

This, then, was the world of the Garths in the summer of 1929. Perhaps the Garth world should be described as a tiny, neglected pool alongside the great rushing river of American life. No one ever left it except to fight a war to protect it. No one ever entered it except to sell or to buy; and the Garth world bought

57

more than it could sell. Thus each year the very momentum of the river's rush would take a little more water from this pool and leave it a little drier and with a little more of its yellow mud exposed to cake and petrify. And as the water grew shallower and more stagnant, the denizens of this pool were forced closer and closer to its mud bottom, and their poverty and ignorance and intolerance and filth were accentuated.

But driving my truck and trailer down the long, dusty road from Garth's Island to Hartselle, I saw only the sunshine. Raccoon Charley and Dan and I would vie to see who could lift the butt of the biggest log, we'd stop at cold, shaded springs along the road and break fat watermelons with our fists and eat them with the juice running off our chins. We'd race the other trucks and turn the summer air blue with fierce, hairy-chested Southern cuss words when we stalled on a hillside. Sometimes Dan would drive and I'd sit back on the rolling, swaying log-load and feel the sun beating down upon me and the fresh hot wind blowing in my nostrils. And I was certain of the eternal and exciting goodness of things.

At home at night I'd plunge into the river and Dan would pour cold water in the shower barrel for me and I'd stand naked in the backyard and feel the cold water restoring the vibrancy to my hardening muscles. I'd drink cold, thick buttermilk and eat turnip greens and pickled beets and boiled ham hocks and red strawberries crushed in cream. Then I'd put on a cool white suit and drive to see Cherry. We'd park out under the moon at the edge of the woods, and as I would hold her in my strong, brown arms, I'd feel her lips grow hot on my throat and her defiant little nipples grow more defiant against my chest.

Hell! Bring on the Great Race! I could lick the world!

58

1929-1933

PAJAMAS AND LIFEBUOY

HAD YOU BEEN riding the Louisville & Nashville accommodation from Decatur to Birmingham on the morning of September 5th, 1929, you would hardly have looked up from your newspaper when the train stopped at Hartselle. There was nothing unusual about the excited knot of humanity on the platform. The dressed-up boy with the flushed face and the lunch box and the cheap, new suitcases would be just another Country Harry going off to college to waste hard-earned dollars, get pukey drunk, and come back with a loud jacket and a swelled head. The wet-eyed woman picking the string off his coat would be just another mother. The hard-handed master-of-baggage, fearful the train would leave, would be just another father. The tall, gaunt old man in the big black hat, who patted the boy on the shoulder, would be just another grandfather. And the red-lipped girl with the black hair would be just another puppy-love sweetheart come for a restrained goodbye after a much warmer farewell the night before.

You would have looked up when the excited chap staggered down the aisle, dropping his bags in his rush to get to a window and wave before the train pulled

59

away. Then, if your coffee had been good, you might have chuckled as he pulled out a *Literary Digest* and tried to read, but kept laying it aside and picking it up again.

"Hell," you would have thought, "that young buck is too excited to give a damn about Hoover's foreign policy."

Yet, while you couldn't have known it, this was another significant morning, not only in the life of Garth Lafavor, but also in the whole lifestream of the American Garths. For many generations the fathers of these Garths grubbed in dirt held in fief by absentee English earls. Then a great chance came to Peter Garth. The chance to join a rabble with a vision and fight for the land which to him meant liberty and freedom and dignity and success and happiness. And Peter Garth fought. Not in well-disciplined ranks with modern weapons, but with Marion's guerillas. Lone individuals with visions, lying in muck behind rocks and trees and pouring hate-heated lead into the ordered ranks of those hired to protect the old system. He carried a conch shell to signal his fellows to disperse or attack, and he needed no morale officer to encourage him, for he had his vision. Only men with the simple vision of liberty for themselves and with the hope of owning and building something for themselves have the courage to fight alone.

In the six generations after Peter Garth, the land he won and the tiny pool around it had been enough for his sons. Between Peter Garth and this lad riding away to the University of Alabama the Garths had lived contented lives just prayin'-and-propagatin', fussin'-and-fightin', and plowin' and plantin' and preservin' the land. None of these Garths had read a book of philosophy other than the Bible. None of these Garths had ever seen a head waiter. Or a manicuress. Or a Catholic priest. Or a New York Jew. None of these Garths had ever slept in a pair of pajamas. Or powdered his feet.

60

Or put "perfumery" under his arms before going to bed with a woman.

The Garths—from Peter Garth to Garth Lafavor—were fiercely patriotic and clannish peasants who, once having achieved land ownership, were content to live and die in their world of the Tennessee. They coveted neither knowledge nor wealth, and except when they went off to fight, they never worried about the complex world beyond the horizon.

Now, progress and its problems were prodding the Garths. And from their languid pool they were sending an emissary out into the main stream to find out what was happening and to bring answers back to them. One Garth, with twenty generations of simplicity and acceptance and faith behind him, was going to rub the lamp of knowledge and plunge into the Great Race.

My heart beat faster when I saw Birmingham's belching smoke craters. This was the Big City to me, a place where big things happened; where successful people from the Tennessee came on big occasions. I had been here twice before, and each visit had been a tremendous occasion. Once was to see Ringling Brothers Circus. For valley folks the prices had been shameful. We had talked for days afterward about the injustice of being forced to purchase a reserved seat. It was the first time I had even seen a reserved seat. I was impressed. Here was proof that we Garths needed more ready cash. Out in the Main Stream you could purchase a Reserved Place for yourself if you had enough money. But despite the cost, we were glad we had gone because Father believed everyone should see Ringling Brothers once during his lifetime and mother had wanted us children to see it.

The other trip to Birmingham had been to see the Alabama State Fair. I had ridden on a merry-go-round which was larger and more colorful than the one which came to the county fair at Hartselle. Also I had sneaked into a hoochy-koochy show where the women were cleaner and nakeder than they had been at the county fair. Apparently this was how it was in the world. As you battled further up the Main Stream, you could ride on even larger and more colorful merry-go-rounds, and you could command progressively cleaner and nakeder women.

At Birmingham, other boys and girls who were obviously college students boarded the train, and I hoped the crowd would force one of them to share my seat with me, but this wasn't necessary and soon we were off on the sixty-mile run down to Tuscaloosa. I had never been beyond Birmingham, so I was engrossed in the countryside with its abandoned mines and decaying tipples when a voice disturbed me.

"Well, freshman, where are you from?"

I looked up to see a handsome chap who might have stepped from an Arrow Collar ad.

"Are you talking to me, suh?" I asked.

"Who else would I be talking to?" He was stern.

"Well, I'm Garth Lafavor and I'm from Morgan County."

"From where?"

"From Morgan County. I live near Hartselle."

"I never heard of Hartselle. What's it close to?"

"It's near Decatur and the Tennessee River."

"Uh-huh. Well, I'm Dave Blocton. I want you to come up to the baggage car and meet some of the boys."

It sounded more like an order than an invitation, but I was delighted. I followed Dave up the train, and he'd stop along the aisle and approach other fellows in the same manner. I wondered how he could be so certain all the fellows he spoke to were freshmen. By the time we reached the baggage car there were seven or eight of us, and inside the car we found that three other upper classmen and Dave had borrowed chairs and a table from the baggage master and had set up court.

"Now, freshmen," Dave explained, "you're all coming to college to get educated. You're a bunch of dumb bastards now, and you wanna start learning things as soon as you can. So my colleagues and I have consented to help you out while we while away these two hours. Chip, hand me the divining rod."

The boy called Chip produced a formidable razor strop, and we seven freshmen reddened and winced. We had heard of this sort of thing, but after all, this seemed a bit abrupt.

"The line forms to the left, freshmen. Step right up here, catch your ankles and give me your full names. You get one lick for each letter in your names this round."

The first boy in line insisted his name was Pat Hicks.

"A slimy rat, huh!" Dave snapped. "You know your name's Patrick Wellington Hicks." And he proceeded to lay on twenty-two lusty licks instead of the eight poor Pat had hoped for.

I was fourth in line and Chip had taken over the strop.

"What's your name, frosh?"

"Peter Garth Lafavor."

"Jesus Christ, what a name! Who hung that on you, frosh? You got a grievance."

I was the only boy in my high school class who had never been whipped by the teacher. My grandfather would have killed a man for threatening to hit me. But now Chip was laying on with all his might and asking for more room to swing. I gritted my teeth and held tight to my ankles to keep from grabbing a chair and braining him. When he had swung seventeen times, Dave stepped up.

"A frosh with a name like that is gonna be slimy. We better give him double."

Dave took off his coat and helped himself to seventeen mighty bats, then surprised me by offering his hand.

He said: "Freshman, you can take it okay. I'm going to enjoy working out on you this year. Of course, I'm not in very good shape now, but I'm gonna go into training so I can do you justice. I'll be looking you up."

The court put us through a course of ridiculous paces and made us learn each other's names. You need only remember Dave Blocton. Then they sent us through the train with rolls of toilet paper, yelling: "Get your morning paper, ladies and gentlemen!" I fervently prayed there was no one on the train who knew me.

During the last hour of the trip I was forced to stand at one end of a crowded car and sing out the time on each minute. At intervals either Chip or Dave would accuse me of being slow and would order me back to the baggage car to be speeded up.

And thus the emissary of the Garths arrived at the New World in Tuscaloosa with blue buttocks and a badly disheveled dignity.

2

From Garth's Island to Tuscaloosa it is about one hundred fifty miles. Yet had I traveled twelve thousand miles from some ancient oasis in the Gobi Desert, the world I found at the University of Alabama could hardly have been more different from what I had known. I spent four years at the university, including the summer sessions, and at the end they gave me an academic degree, a master's degree, and a Phi Beta Kappa key. I learned about communists and fairies and women. I met hundreds of New York Jews. I wolfed away at the first library I had ever seen. I heard the Minneapolis Symphony play Tschaikowsky's Fifth and saw professional actors perform "Macbeth" and "The Rivals." I learned how to dance and how to eat

64

soup. I learned to use a tile bath. To bathe every day with Lifebuoy soap. To shave every day with cool Colgate shaving cream and Gillette blue blades and a biting, clean-smelling lotion. To use Listerine and Mum and Pepsodent and Mennen's for Men. To have my hair cut in a barber shop, and treated with Fitch and Lucky Tiger.

I learned to wear pajamas. Black silk pajamas. And bedroom slippers—something a man never wore in the Garth world. I learned to have my clothes pressed in a pressing shop and to have my shoes shined by a "nigger" boy. I learned how to buy clothes that fitted like Dave Blocton's, and how to tie a neat knot in my necktie. I learned to employ a manicuress and even a masseur. I slept in a Pullman berth and went to Chicago and New Orleans. I checked in at the Stevens and St. Charles Hotels and tipped a bell-hop. I learned that there were other drinks in the world besides cawn whiskey, and that you didn't drink them out of jugs and fruit jars.

I learned that Sunday mornings were better spent sleeping off hangovers than psalm-singing and listening to some stupid salvation-peddler. I learned it was proper to say words like goddam and whore and bitch before sophisticated women. I learned about abortions —that a good doctor demanded two hundred bucks but a quack would do the same job for fifty. And, above all, I learned just how small and shallow and stagnant the Garth pool really was, and how tremendous and exciting was the Main Stream.

Many times the fierce old Garth pride was hurt, but always I fought ferociously to restore it. I was frightened. My first night in Tuscaloosa was the first night I had ever spent outside Morgan County. In a strange bed in a strange rooming house in a strange world, I felt lonely and insignificant and afraid. I wanted to run back to the Garth world and shut the door and never leave. But I got up and looked in a mirror and swore I

65

would make myself as significant at the university as I had been in the Garth world.

Looking back on those four years at the university, I can see some signs of development in the country boy from Garth's Island. His reactions were not extraordinary, but he began to learn that America is a very complex conglomeration of races and creeds, and that terms like "equal justice" and "equal opportunity" are not to be handled lightly by high school valedictorians. I can see also how the shell of cynicism began forming, for at the University of Alabama I experimented with dangerous potions, and I set myself to spinning along a pathway that was to lead me to complete confusion.

3

Until I went to the university I had known only two Jews. Ben Apolinsky, who looked like Soglow's Little King with the beard, ran the Bargain Store in Hartselle. I knew him as a kindly, red-faced man who was said to be "different" from other people. He didn't eat pork, he thought Christ was "just a man," and when he married he had gone back to wherever the Jews were to find a wife. But when I went to his store as a kid, he always gave me candy and reminded me that the Garths were his very best friends because they had never failed to put him up in the years when he had come to Morgan County with a pack on his back.

Ben's daughter, Hilda, was the fat-and-funny girl in my class at school. She never studied, laughed uproariously at everything, and on the class picnics she had inexhaustible baskets of delicious food she shared with everyone.

Ben Apolinsky and Hilda were the type of Jews the people of Alabama had known until 1925. But in that year the university discovered the publicity magic of Rose Bowl football teams and straightway resolved to become a great national and cosmopolitan factory of

66

learning. With low tuitions and nominal out-of-state fees; with sunshine and beautiful, drawling women; and with living costs which looked like Southern hospitality to metropolitan New Yorkers, the university issued invitations to all and sundry to come and drink at its Pierian springs. And the modern Children of Israel, chafing under "restrictions" and "quotas" at the Eastern colleges, accepted with all the enthusiasm with which Joshua's band blew the trumpets and took Jericho.

Four hundred young Americans from the Bronx and the Joisey Side accepted Southern Hospitality the first year. There were eight hundred the next year, and when I arrived "equal justice" flourished to the extent that about one-third of the student body of four thousand were designated by their fellow students as "kikes" and the rest as "gentlemen."

Since no fraternity—not even the old Southern Jewish ones—would accept the New York group, they had thrown up a ghetto of their own fraternities. In the old university barracks, where Southern boys had always found the cheapest quarters, the poorer of the Jews moved in and made the Southerners look like wastrels. They could live six in a room and do their own cooking in ankle-deep garlic and onions. The Barracks Brigade of Southerners was organized for protection against the "Judean Horde." Segregation was demanded and granted. One dormitory was unofficially called "New Jerusalem," and across the quadrangle hot-blooded Brigade leaders stood on second-floor porches and delivered inflammatory harangues which would have made Hitler's diatribes sound like models of tolerance.

There was turmoil in the classrooms. Where once middle-class and ambitious poor-class Southerners had vied for marks with small concern and less jealousy, the law of the tooth-and-fang was enthroned. Where once students had accepted low marks with shrugs or swallows, professors now found themselves pinned to

67

the walls by angry, gesticulating mobs of New Yorkers when they handed out C's and D's. Since the Jews had gone to better preparatory schools and were vastly more aggressive and grade-conscious, the "Southerners" were pushed down to C's and D's and F's. To balance the grades and pass the proper percentage of "Southern gentlemen," professors were urged to discriminate against the Jews, and in oral examinations some professors were said to use a more difficult set of questions on the Jews to drive their marks to the "Southern" level.

At all gentile sororities the "foreigners" were persona non grata. Candidates in the student elections strove to avoid the "Kike-Vote's" kiss of death. And at the football games in Birmingham and Nashville and Atlanta and New Orleans, 'Bama's gaudy, cackling New York group used its pushing, shoving, subway tactics to impress its offensiveness on an ever-widening Southern front.

No group hated the "kikes" as fiercely as the Southern Jews. Before the coming of this new kind of Jew, the members of the two old Southern Jewish fraternities had been accepted everywhere. Sons of the established Jewish families in Birmingham and Montgomery and Mobile, these boys were more Southern than Jewish. They had the manners of high-born Southerners. They had never heard the term "kike" applied to them, and except for their own religious and racial clannishness they could have forgotten they were Jews. But they couldn't forget now. They were still accepted at most parties, but wherever they went they felt compelled to be constantly explaining the difference between Polish and Russian Jews; between "cloak-and-suiters" and the other kinds. The map of the New York area assumed a vast importance on the Alabama campus, for the Southern Jews could take the map and show us the sections where the lousiest of the "kikes" came from. A few New Yorkers gained some

68

degree of recognition after the Southern Jews explained that they had come from a section of New York which produced "fairly decent Jews."

It would be dishonest for me to pretend now that my first reaction to the "kikes" was anything but bitter resentment. While we go off ten thousand miles to fight for "equal justice" and "tolerance" and the "four freedoms," we may as well face the facts of our own personal and national experience. If this war is worth fighting there will have to be some victories at home as well as abroad. We Garths had never encountered people like New York Jews in our live-and-let-live pool. No doubt we were a "decadent, reactionary people," but we waited our turn in line, tipped our hats to ladies, said "suh" and "mam" to all our elders, and spoke softly and slowly when spoken to. We regarded every man as honest until we caught his hand in our pockets. We thought the hair on a man's chest was something he displayed to men only. But these New York Jews seemed incapable of speaking softly. At night you could hear a group of them coming along the street while they were two blocks away. They said "Jeez, goy, what-de-hell?" when they addressed you. They came to class with their shirts thrown open, and they played in front of their frat houses with even their undershirts off. They seemed to take it for granted that everybody was trying to cheat, and in the classroom they regarded every man as a competitor.

I despised the New Yorkers as a group. Not because they were Jews, but because I thought they were a garish, indecorous lot of magpies. During my first week at the university when everything was strange to me, I went one night with a group of freshmen to "listen to the kikes." We were like little boys going to the zoo. We were approaching a great curiosity for the first time. We walked a mile to enjoy the sensation of sitting outside the dormitory known as "New Jerusalem"

69

and doing nothing else but listening to the noises which came from that building.

"They don't sound like folks," remarked one freshman as rural as I. "They sound just like a bunch'a guinea hens who've seen a chicken snake."

The disagreeable word "kike" became part of my freshman vocabulary. The "kikes," I assumed, were a lousy scourge that "my kind of folks" had to endure because of the university's error in trying to expand too rapidly. Alabama should have been preserved for the Alabamians, but now that the error had been made, we'd have to stick it out until the university could purge the unwanted and adopt the Eastern process of "restrictions" and "quotas."

Yet as the months passed, I found myself drawn by curiosity to the barely-tolerated "kikes". The more brilliant among them knew much more than I knew. They had read much more than I had read. They seemed to be my natural opponents in all the literary societies and debating clubs. They hurt me with their sneers and jibes. They called me "another fat-headed Fascist whelp" before I knew what they meant. They embarrassed me by quoting authors I had never read. One night Harry Lerner threw a copy of Gorky's "Mother" at me and jeered: "Go home and read that and see how little you know!"

I went home and read it—and forgot to go to bed. I read all of Gorky and others like him, and the Russian Revolution hit me like a freight train. I never fully grasped it or subscribed to it, but I was fascinated by it. I was afraid of it. I felt all shaken inside. My first understanding of a communist was that he was a person who wanted to rob me of my opportunity to run in the Great American Race. He wanted to abolish the whole competitive process which I thought of as a Race. And the first people who sat in my apartment and told me they were communists were New York Jews. So I concluded that all American communists were New York

Jews—a false and hardly original conclusion which many Southerners share to this day.

There was every reason for me to hate Harry Lerner and for him to hate me. We lived on the same floor at the Cranston Apartments for three years. To me, as a sophomore, Harry was a "goddamed kike-communist." To him, I was a "patronizing Fascist sonuvabitch." No two people could have been farther apart in their background, their thinking, and their attitude toward life. Harry was the son of a one-generation family in Brooklyn which lived over the Bargain Store. He must have spent half his life being shoved by somebody or watching somebody being shoved. He had a meat-saw mind which cut to the bone of everything it examined. He draped his tall, angular frame with loose-fitting, seldom-pressed clothes, and set in his hawk's face were black eyes that burned with the messianic gleam common to people who hate and writhe and reason.

I was the son of a seven-generation family which lived on broad, blood-bought acres on a broad river. I had never been shoved in my life. I was prejudiced because I had always lived on an island that was owned by my folks. I was provincial and stupid, but I loved my conception of America. I trusted people. I liked to wear neat, well-fitting clothes on my compact body. Things as they were looked all right to me. I wanted to preserve this American world just as it was so that I could race in it and win from it all the delights I wanted. Harry had lived on a crowded little island that belonged to other folks. He wanted to tear the world down and abolish the very competitive process which was the basis of my hope. He sneered at what I thought was patriotism and called it chauvinism.

"How does it feel, Lafavor, to live off the blood and sweat of sharecroppers?" he asked me.

"It feels a damn sight more honest than living off

71

four hundred per cent interest from a pawnshop," I replied in the same spirit.

And yet, somehow, Harry Lerner and I found something to like in each other. We wrangled through a hundred bull sessions. We cursed one another both in heat and in jest. But before we left the university we were friends. Even now I am not certain how it came about. Perhaps Harry convinced me by his overpowering sincerity. After Harry had tossed the Russian Revolution at me, I became so curious about the strange beliefs of "foreigners" that I haunted all the bull sessions, and my apartment gradually became the battleground for most of the campus saviors-of-the-world. The fact, too, that I always had jugs of home-made corn whiskey sitting conveniently at hand may have influenced the choice of the battleground.

At first, when I was so obviously the sophomore rustic, Harry and some of his followers delighted in taunting me with their nihilism and superior learning. When they would corner me in an argument, I'd shout to drown them out.

"You goddam lousy bastards!" I would yell. "You've been kicked across the map for three thousand years, and now, by God, when you find a country which gives you free rein to prey on all the ignorant, easy-going dullards you can find, then you want to overthrow the Government. What kind of distorted reasoning is that?"

They'd all laugh and Harry would remark dryly: "Gentlemen, you will please open your mouths and sit in rapt attention while Senator Peter Garth Lafavor, Jeffersonian Democrat of the Old South, recites the Gettysburg Address."

My first concession to Harry came as I was reeling under the Russian Revolution. I succumbed to Gorky as completely as any communist. It seemed perfectly just to me that in a nation like Russia where there was no middle class—only a House of Have and a House of

72

Want, with birth determining in which house one should dwell—the oppressed should certainly smite their oppressors. The Russian Revolution was in the finest American tradition, an effort comparable to Peter Garth's battle to wrest land from the English peerage.

"But if you accept the Russian Revolution as justified," Harry contended, "you must also admit that the Garths should be overthrown by your sharecroppers. Conditions here in the South are the same as in Russia before the Revolution."

"No, they are not the same," I objected. "There are injustices, but the landowning class in the South is not a leisure class. It's a middle class. Any cropper can own land for himself if he has the will to acquire it."

Harry smirked. "Pure Fascist twaddle! The sharecropper is bound as much to the land as any slave ever was. The landowner keeps him in debt so how can he own land? He can't vote so he can't hope for Government reform. He can only look to unionism and revolution."

I honestly wanted to broaden my viewpoint. And when I examined this contention I knew it was near the truth. I knew the cropper couldn't vote, and try as I might, I could remember only one instance where a cropper had become a landowner. But I insisted on attributing this to human inertia and to unjust tariff policy.

"Harry," I replied, "you have a distorted conception of the Southern landholding class. We Garths are peasants who have gained freedom and property and dignity and purpose through revolution. Our energy has come from our system of free enterprise."

Harry laughed. He had me in another of his traps. "You have the perfect supporting argument for the Continuous Revolution. Your ancestor, whom you regard as a great patriot, was really only a sharecropper of

73

his day. He joined a union and fought to get what he wanted."

"You approve then of the American Revolution?" I asked.

"Certainly. But in accepting land ownership for themselves the Peter Garths defeated their own ends. The American Revolution only substituted a new class of landowners for the old ones. We communists are not content simply to change the guard. We are going to create a New Society where the struggle for something to hoard will be abolished."

"And that's where you communists are fools," I snapped. "The impulse to acquire something for himself is the most powerful motivating force in humanity."

"It's a dog-with-a-bone motivation. It will have no place in the New Society."

We were in hopeless disagreement. Nor could I wring from Harry a single kind word for the Garths.

"If the sharecropper is suffering from injustice," I reasoned, "it is the injustice of the colonial system imposed on the South. The Garth farm can't produce more for its croppers because the money value of its produce is constantly falling. Tariff walls are choking us. The cropper's enemy is not the Southern landowner but the Northern manufacturer."

"Now you are close to the truth," Harry said. He always pretended I was saying exactly what he wanted me to say. "You and your croppers and all the other croppers in the world are suffering from tariff barriers which are nothing but a world-wide conspiracy to protect vested wealth. The worker must destroy the whole world-wide system before he can be free, but he must begin by destroying the immediate representatives of the system."

After such a clash I always wondered if Harry had shaken my faith. Had the American Revolution really been a failure? Does land ownership make men free?

74

Did Peter Garth deserve three thousand acres of good land for having fought in the Revolution? No man can till that much himself. Jefferson and the new Government recognized by that very gift that it is proper for one man to distribute the flour and the sorghum to other men. That if there must be paternalism, it should exist between man and man rather than Government and man.

Each time I assured myself that Harry was wrong. America was still the land of broad opportunity for everybody. I still believed in the Great Competitive Race. I still believed every man should be free to win a million dollars as long as he conformed to the rules of the race. I believed it should be the concern of any Government by the people to intrude as little as possible on the individual—to impose the fewest possible restrictions on the runners. I believed that the free man, in order to secure his freedom, had to accept the risks of being free if he were to enjoy the rewards. A Government of a free people had to lean far over backward in its efforts to avoid any semblance of paternalism, lest some act of paternalism destroy the very resourcefulness in a people which had moved them to create a democracy.

But you can't make friends with communists and seek the stimulation of communist argument without losing your fear of communism. By 1933 I had decided that communists, too, were American citizens, and those who tried to persecute them were being both ridiculous and un-American.

There was no denying that the Jews were the most aggressive intellectual force at the University of Alabama. The Southern Jewish fraternities had always led the campus in scholarship until the new frats came in and assumed leadership. When the frat averages were announced, you always had to go down through seven or eight Jewish frats before you found the first gentile frat.

Pug Plagotsky, however, was not an intellectual Jew. He was a boxer who wore gaudy shirts open low at the collar to display the matted black hair on his chest. He couldn't bolster his ego by taunting hostile "gentlemen" with his intellectual superiority, so he sought the physical self-assurance to be derived from cracking them on the jaw. When he saw a woman he wanted to dance with and her partner refused to break, Pug smacked his ears off and danced with the bitty anyhow.

The blond and pure Anglo-Saxon leader of the Barracks Brigade of "gentlemen" was a chap named Cartright Newsome. A product of Alabama's Sand Mountain country, Cartright was an accomplished rabble-rouser, and he and his Brigade hated Pug Plagotsky with that intensity which only racial and religious hatreds can attain. Their Gestapo was watching for the chance to vent their hatred on Pug's arrogant person, and late one Saturday night in 1931 the chance came.

It was an unwritten law that "kikes" could not haze gentile freshmen. "Gentlemen," however, could haze "kike" freshmen—and this they did lustily. One Saturday night Pug Plagotsky and three of his yes-men were likkered and returning from a whorehouse expedition when they decided to stop at a private rooming house and "get" a gentile freshman who had been particularly slimy to Pug. Three or four such freshmen stayed at the house, and they banded together and stood on their racial rights not to be hit with a slat by a "kike." Whereupon Pug's pent-up resentment exploded, and he tore into the freshmen with his well-trained fists.

The Barracks Brigade, too, was properly boozed, and the flashed report that Pug was berserk brought Cartright Newsome and his half-clad hounds howling down upon the house. When Harry Lerner and I arrived in our pajamas, there were five hundred "gentlemen" attacking the house where Pug had barricaded himself. There was a flying report that Pug had beaten two gentile freshmen to death, and Cartright's mob was going to lynch him. A near-naked Brigader was already scrambling up a tree with a rope while the shock troops were battering down the house doors. Reinforcements were arriving in droves, and two cops were shouting helplessly.

I couldn't believe it. These weren't hill farmers come with shotguns and boom poles to lynch a "nigger" for hitting a white man. These were students at a state university hell-bent on lynching a Jew for hitting a "gentleman."

"My God, Harry, what can we do?" I shouted.

"Let 'em alone," he answered. "It's democracy at work."

The crowd surged relentlessly toward the tree. The shock troops had forced the house, smashed Pug with a chair, and were dragging him toward the tree where Cartright was waiting with the noose. Whistles were blowing. Sirens were yowling. Everybody seemed to be yelling, if only from fright.

Two professors, also in robes, had joined Harry and me, and while Harry stood back, the professors and I began fighting toward the tree. Others pitched in to help, and somehow we managed to fight to the circle where Cartright was struggling to put the rope around Pug's neck. I don't know how long we were in that writhing, swearing, hate-maddened mass, blinded by our own blood and swinging our fists. But cold water, played over the crowd's head by firemen, finally halted the mêlée.

Next day Pug Plagotsky was gone and was never seen again on the Alabama campus. I don't know whether or not Cartright and his gang actually intended to kill Pug. Perhaps they only intended to choke him and scare him. But only at trials of accused Negro rapists in the South have I ever felt such mass-hate in the air as I felt that night.

I asked Harry why he didn't help us when we were trying to stop the hanging. "I didn't want it stopped," he answered. "The only way you can cure a boil is to let it come to a head."

Near the end of my college career, some of the university's industrialist alumni suddenly went frantic over the Red menace. They had heard about the communist and anti-God clubs on the campus, so they enlisted the American Legion and began yelling for the blood of a sacrificial lamb.

Harry was then on the "student faculty," teaching some freshman science subjects while he completed work on his Master's. He looked something like a Hearst cartoonist's conception of a Red professor, and he made no effort to conceal copies of the *New Masses* in his apartment. So he was singled out to feel the edge of the reactionary sword. The wolves demanded his dismissal from the faculty.

The campus hustings were hot for two weeks. Most of the state's daily papers sang the dismissal chorus, and the college paper chimed in. Only three professors and a few of us in the student body defended Harry. We wrote letters to the papers and promptly found ourselves branded "kike-lovers" and "fellow travelers." The climax came at a mass meeting attended by two thousand students. Cartright Newsome, assisted by his Barracks Brigade of claquers, led the assault. He really had great talent for public speaking, and in three minutes he had the crowd roaring with him. In the best Tom Heflin-Huey Long manner he called for a crusade against "these conspirers against God," and demanded that Harry be expelled both from the faculty and from the student body.

I had come to the meeting only as a spectator, but as I listened to the applause for Cartright's extravagant

78

phrases, I decided I ought to say something. It was foolish to defend a "kike" and a communist before that crowd, but I tried. The Barracks Brigade booed and hissed. "Kike-lover! Fellow Traveler!" I thought of my old grandfather standing with an automatic shotgun before a mob, and I wondered if reason could ever be substituted successfully for buckshot.

"I am not here to defend Harry Lerner," I shouted. "I am here to defend a dream which caused America to be built. I am here to defend you and me from an ancient enemy more terrible than an army of Harry Lerners. The dream which built America was the dream of a land where every man could believe what he wanted to believe and advocate what he wanted to advocate, and still be safe from the anger of those who disagreed."

The jeers stopped. I pressed hard for five minutes, and I thought I could feel the crowd sway toward me; but then they'd fall back. At the end I risked everything on one last pitch. It was an open-air meeting, and I was already hoarse, so I must have sounded like a tabernacle preacher making his last altar-call.

"If Harry Lerner is discharged from the faculty of this university," I declared, "he will be discharged either because he is a Jew or because he believes something which we do not believe. Therefore, if we concur in this dismissal, we—you and I—will have broken faith with our fathers. We will have done more to destroy the American Way than Harry Lerner can ever do."

There was a moment's awesome silence, but I knew I had lost. The boos of the Barracks Brigade drowned out the scattered applause, and Cartright Newsome took over. He gathered two thousand names for his petition, and shortly thereafter Harry was dismissed from his job, although not from the student body.

When I got back to the apartment after the mass meeting, Harry and a group of the faithful were celebrating his dismissal.

"It was useless, Garth," he said, "but I'm grateful for a friendly gesture."

"I'm not sure it was a friendly gesture," I replied. "In fact I'm not sure I did the right thing, but it seemed the proper thing to do."

I was puzzled. Harry and the Reds were obviously pleased at his dismissal from the faculty. He had entered no defense for himself. He had stood on his "Constitutional rights" and hoped that the Constitution would be violated. Cartright Newsome and the alumni had won a victory. To preserve the Constitution from attack, they had been willing to violate it.

The only ones who were not pleased at the result were the few of us who had opposed the dismissal. In trying to save what we believed to be something fundamentally American, we had been crushed between opposing forces both of which had won victories. And for our efforts we had won the label of "fellow traveler" from the Right, yet we had not won the respect of those on the Left whose liberties we wanted to preserve. They regarded us as naive and sophomoric.

Here, I thought, was a peculiar struggle. Two antagonists, one attacking and the other counter-attacking, and each willing to stampede the mob and destroy the very soul of America in order to destroy the other. But what of us who wanted to preserve the old and still allow our attackers freedom to attack us? On what position could we array ourselves? Did we have to join one or the other of the antagonists?

On the one other front where we liberals fought for tolerance at the university, we were more successful.

During the first few years after the "invasion," no New York Jews were elected to Phi Beta Kappa. Southern Jews were given this honor, but the New Yorkers were not. This struck me as being a loathsome brand of injustice. If we couldn't find the true democratic concept in the greatest society of scholars on earth, where in Heaven's name could we find it?

A group of us brought this question into the open, and a few months before his dismissal from the faculty, Harry Lerner was elected to Phi Beta Kappa, along with another New Yorker named Joe Fileman. They were the first "kikes" to receive this honor at the University of Alabama.

Thus did the "Fascist whelp" from Garth's Island react to Jews and communists. During my first week on the campus, the word "kike" had entered my vocabulary. It had quickly evolved into "goddam kike." Then, under the influence of my relationship with Harry Lerner, the word had slowly faded from my vocabulary. If I didn't come to like New York Jews as a group, I at least came to understand them and to resent discriminations against them. I reached a point where I could see how the many were made to suffer by the use of generalities applicable to only a few. I intend no broad application by linking Jews and communism. It so happened that communism and New York Jews came to Alabama together, and we had to take them together. As for communism, it had, no doubt, deeply affected me. I was opposed to it, but on the day I left the university I believed that Americans had a right to be communists and still be treated as Americans. I believed that if democracy couldn't survive without being isolated and protected from criticism, it didn't deserve to survive.

4

My faith in the democratic competitive concept survived the university, but my faith in my fathers' Living God was destroyed.

What can be said for the young man who deserts his fathers' God and announces he will search alone for a new and true God? When twenty generations of

81

Garths had found peace in their belief that the way of the Cross leads home, who was I to taste a little learning and straightway forswear their God and deny their faith? But in an age where nothing was accepted without analysis and where every adolescent assumed himself a competent analyst, I ate of the Tree of Knowledge and lost sight of the Cross.

What can be said for a young man who sets out to find God by mental exercise? Is he to be pitied? Or derided? Can we ever find God if we insist on searching alone? Or must we search in packs so that the shouts of the pack will help convince us of the authenticity of our search and of our possible nearness to the quarry?

I wish I could piece together the evolutionary process by which I reached the position where in honesty I could no longer pretend that I believed in my fathers' God. Down to this position I traveled a road lined with mental convulsions, for no follower along the road to Golgotha struggled harder to stay within sight of the Cross than I did. I fought the tendency to question with all my strength, and my retreat from my position of acceptance was lined with tears and heartache.

I have told you I cried the day I was saved at the Gum Springs Baptist Church. I was embarrassed by my crying, but for several years I found comfort in the memory that I had cried. It was evidence that some spirit which I could not hope to understand had descended upon me and effected the change necessary for me to enter in unto the Kingdom.

I remember the Sunday afternoon I was baptized in Shoal Creek. Twenty-five of us stood in line in the creek, the water up to our belts. A curious crowd lined both banks, for one of us to be baptized was Matilda Bailey, a perennial backslider who had been baptized many times before and who always shouted as she came up out of the water. The crowd had come to see Matilda do her stuff.

While the choir sang "Washed in the Blood of the
82

Lamb," I struggled to maintain the feeling of deep reverence I knew I should feel. I resented my noticing that Bessie Shaneyfelt's alto was off key. Cherry was on the bank staring at me, and I fought the embarrassment which swept over me. Why should I feel ridiculous at this terribly significant moment when I was signifying my acceptance of the Cross?

Matilda didn't fail her public. As the preacher pulled her up out of the water she was in a Holy Ghost rigor and screaming: "Sweet, Holy Jesus, I'm a-comin' Home!" The woman holding my hand joined in the shout, but I only hung my head and wished the preacher would hurry. It was no comfort to me that I noticed the scragginess of Matilda's neck when her hair was wet, the flapping of her bulbous breasts as she shook and shouted, and the moronic look on a face said to be in God's own image.

When I left high school I still refused to demand an honest answer of myself concerning my religion. The picture of Mary Lafavor at her fireside, in her gown and bare feet, with her black hair hanging in two plaits, with a face glowing with sincerity and acceptance; and refusing to let her two sons go to bed until she had read them a Chapter and heard their prayers—this was a very dear picture to me. How could I smile at my mother and still believe in the goodness and beauty of things, once I had denied her God and concluded the fireside scene was farce? To please her, I had transferred my church letter to a Tuscaloosa Baptist Church and had dutifully resolved to preserve my religion at all costs. But it was no use. Somewhere in the fire of those forensic bull sessions, the last fragment of my faith was consumed, and I could pretend no longer.

Harry Lerner's denunciation of the Catholic Church helped bring me to my final denial of Christianity. I could agree with Harry here, for I despised Catholicism as much as he did. The Garths had preferred "Yellow

83

Dog" Hoover to Al Smith in 1928. But my hatred of Catholicism came by a different line of reasoning from Harry's. I couldn't reconcile democracy and individualism with what little I knew about Catholicism. Democracy presupposes a faith in the common man, a belief that the common man is worthy to be trusted with all the knowledge he can gain, and a belief that once he has gained knowledge the common man can be trusted to reach true conclusions. The common man wants to be and is worthy of being a free moral agent.

"The fight against the Catholic Church should be an individualistic fight by free men to convince their fellows that religion is in itself individual," I said. "Educated men will scoff at any agency which attempts mass production of angels to people the Hereafter."

"You are still compromising, Garth," Harry replied. "The Catholic Church is a sham and a tool of reaction. It is a convicted enemy of the people and deserves no better fate than to die in its own blood."

Harry, naturally, was following his party line in his opinions of Catholicism, and I was still reflecting the attitude of the Garths. I have since learned, of course, that generalities applied to Catholics are as unfair as those applied to Jews or Protestants, and that many Catholics have helped to fight freedom's battles.

On the campus I knew all the common types of adolescent infidels. I knew the members of the Society of the Damned. I attended one of their meetings. The president, who called himself the Great Goddamdest, had done two satirical cartoons of Bryan. One cartoon showed the Commoner sweating in his shirt sleeves at the Scopes Trial bellowing: "Hurrah fer God!" In the other cartoon Bryan lay dead on the floor, having gained "The Fruit of Victory." I was invited to join the society, but I declined. When you are searching for bread you don't appreciate being offered a stone and told there is no bread.

84

Dick Glenn was a frat brother of mine at Beta Rho. He was a strange fellow. Fat, brilliant, and always chuckling. His father was a successful preacher, but Dick pretended to hate the church. He liked to drink whiskey on Sunday afternoons, talk cynically about his experiences as a preacher's son in small towns, and, half-drunk, he liked to go to church on Sunday nights. He'd sit on the back seat and make filthy remarks under his breath about the preacher, the choir members, and the collection takers. At dusk one Sunday I went to his room. He was lying naked and dead in his bathtub with his throat cut. A blood-spattered collection of Browning's poems was on the floor. He had been reading "The Bishop Orders His Tomb at Saint Praxed's Church."

It's hard to think of a fat man who can chuckle ever killing himself.

I remember the one occasion I considered suicide. It was a Sunday in 1932 in New Orleans. A group of us had driven from Tuscaloosa the day before, and the Saturday night had been a riotous one. We had attempted to have a drink in every bar on Bourbon Street, and we had "lifted the skirt" of more than one bar wench. Sometime after dawn I became separated from the others and began wandering aimlessly back toward the St. Charles Hotel. A light rain was falling, and I found myself standing in front of a big Jesuit church at early mass time. I leaned drunkenly against a lamp post and stood there, just watching the faces of those poor-class French and Italians as they went in and came out of the church. I saw how their eyes had changed, and I wondered what they had found inside to give them that lift. I wondered what Harry Lerner and I could fashion for them to replace their church after we had caused it to "die in its own blood." And then I walked away, cursing myself for being a sentimentalist.

Hotel rooms have always been cold and impersonal

85

to me. But my room at the St. Charles that Sunday was the coldest and loneliest I have ever found. The combination of the liquor hangover, the sex odor of those wenches I couldn't get out of my nostrils, and those faces at the Jesuit church almost overbalanced me.

I didn't look out the window that day. I was afraid to look.

By the time I left the university I knew I had no religion. I made no further pretensions. I always enjoyed going to church on Easter, but I discontinued even this practice. You can't honestly go to a church for stimulation or entertainment or curiosity after you have denied the basic tenets. I began piecing together some sort of understanding which must have resembled pantheism. I had concluded finally that there can be no conscious life after death, and I no longer found this conclusion frightening. I didn't suffer from melancholia; I took it all in stride. I was becoming an educated man.

5

The city of Tuscaloosa, Alabama, has a dual claim to fame. It is the location not only of the university but also of the Alabama State Hospital for the Insane. The two institutions face each other with a railroad dividing their spacious grounds, and many legends have grown out of the confusion resulting from this proximity. The railroad station for the university is on the left of the tracks, and the one for the asylum is on the right. It is said that freshmen often get off on the wrong side of the train and don't discover their error for months. Professors often suspect that this error has been reversed and some of their students had been intended for the asylum and simply got off on the university side by mistake.

86

"Are you certain, suh, that you didn't get off on the wrong side of the train when you came here?" is a stock question which exasperated instructors have been asking for decades.

The arrangement, however, makes for convenience in many ways. The university swing band plays for the weekly dances at the asylum. A former big league baseball pitcher at the asylum practices with the university team and gives the college men the benefit of trying to hit his fast-breaking curves. Harmless old nuts, who are allowed to roam about, sit on benches on the university campus and amuse the Damyankees with stories of the Civil War. Visitors assume the old nuts are professors. In the broad woods where nuts exercise by day, gentlemen and ladies can exercise by night. There have been several instances where these have been picked up by asylum guards who found it difficult to believe they had been mistaken.

But the most important benefits from this geographical arrangement were derived by the medical school and the psychology classes. The asylum and the university each had about four thousand inmates, and the medical school could contrast these two groups as to disease prevalence and susceptibility. Syphilis, for instance, ran about seventy per cent at the asylum, but was much lower at the university. Psychology classes, by analyzing groups at both the university and the asylum, could gain a broad understanding of the various types of abnormality.

Meetings of the psychology classes at the asylum were popular. Doctors would bring in representative inmates and explain their case histories and reactions. The professors would then classify the subjects and analyze them in psychological terms. And since mad men are only amusing when they are mad, the subjects would be prodded with questions by both students and professors who hoped for shocking answers. The patient who used the foulest barnyard terms was always

87

the most interesting, and the sorority sister who didn't hear a single vile expression at the asylum considered her time wasted. There was one amiable old nut who when questioned by any girl would snicker and say: "F..k you, wench!" He could be depended upon, and thus he was the most popular of all the asylum subjects.

We Garths were "touchous" on the subject of insanity. It wasn't funny to us. By 1931 my grandfather was raving with *delirium tremens*. Great-uncle Crazy Tom had been partially insane from birth. And there had been other members of the family who had "died ravin'!"

The year I took psychology I accompanied the class on only one of several visits to the asylum. That day, with four thousand inmates to choose from, the smart young doctors chose Case No. 4864 for study. They came leading him in—Case No. 4864. He was a tall, gaunt, red-faced and white-haired old man, with fierce eyes that looked far over your head as though searching for some sign in the distance. He wore a coarse, loose-fitting, prison-like suit and straw sandals.

The sight of him was like a horse-whip across my face! I lunged forward in my seat, determined to strike down the attendants and lead the old man back to the privacy of his cell. I caught myself as I came to my feet and settled down again.

"What the hell, Lafavor?" the boy next to me asked: "Your d. t.'s bothering you again?"

"Yeah," I said. "I suppose so."

Case No. 4864 was Crawford Garth. My grandfather.

I didn't know he had been brought to the asylum. I knew he had gone completely insane. I had been to see him on the Island where Raccoon Charley was nursing him. I had been told he was to be kept there. But, only a week before, he had been brought to the asylum in the hope that something might be done for him. The family had decided not to tell me of his transfer because of the embarrassment I might feel at the university.

Now I was sitting in a front seat, and my pathetic old grandfather, who had been called The Cap'n most of his life, was being led in like an animal and seated on the platform for the amused edification of a hundred sophomores. It was monstrous and inhuman! What if his name should be called? Or the family resemblance noted? Or if he should speak to me as he probably would? Well, what? My next impulse was to stand up and explain the situation and laugh. At least I could protect a proud, helpless old man from further humiliation. But in my dilemma I sat still and said nothing.

The doctor was a smart young Damyankee. You had to be tough to work in a nut house. You had to smack 'em when they wouldn't keep their clothes on. I had heard these boys talk.

He spoke precisely, clipping his words for effect.

"Here," he said, "is Case No. 4864. An unusually interesting case since it affords us an opportunity to study all three of the common causes of insanity in the South. Family degeneracy. Alcoholism. Syphilis. This man is seventy-five years old. He is a member of an old, land-bound Southern family. No formal education. He has had syphilis for forty years and been an alcoholic for thirty. If we could lay his nervous system in a dissecting pan before us, we would find it infected with the micro-organisms of the disease and enlarged and softened by the effect of the chronic stimulant. We would find . . ."

He broke off, for Case No. 4864 was speaking.

"They are kind to me today, Bud," the case said.

The old man had spoken the words directly to me. He sat about eight feet from me, and I had watched him as he peered about the room. Twice I had seen his eyes pass mine with no sign of recognition, but they had kept coming back. The third time the eyes had seemed to settle on me for a moment, and he had spoken the words with no change of facial expression.

"They are kind to me today, Bud," he repeated.

"I'll explain what the patient is talking about," the young doctor put in. "The patient imagines he is persecuted by little animals. From his descriptions the animals are evidently giant potato bugs, a type of bug which he once poisoned on his farm. As a child he probably had to pick the larvae of these bugs off the potato vines, and his childish mind came to associate these worm-like, goggle-eyed larvae with horror. Now he feels he is helpless, and the potato bugs which he killed in his youth are back to take their revenge on him."

Case No. 4864 went on. "Old Big Un bit me yesterday, Bud. But he's laying back under a log today. Jest watchin' me. Old Big Un's kind to me today." The facial expression broke into a faint smile.

The doctor explained further. "The patient is telling this young man here that the potato bugs are not attacking him today. He thinks they are being kind when they don't attack him."

A belle of Kappa Zeta had a question.

"Does he use vile language, doctor?"

The sophomores tittered.

"No, this man is not vile. You see, this man is ignorant and unrefined. He has always used crude, vile language. And when a person goes insane, his habits usually swing to the opposite of what they have been in normality. Our most obscene patients are persons who were normally intelligent, educated and refined. Insanity removes their inhibitions, and they are likely to do and say the things which have normally seemed unreasonable for them to do and say."

"He won't embarrass me if I ask him a question?" Kappa Zeta asked.

"No. He is not likely to."

The girl walked around in front of Case No. 4864 and said: "How do you feel today?"

90

"I'm kind today," he replied. Then he looked back at me. "Old Big Un is kind to me today, Bud."

Kappa Zeta turned to me. "You ask him the questions, Garth. He notices you. Maybe you speak his language."

The sophomores tittered again, and I could stand it no longer. I got up.

"Yes," I said. "I do speak his language. I have always gotten a big laugh out of that story about the son and the father who met in the whorehouse. I guess most of you have laughed at that one, too. As soon as I am gone you can have an even bigger laugh. This man is my grandfather."

I walked up to the rostrum, took Case No. 4864 by the hand, and led him back to his cell. An attendant walked silently along with me and opened the doors.

For some reason they failed to laugh after we had gone. The session broke up, and there were quizzical expressions and even a trace of fright on some sophomoric faces. The doctor was not quite so self-assured.

I suppose my action was nothing to be proud of, but I have always been thankful I did it. Living with myself wouldn't have been easy if I had kept still that morning.

6

You remember I thought sexual intercourse was Something Sacred when I left the Garth world. I knew all about the wenching tendencies of the men in the family, but because of my mother's attitude and of my love for Cherry, I had decided to do all my amorous adventuring with Cherry. The ideal of one man and one woman was worth sacrifice and discomfort. But at the university a variety of influences combined to alter my attitude.

First there was Dave Blocton. You couldn't escape Dave. He was the collar-ad chap who paddled my pants on the train coming down. He became my best friend and fraternity brother in Beta Rho. By his own admission Dave was a Fifteen-Minute-Man. Fifteen minutes after he was alone with any girl he would have so broken down her resistance that he could pat her on the bustle without offending her. He had a colorful collection of step-ins which he displayed on lines hung across his room. Each flimsy garment was labeled with a case history, and from its size and contour and the way it hung on the line you could visualize the type of girl from whom it had been stripped by the artful Dave. There was an exciting story of human conflict connected with each trophy, and Dave would recite these stories with gestures to audiences of bug-eyed freshmen.

"Ah, freshmen, I'll never forget this little bitty," Dave would say longingly as he'd point to a trim, pink creation. "She was a Kappa Zeta, and I had to take her out three nights before I got it."

Dave would then pause to light a cigaret, while his audience drooled in hunger for the details. As my self-appointed instructor in "campus science," Dave considered it his duty to impart to me his seduction secrets so that his art would not be lost to Beta Rho when he had gone.

The second influence was in the circumstance that I lived off campus in two modest rooms, which, taken collectively, could qualify as an apartment. There is something about the word apartment which connotes seduction and assignation. Women, I believe, surrender their virtue more readily in an apartment than anywhere else. I took my meals at the frat house, but I kept the apartment in order to enjoy some degree of privacy. You would think that this reluctance to share the fellowship of the frat house would have made me unpopular with my brothers, but, on the contrary, the apartment made me inordinately popular. Many's the night I have wrestled with Geoffrey Chaucer in my bedroom while a fraternity brother wrestled with a luscious morsel from Sorority Row in my living room.

92

And what with the disgracefully thin walls in the house, such experiences hardly encouraged me to remain a celibate.

Most of the tenants of the apartment house were the more blasé and rebellious boys and girls of the campus. My pink-and-red intellectual pals. An aura of sin hung over the place. It was a port of call for the natty bootleggers who brought the fancy stuff from New Orleans. Adeline Reed, the fabulous rebel from Chicago, lived there. So did the campus dope fiend. So did two effeminate gentlemen whose apartment was said to be furnished in lurid colors and who were subjects of stimulating speculation. The campus humor mag once suggested that a red light should in honesty be hung in front of the building; and both the police and the Dean of Women had honored us with lustrating visits.

At a communal drinking bout one night Harry embarrassed me by announcing to a mixed group that I was still a virgin.

"Oh, how quaint!" Adeline Reed commented through a screen of smoke. "He must be a fairy."

Adeline was the blond, swivel-hipped, free-thinking daughter of a Chicago millionaire. At twenty she had given her life purpose by devoting it to the promotion of revolutions and the smashing of ikons. Her greatest disappointment was that her decadent family had not yet gathered the courage to disinherit her, a weakness that only made her more contemptuous of them. She looked forward to the day when she would present fine, full-bodied, illegitimate sons to the People's State. With her long, lithe, Cossack legs; with hair like October oats in the sun; with her free, abandoned movements under clothes that no communist should afford; and with a full mouth that smirked and brown eyes that challenged, Adeline Reed was a shattering jolt to the son of seven generations of Garths. And she had suggested that I might be a fairy.

Then, too, what the hell! I was a Garth, wasn't I?

93

With seven generations of Garth fathers behind me who had never missed a chance to take a horsin' wench to the woods, what right had I to prate about single standards of morality and doing nothing I wouldn't want my wife to do?

But the first step wasn't easy. Cherry had gone to a girls' school in Virginia where girls were "properly looked after." I loved her. I assumed that someday I would marry her. In my mind Cherry was the clear-eyed combination of freshness and honesty and beauty and desirability, all clothed in an innocent white satin which emphasized the round smoothness of the backs of her legs. Cherry and I had shared every Great Good together. We were saving a *summum bonum* to share. How would I feel if I broke faith and shared it first with someone else?

The apartment where Adeline Reed lived was on the floor above mine. Adeline's bedroom was directly above my bedroom. I went in there once during a party to get some cigarets. It was the first strange woman's bedroom I had ever entered. There was a tormenting odor of evasive powder and perfume about it. Adeline came in behind me, and for a moment we stood facing each other before her mirror. She was as tall as I. She stood erect and looked straight into my eyes. A child of privilege, she imagined she wanted to see all the privileges and pretenses and moral strictures of the world smashed and cleared away. She wanted to see all the ego-props knocked from under the individual man and woman, and the two left standing naked and un-adorned in a communal garden of reality. She was two years older than I. A summer trip to Russia and asso-ciation with Harry Lerner had matured her as a revo-lutionist.

When I kissed her she put her arms around me, but she stood fully erect and kept her eyes open. I imagined she had kissed many men before and liked it, and ex-

94

pected to kiss many others and like it. I was abashed when someone discovered us, but Adeline laughed.

"You're a fool, Garth," she said, "but I like you and I can teach you a few things."

As I lay in my bed directly under Adeline's bedroom, I was tormented by visions of Cherry's high-breasted innocence in white satin, topped by black hair and deep red lips. Then I'd see Adeline standing naked on her long, lithe legs. Adeline was always naked in my visions, and Cherry was always in that white satin.

The frat brothers had wenching parties on Saturday night. The all-night services of two of the town's healthier whores would be engaged, and round-robin contests would be in order. It was as much a fraternity's responsibility to introduce its members to the inner sexual mysteries as it was to teach them to dance and eat soup. A brother's first effort was always an occasion for loud laughter and wisecracks. One of the stock tricks played on a nervous, teeth-chattering freshman was to arrange a mirror so that his first feeble and fumbling effort could provide suppressed laughs for a group of concealed brothers. Dave Blocton was determined to drive me to a fall, but I was equally determined that when the fall came I'd provide no laughs for the brotherhood.

Well, on my eighteenth birthday, I decided it was time I acquired an active sex life. I wanted to be a good sport about it. As long as Dave and the fellows didn't pull any mirror tricks, I'd let them have their laughs. I concluded that the picture of a fraternity man being led to a whorehouse by his joking brothers was ridiculous, but what the hell! There was nothing wrong about it. If my first effort was not to be with Cherry, I wanted it to be with a professional. Above all, I didn't want to make any clumsy, amateurish moves around Adeline. No Southern gentleman likes to go to a grand ball until he has taken his first awkward steps with a dancing teacher.

95

So, fortified with three tremendous jolts of Garth's Island corn, I agreed one Saturday night to be led to the slaughter by Dave and four other brothers. But instead of employing the services of one of the "call" women, I insisted on going out in the country to Mamie's Place. I was taking no chances of having those bastards hiding or rigging a mirror somewhere and watching me. And I knew about those thin walls at the apartment. As we drove out I fought to keep my body from trembling and my teeth from chattering, while they loaded me with mock advice. I had never been inside Mamie's Place, so they escorted me in like five preachers taking one poor soul to baptism.

Seven washed-out country whores in faded negligees paraded for my inspection.

"Look your best, gals," Dave said, "for there's fresh meat on hand to be cured." They all snickered as did two old pimps sitting before the fire.

"You want Louise," Dave advised. "The blonde in yellow."

"For God's sake, why?" I asked. She was certainly the oldest and crumbiest of the lot.

"She doesn't look so hot. But she's got hidden talents you'll learn to appreciate."

"She has them well hidden, all right," I agreed.

Apparently I was to have no choice, for two of my escorting brothers called Louise aside and bargained with her. I saw her take the money and nod to something they told her.

"They're giving her special instructions," Dave explained. "Beta Rhos demand the best of everything, you know."

Louise then took me by the hand.

"Come on, honey," she said. "I understand. I'll treat ya' nice."

She led me down a dimly-lighted hall. I was far too excited to ruminate over the incongruity of a Southern Gentleman first experiencing Something Sacred

96

and Beautiful in a leaking tenant shack with a cotton-patch whore in a dirty yellow negligee.

Inside the room a fire sputtered in the fireplace but I was freezing. The flowers on the wallpaper had faded with dirt, and the black, dirt-heavy canvas under it was exposed in torn gaps. A sway-back mattress hung precariously on a rusty iron bedstead. On a table was a smoking lamp, a torn copy of *True Story Magazine,* and a basin of reddish water. Potassium permanganate. There wasn't a "nigger" on the Garth farm whose place wasn't cleaner.

"How ya' feel, honey?" She was slipping off her dirty negligee.

"I-I-I'm cold," I stammered. Blood was pounding in my ears.

"Git off those britches an' I'll make ya' warm."

She had to help me undress, and when I finally fell clumsily into her long, dirty arms, I must have been nearly unconscious.

The brevity of it all added to my embarrassment, but as the blood-pounding stopped and my hearing returned, I heard something which magnified that embarrassment ten-fold. Roars of laughter were coming from the next room. My shoulders drooped lower in shameful resignation. Those bastards had reached through a hole in the wall, pushed a calendar aside, and had been peering directly into a cracked mirror at the foot of the bed.

"Ya'll fo'give me fer lettin' 'em see ya git ya first, won't ye, honey?" Louise asked. "They paid me five dollars extrey."

I wanted to bash in her head with the washbasin, but I was licked and knew it.

Back with the hilarious brothers I had to be the sheepish good sport who had been made a fool of. But alone in my apartment I stood under the shower for an hour and alternately swallowed and cursed. I bathed in antiseptic. I had lost something, but I didn't resent losing it as much as the way I had lost it. Maybe I wanted to cry. But I took a long drink, powdered my body, put on my black silk pajamas, and crawled between my fresh, clean sheets. What the hell! I was Garth Lafavor, student of life. I was sole arbiter of what was right and wrong for me. I had to try everything just for the hell of it and to see why other people did it. Cherry would never know about such things. Men are different from women. What did the old Saracen tell Sherwood's Virtuous Knight? Western men are fools to pretend to this monogamy stuff.

What the hell!

It isn't easy for a man to recall such sordid little events out of his past. The smart folks will say you are being sophomoric, and those who aren't so smart will say you are being vulgar or sensational. But what the hell? It's dying time again, isn't it? We're on a spot. We've got to go out and fight for mankind, perhaps die, and we're plagued by doubts as to whether or not mankind is worth dying for. I've had one helluva time convincing myself that man is a noble creature bound for some promised land and worthy of governing himself. You have to believe in the nobility of man to believe in democracy, and I realize that the infernal casualness of the sexual relation has contributed much to this shell of cynicism that I am wearing.

I don't pretend to be typical, but I state as a fact that when I entered the University of Alabama I thought God had something to do with the sexual relation; when I left I regarded maids, wives, or widows as proper foils in the bedroom contest. My favorite likkered observation became: "When ya' stand 'em on their heads, they all look alike;" a statement which Adeline Reed always challenged, and with some reason. I learned most of Dave's seduction tricks and developed a few of my own. And while the pursuit of the petticoat was only an avocation with me and not a vocation as it was with Dave, I made my pro rata contribution to the general campus delinquency.

I was caught on a Fathers List. We sophisticated happy-go-luckies knew and practised all modern methods of contraception, but the element of human carelessness persisted and a few pregnancies developed each term. Procedure in such emergencies was standard. When the girl became sufficiently terrified, the several possible fathers were assembled into a Fathers List. The champion Fathers List of all time was submitted by a voluptuous Kappa Zeta from Texas. It had one fraternity's entire roster of thirty-two names on it, so she became known as "The Sweetheart of Sigma Something-or-Other."

The Fathers List I made was a modest one of eight names. Rumor announced in advance who we all were, so we convened at a frat house and confronted the *fait accompli*. One of the fellows, a senior in engineering, presided.

"Now men this is a serious matter," he said. "Do any of us want to deny we belong on this list?"

I was extremely uncomfortable. When an explorer has gained a summit, it hurts his pride to discover that so many lesser men have preceded him.

Not one denial was entered, so we carried on. "Now the cost is going to be $250," the senior said.

There was a low whistle. Three of the fathers were working their way through school.

"Now we can proceed in either of two ways: We can act quickly and prorate the cost and settle. Or we can be stupid and await further developments. Which do you men prefer?"

"Let's pay off." It was a chorus of five voices. The three working fathers claimed they couldn't pay. So it was fifty bucks a throw for the five of us who could pay in cash for our sins.

The working boys got a free ride. It was a snotty, undemocratic act, but as we walked out I turned to them and said: "If you pore bastards can't help look after the cow, why don't you quit drinking the milk?"

In the fall of one of my college years, Alabama's football team played a Damyankee outfit up North, and the trip netted me an experience which I could never live down. Only you who have been a part of that peculiar form of human dementia called "The Football Special" can appreciate it.

The train left the university on Thursday afternoon. Sixteen carloads of insanity. A hundred gallons of corn whiskey. Fat-cat alumni with sheaves of green money to bet on a dice throw, a card turn, a spit at a crack, or that you'd drop dead before sundown. Like "niggers" in a corn crib, painted, heavy-hipped matrons hunched down in a baggage car, cracked dice and prayed for Neena from Pasadena with the Golden Drawers. The train was a rolling madhouse-whorehouse-gambling-house rolling up out of the South to see the Crimson Tide lick hell out of the Damyankees. It was my first long trip, and I was with Addy Reed. After my sexual fall and disillusionment at Mamie's Place, Addy had taken me in hand and introduced me to sophisticated, communistic, and cooperative love. We were not in love, of course, but as fellow suckers at the udders of light, we admitted a physical attraction for one another.

Dave Blocton and two other brothers with their ladies completed our party. By midnight the tumult and shouting had swelled into a riotous pajama dance. Negroes stood at the end of the cars and sang and beat banjos and blew horns; and we who had not passed out weaved and rolled in the aisles, "dancing" in our pajamas. About half the berths were made up in each car, and the other half were being used for sitting and drinking purposes.

"What a piker that bastard Caligula must 'a been!" Adeline shouted into my ear above the roar. She was wearing a blue silk lounge outfit, with her oatfield hair combed page boy to her shoulders. If fuzzy old Karl Marx could see her now, I thought, he would be proud of one convert. Addy was a very brilliant girl. Her favorite trick, when out with some persistent fellow who didn't appeal to her, was to drive him to a whorehouse, give him three dollars and tell him to go in and get it over with while she waited.

At some point during this drunken pajama revel Adeline and I found ourselves in an upper berth in a section in the very center of a coach. We were lost in our own mutual attractions when the catastrophe struck. Lit to the gills, Dave and the brothers wanted to play. They had seen me reel up into the berth, had turned up the lights in the car, and had timed their trick perfectly. Without warning, powerful hands grabbed my heels and gave a mighty jerk.

I hit the floor in my bare feet, dressed in the abbreviated tops of my pajamas and a surprised expression. I was facing a forewarned, howling half-carload of reveling men and women, with every light in the car on!

I dived into the lower berth to my right and was kicked out, I dived to my left and was kicked out. I tried to run back through the portion of the car where the berths were down, but Dave and the gang had clogged the aisle. I had no choice but to run straight through that roaring mob, packed in the sections which had not been made up. I ran. I burst into the washroom at the end of the car. It was the ladies' room, and I was a bit of a shock to the three matronly occupants. I grabbed a towel and had to sit for ten minutes while Dave sent porters up and down the train bawling:

"Has anyone seen Mistah Lafavor's pants? He's in the ladies' room and wants someone to please send him his pants."

Blocton, being a Southern Gentleman, gallantly protected Adeline by turning down the lights and moving her to another car as soon as I had made my scared-rabbit run; but I was hounded relentlessly for months as a bird who was publicly plucked off his nest.

Seven years later I was walking down Hollywood Boulevard early one morning. A slow drizzle was falling, and I was hungry. I couldn't imagine anyone's laughing, but a man meeting me at the Cahuenga corner broke into a chuckle.

"You remember the last time I saw you?" he asked.

"No, I'm afraid I don't," I said.

"You were running down a Pullman car aisle with your pants off."

I suppose my what-the-hell attitude toward sex was the natural companion to my loss of religion and my developing cynicism. Gentlemen at the University of Alabama have always partaken freely of the pleasures of the flesh, but the rules have undergone some significant changes. Prior to 1915, the fraternities kept talented Negro girls to instruct the gentlemen in the mysteries, and when a gentleman foraged forth in the white realm, he confined his hunting to the lower-class whites. After the World War the Negro instructress was ruled out of fashion, and there was a period when the gentlemen reveled in the New Freedom. Even the highest lady of quality became fair game, but the chase was conducted in the spirit of high adventure.

By 1932 the breath of the Depression had blown across the whole process of seduction, leaving it ordinary and casual and taken-for-granted. Communism had made its contribution. The glamour and the thrill of the chase were gone, and only the infernal casualness remained. I devised a neat little explanation for my own attitude. I was only adapting the old wenching practices of my fathers to the new conditions under which I lived. There was nothing wrong about casual sexual relations between educated men and women. Women had once hesitated because of fears which were no longer valid. The hazy idea about it's being religiously wrong was ridiculous. So was the outworn conception that nice girls refrained. What-the-hell, we're all alike, aren't we? Those old fears of disease and helpless fertility were only for the careless and uneducated. They didn't bother the Garth Lafavors and the Dave Bloctons and the Adeline Reeds. We knew what we were doing.

Besides, education and sophistication changed everything. I wasn't a farm boy any longer. I wasn't an ordinary Garth in rubber boots and overalls, lifting some wench's petticoat on a mat of pine needles. I was Peter Garth Lafavor—Phi Beta Kappa, Beta Rho, *magna cum laude,* and silk pajamas with perfume under my arms. I knew "off-the-record" stories about celebrities. I knew which actresses were Lesbians. I was Culture and Refinement and Sophistication Extraordinary. I was the soul of modesty about such accomplishments; but, after all, they do make a difference.

7

In the fraternity bull sessions the propriety of sexual relations with your intended wife was a moot point as late as 1933. Naturally Harry Lerner and Addy Reed and my other Marxist friends had no doubts, since to them even marriage was a farcical institution. But in the fraternity there was a division of opinion. What was most surprising was that Dave Blocton was an advocate for the virgin wife!

"When I find an attractive, honest gal who won't let me have it," he said, "I'm going to marry her."

But his position was hotly challenged both because it sounded so damned unfair and because several of the brothers readily admitted relations with girls to whom they were engaged.

Cherry Lanson was twenty in the spring of 1933 and still a virgin. During my college years I seated myself on a mountain top with a pair of scales and presumed

103

to weigh every established principle in the universe. I weighed my inherited religion, chucked it over the precipice, and fashioned a New Explanation. I weighed my inherited democracy and tempered it with cynicism and doubt. I weighed my provincial ideas of human conduct and decided that I, alone, was the proper judge of what was right and wrong for me. I slept with Addy Reed and found the experience both gratifying and educational.

Then why the hell had I insisted on preserving Cherry Lanson's virtue? Why had I deliberately encouraged that "waiting" every time I had seen her? I wanted her more than any woman I had ever known. Adeline and her lithe-legged, blonde-headed nakedness had only made the dream of Cherry in her white satin and the tight satiny-smoothness of the backs of her legs more tormenting. I was being dishonest. I was acutely aware of my dishonesty. I was like an avowed atheist who secretes a crucifix under his pillow.

Cherry Lanson was a girl who deserved security in mind, soul, and position. Her experience from the time we left our unrippled pool of Morgan County had been as different from mine as a church social is from a bar brawl. At the Mary Scott College for Women in Virginia there had been no murderers of God. No Fifteen-minute Men with comfortable apartments and aphrodisiacs. No what-the-hell attitude. No burning, prying intellects. No Seekers After Truth. No Assayers and Weighers of the Universe.

The verities had been taken for granted at the Mary Scott College for Women. The girls had been taught how to select a pot roast and sew a pleated seam. To dance without sticking out behind and to lead from kings instead of aces. How to sit down so that their legs would cross automatically. How to write correct notes and where a what-not should be hung. They had tittered at shocks supplied by Elinor Glynn and Viña Delmar. They had felt modern and reckless when they had held forbidden bull sessions after lights out and whispered stimulating reports on the love-making of their boy friends. The climax of modern recklessness had come when some exceedingly reckless girl had dropped her voice to a whisper in the darkness and sent them all into pillow-hugging titillations with a match-light reading of some alleged doctor's instructions on how young brides can salvage the most enjoyment out of the drudgery of the marriage bed.

I had invited Cherry to our semi-annual frat dances and parties, and though she was shy at first, she was the kind of girl you enjoyed inviting to your fraternity. She was beautiful and enthusiastic and honest. The other girls liked her and wrote to her after the parties and invited her to visit them. The fellows liked her, and not only did their duty dances with her but rushed her for more dances. They looked at her black hair and black eyes and sensual lips, and remembering that I was one of Beta's two Fifteen-minute Men, they had doubted my claims that our love-making had its limits.

When I was alone with her, either at the parties or on my visits home, I felt strangely content and undisturbed. Life was simple and good to Cherry. When I was with her it seemed simple and good to me, too. Even at twenty it seemed we had known and loved and trusted each other for a very long time. It was inconceivable that she could ever be anything but honest with me. She had dozens of boy friends, but she was mine and neither she nor I ever doubted it.

It hurt like hell the first time I held her in my arms and knew I wasn't being honest with her any longer. My frat brothers had kidded her about Adeline and some of the others, but except for a sly reference, she never mentioned them. Instead, we talked of our love and our dreams and how happy we were going to be. What we believed and why we believed it and all the sluttish things which were happening in the world by 1933—we passed them over lightly. Our only problem

105

was how soon we could marry, and our only disputes came when I pointed out that it might be a year or two after college before we could do so.

Cherry Lanson was a man's woman. No woman ever lived who wanted more than she did simply to be one man's wife and to feel secure always in his love. After her third year at the Mary Scott School, she wrote:

"Garth, I think I've had about enough education. Don't you agree? You know I'm not the student in our family. Remember how I used to write you notes behind my algebra book while you worked out the problems and gave them to me to copy? And how you always wrote out the Latin translations in my book for me? Well, now that I've learned how to feed the baby and how to look after all those big houses we are going to build and how to pronounce the French names on a menu, I find these college books are getting heavier and the words are getting longer. I think I'll chuck 'em and find me a cozy spot to twiddle my thumbs in until you've learned all there is to know. After all, you're always going to know the answers anyhow, so why should I bother with 'em? Besides, if I get too educated we'll have too many dull things to argue about, and right now I am thinking of more pleasant ways that we can spend our hours—if you know what I mean?"

That was Cherry. She heard women in tailored suits lecture about how important it was for modern women to have college degrees so their modern husbands would be proud of them and would not feel superior to them. But Cherry didn't figure it that way. She wasn't afraid of feeling inferior. She'd do the loving. She wouldn't rely on college degrees to hold her husband's love and respect. She'd rely on capable hands, a beautiful body in white satin which made her thighs look smooth and satiny, and a heart to which love was everything.

You can understand why I never introduced Cherry

to Adeline or Harry when she came to the university. They would have considered her simple and provincial. From what they had heard of her, they razzed me after her visits.

"How's the demure little small-town mistress?" Harry inquired.

"You didn't really tell her the moon's not made of green cheese, did you?" Adeline mocked. "I know those little girls' schools. They teach 'em to wear their blindfolds gracefully so they won't ever see anything real in the world."

I let them get away with their kidding because I didn't know what to say. I was a moth like them, beating crazily about the lamp of knowledge. At times I hated them. But when I went back to Morgan County for a visit, the small talk sent me rushing back for stimulation. Perhaps they were my type of people by then.

When I was around Cherry I pretended to be a person I was not. I was changing. The world was changing. But not Cherry. She was only adding a mature veneer to the simple little black-headed girl in high school who believed in fairy tales.

But there seemed to be no end to my rationalizing powers. I soon had an acceptable explanation worked out; and when I accepted it, I smacked my mental lips in satisfaction and looked for new rational worlds to conquer. It was proper for me to be dishonest with Cherry. I lived in two worlds now—the Garth world and the world of knowledge and sophistication. Cherry was of the Garth world. It would be criminal to drag her into the other world. In the world of knowledge and sophistication there were no verities. Only experiment. We analyzed gods and women and emotions and institutions. We kept ourselves constantly under the microscope. We accepted nothing as fact. We subjected everything to ordeals. We broke solid old rocks into bits of sand for analysis.

If I was to have a wife like Cherry it was proper for

107

me to lie to her. She wanted to believe lies. All people in the Garth world wanted to believe lies. They wanted to believe there was a Heaven where you wore golden slippers. They wanted to believe God was a kindly old man who sat on a cloud and whisked the good chillun away from the Devil. They wanted to believe they were Free Americans and Jeffersonian Democrats. They wanted to believe Washington couldn't tell a lie. They wanted to believe that Senators and Congressmen were great and sincere and noble men and that the President was kin to God Himself. They wanted to hip and holler when they saw the flag. They wanted to believe all men were innately noble and free moral agents. They wanted to believe in Faith and Hope and Charity, and they wanted to crucify anybody who said It Ain't So.

Cherry's virginity had been a symbol to me through all the college travail. A symbol which signified that I still respected the Garth world. The crucifix under the atheist's pillow. The safe little haven which the timid explorer maintains while he explores the jungle. I think I was afraid not to "wait" with Cherry. But during the final dances in 1933 I crushed this symbol, too. I tossed the crucifix out the window.

It seems improper to say it, but Cherry had never been too enthusiastic about our noble "waiting" principle. She supposed it was the thing to do. But Cherry was always afraid that perhaps we were passing through our best years. All through the college period we had gone on the understanding that we'd be married on my graduation day, and when we had to retreat again before the uncertainties of 1933, Cherry began showing signs of irritation. For several weeks before she came for the final dances, I noticed sly implications in her letters. If the house was going to be crowded, I needn't be too careful about arranging a place for her to stay. I had lots of room, hadn't I? Cherry had kidded about such matters before, but this time I knew she wasn't kidding. She was through with "waiting."

108

Throughout the dance that May evening Cherry and I knew it was time for something tremendous to happen in our lives again. We didn't say anything; words were hardly necessary. Cherry was wearing a black-and-red combination that gave her the confidence of Cleopatra. I wasn't the only one who had been learning tricks. Cherry had picked up a few tricks, too, at the Mary Scott College for Women. She had learned how effective a party dress can be if worn properly; how and where to exert the proper pressures when dancing; and how to blend perfumes. You know, life would be worth while if you never saw anything but one beautiful woman who loved you on the one night when she felt supremely confident.

After the dance we went to the apartment and turned down the lights. I was nervous as a freshman. Cherry went to freshen and as she came back through the doorway she stopped for me to look at her. She was wearing a white satin gown with a white fluffiness at her throat. She turned around and I could see the smooth tightness and satinness of the backs of her legs—just as in a hundred of my fitful dreams.

"You like me, darling?" she asked. It really wasn't a question. Cherry knew what she meant to me. She had always known it.

"My God, Cherry!" I said. "I feel like I'm in church on Easter morning!"

As she lay on the couch I dismissed the mind-flash that she was lying where Addy and twenty others had lain. I worshipped her. I felt good and clean and noble. Almost honest.

I could feel Cherry's happiness through her tears. "Oh, Garth," she whispered, "we've waited so long."

"Yes, darling."

"Was it worth waiting for?"

"Of course, Cherry. Yes."

"You aren't sorry now, are you? You'll always love me?"

"Yes, Cherry."

"You'll always *respect* me."

I lay there and held her, with the moon shining in the window. Her black head lay on my shoulder. I kissed the wet, black eyes. All her satiny softness lay against my body. My cynicism was gone. There was a God in some Heaven, and there was order and goodness in the world. There was love and faith and hope. Men were not sniveling, filthy, little animals. They were majestic, god-like creatures who could dream and aspire and be whatever they had the will to be. I had been purged of my doubts. Cherry Lanson was going to save me. As long as I could hold on to her, her warm, beautiful body and simple, believing soul would save us both.

That was May 2, 1933.

8

The University of Alabama's centennial celebration was an impressive occasion for the thousands of alumni who attended. It was particularly impressive for the members of my Class of '33. Most of the events were held at night in the new stadium built from the profits of Rose Bowl victories. A stage had been erected on the green carpet of the playing field, and colorful lights played upon the actors and speakers while the spectators sat banked in darkness.

There was a glittering pageant depicting the university's one-hundred-year history. The crowd was noisily excited during the big scene when the Yankee cavalry slashed through the youthful student infantry guard, but a fearful, cold-hearted silence settled over the stadium as a burly, booted cavalryman put a torch to the magnificent Georgian library. Even in make-believe there is something terrifying about the sight of a booted soldier burning a library. It is history's most crushingly awful scene. Force mocking Reason. Bar-

barism surging back to destroy in a flaming moment civilization's golden distillate of the centuries.

The scholarly Claude G. Bowers, interpreter of Southerners and the South, delivered the centennial address. The South's most eminent clergyman, Dr. George Truitt, was the baccalaureate speaker; and the Honorable Benjamin Meek Miller, Governor of Alabama and rugged oak of Black Belt conservatism, added the political plumosity. All of them stood in the economic ashes of that year and foresaw a brave New South marching toward a manifest destiny where industry would be balanced with agriculture, foreign markets recaptured, and the Four Horsemen of the South— poverty, disease, illiteracy and intolerance—defeated by triumphant liberal education.

And so I reached a second significant morning. The May morning the Class Day exercises were held in the sun-filled stadium. The morning Garth Lafavor, first educated son of twenty generations of Scots-Irish peasants, delivered the valedictory for the university's centennial class representing thirty-eight states and four foreign countries. Before him sat six thousand Important People—not dirt farmers in boiled overalls. And before him sat all the people who had mattered in his life.

There was Cherry Lanson. A Cherry who wore a tailored white suit, whose cascade of black hair was topped by an impertinent red hat, and whose black eyes had grown deeper with experience. She could remember when Garth Lafavor wore short pants and rode a horse to school and held her hand under the desk. Last night she had lain in his arms for a long time and felt his heart pounding against her.

Sitting with Cherry was Mary Garth Lafavor and John Lafavor. At Morgan County High School they had been important and self-assured people. But here they were shy and careful, so that the Great One would not be ashamed to present them to his friends. Before they had come on the long journey to Tuscaloosa they had bought clothes they felt they couldn't afford. Not because they wanted them but for Garth's sake. Mary Lafavor had studied both the new Sears-Roebuck catalog and a borrowed *McCall's Magazine* to be certain her blue voile was in fashion. She had starched her husband's collar and pressed his blue serge suit. And now she was glad she had gone to all the trouble. Looking up at her son on the platform she was glad she hadn't made him wear those pants with the microscopic patch on the seat. She was glad she hadn't told him how fierce the battle had been to provide ready cash for his mountainous expenses. She was glad she had worn her old dresses and driven the old car so he could ride the football special to Chicago. She was glad she and Old Mis' Ella had tightened the line on the croppers and borrowed another thousand dollars from the banks so he could go to New Orleans and entertain his friends properly.

Whatever the cost had been, John and Mary Lafavor knew their son would be worth it.

There was Adeline Reed and Harry Lerner. They had done much for this country boy whose temples were now gray and whose eyes were too old and too hard for his years. They had hit him with nihilism and torpedoed him with the Russian Revolution and watched him thresh water and gasp in his struggle to answer the unanswerable with platitudes. They had driven him to trim his lamp in his search for buttresses. When Harry had come upon him rehearsing his speech, he had cracked: "Gonna give us another Lafavor fantasy, eh, Garth?"

"Yeah, with gestures."

"Don't dare let a word of truth escape you. It'd spoil the big celebration for the customers."

"Don't worry. I'm sticking to our Jeffersonian platitudes."

Yet Harry and Adeline had grown close to this country boy who clung to so much that they hated. There was Dave Blocton and a delegation of Beta Rhos. Beta Rho didn't often produce a Phi Bete and a valedictorian. The Lafavor straight A's had lifted old Beta's scholastic standing from third from the bottom to eighth from the bottom. The frat was filing all the Lafavor themes and essays for future Betas to copy. In return, Dave and the frat had contributed much to Garth Lafavor. Dave had begun slatting his pants on the train coming down, driving out his shyness and fierce pride. He had taken him to a whorehouse and laughed at him. He had jerked him out of a Pullman berth and laughed at him. He had taught him about women.

There were the professors. John Robinson Richmond, heavy with degrees and multi-colored braid, a bit impatient with the creaking procedure. Dr. Obadiah Carson, whose black gown was much too short to cover his Lincolnesque shins.

"Lafavor has curiosity," Richmond remarked. "He'll get along."

"If only he doesn't attempt too much," Dr. Obadiah countered.

Then there were two unseen guests. An old man in coarse white clothes was standing at the barred window of his cell less than a mile from the stadium. Mary and John Lafavor had visited him early that morning. Old Big Un and the bug larvae were kind to him now, and he was looking out toward the university. On the front porch of the homeplace on Garth's Island Old Mis' Ella Garth was reading a student paper which carried the picture of the only Garth who had ever gotten beyond the Bible and the blue-back speller.

Who knows? Perhaps old Peter Garth himself was listening from some Valhalla to hear what his son, seven generations removed, was saying about the America he had helped to create.

113

And there I stood. Still chanting the same old emotional song I had chanted in 1929. Still choking like a distempered goat when I pointed to the flag. Still gurgling about the Great American Race. Still captaining souls and mastering fates. Still pretending that a world had not ended. Still ridiculously ignorant of what was happening around me. Still baying at the Great American Moon like a Martin Dies in Hollywood Bowl.

Listen to me. "We have no jobs waiting for us. We face breadlines and temporary unemployment. And, worst of all, we face the ever more insistent charge that the Great American Race has run its course; that some sort of Planned Economy is to be substituted for the Great Race. But we of the Class of 1933 are not discouraged. We have kept the faith. We believe this is the same America it has always been. The challenge of our times is for young men with faith and hope. Young men who can still see the vision which built America shining beautifully beyond these temporary clouds. Young men who will not desert our gods and sell our precious birthright for bread. We accept the challenge."

I used the word "temporary" several times that day. It was very popular with us Great Racers.

"This is an age of changing values. It is fashionable to weigh and assay. But we of the Class of '33 have weighed our gods, and we have decided to cling now and forever to our democratic concept; our belief in the Common American with his dignity, his nobility, his tolerance, his insistence on his right to choose and to strive for himself; equal opportunity and equal justice in the Great Race."

I wanted to sound like a student and not like a politician. But it was no use.

"We believe that in spite of all its defeats, the march of the human phalanx is forward toward the American ideal which would make every man free to run his own race and build his own world. There are brief periods of defeat when the column halts and would seem to retreat: and always at these brief halts there are those who would have us change the line of march. There are those who, to ease the struggle, would have us turn aside to a goal more easily gained. Who would have us accept the collective security of the moment rather than push on to the true objective. If I know the minds of most of my classmates, I do not believe we want to compromise. We want no collective security. We want only a chance to run in the Great Race; a chance to win or lose, to live or die by our own efforts. The American Way gives few hostages to security, and we would give few."

Listen to his heart-rending plea. "We believe that America is still the land of opportunity. Our Race Course where each man can run his own race is still the source of our strength. There are still ample prizes for all of us who would race for them. We ask only that proper inheritance taxes return these prizes to the race course so that each succeeding generation can compete for them. In this way America can stay Young. America can remain the Land of Opportunity. We ask only that the prizes be awarded according to our striving and not be lumped together and divided by some bureaucratic commissar."

My punch line was a killer. I commend it to Mr. Dies. I began down deep and ended in a shout.

"The sons and grandsons of the men who built America will never be content to run their races in the treadmill of collectivism."

The alumni applauded this statement with enthusiasm, but certain sections of the faculty and student body were conspicuously apathetic. Harry Lerner looked as if he had whiffed a foul odor. Then for a conclusion I pointed to the flag.

"In conclusion," I said, "I want to call my classmates' attention to that symbol which flies so gloriously

115

there in the morning breeze. Your grandfather and my grandfather fought in the mud and snow to put it there. It has ridden out many a storm before, and it will surely ride this one out. That banner is a symbol of a nation conceived in liberty and dedicated to the principle that common, ordinary, potato-digging men *prefer* freedom to chains. And a chain, my friends, is no less a chain if we forge the links ourselves. So, as we leave these hallowed grounds to begin racing for the things we want in America, it is my hope that our class and our generation will never lose sight of the true American Vision. May we never compromise with security. And may we be as willing to pay the price for Liberty as were those men who first unfurled that banner in freedom's holy light."

That was Peter Garth Lafavor, A.B., M.A., on May 28, 1933. Education had effected many changes in him, but his political conception of America was still the same as that held by Peter Garth and Old Mis' Ella Garth. America was a place where a man could build a world for himself—a three-thousand-acre world—and it was nobody's goddam business what he did in that world.

1933

THE GOVER'MINT'S A-COMIN'!

PERHAPS YOU THINK IT ODD that I have so casually passed over the tumultuous days of the Great Crash without describing its effect upon myself and the Garth world of the Tennessee. When you think of the Crash you think of dramatic action. Thunder. Black Thursday. Newsboys screaming. A terrified Edward Arnold pulling ticker tape through palsied fingers; then either leaping from a window or heaving heavily homeward to confess to the blasé butterflies: "We're broke. We haven't got a cent."

Good theater, but it didn't happen that way in Morgan County. For while the American prosperity river was at flood, while Mr. Hoover was solemnly proclaiming an end to poverty on these shores, the water in our shallow pool was merely continuing its long process of evaporation. We had no millionaires to go broke dramatically. No one in the county knew how to purchase a share of stock on margin. We had no factories to be suddenly shut down. We had no great body of workers to become unemployed. No bread lines. No communists shouting revolution. Decatur had had no real estate madness, since the loss of the railroad shops had broken its back in 1922.

117

For the Garth way of life, perhaps the Great Crash began on a morning in 1863 when Longstreet delayed the attack at Gettysburg. Perhaps it began on an April morning at Appomattox when an agrarian commonwealth, which had dreamed of unfettered market places, was reduced to the status of a conquered colony. From that moment on the South was condemned to sell in an unprotected world market and to buy only from the protected shelves of her conquerors. We were a colony with an unfavorable trade balance rigged against us. Each year a little more of our vital substance was required to balance the books and declare the dividends in Pittsburgh and Detroit and Wall Street; and thus the eventual bankruptcy of the South should have been an obvious certainty.

But perhaps, in the broad view, the Great Crash in America had its beginning when General Washington and the Congress gave Peter Garth three thousand acres of good land and the right to build himself a private and unregulated world. The Few are so much stronger than the Many that, given the opportunity, they always establish systems which milk the cow dry and in which future Crashes are inherent.

In the Tennessee Valley we heard no thunderclap on an October afternoon in 1929. Among the mortgagors and the mortgagees there was an acceleration of fear and uneasiness, but the drama didn't come until 1933 when the banks closed and the revolution began.

2

When I returned to Garth's Island in the summer of 1933, I brought Harry Lerner and Adeline Reed for a week's visit. When I had asked them to come, they kidded me about inviting the "enemy" to inspect my ramparts, and Addy suggested that she would organize the Garth peons and make ours the first communal farm in America. I had invited them out of curiosity to see how they would react to the Garth fauna, and also out of reluctance to end my long association with them.

We found the Garths fighting an old familiar battle. The battle to maintain the biskit-for-breakfast standard among the hands and croppers, and the no-patched-britches and silk-drawers standard among the Garth men and women. Old Mis' Ella was figuratively standing on the Point with a bull-whip, laying it across the back of any man, woman, or child who "sagged in the collar." She was fighting a panic with the only weapons she knew how to use. Work! Sweat! More food crops! Conservation! Canning!

"It's like Reconstruction, Mis' Reed," she told Adeline. "We're guarding our smokehouses with shotguns. We been whorin' after them automobiles and things the land won't produce. Now we got to pay up, and a lotta folks are gonna starve. But by God and by hell, the Garths'll come through it. And we'll feed our hands, too."

Old Mis' Ella Garth never learned to blame the Government for her troubles. She was ninety-four now, and it was pathetic to see how much the family and the croppers depended on her for courage. She drove Uncle Watts unmercifully. She drove the Garth grandchildren and great-grandchildren even harder than she drove the croppers. Each morning at sunup, two of my cousins rode over the place to see that everyone in the seventy families was up and at work. Old Mis' Ella stomped around the Island on her stick, and when she came upon a cropper's woman who wasn't at work, her old blue eyes would snap and she'd lay on a verbal lashing that'd make Simon Legree's efforts appear weak and ineffectual.

Everywhere something was being canned.

Old Mis' Ella said: "Bud, corn bread and hominy carried the Garths and our niggers through four war

119

and Reconstruction winters, and by hell they can carry us through again."

Harry and Adeline were astonished. They had made speeches about social injustice in the South. But they had never really seen any until now.

They had talked about child labor. Now they saw every kid big enough to carry a pail of water or mind the flies off a baby at work. Not for an hour but from sun to sun. Children ten years old chopped cotton and corn row-for-row with adults.

They had talked about old age slavery. Now they saw ancient women who should have had Thirty Dollars Every Thursday sitting on puncheons and peeling fat peaches or washing tubfuls of vegetables while old men washed fruit jars and fired boiling pots of the food to be canned.

They had talked about bare feet. Now they saw bare feet everywhere. White men and women as well as "niggers." In the fields and around pots. Dirty, bare feet. Times was gittin' harder, and Old Mis' Ella was a-tight'nin' the line.

They had talked about pregnant slaves. Now they saw swollen bellies and suckling infants. Women within a week of birthin' chopping cotton, and four-year-old girls bringing the baby to suck while its mother continued to peel vegetables.

They had talked about arrogant and absolute landlordism. Now they saw it in its most arrogant and absolute form. Old Mis' Ella leaning on her stick at the smokehouse door, cracking that bullwhip tongue at a line of white women and a line of "nigger" women, telling them how to make their food go further. Mary Lafavor watching and checking while Raccoon Charley doled out the week's rations of long sweetnin' and flour and bilin' meat.

They had talked about Southern summary justice. I didn't arrange a lynching for them to study, but the second night we were on the Island, Raccoon Charley shotgunned a black who was trying to break into a smokehouse. The buckshot charge had torn his head half off, and both Harry and Adeline blanched at the sight.

"I see your aim's still good, Charley," I said.

"Yassuh, Mistah Garth. Ah gotta show dem Madison County niggahs dey can't steal Garth flour an' git away wid it."

I turned to Adeline. "What's the matter, Addy? A fine revolutionist you're gonna make if you're bothered by the sight of a nigger with his head shot off."

She and Harry were angry. "Can you imagine men being shot trying to obtain food in a country where we have too much food?" Harry asked.

I answered him with a question. "They shoot them in Russia, too, don't they?"

It was interesting to watch Harry and Adeline in the Garth world. They were kind and gracious to my parents. My father had never talked to anyone from New York, and he plied Harry with questions about the Statue of Liberty and those big skyscrapers he hoped someday to see. Harry answered with more enthusiasm than I had ever seen him display.

"Can you really stand up in her little finger?" Father asked. And Harry amazed him with a detailed description of Miss Liberty's immensities.

Adeline dispelled mother's shyness by insisting on looking at her flowers and listening to the history of each little pink begonia in a painted tin bucket on which the words "Pure Lard" were still visible through the paint. Mother asked Adeline about her mother in Chicago and if she kept flowers and if the cold Northern winters killed all the flowers. Addy answered evasively. She didn't tell mother that Mrs. Reed spent more for flowers for one party than Mary Lafavor spent on food for a year.

At meals we all sat together around the big table.

121

Harry and Addy and I, with mother and father and my brother, Gene, who was sixteen now, and my little sister, Leslie, who was nine. We ate without formality and passed mountainous dishes of fried chicken and turnip greens and corn bread and biscuit and beans and squash and pickled beets and peaches with cream. We talked about simple things and laughed easily at remarks we would have considered trite at the university.

Hell, Harry and Adeline were just a couple of kids who had smoked some cornsilks behind the barn! All three of us were happy, well-fed young Americans. At school we had tried to make ourselves old and hard. Harry had been judged a dangerous criminal, and Adeline had sneered and jeered and cursed. I had played with some chemicals whose fumes had hardened my skin, but hard skin sloughs off rapidly. Laughing and eating fried chicken with our fingers in my mother's house on Garth's Island, we were ordinary life-loving young folks. Adeline was a lithe, bright-eyed girl who could marry some honest boy who ran a filling station and have a baby she could love and a begonia she could cherish. Harry was a tall, happy chap who could marry a gazelle-eyed Hilda Apolinsky and eat good kosher food and have the best damn Bargain Store in New York. I could marry Cherry Lanson and laugh and go fishing and grow cotton and be a deacon in the Gum Springs Baptist Church and have a son— Peter Garth Lafavor the Second. And ten years from now Harry and Addy and I could meet again and get drunk on elderberry wine and laugh about how seriously we took ourselves in college, and then give fifteen rahs for the old alma mater.

Or could we? I knew I was kidding myself with such thoughts. We were not youths any more. We were old. Harry and Addy were twenty-three. I was nearly twenty-one. We were Masters of Art. We were Weighers and Assayers of the Universe. We were godless. We were visionless. We were free-livers and free-lovers. Imagine Addy with a madonna look and a baby in her arms! She had already had one abortion. Imagine Harry behind a bargain counter with Hilda Apolinsky! He was a "sneaking, conniving communist!" Imagine Garth Lafavor at a meeting of the Board of Deacons! He sneered at "organized religion" and his intended wife was already his mistress!

I introduced Harry and Addy to Cherry, and they were friendly to her. Cherry had been embarrassed by the gossip over my inviting Adeline home. Garth Lafavor taking up with the Yankees! This young woman may be rich, but she can't be *much*—going around with two men. And I'll bet she's more to Garth Lafavor than just a friend. I know these Garths. They don't have women friends. Cherry had answered by explaining that Harry and Adeline were engaged. Cherry knew how to keep everything proper.

The four of us went in the boat to Muscle Shoals for a look at the dam and nitrate plants, and Cherry sat pretty and amused while Harry and Addy and I wrangled over the social aspects. All three of us damned the Republicans in black language for letting the dam stand idle, but I wanted the project leased to Henry Ford while Harry and Addy envisioned the day when the dam could be the heart of a vast communal enterprise like the dam at Dnepropetrovsk.

I tried to give Harry and Addy an intimate glimpse into the Garth world. With Old Mis' Ella I ushered them into the Inner Sanctum and showed them the precious Memorabilia. I told them the story of Peter Garth and his conch shell and Marion's guerillas. I showed them the Great Deed and the old letters from the Presidents and generals. I showed them the pictures of the Garth war dead and the old guns and sabers and the Garth family cemetery. I watched their faces as they listened to Old Mis' Ella's stories of war and famine and flame and raiding Yankee bastards. I pulled

123

aside the curtain and let two Fellow Assayers examine the old, dear, dark pathetic chauvinism of the Garths.

I felt a tinge of guilt when I watched Old Mis' Ella talk to those two enemies as though they were friends, when I saw Harry hefting the conch shell and Addy testing with a fingernail the Great Seal of the United States of America on the Great Deed. They were unbelievers defiling the shrine. What could they know of fierce patriotism and the love of a family for its land? How could they understand the Garths and our conceptions of life? Who were they to consider us "fascists" and "obstructionists" and "enemies of the People"?

Swimming in the river in the afternoons and lying in the sand, we talked of the Garth world.

"Don't you honestly feel that there is something good and enduring here?" I asked them.

"No, Garth, it can't endure." Harry pronounced the sentence almost regretfully.

"But here on Garth's Island, Harry, is the essence of the American Dream. The spirit which built this Garth world is the spirit which built America."

I was never more serious. And Harry was calmer than usual.

"Garth, look around you," he said. "America hasn't been *built*. America has been *depleted*. Look at the end-products of this divine process by which you say your Garth world and America were *built*. What do you see? Disease. Ignorance. Stunted children. Slavery. A man shot down for trying to steal something to eat, and you commend your faithful slave for his watchfulness and steady aim. Is this your conception of a proper way of life? How can you call a process with such results a noble process?"

"But these end-products in the Garth world," I reasoned, "are the result of national mistakes. Mistakes we can rectify. When the Garths can make more money with the farm unit, then everyone dependent on the farm unit will benefit."

Harry had driven me to the defensive. "I understand you, Garth, of course. I can see how you people can live in a place like this, forget the world outside, and imagine you are lords of creation and that everything you have done is good. You cringe from the truth. But the truth is that your paternalistic set-up is filthy and you know it. Mistakes can't be rectified because the whole competitive, land-grabbing system is fraudulent. We must tear it down, and rebuild it on a sound base."

"But where do you expect to find the energy for this noble rebuilding process, Harry?" I asked.

"Why the energy will come from the people building for the people."

We had reached the impasse again. "That's where you Groaners make yourselves ridiculous," I said. "You try to imagine that people are nobler than they are. The people have no energy. The people are dependent on the few who have the git-up-and-git. How much work do you think a cropper would do if he didn't have someone to make him get up in the morning, sharpen his plow for him, and show him how to work? There will always be paternalism in the world, and I suppose you Groaners will always be there to call it 'slavery'."

Cherry came out to the Island and spent two days with us. She helped me answer the endless questions which Harry and Addy asked about the strange ways and strange people. We circumnavigated the Island. We examined the cropper houses, and I gave Addy a pair of genuine cropper flour-sack drawers with "Angel's Food" on the seat.

"You'll have to wear these, Addy," I told her, "to get in the proper mood to understand the peasantry."

I gave Harry a corn-cob pipe, and we visited a likker still and drank some freshly distilled corn out of a fruit jar. Neither Harry nor Addy had ever seen a person dip snuff, so I put two of the more dexterous dippers through their paces and had them explain the relative merits of the lip-dip and the jaw-dip.

125

We went to a "Nigger Meetin' " and sang "Swing Low, Sweet Chariot" at the top of our voices. We watched the wild, weird frenzies of the shouters and saw the young bucks run out the back door with their gals. We went to a Holy-Roller tabernacle and sang "On the Jer-i-cho Road" with the mock fervour of Holy Rollers. We watched men and women wallow deliriously in the dust and gabble in the Unknown Tongue. Harry and I kept daring Addy to go to the altar and get a working-over by the battery of soul-savers, but her courage wilted. We went fishing with Raccoon Charley and Dan and drank likker from the jug and lay in the sand under the stars. We pulled the big catfish off the trot-line and ate brown, toasted slices with cawn pone and black coffee.

"Now you see, Harry," I said, "if you had only been born here instead of in Brooklyn, you could lie in the sand with a bellyful of catfish and corn whiskey and dream of what a beautiful world you live in. Instead, you groan because life's tough, and you want to revolutionize the world and give it to the People who don't want it anyway."

We all laughed and Charley passed around the jug again.

"And, Addy, if you had been born here instead of in Chicago, you would already have been married five years and have five bouncing babies. You'd be a good Baptist, you'd hate the goddam Yankees, and the only revolution you'd know anything about would be the one your great-grandpap fought in."

I chided Harry mercilessly for not accepting my invitation to partake of the favors of one of our more talented yellow wenches.

"Hell, Harry, you don't believe in discriminating against these niggers," I told him. "What'll they think if you spend a week here and don't give them a single indication of what they can expect after the Revolution?"

126

He took it good-naturedly. "Just wait until the Revolution," he countered. "Then they can enjoy all the communal delights."

Harry did, however, condescend to make a close, personal examination of one of the more enthusiastic white wenches. He took three slugs of likker and accompanied the seventeen-year-old Southern girl on a moonlight stroll under the pines. It was a hot June night and he was gone two hours. I didn't press him for a report on his scientific observations, but the revolutionary fire in his dark eyes had been reduced to a bank of contented embers.

Apparently Harry Lerner found one phase of the status quo in the South which he was willing to accept without change.

Our last night on the Island, Addy and I went for a late swim. A freight boat was chugging up the South Channel toward Chattanooga. We could see her clearly in the moonlight. We swam far out and rode the backwash from her wheel, then returned, puffing and dripping, to sprawl on a blanket in the sand.

"Ours has been a strange friendship, hasn't it?" she said when I had lighted her cigaret.

"It certainly has. How do you suppose we ever got together?"

She blew smoke slowly from her pursed, rougeless lips. "We're both curious. With the world as it is, I suppose it's natural for the curious people to be drawn together. We can share our curiosity even if we can't share our conclusions."

"I guess that's it. You know I can't understand you, Addy. I can understand Harry's being a communist. He has always been kicked around. But you have everything. You've never been pushed around. You can feel superior in every way. Then why in hell do you want to change things?"

She flipped her cigaret into the water. "Garth, do

you ever look up at the stars and listen to the stillness and feel something Big and Unknown bearing down upon you and challenging you? I do, and I feel that something. I feel it terribly. I am one of those people who must do things. I like to believe I am a part of the positive element in humanity. If I had lived in '49, I would have been in a covered wagon. I'd have deserted all the beauty and security of the Blue Ridge Mountains and gone out where the mountains were bigger and uglier. Maybe I'd have died along the way, and maybe I'd have found the pot of gold. But, by God, I'd have been in the Rush. I want to feel that I am a part of something big and challenging and worthy of my life. I can't stand still and conform."

She propped herself up on her elbow and went on. "Well, where in the world today is there something that is new enough and grand enough and throbbing enough to challenge your life and make you want to be a part of it? There's only one such movement left in the world, Garth. I went to Russia and saw it. I felt it. And Russia is the only place today where you can feel it happening. Maybe we can't explain it, but somebody has dared to start something in Russia. It makes you think of—of a titan testing his bonds. It's so rough and ugly and new and powerful it overwhelms you. It's the only clean and honest and young thing in the world. You feel that it's worth living for and worth dying for."

A cloud had come over the moon, but I could see her brown eyes flashing even in the semi-darkness.

"What are you going to do now, Addy?"

"What can I do except join the battle somewhere? Anywhere where I can be effective."

"What happiness do you expect to find?"

"I expect to find action and the feeling that I am a part of some worthy something."

We lay listening to the water lapping against the

128

rocks for what must have been a long time. Then Addy sat up and looked down at me.

"Now it's my turn to ask the questions," she said. The fire in her eyes had subsided to a glow.

"As if you needed to. I've been under your scalpel for three years. You know my history back to 1776."

"What are you going to do?"

"Oh, I don't know. Read a little. Help around here this summer. Perhaps teach a year or two."

"When will you be married?"

"About next Christmas, I guess."

"You think you'll be happy?"

"Sure, as far as the marriage is concerned. That's the one thing I'm certain of, Addy. Cherry and I have always loved each other."

"She's lovely," she said. Then she added: "I hope she'll be very happy."

There was something ominous in the way she said it, but it was an honest statement. Not a cynical remark by one woman about another.

There was another interlude of silence. Tomorrow Adeline and Harry would be gone, and I'd be left alone back in the Garth world. The university era would be over. I'd be removed from all the strange, foreign forces and left to adjust myself again. I suddenly felt afraid. Sitting on my mountain top in college, weighing and assaying, I had felt assured. But now I was afraid.

"Addy, I'm going to miss you," I said. "Do you suppose we'll ever see each other again?"

She had pulled off her swim-cap and fluffed out her hair. She saw the fear in my eyes. Maybe she saw much more, for Adeline Reed was a very brilliant girl. Her eyes went soft, and she no longer looked like the brilliant, sneering master of economics and sociology. She looked like a lonely, lithe girl. Her eyelids drooped low and the corners of her mouth came up in an intimate gesture as old as woman.

"What do you think?" she said.

I kissed her and we forgot wars and depressions and yearnings. We clung to one another, for we were afraid. We were afraid we knew too much and afraid we didn't know enough. We were afraid of our pasts and afraid of our futures. So we forgot both past and future and poured everything into the throbbing, all-encompassing present.

Afterwards, she lay in my arms, her mass of oat-field hair on my shoulder, and her lithe, beautiful body as tall as my own lying naked against me. There were no tears in her eyes, but her lids were moist when I kissed them. Only the trace of hardness in her lips from too much whiskey and too many cigarets kept her from being completely feminine. Then, without benefit of swim suits, we swam back out into the current.

We were swathed in towel robes and walking back through the trees toward the homeplace before either of us spoke. Adeline said: "Realists should never risk themselves sober in the Southern moonlight, should they?"

"Why sober?"

"Well, if you are drinking you can blame it on the likker. But if you are sober, you have to consider feelings and impulses it's safer not to consider."

Walking under the old moonlit water-oaks in our white robes, past the neatly-whitewashed wellhouse and smokehouses, a wisp of the old romantic South brushed my heart. "What do you suppose would have happened, Addy, if we had met here on Garth's Island a hundred years ago tonight?" I asked. "That would have been June, 1833, when America was young and vital and stimulating and the South was genteel. This was a place of love and laughter and music. Democracy was at flood, and no sordid end-products had developed. Peter Garth had already built his New World. He had stood on the Point and looked down on what was his and his sons' forever, and his old Irish heart had burst with rapture, and he had been buried in earth he owned. His sons had only to accept and work and dream and love. Suppose you and I had . . ."

I broke off suddenly. Up on the Point an automatic shotgun was powing away. Raccoon Charley was firing at two niggers sneaking up in a skiff from the Madison County side.

"What were you saying, Garth?" Adeline asked.

3

In August, 1933, it came. The beginning of the end of the Garth world.

The years from 1928 to 1933 had been plain hell on Garth's Island; but we liked to believe that Old Mis' Ella's formula would pull the farm through. It was an old formula and a simple one, but it had never failed. It was the old formula of work and sweat and sacrifice and atonement. There was something of our religion in the formula. We had been whoring after what we couldn't afford, so it was proper that we should now pay the madam. And most important of all, we looked to ourselves for our salvation, and we recognized that no sacrifice was too great to preserve the heritage of the Garths.

Old Mis' Ella's last fight was worthy of her first one in '61-'69. She fired the farm and family units with a furious spirit.

She made most of the croppers realize that the unit was fighting for its life; that there was a direct connection between Garth pride and the breakfast biskit on every Garth cropper's table.

But it's easier to break a battle line with a rumor than with a bayonet charge. And during the Summer of 1933, while Old Mis' Ella cracked the bull-whip and the croppers sweated under the sun, a rumor crept into the Garth world.

The Gover'mint is a-comin!

You could hear it everywhere. It charged the fields like electricity.

Yessiree! The big Gover'mint in Washington. A-comin down heah to look after us. Nuthin to worry 'bout now. Mistah Ruseyvelt hisself is gonna look after us.

There was the typical story of two "niggers" in an argument. One says to the other: "Nigger, ya knows dis man Ruseyvelt he shore is a great man. Ah believes he's ax'ly a greater man dan Jesus Christ!"

But here the other objected. "Now ya wait, nigger," he says. "Mister Ruseyvelt he's a great man aw'rite, but he aint no greater'n Jesus Christ."

"Well, all ah knows is dis," the first comes back, "Jesus Christ, he says, 'come unda me an' ah'll feed'je,' but Mistah Ruseyvelt he says 'jest sit on yore ass, nigger, an' ah'll bring it to yuh'."

The rumor said: "Take it easy, boy. The Gover'-mint's gonna take care of ya from now on. Ya can work eight hours a day. No more sunup and sundown stuff. Why eat Ga'th food an' have to work like hell for it when the Gover'mint's got so much to throw away?"

Mistah Watts said: "Boy, ya wanter eat this winter, dontcha? Well, by God, don't let me ketch you lyin' in bed at sun-up in the morning. Ya better be out here gather'n' this hay when I come by here."

In August it came. The first leaves to rake and shovel handles to lean on. And since it had been most hurriedly thrown together, it was the effort most sloppily administered by the political shysters. Anybody could get on. The more the merrier.

Nine families deserted the Garth standard. Seven white families and two Negro families out of fifty-two decided to "jine de Gover'mint." The workers sneaked off to Hartselle and Decatur to "git on de cw an' a."

The attitude of the croppers who chose to stay ranged from hesitancy to unquestioned loyalty to the Garths. Raccoon Charley and his like regarded the de-

132

sertion as treason and expected to lynch the deserters.

"Na suh, de Cap'n an' Old Mis' Ella's been good to us. My pappy worked fo' deir pappy and his pappy befo' him. Dey's allus been good to us. Hell, we'se Garths, too, aint we? Dis is our home, aint it? Maybe we does have to wuk hard, but we has biskits fo' breakfus. An 'lasses. Dis Gover'mint business may be a trick. We'uns bettah stay on de land."

The deserters were, of course, the ones who had never wanted to work anyway. The ones who had always given the most trouble. That portion of humanity most afflicted with goddam cussedness. The ones—happily, I suppose, for the cause of progress—whom the reformers can always turn against us "fascists" most easily.

"I never thought I'd live to see this day, Bud," Old Mis' Ella said. "I've seen the carpetbaggers drive our niggers off to starve, but I never thought I'd live to see the politicians using our money to hire our hands away from crops in the field."

"It's a big problem, Grandmother," I explained. "The Government is trying to help. It'll take a little time to organize proper administration."

But she'd have none of it. "Bud, it can't be done. Why should any of 'em work if the Gover'mint's goin' to take care of them? Don't those folks in Washington know that hands won't work unless they have to? Hell fire, Bud, I ain't never been outside the Tennessee Valley and I know better'n this."

Everybody on Garth's Island was mad. Houses of the deserters were shot into at night by Loyalist guerillas. The deserting workers were afraid to return to the Island for their belongin's and their families, so we set Saturday as the day when they could return and move their things under convoy.

We had to carry shotguns and accompany all the returning deserters to keep them from being bushwhacked. And while we could protect the traitors from

133

buckshot, we could not protect them from abuse. I almost felt sorry for one of the Negro deserters. I thought Old Charley was going to throw down his gun and strangle him in spite of all we could do.

While the Negro loaded his belongin's on a one-horse wagon, Charley cussed him continuously. "Ya goddam black sonuvabitch, ah oughta tuk mah gun an' blowed yore black haid off long ago. Aftah all de Garths done done fo' you. Den ya go off lak a skunk an' leave yo' crop in de field. Ef ah evah ketch ya in a mile o' Garth lan' ah'll fill yore ass so fulla buckshot it won't hold shucks."

By afternoon the nine families had loaded their pitiful little knots of belongin's on patched-up wagons and were lined up at the Island landing, waiting to be ferried over to the Morgan County side. At a glance you might have taken the scene for a Hollywood movie set of the Children of Israel waiting to cross the Red Sea. Nine wagonloads of the wretched impedimenta of Southern sharecroppers. Bedsteads and washtubs and a broken mirror and a hickory-bottomed chair. The picture of pappy and the scarred kewpie doll won at the last county fair. A frowsled, dead-eyed woman sprawled atop the load with twin babies hanging from her long, flopping breasts. A sullen, overalled, unshaven man holding the bridles of a pair of "crap-shootin' " mules to coax them onto the ferry. Barefooted urchins in patched overalls and faded gingham dresses driving a muley cow behind. They were "desertin' to the Gover'mint." No longer would they have to endure Garth tyranny. No longer would they have to work like hell from sun to sun. The Gover'mint was a-changin' things.

Around this curious procession milled two hundred white and black Loyalists. The Garths and our loyal croppers. Croppers who either felt too much a part of the Garth world to break away, or who were afraid to discard known security for unknown security. They

134

had come to view the exodus in dumb curiosity or to hurl insults and jibes at the deserters.

The climax came when Old Mis' Ella hobbled upon the scene. She held to my arm with her left hand and used her stick with her right. The crowd saw us coming down the path from the homeplace, and everybody took off his hat. Even the deserters, holding their mules, took off their hats and lowered their eyes. Any one of them would rather have been whipped than to have to listen to what the Old Mis' was going to say.

She was ninety-five now and very feeble. We had tried to persuade her not to come down to the Landing. But she had been determined. She knew both the Loyalists and the deserters would be expecting her, and she hadn't wanted to fail either of them. As we walked down the path I thought that she would have made a great actress. She had more fire and energy than ten average women, and she knew how to time an entrance. She wore a plain gray cotton dress, and her blue bonnet was pushed back to reveal her lamb-white hair.

Her old eyes counted the deserter families. "Well, folks, you're loaded up and ready to go," she began. "You're goin' off an' join the Gover'mint. The Gover'mint's a-goin' to take care of you. Pay ya wages and buy ya remedies. You're gonna get a new deal. Ya're gonna have it easy. Well, ya don't belong on Garth's Island. For there aint nothing new and there aint nothing easy on Garth's Island. We been here a hundred and fifty years and we aint found no way yit to turn land except to git up at sunup and start plowin'. We aint found no way to git cotton chopped without swingin' a hoe. We aint found no way for folks to live without workin'. And when hard times comes we aint found no way out except to work harder and longer and spend less. Maybe smart folks somewhere have found a new way to live without workin', but I don't believe it."

She paused to catch her breath and one of the deserters ventured a defensive question: "But Mis' Ella, yo' kaint blame us fo' tryin' to bettah ourselves, can you?"

She looked at him in disgust. "No, Saul Riggs, I don't blame you 'cause you're a lazy bastard and a damn fool anyway. I blame the bastards who're a-leadin' ya. And lemme tell the rest of you this. I remember when a buncha fat Yankee bastards came down here offering everybody forty acres o' land and a mule. And a lot o' your granddaddies and grandmammies thought it was the Second Coming. But they starved to death, an' them that lived come a-runnin' back for us to show 'em how to get something to eat. All the goddam carpetbaggers had wanted was their votes."

Her voice was rising and her shoulders were shaking now.

"Now I want you all to listen to this," she hammered, "for I'm goin' to tell ya' something. The damn yellow-bellied politicians may be able to steal enough from us to keep ya livin' easy for a while. But the day'll come—I want you all to remember this:—the day'll come when the politicians'll step on you and shoot ya like dogs and leave ya to starve, an' ya'll have to go crawlin' back to the land to dig it out with ya bare hands. And when that day comes ya'll find that the Garths an' the folks who tried to make ya work were ya friends, an' the carpetbagging politicians are the same yellow-bellied bastards they've always been. Now you deserters get the hell offa Garth land, an' if you or any of your children ever put a foot back on it, I'll have ya shot like I would'a belly-crawlin' blacksnake."

We walked back up the path, while Les Winters lowered the bars and let the traitors begin loading their wagons onto the ferry.

Four weeks later, on a warm, bright September afternoon, Old Mis' Ella Garth died in her bed on Garth's Island.

136

She had lived much too long, yet, strangely, she could not make herself surrender to death. She remained conscious and struggled up to her last gasp. Her granddaughters, hovering about her bed, had hoped that peace might descend upon her and she could die quietly with a smile. An hour before she died one of them inquired anxiously: "Are you at peace, grandmother?"

"No, child," she replied, "I have lived too long to find peace at the end. Open the window and let me look out at the river."

Those were her last words. We buried her the next afternoon in the family cemetery on the Island while the sun beat down upon two thousand bared heads. Six of us great-grandsons served as pallbearers, and a chorus of great-granddaughters sang the old songs she loved. The great-great-grandchildren, from three to five years old, walked before us and strewed wild flowers to her grave. We opened her white casket at the graveside, and the thousand whites marched by first, and then, while a Negro chorus sang spirituals, the thousand blacks shuffled by. And every Garth Negro wept, for they are a sentimental race with an old dark longing in their hearts, and Old Mis' Ella Garth had believed that niggers should have biskit for breakfast.

In accordance with her wishes, we buried her in a white shroud, and in a plain, white, pine casket, and the body was not embalmed. She liked the smell of pine, and as quickly as possible she wanted her body to become a part of the land on which she had spent her life.

As Raccoon Charley and the Negroes were filling the grave, I noticed the headstone next to it. It seemed unnatural that a woman ninety-five years old should lie in death with a husband who had been but twenty-four when he died. The stone bore the inscription: "Capt. Judson Garth. The Fourth Alabama Infantry.

At the top of the charge at Chickamauga on Sept. 19, 1863, he died gallantly for a Cause he loved."

I was glad Old Mis' Ella was dead. She didn't believe in democracy, for she didn't believe that all men are created equal. She didn't believe that the meek will inherit the earth. She didn't believe in majority rule. She believed that, by and large, the strong will always be the custodians of the earth, and that the concern of the weak should be to seek out the strongest and most desirable masters. She believed that Responsibility is the proper companion of Strength, and that civilizations span highest when the strong are free to provide for the weak who depend on them. And above all, she believed in the Land, not as an industry, but as a way of life.

Yes, I was glad she was dead. She had lived too long. Bodies as old as hers don't bend in the wind: they only break.

1934-1935

COSSACK AND BOLSHEVIST

BIRMINGHAM IS A smoke-belching automaton standing in an Alabama cotton patch and manipulated by wires from the Northern offices of Steel. Clustered around the automaton are the mineral resources of an agrarian commonwealth, all either owned or commanded by Steel. The automaton is vital to Alabama. It is the only automaton Alabama has. Yet it is only a reserve cog in the vast Steel Machine and is set in full motion only when the Pittsburg and Cleveland automatons are overworked.

The automaton is selfish and vain. He demands that in his shadow there must always live enough hands to operate him at full 100 per cent capacity. Yet he rarely operates at 100 per cent capacity. In 1933 he was operating at 38 per cent capacity. And thus a varying percentage of Birmingham's 300,000 automaton-dependants are condemned to idleness and poverty and starvation and debt. They are forever listening for the whistle to blow over the portion of the automaton's metallic anatomy which they manipulate.

Birmingham's business barometer is your shirt collar. If your collar is grimy at noon, business is good. But if your collar is too clean at closing time, the cash registers are clean, too.

When the automaton is belching smoke from all his apertures, fifty thousand stokers and manipulators receive weekly wages from Coal and Iron. Every worker, from automobile salesman to scrubwoman, watches his wage wax and wane with the density of the smoke. Birmingham is a heavy industries town which makes steel rails and freight cars and bridge beams and heavy struts with which to build and expand. All its eggs repose precariously in one massive iron basket. It is a community wholly dependent upon risk and confidence, and thus it wilts under the first whisper-breath of depression, and is slow—very slow—to revive.

So, late in 1933 when I became a reporter for the *Birmingham Press,* Birmingham and the Man of Steel were sick. Very sick.

A Mountain of Iron separated the House of Have from the House of Want. Like the rot in the heart of a pine log, Birmingham's poverty began at the railroad tracks where the matchwood dials of Negro huts clustered. Six one-room cribs fanned out around a single water faucet and a water closet partially enclosed by slabbed-on Coca-Cola signs. Here collectors of rents and installments worked in pairs, one going to a crib's front door and the other appearing simultaneously at the back door. A single collector could never catch a delinquent, and the pairs had to swoop quickly, for news of a collector spread through the clusters as though by some ancient mumbo-jumbo telegraph.

Around this putrid heart was the next stratum of rot and degradation. The lowest white stratum. Vast, decaying, old rooming houses, mansions of fifty years past, now foul-smelling caverns of decadence where lurked hop-heads, whores, pimps and all those with rotten hearts and rotten bodies who could expect employment only between 95 and 100 per cent Capacity.

In the next stratum lived those who could expect employment until the automaton slumped below 75 per cent. Waitresses and hack drivers and peddlers of all the assorted notions of the earth. They ate more regularly. They lived only eight families to the rooming house. They bathed once a week in the cracked communal tub.

From here the strata became progressively better until close to the foot of the Mountain you reached the homes of those who enjoyed regular employment. They lived in six-room installment houses with a bathroom for every family.

Over the Mountain—out of the smoke zone and into the ozone—stood the Houses of Have and the Houses of pretenders to the Houses of Have. These houses, too, were arranged in strata, beginning with the brick-veneered "1928 Specials" of the lesser pretenders and progressing outward until finally, far back on a terraced, barbered knoll, stood the mighty pile of the viceroy. The dimensions of this mighty pile were obscured in legend, but one wide-eyed report could be heard even in the Negro clusters.

The viceroy had ten bathrooms!

India was far less dependent on the whims of The Old Lady of Threadneedle Street than was industrial Alabama on the whims of Steel. For Steel owned Alabama's mineral resources, and thus the viceroy possessed the power of life and death over all lesser business. The coming of a new viceroy was an all-eclipsing event. It was the occasion for a levee at Mountain Brook Country Club, for kotowing and the sending of lackeys bearing gifts. With extreme ceremonial and the pouring of libations, the viceroy was ushered into his inherited memberships in the Rotary Club and the Country Club, and he humbly donned the robes of the chairmanship of the Community Chest.

On those rare and tremendous occasions when the Chairman of Steel's Board was pleased to visit the Alabama dominion with his royal retinue, it was like Victoria visiting Delhi. A special company train toured the Empire, carrying the dignity of Great Men in one decorated car and the commonalty of reporters and photographers in another car. We hung on the words of the Great Men. We read meaning into their every gesture. We waited. Waited. Waited anxiously for the momentous moment.

The momentous moment would come when the bespatted public relations officer, after plying us with golden whiskey bearing black labels, would usher us into the Supreme Presence. The presence would clear its throat: "Gentlemen, in spite of the dark General Situation, I am pleased to announce that because of the continued Splendid Cooperation of the State of Alabama in discouraging Unrest and Instability, and because of the Splendid Work being done by our Viceroy here, the Board has decided to spend an additional Ten Million Dollars on a new mill to develop the resources of this great state."

The presses would roll, and Judgment Day type would inform the subjects of this new beneficence.

The nerve center was a cluster of skyscrapers and the most imposing of these were the Houses of Steel. On the top floor of one of the houses—in the corner with the best light and ventilation—was the viceroy's royal suite. Here the viceroy sat, dividing his precious time between listening on his private line to New York and receiving the reports and the homage of the lackeys.

Under the viceroy, in each lower story—but with the well-lighted and well-ventilated corner office as the sanctum—his assistants labored at the Company's business. Here were his attorneys examining political records, searching for tax loopholes, and readying themselves to pounce on the constitutionality of any social security law. Here was his First Vice President, who was the Company's gladhander and lobbyist, practicing a new batch of sex stories to tell at the next barbecue. Here was his director of public relations chiding the reporters for insisting that the relief situation was acute. Here was his land agent scrutinizing maps to

142

make certain that every foot of land with conceivable mineral value was under company option. Here was his sales manager. His mine boss. His transportation expert. And here was his chief of company police receiving spies and laying battle plans against the Commies and the Labor Racketeers.

Across the street, in offices much lower and much smaller, sat the ministers from other Steels, and under them sat the ministers from all the lesser coals and fabricators. All were competitors. Yet the making of golf dates, the swapping of mistresses, the worrying about Roosevelt, and the battling against Commies and taxes had made them all kin.

Across another street was the temple of the Great National Bank, and over the bank were the offices of Coal. The little fish who mined coal for sale to the public and not for use in converting iron into steel. Some of them had started with shovels in their hands, but all had won riches during World War I. Now they lived in the Ozone, talked on direct lines to mine superintendents, sold coal, made golf dates, and cussed taxes and Roosevelt.

On another corner stood the House of Power, and on its top floor in the best lighted corner sat the puppet governor of this puppet kingdom. He listened on his private line to Washington and New York, while under him his assistants cussed Roosevelt and labored to dispute the constitutionality of the Tennessee Valley Authority.

Ten thousand dollars' worth of executive time was lost with the circulation of each new obscene Roosevelt joke, for each minister and assistant viceroy would have to call up all the others and share the laugh. "Hi'ya, Jim. Hi'ya this morning. Oh I'm okay. Say, I just had'ta take three minutes ta call ya an' tell ya th' latest one. Have ya heard it? The one about Eleanor. . . ."

At two o'clock the 18-hole ministers and assistant

143

viceroys summoned their chauffeurs and unharnessed themselves from worry. At three o'clock the nine-holers would depart, and on tee, fairway, and green, they all chose drivers—cussed Roosevelt—wrangled over stakes and concessions—repeated the current foul story about Madam Perkins—drove—cussed Jawn Lewis—pitched—cussed Eleanor—putted—and muttered: "How long, oh, how long!"

At night they sat on the country club ver-andas—moaned—sipped Manhattans—moaned—dealt—moaned — lead trumps — moaned — took tricks — and moaned. When an attorney announced a new income-tax loophole, they chattered around him like old hens around a rooster who has discovered a worm.

Spreading in the other direction from Birmingham's rotten, Negro-clustered heart and at the opposite pole from the viceroy's royal residence were the production units of this Empire of Coal and Iron. Ishkooda and Muscoda and Winona. Docena and Tuxedo Junction. Ensley and Fairfield and Bessemer. Sayreton and New-castle and Thomas. Coal mines where all was black. The shacks around the monster-mouth. The faces of the young-uns. The occupational color. All black. The ore mines where all was red. The sheet mill. The rail mill. The plate mill. The wire mill. Mills and mines. Bodies and souls on conveyor belts. Company houses. Company commissaries. Company scrip. Company men. Company orders. Poverty. Filth. Hunger. Hate. Boiling, bonds-bursting hate. Black "nigger" hate. The cankerous hate of whites doing "nigger" work with "niggers." Blood. Dirty, grimy blood in the ore dust.

A hundred thousand men and women. Working in the mines. Working in the mills. Working in the offices. Jammed together. Afraid. Afraid of the Shut-Down. Afraid of the bosses. Afraid of the union racketeers. Praying for more capacity and more security. Standing in line for advanced company scrip to spend

144

in the company commissaries. Praying for smoke and more smoke. Praying for dirtier collars and dirtier dresses.

And somewhere in the shabby offices in the shabby mill towns there were other viceroys and ministers. Shabby viceroys and shabby ministers with fire in their eyes. With muscle-men and machine gunners and dynamiters waiting in the outer office to do their bidding. Listening on the long distance wire to the beetle-browed master in Washington or to the sallow-faced party secretary in New York. Organizers.

Red "rats" scurried from hole to hole. Gnawing. Whispering racial equality into hungry black ears. Black men have the same right to sleep with white women as white men have to sleep with black women. Red "rats" scurrying and pursued by company dicks with blackjacks and Thompson guns.

Here, in the Birmingham district from 1933 to 1937, the American cossacks and the American bolsheviki locked in mortal combat. It was a raw, brutal, primitive, internecine battle. It was fought with bare fists, sticks, stones, hawkbill knives, shotguns, machine guns and dynamite. It was fought in cotton patches and potato patches and in mine pits and in mill yards. There was no middle ground. You were either a cossack or a bolshevik. You were either a Great Democrat or a Goddam Communist.

Nowhere in America was the issue drawn so clearly. Nowhere was the battle so fierce. Nowhere was blood so hot. For all the old, dark, writhing emotionalism of the South was thrown into the conflict. Racialism and sectionalism contributed their bloody lances. And those who directed the battle were not on the scene. They sat safe and serene in the House of Capital in New York and the House of Labor in Washington and the House of Nihilism in Moscow. Even the newspaper of which I was a part was directed from some House in New York.

145

I was a part of this struggle. As a confused Old Southerner trying to be a New Dealer; as a chauvinistic son of Peter Garth with a devotion to some nebulous something called Americanism; as a lover of the simple and the old, who had been taught to experiment with the complex and the new; and as an ordinary, curious American, I fought first with the one force and then with the other.

Harry Lerner was a part of this struggle, for in January, 1934, he had returned to Birmingham as Southern Secretary of the League for Promotion of Proletarian Propaganda. And Adeline Reed was a part of this struggle, for she became Southern Secretary of the Committee to Oppose Political Persecution.

By May Day, 1934, I had developed into a reporter worthy of a bona fide assignment. Which means, of course, that Peter Garth Lafavor, A.B., M.A. and Phi Beta Kappa, had undergone a painful transformation. Six months of teeth-grinding hell at fifteen bucks a week. Six months in which I quit four times and was fired twice for insubordination. My first day was a horrible mistake. I swung jauntily into the city room wearing a freshly pressed blue sports suit, with my Phi Bete key glittering like a headlight from my vest. Every desk man from the assistant city editor to the editor looked up and started smacking his chops in delicious anticipation. Thereafter I was defiled, defamed, spit upon, abused and enslaved. For agonizing weeks I wasted my great talents hustling bottles of coffee and writing church notices.

Now I had survived the ordeal of indignity. I was a shabbier and a wiser man. I no longer wore the Phi Bete key. My salary had been boosted to twenty-five bucks a week, and I had been assigned to cover the expected May Day riot in Wilson Park.

I had once thought of May Day as a festival day when children laughed and made flower baskets and wound

Maypoles. But now I discovered it was a day of Social Significance, when the Workers of the World paraded, made speeches, and smashed ikons.

A week before May Day, Harry and Adeline had sneaked up out of their holes and appeared at City Hall to ask for a parade permit. Their request was denied, and the Red Squad ushered them to the city limits and ordered them to stay out of town.

Eight months with the Communist Party workers in New York had changed Harry and Adeline. They both seemed years older. The messianic glow in their faces had grown brighter and more deadly. Addy tied her hair back now, and wore a beret and skirt and sweater. Harry seemed taller and more angular and less inclined to laugh. They shuttled between Birmingham and Chattanooga where they had an underground press on which they printed *The Southern Masses.* They played hide-and-seek with the Red Squads and with the more deadly private detectives and company dicks. Occasionally one or the other of them would spend the night in my room at the Birmingham Athletic Club. I was opposed to what they were doing, but what-the-hell? They were my friends. They were harmless. And besides, they were no worse than the arrogant bastards who chased them.

Late one afternoon I was working alone in *The Press* city room when a furtive figure slipped through the door and ran breathlessly to my desk.

"They're after me," he panted. "Addy Reed said you would help."

There was no mistaking him. The glowing face. The filthy clothes. The thin, set lips. He was one of the apostles.

"Who's after you?"

"Biff and his boys. Biff Bargin. They chased me here."

I went to the window and looked down into the street. Biff Bargin, a private detective with a reputation for getting things done, was scrambling out of his car with two of his hulking assistants. I locked their Red quarry in the file room and was back at work when they got up the stairs.

"Hi, Lafavor," Biff said. "You haven't seen one o' them Red rats run through here, have you?"

"No I haven't. You looking for one?"

"Yeah. We wuz tailin' one o' the sonsobitches to the edge o' town to pick 'im up. We saw him run in the front door downstairs. I guess he ran on through the circulation rooms and out the back door. We'll get after him. Call my office if ya see him, willya?"

"Okay, Biff. Hope you find him."

I went to the window and watched until Biff and his boys had driven away.

That was seven years ago, but I remember plainly how puzzled I was at my own actions. What-the-hell? I thought. Here I have a man under lock and key who is an avowed enemy of everything the Garths have valued for eight generations. A man who is risking his life to promote the destruction of our family, our religion, and our land ownership. If I don't want to turn him over to a professional ruffian who lacks authority to arrest him on a public street, why don't I call the police? I didn't know. There was something Voltaire had said. I unlocked the file room and showed the "rat" the way down the back stairs.

We had played the threatened May Day riot for all it was worth. The Commies would have their Constitutional rights. The Mayor and the police chief would Preserve Order and Protect Property until the last skull was cracked. It promised to be interesting.

I'll never forget the scene in the park when I arrived about ten o'clock. The police department had issued new night sticks to the entire force. Sturdy oak bludgeons almost as large as baseball bats. And as the heavy Irish Infantry swarmed over the park, every Irish Jack among them was afraid: He was afraid the

148

Commies wouldn't show up, and he wouldn't get to use his new bat.

At the main entrance to the park the police inspector had set up field headquarters. He had two-way radio communication with scout cars and motorcycles. In reserve he had the Riot Squad drawn up with Thompson guns and tear gas. The Red Squad had sawed-off shotguns. A company of Legionnaires was available.

There was tension and expectancy. If it had been announced that a Panzer Division, aided by the Luftwaffe, would attack Birmingham at noon, no more war-like preparations could have been made.

I could hardly believe my eyes! What in the name of God were these people afraid of? One playful brute on the Red Squad prodded my ribs with his bat. "God, I hope that lanky Jew bastard comes up here," he said. And he brought his bat down hard in his hand.

"Ya can have the Jew boy," another one put in. "Jest give me one crack at that little yaller-headed whore."

I stepped aside to keep them from seeing my amazement. They weren't talking about two gangsters. They were talking about Harry and Adeline. Two people who wanted to make speeches without a permit.

There was a flashed report. The Commies were gathering in a vacant "nigger" house by the freight depot. I leaped on the running board of a riot car as it sped off. We surrounded the place. Rushed it. And found five black boys shooting craps for bottle tops.

The hours wore on, and the Defenders of Liberty became more and more impatient. Down in the Steel and Coal offices thousands of dollars' worth of executive time was being wasted as all the ministers and assistant viceroys paced the carpets, called each other on the telephone, and wondered if the insurrection could be quelled. Golf scores had skyrocketed the day before.

Two o'clock came and the big cops hefted their new bats and wondered who would get the first crack at a Red rat's skull.

"Now when they come, boys," the inspector cracked through the loudspeaker, "two of them will probably dash for the flag pole, and they'll try to lock themselves to it. Just let 'em have it. Don't kill 'em, but let 'em have it."

The most heroic cops stood at the flag pole.

What a travesty, I thought! The United States flag floating over such a scene. Thick-skulled simpletons standing ready to defend the flag pole! Against a group of people armed only with words.

Attention again! An unshaven chap about thirty had stepped from the crowd across the street and was sauntering toward the press cars. The inspector had seen him. Yeah, he was a Red. Ill-fed, long-haired, and bored. Six big cops pounced on him with raised bats, hoping he would offer some resistance. When he showed nothing but surprise, they hustled him toward the nearest black maria. The crowd chattered. The inspector barked. The cossacks hefted their bats. Maybe the Revolution had come.

A photographer and I fought our way toward the victim. He was obviously trying to discover what the hell it was all about. But everybody around him was shouting: "Ya goddam Red bastard!"

He was yelling that he was a reporter, and he finally managed to produce a press card. A cop took one look at the card and exploded.

"You dirty Red sonuvabitch!" he shrieked, and Victim No. 1 was hurled, kicked and slammed far back into the patrol wagon.

It was a New York press card.

Two reporters from *The Birmingham Beacon* had pushed into the crowd, began yelling: "We know the guy! Wait a minute! He's okay!" In the confusion they explained that Victim No. 1, a former reporter for the

150

New York Herald Tribune, had only that morning
been given a job at *The Beacon.* He had been rushed
over to reenforce the boys at the riot scene and had
not had time to get either a shave or a Birmingham
press card.

Victim No. 1 later became a star police reporter for
The Beacon, but he never forgave that copper who
back-handed him and called him: "a dirty Red sonuvabitch."

It was a long hour before the next flash crackled: "A
truck load of rats has just been sighted on the way to
the park!" And sure enough, within five minutes, a
battered truck came wheezing through the traffic. It
was loaded to the gunwales with ill-fed Negroes and
was surely the advance guard of the Revolution.

Like pirates boarding a treasure galleon, those big
coppers swarmed up the sides of the truck and put their
ball bats into motion. Women screamed and cossacks
cussed, while our photographers snapped away and we
barked at our messengers.

A dozen skulls were laid open before the cossack
wrath subsided, and the Negroes were sent to County
Hospital. They were a group of Baptists going to a
baptizing. They would have guessed that Karl Marx
was the father of Groucho and that Lenin was something the white folks put on their tables.

At four o'clock our last deadline had passed, and
the Home Guard began to disband in sheepish disappointment. I felt very tired, so I dropped into the nearest speakeasy and had a double bourbon.

Sometime after midnight that night there was a soft
rap on my door. It was Addy.

"Hiyah Thomas," she quipped as she came in.

"Whattayah mean, Thomas?"

"Why Thomas Jefferson Lafavor. It was a great day
for you Jeffersonian Democrats."

She was celebrating a Great Victory. She and Harry

151

had sat at a window in an office building and laughed at the performance in Wilson Park. "Look at old Garth," Harry had jeered. "He'll start vomiting any minute. Just give these Great Democrats a chance and they'll sicken of their own kind."

Now Addy was as fresh and confident as morning. She tousled my hair. She jerked the paper out of my typewriter and threw it on the floor. She jumped on my bed and rumpled it, something she knew made me want to commit mayhem.

"Addy, you got to get the hell out of here," I said. "You're gonna get your damn fool self killed."

"Nonsense, Thomas Jefferson," she laughed. "We've only begun to fight. Have you got a drink? And can you put a Red bitch up for the night?"

I dragged out the jug and we had a drink.

2

What the hell does it take to make a guy happy and hopeful?

It seems I should have been happy and hopeful by the fall of 1934. I was a damn good reporter making forty bucks a week. The work was interesting enough. Labor war. Rape cases. Politics. A lot of laughs. Smart talk. Lousy puns. I had plenty of friends and not a real enemy in the world. My room at the B.A.C. was comfortable. I could swim in the club pool, play deck tennis on the roof, or just sit in the bar and talk or play the slot machines.

Yet I know now that my skin was hardening through that period. I can understand how most reporters get hard and cynical. You see some of the good human stuff that holds the world together, but you see a lot more of the stuff that pulls it apart. Looking at the seamy side so constantly, you get the idea that men are not noble masters of fate, but only selfish and hopeless little stumblebums fighting one another inside an unbreakable mold of environment. Aw-what-the-hell-anyway becomes your favorite expression, and you gradually drift into doing little things yourself that you never thought you'd do.

While the world turned flip-flops, my life was reduced to a comfortable routine. I got up at seven o'clock when the telephone rang, pulled pants, zipped zippers, gulped coffee and was doing rewrites by seven-thirty. From nine till two I was out on the news front asking questions, supplying answers, laughing, cussing, crabbing, and hanging on the telephone. By four o'clock I was through for the day, and the whole world of entertainment stretched out before me. I could join the crap game or the poker game. I could swim or play tennis or golf. I could argue about the General Situation with a dozen damn clever arguers, including Harry and Addy if they weren't engaged on some picket line. Or I could take a drink and pursue a petticoat.

Virtually everything was free. My cop pals gave me all the whiskey I could use. They were good guys. They couldn't see any use in pouring good whiskey down a sewer even if they had picked it up in a raid. And then I was a good guy who remembered to credit them with an arrest now and then and spell their names right. I ate free at a big restaurant chain. The proprietor was a good guy who liked me. I tipped him off when I thought there might be a beer raid. What the hell? No use letting the guy get caught with his pants down just because some politician ordered an occasional raid to keep up appearances. My rent was free. I put in a few publicity licks for the club. All greens fees and court fees at the city parks were taken care of by my friend Happy Richards on the city commission. When Steve Leonard, my managing editor, and I went out to the gambling house on the county line, the big guy out there usually slipped us a nice stack of chips to toss around. Steve and I were both honest newspapermen, but what the hell? If they had a little Saturday night riot out at the gambling house and a few folks got smacked, no use smearing it all over the front page.

If I wanted to go anywhere on an airplane, Steve could get me a pass. We sort of took care of the air lines. If there's a plane crash what the hell's the use plastering wreckage all over the paper? It's sickening. Besides it cuts down plane travel, and you can always run through the picture service and find the Queen of the Titusville Peach Festival in her cute little panties. Keep the Great Public Mind off the realities. Give it Beauty.

Steve dearly loved to crusade against the loan sharks. He owed money to every one of them and whenever they'd pinch him too hard I'd have to grab a photographer and go into my act. I'd head for Poverty Row and find a hungry and pitiful young mother and slip her two bucks to pose for me. Next day there'd be a story on Page One that'd rip your heart out. This poor, deserted leaf in the storm, without milk for her babies, had been paying a dollar a week interest on a fifty-dollar loan to protect her wretched furniture from confiscation by a heartless usurer. *The Press* understood that "several legislators" were already drafting bills to curb this foul practice. Then the sharks would lay off Steve for another ninety days.

Sometimes, however, Steve would get generous and give the sharks a rubber check, and they'd be momentarily looking down his throat. I'd have to make Steve a loan and rush over and take up the check. On my next trip out of town it was understood that I'd pad my expense account the amount of the loan, Steve would okay my claim and we'd be even again. And Steve would be even with the penny-pinching Big Guys who wouldn't pay him enough to keep his mistresses in the style to which they aspired.

Steve was a great guy and a great newspaperman. He gave me my first job, and every reporter reserves a

154

special place in his heart for the guy who gave him his first job. In the air force Steve had done his bit for Democracy in World War I, and now he lived just for the hell of it. He wore ridiculous sport coats, made foul puns, owed everybody in town, always needed money, had a wife who adored him, yet he pursued petticoats relentlessly and would cuckold his best friend and laugh like hell about it all over the office.

One week there was a beauty operators' convention in Birmingham. It was a dull week and Steve sent me down to pick up a feature or two on goofy hair styles and beauty aids. Good God! Every man who attends a beauty convention must feel like a Jersey bull in a pastureful of succulent heifers. Five hundred hair-bending gals from the provinces all come to town to Do Something. Golden-haired dolls with painted claws come to demonstrate the company's new products. A big assignment for one reporter to cover.

By three o'clock I had shaken down all the factory representatives who wanted pictures of their displays in the paper and had knocked out a couple of features on a hotel typewriter. I called Steve.

"Hello, Steve. Looks like it's gonna take a little longer to cover this assignment than I figgered. It's pretty hot stuff."

"Sho' nuff," he snapped. "What room ya in?"

I gave him the number of the room the hotel had contributed to the cause.

"I'll be down soon's I get the green-stripe to bed," he said.

It was two days before we got back to the office. Cops had been looking for us. We had both been fired. It was another day before we got our jobs back. But we had done our damndest to cover the convention.

Happy Richards was a lawyer turned politician. A dangerous combination for the commonweal. All politicians will promote a few cash rebates, I suppose, but a lawyer knows more ways to do it. Happy was about thirty-five when I first met him. He was one of Birmingham's city commissioners. The smart young White Hope of Democracy who promised everything for everybody and damned the filthy corporations with fire and fury.

Soon after his election Happy bought three thousand dollars worth of furnishings for his office. His opposition castigated him and the papers ribbed him, for spending tax money so lavishly. But Happy didn't give a damn. He interviewed secretarial applicants on the new studio couch, and we shot craps on the new carpet.

Just get this picture of "Democracy" at work. The time is two o'clock one afternoon. The scene is the private office of Commissioner Happy Richards. On the floor is a new thick-pile carpet, and on the carpet six gentlemen are on their knees shooting craps with much vocal enthusiasm. Three of them are nondescript gentlemen of the press. The Commissioner is rattling the dice and pleading for Big Dick from Boston.

In the outer offices fifty taxpayers are waiting to see the Servant of the People. But his three efficient secretaries are turning back all calls and callers.

"Sorry," they chirp, "the Commissioner can't see you now. He's in an important conference with the press."

In the next room, Police Court is in session and the judge is solemnly assessing fines against sundry nigger-boys for shooting craps for pennies in back alleys. The flat-footed assistants of the chief of police are giving solemn testimony to crime, and the ambitious young assistant to the official attorney is demanding maximum punishments.

A call does get through to the inner sanctum, however, and Garth Lafavor, reporter, is interrupted. Steve Leonard barks at him.

"What the hell, Garth? We gonna get anything out'a City Hall today?"

"Don't know yet, Steve," is the reply. "I'm with Commissioner Richards now waiting for a statement."

"Y'are, huh. Well, tell that bastard to put the dice down long enough to deplore the relief situation."

After the crap game the Commissioner draws the blinds and proceeds to more official business. He receives a city employee who owes her sinecure in some department to him, and for half an hour he gives her personal instruction in how to render more satisfactory service. And while the fair employee is earning her salary, the judge in the adjoining police court is plastering the regular ten-dollar-a-month fines on the prostitutes for soliciting.

After Happy was defeated for re-election but before his term expired, Steve and I helped him in a hell-raising crusade for Better Conditions and a Safer Life in Birmingham. Early one morning a speeding fire truck swerved to miss a trolley and crashed into a telephone pole. One fireman was killed. In less than an hour Happy had called a press conference and outlined his plan. It was a stingeree. Worthy of Old Happy at his best. It went like this. We'd sling the slobber over the dead fireman. Play up the sorrowing widow and the pore orphan kids. And over it we would banner-line the Commissioner's brave charges that this heroic fireman had been a sacrifice to False Economy. He had died because of the city's antiquated fire equipment and because of the Big Taxpayers' stubborn opposition to the purchase of new fire equipment.

"We'll put over a coup," Happy chuckled off the record. "As a parting gesture I'll nail those fat bastards' hides to the wall and spend $200,000 of their money. It'll be a Great Humanitarian Stroke I can use in my next campaign."

The set-up was a little too raw for me to take, but Steve talked with Happy and then told me to play ball. I needed no further instructions. Everybody knows that the rebate pay-off on fire equipment is usually fif-

157

teen per cent, and if Happy could drive through the purchase with newspaper help, there might be thirty thousand dollars floating around for the machine and its cogs. I called a photographer and went to work.

We got the Commissioner in a new fighting pose. We got the grief-racked widow with the orphans tugging at her skirts. We got Happy laying a wreath on the grave of the brave man who had been sent out to die in a Death-trap because the Big Mules had clamored for Economy.

"But this man will not have died in vain," Happy tearfully declared, "if by his death we public servants of this great and wealthy city can provide modern trucks with four-wheel brakes for his brave comrades to ride in."

For a week I slobbered all over Page One. I got statements from garagemen about the obsolete two-wheeled brakes of the city fire trucks. The dead man had had a premonition of death the last time he examined the brakes on the Death Truck. All the firemen were doomed to ride in Death-traps until the city softened its great heart.

Happy jammed the order for the new trucks through the City Commission, but the opposition machine challenged the order in the courts. A circuit judge, belonging to the opposition, issued a restraining decree holding up the order for "further investigation." If the order could be "investigated" for two weeks, Happy's term of office would expire.

They beat us. Time ran out, and Happy didn't get to place the order. Happy lost, but the taxpayers didn't win. Four days after the new administration came in, the judge rescinded his decree, and an order was placed for new fire equipment.

Happy was unhappy. "There ain't no justice," he wailed. He had been turned out of City Hall, but in two weeks he was on some Federal agency's payroll at six thousand a year.

158

3

As my months on *The Press* dragged out into a year, I knew that Cherry was unhappy. When I finished college, I couldn't marry her and settle down in the Garth world, for there was no place for me in the Garth world. At tremendous expense I had been prepared to Go Somewhere and Do Something Big. It was inconceivable to any member of the Family that I should waste my great college-trained talents on any of the ordinary tasks connected with the operations of the Garth enterprises. Yet when I went to Birmingham to make my start, I had nothing but a job at fifteen bucks a week. I couldn't marry a girl like Cherry until I had much more.

Everything at home was unpleasant for Cherry. All the banks in Morgan County had closed. Her father's business had gone bankrupt. She couldn't remember when she hadn't been waiting. Waiting. Just waiting to marry me. And now that I was gone, those unspeakable bitches who haunt the lives of women were whispering that I probably would forget her.

Cherry was brave about it. Yet women like Cherry Lanson can face hell fire with more grace than they can face waiting and uncertainty. They are not adventurers and experimenters. They are like a flower which remains a flower with love and care and security, but which degenerates into a weed without these. I suppose it was inevitable that Cherry should fall prey to fear. The fear that I might be losing my respect for her. That I was becoming tired of her. That she didn't come first in my life. That she was becoming tarnished and less exciting to me.

Cherry didn't tell me of her fears. I saw them in her eyes. When we met in Birmingham we were deliriously happy. We ate good food together. We listened to music. We saw good shows. We laughed. We loved. We dreamed. But as our time ran out we grew nervous and irritable. Weeks of separation were before us. Weeks of doubt and fear and confusion and loneliness. Weeks in which another bastion would crumble. Weeks in which skins and hearts would grow harder and belly-knots of cynicism would petrify into stone. We clutched each other. We cried.

A climax came in October, '34, when for three weeks Cherry feared she was pregnant. I don't know which one of us suffered the most. I couldn't sleep for thinking about her lying awake hoping and waiting. It must have been hell for her. Acting, pretending, to keep her mother and her friends from sensing her worry. Knowing that even if we were married now, Old Dulcina Crabtree, who "marked the calendar" on all marriages in Hartselle, would mark us with her fate-like finger and our son would grow up under the shadow cast by parents who had sinned in the sight of God. Each day she wrote me of her confidence that everything would be all right, and each night I paced the floor and gulped down liquid fire and sent her as much comfort as I could put on paper. I knew the proper doctor in Birmingham. It could be done at the club. It wasn't really dangerous. No one would ever know.

Well, Homer had not nodded. Cherry wasn't pregnant. I had on the headphones, taking the play-by-play detail of a football game in Tuscaloosa, when the telegraph editor tapped my shoulder. A message was coming in for me on the relay printer.

"Hold a second," I said to the reporter in Tuscaloosa.

I walked over to the machine and pulled out the tape. Ten words. "Darling, I am feeling painfully divine and I adore you. Cherry."

I went in the washroom and took a shot of alcohol and glycerine. Then a long glass of water. I threw up the window and took a deep breath. I went back and adjusted the headphones. The crazy guy was squawking about a touchdown I had missed. "Aw, keep your shirt on and pick it up," I said.

A week later Cherry came to Birmingham and we celebrated. It was swell. But Cherry had a mild attack of hysteria during the night.

4

Nothing disgusted me so much as the Scottsboro Case.

I covered some of the Decatur trials. Harry and Adeline and the apostles were on hand with circulars and bitter arguments as to what constitutes rape. I visited the Negro defendants several times in the Jefferson County jail. Once I took Addy's picture with them for one of the picture services. As "political prisoners," they were her most famous charges. They were also her committee's most profitable charges. I tried to persuade the Negroes to kick the communists out of the case and let us obtain an Alabama lawyer to defend them. Once I had them ready to sign a statement disavowing the communists, but when I arrived at the jail with the story I found Adeline and an attorney distributing new shoes and tobacco money to the Negroes. They did not sign.

What impressed me most about the case was not anything I saw in Decatur but a scene I witnessed while on a trip to Chicago. In the hotel where I stopped I saw a notice of a lecture in one of the club rooms on the Scottsboro Case. Out of curiosity I attended. There were about two hundred apparently intelligent and educated men and women present. The speaker, an impassioned chap about thirty-five, proceeded to depict all the "horrible tortures" which the Negro defendants had endured during their four years of imprisonment. He described the "loathsome dungeon" in which these "innocent Negro boys" were forced to sleep "with rats and stagnant water" all around them.

161

He told of how they were starved and beaten by their cackling, snuff-spewing jailers. And after he had made his appeal for funds to continue the trials, he opened a discussion and question period.

I was amazed! Not by what the speaker had said, but by the fact that the people around me seemed to accept without question the truth of his statements. I rose and requested permission to say a word.

"How many of you people believe that this man has told you the truth?" I asked. They hesitated in surprise, then every one of them except one man raised his hand. He later told me he was a reporter for the *Daily News.*

"I can't believe it," I said. "I can't believe that you people can be so clever about most things, and yet be so damn gullible about what goes on in the South. This man has probably never been to Alabama. He is either misinformed or he is a liar, and if you'd like me to tell you the truth, I can tell you in five minutes."

The crowd added to the discomfiture of the lecturer by insisting that I speak my piece.

"Very well," I said, "I'll tell you first that the Scottsboro defendants are kept in the Jefferson County jail in Birmingham. Instead of being a 'dungeon' that jail occupies the seventh and eighth floors of a magnificent new fireproof courthouse. The jail is the most modern type. There are showers and toilet facilities in every block of four cells. The dietician at the jail is a college graduate. The Scottsboro defendants exercise every day on the roof. They are fat, slick, healthy Negroes, and if one of them has ever been struck a lick by a jailer, they have neglected to tell me or any of the people who are handling their defense about it."

The lecturer tried to remonstrate, but the crowd would have no more of him. "But the Negroes are innocent," a woman rose and declared, "and even if what you say is true, the fact that they are in any sort of jail is a great injustice."

162

"Well, I'll tell you about the innocence which you people so readily assume. The facts are simple, and, except for the record, they are admitted by everybody concerned with the trial. Nine Negro boys were riding a freight train. In the next car, an open gravel car, there were two white women. The women were 'lint-heads,' cotton mill workers. Whatever the status of the women, they resisted when the Negroes approached them. Forcibly, the Negroes threw the women in the gravel, ripped off their underclothing, and held them while, one by one, seven of the Negroes ravished one or the other of the women. Two of the Negroes were too young to be sexually competent, but they assisted in the holding."

Some members of my audience of intellectuals were recoiling from my language. "Well, in your books, does that constitute rape?" I asked them. "In my book it is rape, and Justice need not bow her head if every one of the seven rapists goes to the chair."

One elderly gentleman rose and stammered self-consciously but bravely. "But, sir, a woman on a freight train—a hobo—you can't accuse boys of rape in such a case."

"Yes, sir," I answered. "Even a prostitute is entitled to the protection of the law. Suppose I walk down to one of your Chicago brothels and murder a prostitute? Will your courts allow me to go free? Her person is legally as inviolable as your own."

It remained for the reporter to hit me in the soft spot. "But what if a gang of white boys had done this thing?" he put in. "They wouldn't have been arrested, would they?"

"Probably not," I conceded. "And, of course, you have brought up the only debatable aspect. Had the rapists been white boys and had they been arrested, the case would have been thrown out of court. They would have deserved extreme punishment, but they would not have been given it. When we say this we admit that there is racial discrimination in the South. We admit that white boys can do things with impunity that Negro boys cannot do. We hope that some day this will not be true. But should we free Negro rapists because we cannot convict white rapists? Or should we punish Negro rapists, as they deserve, and hope that we can some day punish white rapists, too? Our racial problems in the South are very real and very terrifying. We need your help in solving them. But you can't help us by listening to crackpots who recite *Uncle Tom's Cabin* to you before taking your money."

During the lively discussion which followed, our lecturer slipped out and there was no money collected that night for the Scottsboro Defense Fund. Once they get the facts, Yankees can be reasonable folks. But about the South—and particularly about Negroes and rape—most of them are as naive as your maiden aunt.

5

The case of Roosevelt Wilson never became a *cause célèbre*. In fact, you never heard of Roosevelt Wilson. But I knew him, and I'm quite certain I'll never forget him.

To understand Roosevelt Wilson you'll have to visualize the loneliest, most insignificant human being in the world. The cipher in a social system. He never knew who his mother was. He just appeared as a nameless black brat in a cotton patch. He breathed. He grew. He chopped cotton for bread. He stole. And somebody, somewhere, labeled him Roosevelt Wilson. Just think of him as a black, burr-headed creature who could not have felt superior to a hound dog, and whose death would not have brought a waft of regret across any heart in America.

When I first heard of Roosevelt Wilson he was a dog being chased by other dogs. He was a scurrying black animal to be shot on sight and left naked to rot in a ditch and be picked by buzzards. He had raped a white woman in a potato patch at Bug Tussle, and bloodhounds and a posse were chasing him. It's the old familiar fabric to every Southern reporter, so I methodically ground out eight paragraphs on the Chase. And when the black quarry had been captured by a sheriff and "spirited away for safekeeping," I ground out two editorial paragraphs congratulating the sheriff for preserving Alabama's proud record of not having had a lynching in three years.

When I arrived at the county courthouse to cover the trial there was nothing unusual about the scene. The AP reporter and I sat in a dysentery parlor across the street, drank coffee, griped about the assignment, and hoped Justice would act swiftly so we could get back to Birmingham before night.

There were two or three thousand people massed in the streets leading up to the courthouse square. A scattering of sticks and shotguns. Two companies of National guardsmen had mounted machine guns around the courthouse, and an officer with a loudspeaker kept issuing warnings against anyone's crossing the street to the courthouse. Only those who had stood in line and obtained tickets for the two hundred seats in the court room were allowed to pass into the courthouse; and these, both men and women, were searched for weapons.

The scene in the court room was usual for such trials. State police and guardsmen, with side-arms and nightsticks, were stationed around the walls and in the aisles. The jury had been selected when I seated myself at the table which the sheriff had hastened to provide for the two out-of-town reporters. We had not been expected. It was a routine trial. We would not have been sent to cover it except for a dull news week. The jurors were farmers and townsmen, and I observed that they appeared more intelligent than the average Alabama jury. This was because the verdict was a foregone conclusion, and thus counsel had not made the usual effort to strike out the more intelligent men but had simply taken the first twelve in the venire.

I looked across at the plaintiff. She was a husky, loose-jointed farm woman, perhaps thirty, with big red hands, big feet, and a matted mass of blond hair which some amateur barber had chopped squarely and roughly off. She reminded me of a gangling battleaxe I had once seen in a brothel, whom the madam used only as a shock trooper to take on the heavier and more bellicose Polacks who came in very late and very drunk. The two great press services dryly agreed that young Roosevelt Wilson had shown damn poor taste in his selection of a queen bee worthy of his life.

Next to the plaintiff sat her husband, a burly farmer whose cheap clothes were much too small for his bulging muscles and whose flushed face gave evidence of the great rage pent up inside him. Around the two sat the imposing array of counsel for the State. The Attorney-General himself was on hand, his hackles up, and issuing brash statements by the bucketful. Every elected prosecutor in district and county was present, with assistants and volunteers, to see that swift justice was done. Such a case provides rare political opportunity, and every attorney who plans to run for office rushes in to participate gratis in the prosecution and make a hell-raising speech to the jury.

"Oh, hell," moaned the AP. "If all those bastards have to make speeches, we'll be tied up in this hick town for a week."

You had to look at the counsel for the defense to appreciate the contrast. Two lawyers had been appointed by the court, and in this county they use a system whereby lawyers for such thankless tasks are chosen by drawing names from a box containing the names of all the practising members of the bar. Fate had frowned on poor Roosevelt again; for he had drawn a couple of old ninnies who were in mortal fear that the popu-

166

lace would get the idea they had willingly taken Roosevelt's case and that they believed him innocent. Before the trial began one of them rose and addressed the Court.

"Your Honor," he stammered, "to avoid any misconceptions here, my colleague and I would like you to publicly explain that we have been drafted by the Court to safeguard the constitutional rights of the defendant and that no sympathy for this defendant is implied by our actions."

This the judge did, solemnly, in the presence of the jury. The judge, a graying figure about sixty, was nervously trying to rush the procedure. He wanted the trial over and the defendant safely back in state prison by nightfall.

There was a rumble in the court room. The big coppers and the guardsmen hefted their nightsticks. You could feel the hackles rise and the hate charge the air. The defendant was trudging in with an escort of troopers. I gave him an unconcerned and half-amused glance and jotted down a note. Barefooted. Faded and patched pair of blue overalls and jumper. Hundred and thirty pounds. Five feet six. Burr-headed bastard. The troopers handcuffed him to a chair directly in front of us. With the trial about to start, his attorneys spoke contemptuously to him. It was the first time they had seen him.

"What's ya' name, boy?"

"Ruseyvelt Wilson."

"How old are ya?"

"Ah thinks ah's twenty-two."

Then they sat back and announced themselves ready. They assumed the defendant had no witnesses and that he should be pleaded not guilty so as to be certain of the death penalty.

The state called the plaintiff and recorded her story. Her husband had been away working in another county. While she was digging potatoes in one of the

167

more remote fields, the nigger had sneaked out of a thicket and accosted her with a shotgun. He had threatened to kill her if she didn't go into the thicket with him. So with a choice between death and such a sacrifice she had complied with his demands. After he had run off, she had heard the shouts of some women who were looking for her, and she had rushed to them and reported the crime.

The defense cross-examined softly and sympathetically: "Not that we doubt your story, ma'am, but just for the record." In reviewing her testimony the plaintiff agreed that the nigger had laid down the gun before the rape occurred, but the judge promptly explained to the jury that she had been intimidated with the gun and was thus in mortal fear for her life even though the gun had been put aside before the actual crime was consummated.

The irreverent AP cocked an eyebrow and shook his head. The plaintiff weighed a good thirty pounds more than the defendant and could obviously have smacked him silly when he laid the gun down.

Then followed a succession of witnesses who established that the defendant had run when approached by the posse, that he carried the gun, and had resisted arrest. Two women testified to the nervous state of the plaintiff after the crime.

At the noon recess I overheard a conversation between Roosevelt and his attorneys. They were telling him that there would be no need for him to take the stand; that it would be best just to submit the case when the state closed. But Roosevelt objected.

"Naw, suh, boss," he said. "De truf aint being tole heah. Ah got ta git up deah an' tell de truf. Ef dey kills me, ah got to git up deah an' tell de truf."

Believe me, it was no noble motive which inspired my intervention. I only wanted to blow up a dull story. I stepped up and said: "That's right, Roosevelt. If they're not telling the truth, you get up there and tell it. They've got to listen to you."

The lawyers then admitted to him that "of course the Court couldn't deny him his constitutional right to testify in his own defense," but his testimony would do no good. When they had gone I stepped back in and gave Roosevelt some more encouragement.

"Get in there and give it to 'em straight, Roosevelt," I said. Then, in that burr-headed Negro's face I saw something I didn't want to see. I must have been the first white man ever to have spoken a civil word to him. He reacted like a dog when you pat him on the head. He let down his guard, and I saw that he wasn't a nameless animal but a living, breathing, feeling—even aspiring—person. He showed me all the loneliness and fear of his wretched life. The loneliness and fear of the swamp with bloodhounds baying. The loneliness of the cotton patch and a dog howling under the moon. The loneliness and fear of a jail cell and a thunderbolt exploding in your body.

I shrugged and turned away quickly.

Shortly after noon the state rested and defense counsel rose to inform the Court solemnly that counsel had advised the defendant not to testify but that he insisted on his constitutional right. The defense, therefore, was calling the defendant, Roosevelt Wilson.

If you had struck a match while that boy was walking to the stand, the court room would have exploded. I have never felt such tension, such organized hate focused on one insignificant object. Everybody leaned forward off his buttocks and was sitting on the backs of his legs. Troopers clutched their nightsticks, and the judge unconsciously rapped for order though the room was breathlessly silent.

"Now, Roosevelt, just go ahead and tell your story," defense counsel said. "And make it short." There was no effort to guide his testimony or to help him in any way.

"Well, jedge, it wuz lak dis," he began. "Ah got up dat mawnin' an' ah borr'd Sam Winson's gun to go rabbit-huntin'. Ef Sam wuz heah he'd tell ya ah did. Ah went ovah tow'd de nawth fawty an' ah seed dis lady a-diggin' taters. Ah'd seed her a time o' two befo' an' she'd tole me she wanted a ring ah had. Ah wawked up to her, an' ah show'd her de ring an' we tawked a minute. Den ah exed her de question an' she luked aroun' an' said she wuz willin'. . . ."

The room exploded. In a split second the husband had yanked open his britches and from somewhere under or between his legs had come up with a forty-five. And he had come up shooting. The crowd rioted, and the guardsmen began laying them in the aisles with the nightsticks. Two big troopers dived on the hate-crazed husband and wrested the gun from him. Two reporters who had been standing up to hear the story better had done a dual jackknife under a table. The judge, barely missed by one of the bullets, made an undignified retreat under his desk; while the defendant, scared but unhurt, sat unguarded on the witness stand.

It was half an hour before order could be restored. The jury, the husband, and the defendant were removed from the court room, and AP and I began burning up the wires with flashes. I asked the judge if he wouldn't have to declare a mistrial.

"I suppose I should," he said, "but, hell, we've got to get rid of this mess." He looked as if he were bothered by an offensive odor.

I went in to see Roosevelt, and his lawyers were upbraiding him. "We told you so. We told you not to get up there. Now you see we were right. When the Court goes back in session, we'll just close the case."

"Naw, suh, boss," Roosevelt objected. "Ah's jest got started good. De whole truf aint been tole yit."

By now Roosevelt had me pulling for him. "Get

170

back up there, Roosevelt," I told him. "Don't let 'em scare you. Tell it all."

When trial was resumed, the defense, apologizing profusely and explaining again that they had urged the defendant not to testify, moved for a mistrial. The motion was denied, and Roosevelt went back to the stand, completely surrounded by troopers. In a deadly silence, broken by the crowd's heavy breathing, he finished the story of a pine-needle intercourse, hastened near the end by "some women hollerin' fo' dis lady."

The cross-examination thunder began to roll. The prosecutors began jumping and yelling and shaking their fists.

"If you hadn't committed a crime," the Attorney-General bellowed, "why did you run like a scared rabbit when these men found you over there in that field?"

The reply was cool. "Ah seed a buncha men come a-runnin' at me. Dey wuz a-cussin' an' a-shootin'. So ah jest run. Dey kept a-chasin' me, so ah kept runnin'."

For an hour the state battery took turns working out on Roosevelt. They attempted to cross him in every way. But his story never changed. The woman had gone to the woods with him willingly in exchange for the ring he had given her.

The county solicitor was sweating and trembling with anger. He shouted: "If this good woman had submitted to your filthy embrace willingly, then why in the name of Heaven would she tell anybody about it? Don't you know she would have been ashamed of it, you lyin' black bastard?"

"Ah don't know, boss. We heard dem other women hollerin' fo' her an' ah run. Ah guess she figgered dey had seed us go to de woods togedder, an' she figgered she bettah tell 'em ah fo'ced her."

During the prosecution's impassioned oratory to the jury, I convinced myself that the plaintiff had smuggled the gun into the court room. The husband could hardly have brought it in, for he was the most suspect

171

of all the spectators, and two deputies had searched him thoroughly. But the matron admitted a perfunctory search of the woman. The woman had known the story Roosevelt might tell, and she had brought the gun in to have her husband kill him before he could tell it.

The jury required four minutes to go out and bring back death. While it was out, I whispered to the judge: "Judge, I've lived around niggers all my life, and if I ever heard one tell the truth that little bastard was telling it this afternoon, wasn't he?"

The judge crouched down low behind his desk, nodded his head, and grinned.

When the jury had been discharged I spoke privately to several of the jurors. To each one I made the same statement I had made to the judge. In each case I got, in effect, the same reply.

"Shore he was telling the truth. But what the hell? The bastard deserves the chair for messin' around with a white woman. Besides, if we'd turned him loose, that crowd outside would'a lynched us. We gotta live with these folks."

After the troopers had rushed Roosevelt through the crowds and away toward the penitentiary, the judge called the husband back to reprimand him for creating a disturbance, not to mention attempting to murder a man still presumed to be innocent. The husband told the judge:

"Judge, I felt like I had to kill that sunuvabitch. I intended to do it this mawnin' while he wuz a-settin' over there at the table. But ever' time I'd reach down to pull my gun, the Lawd would tell me not to do it fo' them two newspaper men wuz a-settin' right smack behind him."

"Whew!" AP turned white around the gills. "We got something to thank the Lord for, haven't we, boy?" he said.

As we rode back to Birmingham that night, I kept thinking of Roosevelt Wilson in his faded overalls and bare feet riding alone toward Death Row with a hundred and twenty guardsmen to see him safely in the chair. I thought of Pontius Pilate. I thought of Emile Zola and the few men who have had the courage to defy the Mob. Then I sneered. What the hell! AP pulled in toward a roadhouse.

"Let's have a drink," he said.

We had several drinks. We told the waitress some stories and pinched her on the thigh. To hell with Roosevelt Wilson. Smart guys don't go around butting their heads against stone walls. Smart guys live for the day and gather flowers for themselves.

Next morning in my clean-up story I inserted two paragraphs about Roosevelt's testimony. In polite language I hinted at its substance. I was watching Old Steve when he picked up the story at the copy desk. He looked over at me, made a wry face, and jerked his nose to tell me it stank. I saw his pencil go down in an impatient gesture, and I knew those two paragraphs would never see print.

No one reading my story could have guessed on what claim Roosevelt based his plea of innocence. The story recounted that the defendant had pleaded not guilty, and while he was testifying the husband attempted to assassinate him.

I suggested to Steve that we use a picture of Roosevelt Wilson. His face might impress somebody with his innocence. But most papers in the South have a policy against using pictures of Negroes. We had never run a picture of Joe Louis or of Dr. George Washington Carver or of the Scottsboro defendants. So we didn't run a picture of Roosevelt Wilson.

Instead, we used the latest shot of Marlene Dietrich's legs. Nothing brightens a front page like a good piece of leg art.

Now that I am a soldier in the New American Army and going off to fight Hitler and Hirohito, I wish I could tell you that the case of Roosevelt Wilson perched on my shoulder like a raven, and that I never rested until I freed him from his cell and threw him back into the faces of the Pontius Pilates. I wish I could tell you that I made a brave speech to Steve Leonard, that I flung my job in his face, and that I fought for Roosevelt's freedom with pamphlets printed on a hand press.

But none of these things happened. I told Steve the filthy facts and suggested a further story, but when he said: "Hell, Garth, you're crazy," I nodded and said: "Yeah, I guess you're right."

I told the Governor the filthy facts. He shrugged and said: "Boy, you're crazy. What the hell can I do? You know what it would mean if I intervened in a case like this."

"Yeah, I guess you're right," I said. "But you know I've read of governors who couldn't sleep after they had let an innocent man go to his death."

He laughed. I laughed, too. The kind of laugh you laugh to keep from crying. Then, incredible as it seems, I forgot Roosevelt Wilson, and it was quite by accident that I saw him again.

Thursday night is execution night at Alabama's big Kilby Prison. Most every week the state fries some Black Meat and occasionally a little White Meat is thrown in for good measure. There was a young cop-killer sent up from Birmingham. I forget his name. He was a white boy from somewhere out West. He had been in the Marines and had hit the highways. He had gone jittery during a hold-up and plugged a cop. We had played the case with a lot of sob stuff, and Steve sent me down to Montgomery to cover his burning.

The warden was impatient. "Come on, you guys," he said to the reporters, "let's get started. We got eight black boys to burn after we finish off this yellow cop-killer."

The cop-killer was yellow all right. There were six preachers with him when they brought him into the Death House—all anxious to get their names spelled right. He went hysterical and guards had to throw him into the chair. Then they hit him with that extra five hundred volts which jail wardens always reserve for cop-killers and burned his eyeballs out.

I had filed my story, cleared my nostrils of that sickening odor of burning hair and flesh, and was ready to leave the prison when I remembered I had left my coat in the corridor near the Death House. I went back for it and just happened to notice the black boy who was being led toward the Green Door.

It was Roosevelt Wilson.

In his white prison clothes the burr-headed little bastard looked smaller and less significant than he had looked in his overalls. Friendless and alone, he was going to his death. During his weeks of waiting he had not a single visitor nor communication from the outside world. His eyeballs were rolling in fear, but he was walking without support.

I tossed down my coat and called to the warden to wait a minute. "You're Roosevelt Wilson, aren't you?" I said. "The boy from up in Webster County?"

He recognized me. "Yassuh, boss, ah is. And yore de news-paper genmun who wuz at mah trial, aintcha?"

The warden was annoyed. "Come on, Lafavor," he snapped. "We're in a hurry. We got three more to go and it's gettin' late."

But I insisted, and he reluctantly agreed to take another nigger on and get Roosevelt last. He locked us back in the cell and I had a few minutes to talk to him.

"Roosevelt, would you like to see a preacher before you go?" I asked him.

He said he would, so I called an attendant and sent him for a preacher. But the only preacher around then

175

was a Negro preacher, and he was in the Death House. So I borrowed a greasy little Testament from an old white prisoner on the Row. I couldn't remember a suitable passage in the *New Testament*, so I opened the little Bible, pretended I was reading, and recited the last five verses of the Twenty-Third Psalm. Roosevelt repeated after me.

I fumbled for something to say to that Negro boy. I wanted to say something appropriate. Something that would give him faith and comfort and hope. Something he could understand. Finally, I said: "Roosevelt, before you go in there, I want to say this to you. You are not guilty of the crime for which this state is going to kill you. All of us who heard your story know that you are innocent. The judge knows you are innocent. The jurors know you are innocent."

"Den why is dey killin' me, boss? Fo' God ah didn't fo'ce dat lady."

"I know you didn't. We all know you didn't. But we couldn't help it."

"Is dey killin' me jest fo' messin' aroun' wid dat lady?"

"Yes, that's one reason. And there's a bigger and more awful reason that I haven't time to explain. But what you want to do now is buck up. Everybody has to die. It's not bad in there. You never feel it at all. So don't be afraid."

He thought for a minute. "Does ya reckon ah'll go to Hebben, boss?" he asked with sincerity.

"Well, Roosevelt," I answered, "I've heard it said that the folks here on earth who are done wrong to like you, and the folks who have the worst luck—they are the folks who go to Heaven, and they are the ones who get the biggest crowns and the most gold. So I think you deserve to go there and I believe you will."

"Thank ya', boss," he said. The warden was coming, and he turned and asked: "Will ya go in wif me, boss. It won't be so bad ef ya'll go wif me."

God, I hated to go back in there. It always made me sick. But I nodded. The Garths don't shake hands with "niggers," but I took Roosevelt by the hand, and we walked down the corridor. An old white-headed Negro preacher joined us, and the Negroes waiting along the Row moaned their old jungle death chant.

You would have been proud of Roosevelt in the death house. He was scared, but there were no hysterics. At the chair he turned around and said: "G'bye, boss. G'bye, parson." I bit my lip and clasped my hands in front of me in the old buck-up gesture. The attendants clapped on the hood and adjusted the electrodes, and the old preacher broke into "I am the Resurrection and the Light . . ." For a second the frail form quivered in the chair, and then the sovereign State of Alabama exploded twenty-three hundred volts of lightning. The black body was flung against the straps, and Roosevelt Wilson had paid his debt to a great democratic society.

They buried him in the prison plot for unclaimed bodies. And while I lay drunk and sick in a Montgomery hotel, my paper ran a brilliant story under my by-line. It was a stinking account of the execution of a yellow cop-killer.

The last paragraph of the story was inconsequential. It would have been killed by the make-up man had it run over the column. It said: "Among the eight Negroes also executed last night was Roosevelt Wilson, 22, convicted of rape in Webster County."

Whenever I think of racial injustice in America, I think of Roosevelt Wilson and not the Scottsboro Negroes. Whatever the mitigating circumstances, the Scottsboro defendants were guilty of criminal assault upon two women who resisted them. I knew the Scottsboro Negroes, and I could have watched them executed without feeling anything more than a natural sympathy for unfortunate people who fall victim to circumstance and human weakness. But Roosevelt Wilson was innocent. I knew he was innocent. My editor knew he was innocent. A judge, twelve jurors, and a governor—all of us important cogs in the democratic machinery—knew he was innocent, and we allowed him to go to his death while we looked complacently at each other and asked: "What the hell can I do?"

It was not until a few months ago, five years after his execution, that I realized the full significance of my complacency and what-the-hell attitude toward Roosevelt Wilson. When I at last saw the meaning clearly, I could understand those anguished wails of what-the-hell we heard in America before Pearl Harbor. I could understand some of my own cynicism and what-the-hell. Complacency is a cancerous disease. Neither a man nor a nation can stand by silently and watch a great injustice done without having his own faith and self-respect impaired. A man or a nation must fight injustice wherever it appears, and if either of them chooses to ignore rather than oppose injustice, he will one day be surprised to find that his own strength of heart and strength of soul have been sapped in the process.

But who am I to go marching off to fight for tortured Jews in Poland and bombed children in China when I wouldn't raise my voice to stay a state-lynching in America? And who are we to espouse the dream of international democracy when we have expediently nurtured Hague gangsterism in our own country? These questions puzzled me for a while, but I can see the answer to them now. The answer is that here in America we at least recognize and pay homage to the ideal of justice to all men. We have reason to hope that we can some day overcome our personal and national shortcomings. But the berserk brute now threatening us denies the ideal and seeks to set mankind to marching back toward darkness instead of toward light.

I don't believe that dogs and apes can destroy the great dream of liberty and justice and dignity. But they can devour the dead carcasses of men and nations whose strength has been sapped by complacency and concession.

6

On a November afternoon in 1935—on her twenty-third birthday—Cherry Lanson and I were married at her home in Hartselle. And Mis' Dulcina Crabtree "marked the calendar" and hoped our first child would come in less than nine months.

Our marriage came nine years after our first kiss, seven years after our first formal date, and two and a half years after our first bedroom scene.

Had you been among those present at our wedding, maybe you would have pitied us. Maybe, considering what had gone before, you would have called the simple, moving, little ceremony a mockery and a sin in the sight of God. Maybe you would have read social significance into it. Maybe you would have found no freshness at our wedding. No young hearts leaping up to behold the rainbows in the sky.

But I thought our wedding was sort of nice. Cherry was the most beautiful girl I had ever seen. She was a Deep South combination of Hedy Lamarr and Dolores del Rio, dressed in a tailored red suit trimmed with black fur, with her black hair topped by a saucy red, fur-trimmed, cossack hat with a little veil business. She was radiant. All her doubts and fears were gone. Her years of waiting were over. Never again would she have to be afraid someone we knew would see us ride down a hotel elevator together. Never again would she have to leave me and go back to the monotony of waiting in a small town.

It was a moment of triumph for little Cherry Lanson

who had been my girl since we were ten years old. She didn't look tainted to me. She looked like a vibrantly beautiful and honest woman who deserved all the best in the world. Her soft black eyes were swimming with happiness, and for her I was happier than I ever thought I could be.

In Birmingham the fellows had been swell. The boys at the office, the cops, the gamblers, the politicians, the bootleggers, and even a couple of labor organizers, all of them had sent gifts and wrung my hand. There had been a dinner the night before, and everybody had gotten drunk and pounded me on the back. The Front Office had crashed through with a hundred-dollar bonus. A friend at an automobile agency had insisted on lending me a sixteen-cylinder Cadillac for my wedding trip. Three gentlemen who had nothing in common but their friendship for Garth Lafavor rode with me from Birmingham to attend the wedding. They were Dave Blocton, Harry Lerner and Steve Leonard. Dave, Beta's old fifteen-minute-man, was now vice-president of his father's soft drink business. He had come up from Montgomery to be my best man. Harry, for this one occasion, had forgotten that he was Secretary of Proletarian Propaganda and was only a well-dressed, wise-cracking member of the bourgeoisie. And Steve Leonard, the ideal boss, was making his foul puns and looking at Cherry and probably wondering how she would act when he got her in a dark corner at the gang's next party.

I had written a lot of satirical stuff about weddings and Lohengrin and O, Promise Me, but, you know, it all sounded pretty clean and pretty proper and pretty honest when I heard it. Even the preacher was a nice guy. He was a young fellow who looked at you straight and spoke with sincerity, and then laughed as if he enjoyed life when he shook hands with you.

I felt clean and honest and hopeful myself. I had

spent sixty dollars for a new tailored gray suit. My equity in a Ford car was growing more substantial each month. I had rented a bedroom apartment in a pleasant section of Birmingham. I had four hundred dollars in the bank. Even without the borrowed Cadillac I could feel reasonably important coming back to Hartselle. I had dusted off the old Phi Bete key and hung it across my chest.

The ancient, high-ceilinged room where we were married was banked with lilies and smilax. My mother and father and brother and little sister were there, and the house was overflowing with Garth aunts and uncles and cousins. Everybody was swell. I kissed everybody and everybody kissed me. I didn't know Cherry had so many friends. The entire Mary Scott College for Women Alumni Association must have attended. It would have taken a moving van to cart off all the gifts.

After the wedding we drove to Birmingham and spent the night at the new apartment. We were perplexed as to whether I should carry her through the main entrance or through the apartment door, so while the maid and janitor grinned, I carried her over both thresholds. On the living room floor we found a Special Extra edition of the *Press* announcing the wedding under a "War Declared" banner line. A four-column cut of me mulling over a bob-tail flush in a poker game bore the caption: The Groom at a Moment of Decision. Next day we drove to New Orleans where that damn Cadillac caused every bell-hop to mutter about the Revolution when I tipped him only a quarter.

"Are you happy, doll?"

This seemed to be the only question I could think to ask Cherry, and I must have asked it a hundred times during the week we spent eating rich foods, prowling in quaint little shops, dancing and loving.

"You know I'm happy, Garth," Cherry replied. "You see I've sort of been thinking of this for some time."

"Is it as nice as you thought it would be?"

"Much nicer. And I think it will get nicer each day as long as we live."

"Remember how you used to be afraid that our high school days were the happiest days we would ever know? What do you think now?"

She laughed. "We were just children then, weren't we? We have been children groping for something. We have done some experimenting—some of it pretty dangerous, I guess. But I believe we've built a solid foundation for our happiness together. From now on we're going to build on that foundation. I think we ought to build about the biggest and finest life that two people ever built together."

She was right.

I felt that marriage was going to bring a great change in my life. From now on there would be meaning and purpose. Why, just making a girl like Cherry happy and secure was purpose enough for any man. There would be no more restlessness. No more groping. No more disorder. No more eating in restaurants. No more despair at five o'clock. No more skirt chasing. From now on I would have a home, and order, and someone waiting for me.

The world's problems would no longer vex me. I could work hard and make more money and save some of it and grow conservative. I could build a world around Cherry and me, and then work to improve and defend that world.

What the hell! It was all as simple as that anyhow. That's what marriage is for. To give a man purpose. To resolve his doubts. To convert him from a revolutionary, who wants to tear down, into a solid citizen who wants to adjust and conserve and build and accumulate. No happily married man ever tried to overturn a world. He wants a safe world. He wants law and order and protection.

182

It all seemed clear and simple to me. I had made many mistakes, but marrying Cherry Lanson was not one of them.

I was certain of it.

1934-1938

WORLD'S END

IN THE PERIOD from 1934 to 1938 I watched the breakers of revolution beat against two worlds. One, an agricultural world, was destroyed; the other, an industrial world, was badly shaken.

With the creation of the Tennessee Valley Authority the entire valley became one vast Project. From the river's confluence with the Ohio clear back into the Tennessee and Carolina mountains, the valley was lifted up and pegged out on the drawing boards of the architects and planners. Sketches and blue-prints and stark, brilliant drawings were made to illustrate how decadence and decay were to be converted into New Life and Order and Concrete and Power.

It was a fateful day for the Garths and the Tennessee Valley when Senator Norris at last induced Congress to embark on the vast experiment. The experiment was so vast in its scope and implications that even now I am not certain how to assess the complete and final result, but the immediate result in 1934 was to start the second Yankee invasion of the South. The Garths awoke one morning in 1864 to find Sherman's raiders pouring across the river. They awoke one morn-

184

ing in 1934 to find the smart young political friends of Senator Norris and Senator Wagner and Senator Guffey pouring across the river. The new invaders were the sexless social service workers in plaid skirts and saddle oxfords, the boys with the graphs and the gadgets and the slide rules.

The old invaders came openly to pillage and destroy; but the new invaders came bearing gifts.

Everything was to be streamlined and electrified.

A streamlined pit toilet with a light in it for every family!

A streamlined refrigerator with a light in it for everybody!

A lighted playground for every community!

A streamlined, lighted housing project for every community!

New soils for old! Lakes in which to fish and swim! Power to burn! Jobs for the accepting! Order and Design set in concrete. New Order and New Design! New economy! Planned Economy! Streamlined Power Planned Economy!

Good God! It was the millennium in the midst of depression!

There was only one hitch in it. We "fascist" Garths were for the millennium one hundred percent, but what-the-hell good was the millennium going to do us if every foot of our land was to be buried under ten feet of water!

"Now listen, son, maybe it's all right to plan, but, by God, if you're figgering on covering up this Island, you got another plan coming. You're talking through your hat. The T. V. and A. may be all right, but Garth's Island is a part of America. It's a helluva lot older than Senator Norris and a helluva lot older than any of you Johnny-come-lately planners and social workers. The New World may look fine in them drawings, but if it means washing out the Old World, you

185

just take your plans and go back to Washington or to hell with 'em."

The prospect of the Garth world's being flooded put me on a terrible spot. I was a pretty good New Dealer in 1934. Not an Original Roosevelt Man, but a fairly enthusiastic New Dealer. I had been able to take the spectacle of the Government "hiring hands away from crops" without bitterness. In spite of Old Mis' Ella's fierce anger and the loud cussing of the older members of the Family, I had been able to hold the broad, detached view of that difficulty. But the complete erasure of the Garth world from the face of the earth was something fearful for a man named Peter Garth Lafavor to consider!

Looking one way I could see that Garth's Island didn't really matter in the broad scheme of things. Nobody outside the valley had ever heard of it. It was too small to appear on the map of Alabama. I had to think of progress. I had to think of the mighty laws of eminent domain. I had to think of how small and stupid it would be for an individual or a family to obstruct progress for the many. I had to think of the dog in the manger. Of one old reactionary fossil holding up a great social experiment. An experiment in which socially minded legislators were trying to make belated amends to the South. Trying to return some of the wealth which a near-sighted Congress had sucked away with tariff barriers. I had to think of how improper it would be to plague with a petty grievance a great President who wanted to get things done.

We Garths who had always believed that we had helped to "build" America couldn't turn into obstructionists now. We had to make the sacrifice and welcome the waters which would erase our Homeplace from the face of the earth. The Government would pay for the land.

As long as I stayed in Birmingham, as long as I talked to Harry and Addy and the fellows on the paper, I

186

could see that, however sad it might be, it was proper for the seventy-two families in the Garth world to move out onto the neat little resettlement plots and make way for the New Society. I wrote to Mother and Uncle Watts and told them there was nothing else for us to do.

But I made the mistake of going back to the Island to talk to them all. And Garth's Island was no place for a Garth to reflect calmly on such a prospect.

"Remember your name, Bud? You are named after Peter Garth. Remember who Peter Garth was? Remember how one peat-digger lay in a ditch and pumped lead at a bunch'a hired Hessians and dreamed of a day when he'd own something that would be his and his family's forever? That was the dream which built America, Bud. Don't let 'em kid you about that. Garth's Island may be insignificant in the big scheme of things, but it means everything to a Family which is still an institution in the heart of the last fortieth cousin. And if they're going to destroy the family-unit and the farm-unit and leave only one individual standing naked and impotent before the Great Omnipotent Federal Government, there isn't going to be any America left.

"Remember the Great Deed? General Washington signed that deed. Garth's Island is the symbol of the individual in this struggle. The preservation of a Family and its stake in America is more important than a few feet of height on the top of a dam.

"When the millennium comes to the valley, what'll we have? One man and his wife and kids living on a Government plot. One of those little plots that look so neat in the drawing. He'll have a pre-fabricated house and an electric refrigerator. He'll have a pit toilet with a light in it. He'll have a Smart Young Thing to advise him about calories and vitamins and pre-natal care. He'll enjoy 'supervised recreation.' He'll have the more abundant life. He won't need a

187

church-unit for the Government will give him Heaven-on-earth. He won't need a farm-unit to feed him in the bad years, for he'll have his Government. He won't need a family-unit to care for him when he's sick and old and unlucky, for he'll have his Government to benefit him and compensate him and adjust him and pension him. He'll even have his burial insurance to bury him.

"Just one man and the Government. No intermediate safeguards either wanted or needed. An ant in an ant-hill. That's a dangerous disproportion, isn't it, Bud? What can the man feel that he is a part of? The proletariat? The workers of the world? One big union? What stake will this man have in America? His streamlined pit toilet which will be his in thirty years? How strongly can he be counted on to defend this stake in America? Men won't die for anything except land and dreams. What dream will this man have worth dying for?"

I suppose the little liberal veneer I had acquired in college and during one year on a newspaper was insufficient to stand against the rush of that old hot Garth blood. My mother had stepped into Old Mis' Ella's shoes and was talking about as Old Mis' Ella would have talked. When I stood on the Point and looked down on those acres, I could see Old Mis' Ella clutching the Deed and cussing the Yankees while they burned the houses and stole the gold. Goddam it, those acres belonged to me and my folks. The Garth world meant something to us, and no man had a right to tamper with it.

In a Birmingham hotel lobby one morning I recognized old Colonel Sammy Johnson and his son, Tom Johnson. They managed the old General Johnson Place which was ten miles up-river from Garth's Island.

"You're Colonel Johnson, aren't you, suh?" I said to the old gentleman.

188

"Yassuh," he answered. "And you're a Garth. I can see it."

We talked for a few minutes, and they told me they were on their way to Washington. Both of them were fighting mad, and the Colonel's voice rose as he told me his trouble.

"Son, you know that row o' twenty-four big maples in front o' the homeplace? Everybody in Alabama knows that them trees was planted by the Old Gen'al himself. Well, ya know what these little bob-tailed, latter-day bastards are a-sayin'? They say they got to cut them trees down. That their blame little road's got to come through there, and that it can't go nowhere else. Well, by God, we'll show 'em. We've put niggahs out there with shotguns. We're goin' to Washington to see Jawn and Will. We'll spend every last nickel the Johnsons' a' got. And we'll see every lyin', thievin', Yankee bastard in hell with his britches on befo' we let 'em cut a tree."

In the end, blood made my decision for me in 1934. I decided that if Peter Garth could give his life to the building of the Garth world, and if six other generations of Garths thought it was worth dying for, we could risk our time and dollars in a battle to preserve it. So we hired the two best attorneys we could find in Birmingham, and lined up with the Johnsons to oppose the millennium and the Tennessee Valley Authority.

I wasn't bitter when we began our long court wrangle with TVA. The Government couldn't help the fact that the Garth world lay near a desirable location for a dam. What I wanted most was to protect the Family from drastic and unkind handling by the Government. I didn't want to feel that the Government was my enemy. If a compromise couldn't be effected, I wanted the courts and the TVA to help me explain to the Garths that we were making a great sacrifice for a

189

great cause. The Garths know how to sacrifice, but they are a simple and proud people. They like to feel that their sacrifices are for something great. They like to feel that their pride and their dignity have been respected. They like to be persuaded and not forced.

The Garths "wanted to do the right thing" toward TVA. Our lawyers consulted engineers and were told that if the proposed Joe Wheeler Dam was built as a power-generating dam it would have to be very high and all our land would be flooded. But if the dam was built only for navigation and flood control, it could be much lower, and only a small portion of our land would be flooded. We based our case on the compromise plea for the lower dam, and we buttressed our plea with the Congressional Deed and some talk about national honor and the Government's responsibility to the individual.

But I was bitter and resentful before it was all over. Not because we lost, but because of the way we were treated. The lawyer who represented TVA in the lower courts was a haughty, supercilious Harvardian. He appeared bored with the proceedings. He couldn't conceal his contempt for us, and I'm sure we displayed the same contempt for him. He treated the two University of Virginia gentlemen who represented us as though they were ancient Chesterfields who had to be endured until concentration camps could be arranged. He questioned our motives and insisted on trying us as enemies of the People.

We were preparing the record in the Federal District Court in Birmingham when he first questioned me. Uncle Watts and Mother and Father and Aunt Lilly had made the long trip to be present.

"Mr. Lafavor," the lawyer said, "are you aware, sir, that the plans for the Tennessee Valley Authority construction program have been prepared by the finest engineering talent in the country?"

"I have no way of knowing," I replied. "Was the en-

190

gineering talent selected the same way the legal talent was selected?"

The reporters snickered, and the judge rapped for order.

"For your information, sir," the lawyer continued in his surly manner, "these plans have been drawn with the most meticulous care and after months of scientific surveys. Don't you think then that it is rather presumptuous of you and your family to ask that plans affecting the lives of so many people be reconsidered because of your selfish interest?"

"No, I do not."

"Are you opposing this social development in the hope of raising the price of your land?"

"Hardly," I said. "We know you can set any price you choose on it. If we were interested in selling land we'd want it all covered up instead of only the thousand best acres as we propose."

"I believe you contend your land has some sentimental value. You Southerners are supposed to be sentimental, I believe."

"Yes, this land has been in the family for eight generations. It's our home. It was given to our ancestor by Congress. We'd like to preserve it."

He sneered. "Yes, a remarkable motive. But land is land, isn't it? When TVA pays you, you can purchase new and better land."

"I suppose land is land to a communist," I replied, "but hardly to me."

This time the snickering ruffled him. "Nor to a Fascist obstructionist either, I dare say," he snapped.

It was in this spirit that the hearings were conducted. Who were we to question a Government blue-print when the Government was creating jobs and spending so much money for the People? The lawyer and his experts sat with cases full of drawings and estimates. When our attorneys talked about honor and the rights of the individual, the TVA battery looked as if they were amused; as if they had heard stories of such strange people but never quite believed they existed.

Our display of the Great Deed and the reverence with which we mentioned it irked the TVA lawyer. "Your Honor," he popped off, "will you not inform the contestants that neither TVA nor the Court is interested in how title to this land was acquired. We have admitted title, and we are not interested in sentimental displays of old parchments. If the contestant has scientific data to support his plea, let us hear it and be done. This is a court of law and not a theater."

All our resentment was forgotten, however, when, after our plea had been denied by the District and Circuit Courts, the Supreme Court of the United States consented to hear us. Now at last we had found a bar before which the Garths could stand on equal ground with the arrogant bastards who personified TVA to us. Now, no matter what the Court decided, the Garths could accept it without bitterness; for no Garth could question a decision by the Big Court. The Big Court's action meant that our case was of some importance, and that at last we were to be treated with consideration and respect.

The hearing gave me my first trip to Washington. I wandered around and looked at the Lincoln Memorial and the Washington Monument and the Capitol and the White House, and I thought of all the other Obstructionists who had come to Washington in the past. Colonel Johnson coming to save his precious trees from the TVA road-builders. Garth Lafavor come to save the precious Island of the Garths. Obstructionists. The selfish few of us. Always trying to save our insignificant private domains from being inundated by the rush of the socialistic river. The arrogance of us! To think that a part of this universe should be forever ours! To think that a nation should have been brought into being for our benefit! To dare to interpose our selfish objections to the will of the majority!

Inside the great marbled Hall of Justice and before nine austere gentlemen, our attorneys made the last plea for Peter Garth's World. As I listened to the pleas, I felt very lonely and weighted with responsibility. No member of the Family had come with me. It was too far. As the educated Garth I was the logical one to represent the Family when so much was at stake. I'd have to tell them about the hearing before the Big Court, and I'd have to explain the decision.

Even after two eye-opening years as a reporter, I was tremendously impressed by the solemnity of it all. On that bench were men who were not politicians. They didn't win their places by contributions to the National Committee or by carrying water to elephants or to donkeys. Presidents forgot their politics and remembered only the American Dream when they considered an appointment to the Supreme Court. For the Court was the custodian of the Dream.

Yeah, I knew how the district judge got his job. Carrying water for his Senator. And, yeah, I knew how the circuit judge got his job. Hat-passers and water-boys! "Dear Tax Assessor: the committee needs twenty-five bucks out of your salary." But the Supreme Court of the United States was different. Here was majesty and honor and stateliness and quiet dignity. Here an unknown farm boy from the Tennessee Valley could come and feel that this Court stood ready to protect him from the great, blind mass called Government. I felt as if I were in the presence of the American Vision the day I sat and listened to our attorneys pleading for the world of the Garths.

Well, what the hell! There is no need to recall any quotes from those pleas. You know how they ran. A lot of talk about an Irishman's dream and a Family's heritage and what a democratic society owes to the individual. Your Honors, where will it all stop? There are five hundred descendants of Peter Garth in the Tennessee Valley. Garth's Island is their stake in America. . . .

It was a six-to-three decision for electricity, and the TVA bought the Garth world for $210,000. Fifty dollars an acre for three thousand acres, plus sixty thousand dollars for buildings and improvements.

A huge pile of money. The value of the Garth world. An incidental item to the land department of TVA. Watts Garth died three days after the Big Court decision, and I was made administrator. We sat down with the boys with the slide-rules and blue-prints, and they told us what our world was worth. We didn't haggle. We had never considered its dollar-value since we had never expected it to be sold. The boys set the price, and we accepted without contest.

"You know the Government wants to be fair with you people," the TVA land agent told me. "I can't understand why you aren't grateful. You know the money to do all this comes from New York and Pennsylvania and Ohio. Alabama doesn't pay enough taxes to count."

"I suppose we should be grateful," I said. "You people up North have more money, more education, and more energy than we have. You pay your relief workers twice as much and have ten times as many as we have. You're the successful part of America, while we are the unsuccessful part. Now you've taken over and ordered us out. For the sake of all the people who are going to be dependent on you, I hope it works out for the best."

"Well, we can't do much worse, can we?" he retorted.

"I'm not so sure. My grandfather dreamed of Muscle Shoals being used to produce cheap fertilizer for this valley. He was disappointed when the dam wasn't

194

leased to Henry Ford. But I doubt that he had the same dream which you fellows have."

"He was one of those guys who wanted Government wealth poured out at the top with the hope that a little of it might filter down, huh?"

"Perhaps, he was," I replied. "He wanted the valley to have cheap fertilizer and lighted toilets, but he didn't want to pay too big a price for them. He didn't want to break the cement which holds this world together down here. You latter-day Yankees with your overpaid political jobs don't know anything about this cement."

"What kind of cement is it?" he asked.

"Well, it isn't the kind you buy in sacks," I said.

It took a year for our attorneys to liquidate the Garth world.

Since the death of Peter Garth in 1823 that world had been held and operated as an estate. It provided houses and land for Garth sons when they married at seventeen and eighteen. It provided dowries for Garth daughters when they married at sixteen and seventeen. When they got on their feet, some of the sons and daughters had moved out into the valley to acquire more land for themselves, and always the three thousand acres had remained intact to give the young-uns their starts in life. The estate provided money for Garth enterprises and for Family emergencies. The estate provided the haven for the old, the feeble, and the unsuccessful. And, above all, the estate provided the foundation stone for a Family. The magnet which held all the brothers and sisters and uncles and aunts and cousins together in a family-unit.

Once each year they all came back to the Island for the Garth Family Reunion. They sang the old songs and strewed flowers on the graves of their dead. They hugged and kissed and slapped backs and laughed and cried and remembered. They ate too much barbecue and drank too much whiskey. They crossed the threshold of the homeplace and took off their hats and shuffled into Old Mis' Ella's room and looked reverently at the memorabilia. The young mothers told the daughters about the great deed. The fathers showed the sons the conch shell, and where the Yankees hanged old Uncle Nap. And every Garth, from the oldest grandmother to the youngest fortieth cousin, knew that he was a part of something Very Great and Very Dear and Very Old.

After the Court decision we decided to hold one last reunion before the floods came. It was a May Sunday in 1936. More than two thousand people ate dinner that day on Garth's Island. There were four big steamboats and an extra ferryboat at the Landing. Hickory coals glowed in the barbecue pits all night Saturday night, and over them Raccoon Charley and his aides turned fat quarters of beef and pork and lamb and kid. Of course not all the two thousand were Garths by strict genealogical rule. There were at least twenty families represented. But they were all related to some generation of Garths by some marriage tie, and thus they felt welcome to the reunion. In addition, every Garth had invited his preacher and his string band or quartet.

One of the Garths had a friend in the radio business who had supplied a loudspeaker like those the politicians use so everybody could hear. In the afternoon, after all the bands and quartets and preachers had been heard and after some of the older aunts and uncles had talked about the Good Old Days, it was my turn to tell them about the Family's business.

"Well, folks," I began, "you all know most of what has happened and you know what we are up against. We have done all we could to prevent the Government from taking our land. But they've taken it. Every last foot of it. It seems a strange thing to say, but today the land we are standing on doesn't belong to the

196

Garths. It belongs to something called the TVA. The land our fathers died for is to be covered by water which will generate electricity to be used in rebuilding the valley. Six months from today the Island will be only a memory. The deal was closed a month ago when TVA gave us $210,000 for our land and buildings. As soon as debts are paid, each of you will get his proper share of what is left."

I looked over the crowd for evidence that somebody was glad he was going to get his part in cash. But there was no such evidence. Every Garth realized that as long as the homeplace remained intact, it was a great and valuable source of pride and security. But, broken into little pieces, it would be nothing.

"Now there was a time," I continued, "when we'd know what to do under these circumstances. We'd make some fighting speeches. We'd blow the old conch shell. We'd strike up 'Dixie.' We'd go get our guns and die in our own blood before we let a gang o' Yankee bastards push us around and take our land. This is the way the Garths would have acted in years which some of you can remember."

Some hips and hollers rose to remind me that those years were not so far gone, so I rushed on. "But today we are living in a different sort of world. The America which Peter Garth and Old Mis' Ella knew is gone. The President and even the Big Court have told us that we must build a new kind of America. A new kind of America in which the Government is going to run things and regulate things and try to see that everybody gets his share.

"Now, sight unseen, we Garths can tell you that we don't believe in this Government stuff. We've spent ten thousand Garth dollars trying to save the Old America, but we've been licked. And now we have a choice to make. We can continue to hang on the backing-straps, or we can dry our eyes and pitch in and help build this new kind of America. God knows what

197

this New America is going to be like. I don't know. The President doesn't know. We've got nothing left to guide us. We are throwing the Constitution overboard. The Constitution today is only an old piece of parchment worth no more to America than that old Deed is worth to the Garths.

"Building this New America is not going to be easy. Some heads will be cracked and some blood will be spilled. But apparently we've got to build it. And we Garths and the people like us have got to help. We've got to go further than just help in the building. We have got to get in there and see that this rebuilding is done according to the way we think and believe."

Then I got down to immediate problems. It was for the family to decide whether or not the cemetery was to be moved. All up and down the valley the moving of old cemeteries was being discussed. Some were being moved and some were being left for the water to cover. The Garths had been discussing the possibility of having to move ours for months, and now it was time for a decision. I had heard the various arguments.

"Shucks, ya' can't move a graveyard's old as our'n. They aint nothin' t' move."

"Remember what Old Mis' Ella said. She wanted a pine box an' no embalmin' so's she could go back to dust an' the land soon's she could. She couldn't rest nowheres 'cept on Garth's Island."

"But we'se all got to be bur'd together. How's it gonna be with us bur'd off yonder some'res an' mammy an' pappy bur'd heah under the rivah?"

"Taint right for bodies to be bur'd under a rivah. What'll happen on Judgment Day?"

"But, shucks, are we gonna just take a box of dirt from under Peter Garth's headstone an' call that dirt Peter Garth an' bury it some'res else?"

"Remember the night Watts died after the Co'at decision? He said he wanted to be bur'd on Garth's

198

Island an' he didn't want nobody to move him anywheres else."

"What'll we do on next Decoration Day? The biggest family in the valley won't have no graves to put flowers on!"

"Let's let 'em rest in peace. They wouldn't like this new Gover'mint world anyhow."

"Good Lawd, niggah! De Garths is a-tawkin' 'bout not movin' de buryin' groun'. Mah last ole lady couldn't swim a lick. She'll nevah git to Hebben on Judgment Day. She'll rise jest ta git drown'd again."

"Crawford and Crazy Tom's both bur'd on the Island. Both a-ravin' when they died. They'll haint us sho' if we let the water cover their graves."

After much discussion we decided that we would take no concerted action to move the cemetery. All the old generations would be left undisturbed, but if any immediate family wanted to move the bodies of more recently buried relatives they could do so. Before the water came all the headstones would be moved to Gum Spring Cemetery where the Family would set up a new plot. The Negroes were hardest hit by the decision, since they could only count as lost all the water-covered souls. Even if a soul could rise with tons of water on top of him, he would either be drowned or have to face the Judgment wet as a rat.

We also agreed that financial assistance should be extended to the twenty families of Garths living on the place who would have to become renters or would have to begin purchase of new land plots. The fifty-two croppers' families were to be helped toward securing new places to live, and the Garths would try to reassimilate the old Negroes and whites who were too old to rent land plots or find employment.

Late in the afternoon, after I had told them about the Big Court trial and about what I saw in Washington, and after the more distant relatives had begun to leave, the Family did me a very great honor. My older uncles and aunts, together with my mother and grandmother, decided that I should be custodian of the memorabilia. Before the homeplace was demolished I would take the great Deed and the conch shell and the old Bible and the old papers and letters, and I would put them in a bank vault in Birmingham until I had a home for myself. Then I could keep them and hand them on to my son, but they would always be the property of the Garths.

Thus did we Garths dispose of our Old America. After we paid off forty thousand dollars in mortgages and ten thousand dollars in litigation costs, and after we helped seventy-two families to move and readjust themselves, there was approximately $120,000 to be divided among 348 heirs of Peter Garth. The largest check was for $748.92, and the smallest was for eleven cents.

Raccoon Charley and two of his sons came to live on a little forty-acre place which my mother and father rented near Hartselle, and Mother assumed the responsibility for seeing that they never lacked their remedies and their biskit for breakfast. Five more Negro families found refuge with Garths, but twenty-eight faithful Negro families had to be abandoned to the Government. I have often wondered if the bureaucrats are supplying them biskit for breakfast and quatahs for snuff and candy. The twenty white cropper families went into the resettlement projects.

In November Cherry and I drove up for our last look at the disappearing world of Peter Garth. The moon was shining, and we stopped the car at the Point where we had parked the night we graduated from high school. For a moment we felt very old and very melancholy.

"Some day," I said to Cherry, "when the world grows stable again, I am going to write the history of Garth's Island. I am going to say that it was born in the dreams of an Irishman on July 4, 1776, and that it died by Supreme Court decree on March 12, 1936."

2

In 1933 Old Buck Delancey was sixty, worth five million dollars, and master of a world all his own.

Old Buck was the industrial counterpart of Old Mis' Ella Garth. His fathers had mined the first lump of Alabama coal. In a valley surrounded by high, fence-like hills forty miles from Birmingham, they built a world and posted signs around it subtly announcing that trespassers would not be prosecuted but shot. In this world of the Delanceys two thousand families, white and black, lived, dug coal and died. When a denizen of the Delancey world was born, a Delancey doctor presided at his birth. He went to a Delancey school, he went to a Delancey church and listened to a Delancey-paid preacher. He swam in the Delancey pool, recovered from his injuries in the Delancey hospital, and got his groceries at the Delancey commissary. When he died, he lay in a Delancey coffin, the Delancey preacher preached him into a Delancey Heaven, the Delancey Quartet sang "Shall We Gather at the River?" and he was buried in the Delancey cemetery.

In family, school and church, the Delancey denizen was taught from infancy to love God and Buck Delancey and to hate the Devil and John Lewis. For all practical purposes Buck Delancey was God from whom all blessings flowed, and John Lewis was the beetle-browed Menace who condemned little chillun to starvation and cut old men adrift without hope or promise. Every Delancey denizen qualified as an expert marksman with rifle or shotgun, and learned to work with his gun at hand. In times of stress and strike, whether he was principal of the Delancey school or the lowliest Negro mule-boy, he knew how to throw down his work, pick up his gun, and race to the Delancey property line

201

to protect his world from invasion by the bastard legions of John Lewis.

It wasn't hard for the denizens to love Old Buck, for he was a benevolent despot. He stood on the tipple and cracked the bull-whip, but every slave knew that as long as Old Buck ate he would eat, too, and that when he had a grievance he didn't have to take it to some superintendent but could stride unchecked into the open office and sit down with Old Buck himself. When the Lewis minions came to attack, the denizens didn't have to follow some company deputy to the firing line. Old Buck, wearing his big hat and leather boots, carrying his automatic shotgun and spewing a stream of elegant profanity, was at the head of the column, and every denizen coveted the privilege of fighting next to him.

Old Buck Delancey had not fallen into the errors of his fellow mine owners. He didn't live in a massive pile hidden far over in the Labyrinth of Have. He lived in the Big House on a hilltop where every one of his serfs could see him and where any serf could find him if catastrophe came in the night. He didn't spend his afternoons on golf courses nor his evenings sipping brandy in a secluded alcove of a Country Club. He didn't sit in a downtown office tower and telephone to superintendents to see how things were going. He lived in his own world, and, like Caesar, he knew the names of all his soldiers. Instead of golfing with the other Haves, he cheered on his baseball teams. Instead of sipping brandy with the butterflies, he was on hand to likker up the string band in the Delancey playhouse and urge on the dancers. Instead of allowing his sons to race around in sport cars and acquire divorce records, he sent them into the mines to work and to learn the names of all the soldiers. Instead of spending money and time on sales promotions, he advertised that no Delancey mine had ever been shut down an hour because of labor trouble, and thus Delancey deliveries were as certain as sunrise.

Old Buck Delancey knew something about human nature. He knew what it takes to make workers contented and efficient. He knew how to make every worker feel that Old Buck Delancey was his powerful friend and confidant. In short, Old Buck Delancey knew how to hold his world together. He knew the importance of family-units and farm-or-factory-units. So when the lieutenants of John Lewis launched their new streamlined attacks against the crumbling industrial citadels of 1933, they found the world of Buck Delancey as stubborn and formidable as ever.

When dawn broke on one winter morning in 1934, I was soaking wet. I was lying in the mud behind a rock on a hill over-looking the main approach to the Delancey properties. It was cold, and raining one of those slow, steady rains which you are certain will go on forever.

The Lewis legions were preparing to attack. Looking back down the road with my glasses, I could see the cars stretched out for four miles. Three thousand desperate men. A thousand whites and two thousand Negroes. Enough for an infantry regiment. Armed with clubs and pistols and shotguns and rifles. The American proletariat going into action against the cossacks. I had watched them gather in a baseball field forty miles away. As representative of a paper which espoused their cause, I was their friend: I had listened to the wild-eyed harangues of the Lewis lieutenants.

Buck Delancey is the enemy of every man who works in America!

Buck Delancey is takin' bread outa my chillun's mouths!

How can we win a strike as long as Buck Delancey's mines run three shifts a day seven days a week?

203

We're goin' over there and free them slaves! Buck Delancey's slaves!

Before sundown tomorrow Buck Delancey's mines will be closed if we have to blast hell outa 'em!

I had watched the Lewis lieutenants pass the whiskey jugs which, God knows, those poor fellows needed in the cold and rain. I had watched the old dark fury mount in terrible black faces, and I had stepped back in fear and wondered how these leaders dared to whip up this fury which once unleashed they could never control. I had watched Harry Lerner confer with the deadly, World-War-trained gunners assigned to the front cars, and I had counted the cars as they stopped at the union gas pumps to be filled for the eighty-mile round-trip to the Delancey mines. I had ridden with the column until it halted a half-mile from the battle line, and then I had run on ahead to find a hill and a rock from which to observe the battle.

Off in front I could see Old Buck with his minions. The Lewis legions had hardly hoped to catch Old Buck napping. The Delancey searchlight which stood on the highest mountain could spot a man sneaking through the woods three miles away. It revolved constantly during strikes, and picked up every car which approached Delancey agents. Every entrance to Delancey property was guarded by a manned stockade, and there were Delancey road-riders to keep Old Buck informed of the movements of Lewis's men.

I could see Old Buck stamping around with his shotgun, impatient for the attack. His superintendents and deputies fondled well-oiled Thompson guns with their big bandoliers, and adder-like black snouts darted out of holes in the stockade. Behind this heavy-weapons detachment Old Buck had deployed five hundred "infantrymen" armed with shotguns. They lay on their bellies to be called up in the event the Thompson guns proved insufficient to halt the charge.

Back further in the valley I noted something truly

characteristic of Old Buck. Every damn one of the eight Delancey mines was running. Maybe the crews were skeletons and maybe every miner had a pick in one hand and a shotgun in the other, but, by God, coal trams were snaking out onto the tipples, vomiting their loads, and snaking back into the mines. Not in thirty years of warfare had John Lewis ever shut down a Delancey mine, and Old Buck was preserving the record. Mine whistles screamed defiantly while the Lewis legions took battle positions.

The engagement was pitifully short. A crudely-armored car carrying three gunners formed the spearhead of the assault. It advanced along the road, flanked by the ragged, overalled, white-and-black infantry which advanced through the adjoining cotton patches. When the car was within a hundred and fifty yards of the stockade, each side nervously holding its fire, Old Buck exploded a thunderous charge of dynamite with which the road had been mined and blasted the armored car off the road. As the car landed on its side in a ditch, the Delancey Thompson guns began chattering.

The explosion and the rapid fire were too much for the Lewis infantry. A few of them fell to their bellies in the mud and began firing toward the stockade, but the main body turned tail and fled in disorder down the road toward their cars. The Delancey fire held up and allowed those who had stuck to scramble off to safety.

When the smoke cleared I ventured out from behind my rock. I had counted the Lewis casualties at nine dead or wounded, including the three gunners in the blasted car. There might just as easily have been nine hundred casualties, but the Delancey gunmen had sent most of their fire into the ground in front of the attackers. Before looking for a telephone I decided to approach the stockade to see if there had been any company casualties. In my best military manner I pulled out my soggy handkerchief and held it over my head as I plodded up the road, my feet gathering more mud at every step. Some of the Lewis men were coming back now, with their hands up, to pick up the fallen, and I shared their surprise when Delancey men came running out to tell them to bring all the injured men to the Delancey hospital. This gesture saved carrying the injured men forty miles over clogged roads; some of them would certainly have died.

Old Buck had nothing but pity and contempt for the grimy-faced relief clients who came to attack his fortress. He regarded them as pawns in the hands of his arch-enemies in Washington.

As I neared the stockade, six black and white gunners flanked a heavy white man who came out to meet me. They said nothing and their silence bothered me.

"You boys goin' rabbit-huntin'?" I managed, in what I hoped was the voice of self-assurance.

"No we ain't. Who are ya?"

"Just a reporter. I'd like to see Mr. Delancey, and I'd like to use your telephone."

"A reporter for who?"

"For *The Press*. I want to use your telephone."

"*The Press*, huh? Git the hell offa this land an' git quick. Don't ya know Old Buck don't allow *The Press* in this county?"

It was the truth. Because of our support of the union, Old Buck was a fierce enemy of the paper. He didn't allow our circulation men on his property. But since Old Buck would probably recognize me if I saw him, there was no use pretending I was with another paper.

"But this is different," I argued. "Mr. Delancey will want to give me the facts about what has happened."

"Like hell he will," the superintendent came back. "If you'd bother him now he'd probably give you the butt end of a hoss-whip. You'd better git while the gittin's good."

Had there been more time I would have risked seizure in an attempt to get to the company office. But I had to think of a deadline. I back-tracked down the road and soon caught up with the tattered and dejected Lewis legions retreating in blood and rain and mud from Moscow. Traffic was so badly snarled along the narrow muddy road that I found it quicker to walk the three miles to a cross-roads store on the main Atlanta-Birmingham highway. The place was serving as a base of operations for directing the retreat, and some of the Lewis lieutenants were there. After I had shouted through a bad telephone connection for twenty minutes, I slumped down on a feed sack and offered the storekeeper a dollar if he would go out to his house and make me a pint of coffee. I had been wet all night and my feet were numb blocks of muddy ice.

But, hell, I couldn't drink the coffee. The storekeeper came, bringing it in a milk bottle, and as he made his way through the mass of hungry, wet and bedraggled men, each one of them looked at the bottle and swallowed like a street urchin looking through a bakery window. Just as they handed me the coffee, they brought in a white man whose cheek bone had been smashed by a rifle bullet and a huge Negro whose arm had been torn by buckshot. I split the coffee between them.

There was a rumpus outside, and I found that the Lewisites had captured two Delancey slaves and were holding them as hostages. The slaves were defiant under taunts.

"Relief hounds! Goddam relief hounds!" the Delancey slaves sneered back at the Lewisites. All the union men were on relief during the strike. "Look at 'cha. All of ya on ree-leef an' ya children howngry, an' ya come off ovah heah ta try to drive we-uns offa our good jobs."

"Slaves! Bootlickers! Ass-kissers! Nobody don't own us," the Lewisites retorted.

"The Gover'mint an' Jawn Lewis owns yuh dirty

207

souls. There aint nevah been no damn ree-leef hound on Delancey land an' ther' won't nevah be."

"By God, ye're gonna join up with us or we'll kill ever' las' one uv ya."

"Like hell ya' will. The onliest way ya'll ever cross a Delancey line'll be when ya' larn to fly."

The Lewisites took this last to heart. They whispered excitedly that the union leaders would hire airplanes to drop bombs on Old Buck's mines.

A photographer arrived in one of our press cars, and we circled the Delancey property and checked on casualties. I sighed every time I thought of missing pictures of the mass attack, but I had promised the union leaders there would be no pictures until after the fighting was over. We stopped at a commissary, long enough for me to eat and buy some socks, underwear and shoes. Perched on a lard can, I sat in my underwear while my suit dried over a cook stove.

At another entrance to Delancey property we found where a second detachment of union men had been turned back. It was the same story. The Delancey denizens had taken cover on a hill-side, then turned the fast-shooting guns loose at the attackers. A blond, overalled young man about twenty-three lay in a ditch at the side of the road. His face was turned up to the rain. His eyes were wide open. Muddy water swirled around his legs. A .38 calibre revolver, fired three times, was clutched in his right hand. The photographer and the coroner counted eighteen holes in his body. Those little sub-machine gun bullets don't lodge in a body. They go all the way through. His pockets contained three matches, fourteen cents, a crumpled sack of smoking tobacco, and two cards. One card said he was a member of the United Mine Workers of America. The other card said that he, his wife, and three kids could draw four dollars a week relief from the United States of America.

I looked at him lying there in the ditch in the rain. He was about my age. What had he died for? What vision had John Lewis unfolded to him which could make him leave his wife and kids two days after Christmas and come charging into machine gun bullets with his pitiful little pop-pistol? What had he endured, what had he hoped, what had he dreamed, to make him willing to risk a bloody, muddy death in a ditch? Was he a martyr, a criminal, or a damn fool?

I tried to figure out an answer, but I couldn't. It would have been easy if I could have looked around at those who machine-gunned the boy in the ditch and seen a group of sneering Pinkertons blowing smoke out of their guns. Yes, I could have said, the boy in the ditch is a martyr. Some day, when the workers of the world are free, they can strew flowers on this boy's grave and say that he was one of the heroes who died along the road to victory.

But it wasn't that easy. For when I looked around I didn't see any Pinkertons. I saw the grim, white faces of boys and men who thought they were protecting their homes and their jobs and their blood-bought American right to choose for themselves whether to serve Buck Delancey or John Lewis. The boy who had machine-gunned the boy in the ditch was no thick-skulled company thug. He was twenty-three years old, too. A young mining engineer from the university. A classmate of mine. A boy who had known a year of jobless heartache before Buck Delancey gave him a start in these mines. A boy whom the United States of America had taught to use a machine gun in the ROTC. A boy who had a young wife and a baby living in a company house a quarter of a mile from where the boy lay in the ditch. He had grabbed the company gun and gone out to defend his home and his family and his job and his American rights against attack by an armed rabble.

The great leaders of America who sit off somewhere in comfortable offices can tell you in a flash which one of these boys was the hero and which one was the villain. But standing in the rain and mud looking at them, I didn't know which to accuse.

About midnight I dropped into a café on the highway near the Delancey property. I found an edition of my paper, and I sat down to read it over coffee and eggs. I wanted to see what we were saying under my by-line. The piece was unmistakably anti-Delancey. Yeah, I expected that. The union men had been on an "organizing expedition." UMWA headquarters explained the guns by saying "a few of the men" had carried guns because they feared violence at the hands of the Delancey "company deputies." The report of the battle was fairly accurate. The company deputies had blasted the road and fired first. Well, they HAD fired first, and there WAS a company deputy among the four or five hundred company men who fired. The re-write man who had taken my stuff was a Socialist and a passionate supporter of unionism. We were carrying the flag for Labor. We represented the Weak against the Strong. So it was natural for the story to carry an undertone of sympathy for the union and to portray the company men as hired minions of Entrenched Greed.

While I was eating, two men in a car stopped in front of the café. One of them came inside, and I recognized him as Manny West, my former classmate who had machine-gunned the boy in the ditch.

"Hello, Manny," I said. "Sit down."

He was not cordial, but he sat down and said: "Hello, Garth. You still around?"

"Yeah, I thought I better stick around for a day or two. You boys might be hunting some more rabbits."

"You don't think they'll come back, do you?" he asked.

"God knows. I wouldn't think so after what you gave them this morning. But you can't tell what men will do now."

210

As he sweetened his coffee his eyes fell on the paper I had been reading. "I read your story," he said.

I waited for him to go on, but he was obviously waiting for my question. "What did you think of it?"

He sneered. "You know what I think of it. I think it's rotten and unfair. I was surprised, too. I always thought you were a pretty fair-minded fellow in spite of the way you hung around with those Reds."

"I'm sorry to hear you say that, Manny," I replied. "It's pretty hard to be fair about something as tough as this."

"I don't see anything hard about it," he said quickly. "When a gang o' drunken thugs attack your home and your job, you don't have to pray over it to know what to do. We are living in peace up here, and all we ask is to be let alone. What would you have done if you had been in my place this morning? Stood aside while those drunken relief hounds tore up your house and blew up your job and drove you on relief like they are?"

You couldn't doubt his sincerity. "No, I guess I would have done just about what you did, Manny, if I had been in your place."

"Then why didn't you treat us fair?" he shot back. "Why did you make it look like we were wrong and those drunken Lewis bastards were right?"

I wanted to explain it to him if I could. I wanted to understand the explanation myself. "Well, I guess it's because I'm in *my* place, Manny, and not in your place. You work for Buck Delancey. You think Old Buck is a swell fellow because he gave you your first job when you needed it. You are part of Old Buck's world up here in the hills. You are doing all right for yourself and for your wife and baby. Some day you'll be chief engineer for Old Buck or for the next Young Buck. So you are interested in keeping things like they are up here."

"Sure I am," he said. "Wouldn't you be?"

"Yes, I guess so. But you see I'm in a different position. I work for a big newspaper chain. We have papers all over the United States. We have papers in Pittsburgh and Cleveland where every miner belongs to the union. Here in Birmingham there are twenty-five thousand miners who belong to the union as against the two thousand up here who don't."

He cut in. "You know why they belong to the union. They know their homes will be dynamited if they don't."

"Well, yes," I admitted, "that's true in some cases. But whatever their reason for joining, the fact is that 'most every miner belongs to the union. Now my company has to take a national view of this thing. The men I work for are just as sincere as Buck Delancey. They want to find what's best for the men in Cleveland and the men in Pittsburgh and the men in Birmingham. And they have decided that, by and large, it is best for ALL miners to belong to the United Mine Workers."

"Well, that's okay," he said. "Let everybody belong who wants to join. It's a free country. We don't want to join. They leave us alone and we'll leave them alone. That's Americanism."

"Yes, I'll admit that sounds pretty good to me, Manny. But I'm afraid it isn't that simple any more. You are shipping coal by the trainload out of these hills every day. Maybe there was a time when that wouldn't have affected anybody but you. But now these Delancey coal trains affect every man who mines coal in Birmingham and every man who mines coal in Cleveland and Pittsburgh. You are all inter-dependent. So we are revising our definitions of a Free Country and Americanism; and the men I work for believe that the sooner you join the union the better it is going to be for everybody. That's why sympathy for unions creeps into our stories. I'm not looking at this fight from the same angle you are looking at it."

"No, you are not," Manny said. "You didn't have to cram furnaces to get through school like I did. You didn't have to pound concrete for a year looking for a job like I did. If you had, you'd know that every man has still got to look out for himself up here in these hills. When anybody bothers us we are going to give 'em the same treatment we gave 'em this morning."

He was ready to go. He was an honest fellow from a small town. In college he had always worked hard and lived to himself. I offered him my hand. "Well, whatever happens, I hope it all works out for you, Manny. You deserve all the best."

He softened. "Thanks, Garth. I'm sorry if I gave it to you a little stiff. I don't have to kill a man every day, you know."

I walked to the car with him. Two submachine guns lay in the car seat. He got in beside his companion, stood one of the guns between his knees, and they drove off down the road toward Birmingham. They were two of the outriders protecting the Delancey fortress.

The litigation growing out of this Delancey-Lewis war dragged out for weeks and months. The Delancey world lies in a rural county adjoining sprawling Jefferson which contains most of the mines and mills of the Birmingham District. All the trials were held in this rural county where Old Buck enjoyed a tremendous advantage. A second or third Special Grand Jury finally indicted Old Buck and ten of his people, including Manny West, for murder. They were all tried together in a two-by-four country courthouse around which hundreds of families spread dinner on the ground and waited for the High Sheriff to announce developments from an upstairs window.

There were sixteen lawyers representing the State and the union, and twenty-two lawyers representing the Delanceys. To keep damage suits down, Buck Delancey had a policy of retaining many members of the bar in his county. We got a laugh out of six of Buck's old-time country lawyers, for their sole contribution to

Delancey defense was always the selection of the jury. The six of them together were certain to know every man in the county back to the third generation, so Old Buck depended on them to pack the jury with Lewis haters and Delancey lovers. They studied the venire for hours and would fall into long, heated arguments over whether some prospective juror's sympathy for the company extended back two or three generations.

"Now I 'pear to recolleck that this boy's grandpap got into a spat with Old Hoss Delancey about a option, didn't he?" one of the Jury Fixers would ask. And if it was agreed that the spat had occurred, the "boy" would be deemed unfit for jury service and would be marked to be struck.

At the outset, the country lawyers sprung the hoariest of all technical coups on the city slickers in the prosecution by winning the prosecution's consent to try all the defendants at the same time. In choosing a jury the defense usually has two strikes to the State's one; but, under Alabama law, when there is more than one defendant the defense can strike once for each defendant each time the State strikes once. Since there were eleven defendants in this case, each time the union attorneys struck one prospective juror from the venire, the Delancey lawyers went into their huddle and struck eleven. This made it possible for them to eliminate from the jury every man about whom they had the slightest suspicion of disloyalty to the Delancey cause.

As the trial wore on, I noticed that the six old country lawyers sat far down the defense line and were allowed no part in the conduct of the trial. I said to one of them: "Judge, when are you going to earn your money in this trial? Looks like these fancy boys are gonna do all the talking."

He chuckled. "Listen, son, that fancy talk's just like lace on a petticoat. When I picked this jury I fixed it so Buck Delancey couldn't lose this case if a blind Jew an' a deef-an'-dumb niggah wuz a-pleadin' it for him."

The laugh came when it developed that the country lawyers had nodded. They had allowed one man to reach the jury who nursed a grievance against the company. Three weeks earlier a Delancey truck had run over his red rooster, and the company had not yet paid him for it. So instead of bringing a summary verdict of acquittal, the jury stayed out for three days and a mistrial was declared.

When we learned what had happened in the jury room, we had to intervene forcibly to prevent the six country lawyers from assassinating one another with hoss pistols and hawk-bill knives. Each one accused the other of criminal negligence in not being apprised of the rooster incident, and all six were deeply humiliated at this blow to the board's reputation.

The union attorneys, however, gave up the struggle. They reasoned that if all their eloquence plus a display of seven widows and twenty-two orphaned children could win them only a single juror with an unrecompensed rooster, then there was little hope of ever convicting any of the Delancey clan of manslaughter. The individual damage suits against the company dragged on for three years, and though it cost Old Buck a fortune to defend them all, he never paid out a penny to the pitiful heirs of the labor martyrs who died storming the Delancey fortress on a cold, rainy morning in 1934.

I believe Old Buck Delancey would have won your admiration if not your sympathy. He was like the hero of a Greek tragedy. His doom was apparent to all but himself. You knew he would die, but never compromise or surrender. His fellows among Alabama's coal barons were smug little men who retreated and compromised and appeased and struggled only to maintain their own selfish little positions in the Reserved Seat Section—to pay their Country Club dues and the cost of coming-out parties. They deserved little better than the contempt in which they were held by Mr. Lewis and Mr. Roosevelt. When they have been liquidated or inundated by the forces of Revolution, the positive element in the human phalanx will have suffered no noticeable loss.

But Old Buck was different. He wanted to preserve his own Reserved Seat ticket. But he wanted much more. He wanted his world and his way of life to survive. He was willing to risk his own safety to save his world. He wanted to prove that his world was stronger, better and more fit to survive than the bigger, newer world advocated by his opponents. He knew that John Lewis was a realistic and relentless foe. He knew that Mr. Lewis's lieutenants would machine-gun and dynamite his people if he gave them the chance. So Old Buck fortified his hills and erected searchlights and never hesitated to use dynamite and machine guns to make the Lewis minions keep their distance. He built armored cars to transport the Delancey workers in safety. He built homes in the fortress so Delancey workers could sleep without fear of dynamite.

But if Old Buck was to demonstrate the superiority of his world he had to do more than protect it. He had to make his world provide the workers with more than the New World of Roosevelt and John Lewis could offer them. He had to pay his workers at least as much as the union scale. He was already providing hospitalization and better housing. In the long lay-offs caused by depression and falling coal consumption, Old Buck could not throw his workers on relief offered by the New World. For Old Buck was proud and honest. He admitted that if a Delancey worker had to become dependent on the New World then the Old World would have failed. Old Buck's competitors—the compromising and retreating moaners for whom he had less respect than he had for Roosevelt—didn't worry about their workers in the lay-offs. Relief took care of them. But Old Buck would have no relief. He hired agricultural experts and canning experts and bought more land so that his workers could raise food when they were not digging coal. He boasted that social workers were neither needed nor allowed in the Delancey world. The Delancey world could take care of its own. John Lewis' assistants never missed an opportunity to plague Old Buck. Madam Perkins had an agent sitting in Old Buck's office every week. Old Buck would throw him out and give him a message to take back to his boss.

Old Buck died in 1938 cussing Roosevelt, Hugo Black and John Lewis. He tried to cuss Madam Perkins a final cuss, but when he mentioned her name he went into such a paroxysm that he never regained his breath. I think he could have lived longer, but by 1938 he saw the prospect of the Third Term, and it was too much for him. On his death bed he swore his sons to carry on the fight and to dynamite the mines before allowing "a Lewis bastard" to enter one of them. Most of his personal fortune was gone, sacrificed in the unequal battle.

The sons continued Old Buck's fight; and I am told that they are still able to repel the attacks of the Lewis legions. But the inevitable end is in sight.

When I think of the Garth and Delancey worlds, I sometimes feel that the Garth world met the kindlier end. It, at least, was covered by cool, clear, clean Government water, while the Delancey world, its warming fires of paternalism extinguished, must go on as a grimy, cold, mechanical production unit.

1936-1938

DEFENSE AND DEFEAT

I WAS TWENTY-THREE in 1936 when I cast my first ballot. I voted for Roosevelt. It wasn't easy, for the rest of the Garths voted against him. My mother got up out of a sick bed to go to the polls and vote against a Government which had hired hands away from crops and then destroyed the Garth world. I distrusted expanding Government, and I seemed to have an inborn contempt for Government employees. Also, as a newspaperman I suffered from a growing, almost blinding cynicism toward all politicians. "Our kind of folks" in Alabama opposed the New Deal in most of its manifestations. With some justification, it was charged that only the political opportunists and the mass of folks who "wanted to get some'pin' " supported Roosevelt.

Still I felt I should vote for Roosevelt. I knew the filthy aspects of the local labor set-up, but I felt that unionism should be encouraged. I felt that my education and my broader experience had put me in a position where I could no longer take the limited view of the Garths. I had to take the broad view. I had to look forward toward the distant goal of the New Deal and not be confused by the immediate consequences of change. Change meant a larger degree of socializa-

218

tion. Change meant the bigger governments I instinctively distrusted. Change meant the end of little private worlds. But change was normal and necessary and inevitable.

I still maintained a tolerant attitude toward communists. I had had some lively bouts with Harry and Adeline over the way in which they exploited the racial issue, over the Scottsboro Case, and over some of the "direct methods" they employed to aid the labor organizers. When Earl Browder came to Birmingham during the Presidential campaign, I helped them in their efforts to obtain the City Auditorium for their meeting. When the Interests kept them out of the Auditorium, I told more than one representative of the Interests how short-sighted he was.

I liked Browder when I met him. Harry took me to his hotel, and I spent the afternoon talking to him and watching him receive the homage of the hungry, apostolic "rats" who sneaked up out of their holes to sit at the feet of the Great Man. I realized that afternoon that communism is more than an ideology; it's a religion. I knew many of the fiery-eyed young men and women who came in to see Browder. I knew that they had been shot at, kicked and slapped around by Red Squads and company dicks. But when they came in to shake Browder's hand, they looked as my mother would have looked had she walked up to the Great White Throne to shake hands with Christ.

At the meeting in a labor hall that night Browder invited me to sit on the platform with Harry and Addy and the four Columbia University fellows who traveled with him. But I declined. I sat down in the audience, and, as luck would have it, the man who sat next to me was the chief of Steel's police. He told me he had come "just to see who's here," but he made a poor watch dog, for he was sound asleep before Browder had half finished. After the meeting I drank some coffee with the Red retinue, and Addy ribbed me by saying:

"Garth, there were six Phi Betes in the hall tonight. Five of them sat on the platform where they belonged, and you sat down in the audience with the noblest cossack of them all."

They all laughed, and I said: "Yeah, I guess I'm still out of step."

Next day Browder and the gang went out to Bessemer, a Steel-dominated suburb which used an antisedition ordinance to lock up Commies caught within its city limits. One labor martyr had been in the city jail there for several months, and Browder went to visit him. I remember how I resented the sullen contemptuousness with which the Bessemer Mayor and police chief and jail warden treated Browder and his retinue. They made Browder wait for an hour in an anteroom before they decided to let him visit the political prisoner. It was only out of fear of the newspapers that they let him in at all.

We took a picture of Browder reaching through the bars to shake hands with the pitiful bit of half-starved, tubercular humanity inside the cell.

"Don't worry, son," Browder told him, "we're gonna get you outa here."

The prisoner's burning eyes looked out of place in his emaciated body. "I'm not worrying," he said. "And don't you worry about me. Every day the Fascist swine keep me in here they're gettin' sicker."

When Browder had gone, I said to the warden: "What you got that boy in here for?"

"Ya mean ya don't know!" He was surprised. "Why he's the Red sonuvabitch who lives with niggers an' tells 'em they're as good as white folks!"

"You mean he lives with niggers?" I asked with mock concern.

"It's the God's truth." And then darkly: "He tells niggers they got a right to sleep with white women. Now ya kin see why we don't want them New York bastards a-comin' in heah a-pattin' him on the back.

220

Why that yaller-headed bitch has been in here a dozen times worryin' us to death."

"You mean Miss Reed?"

"Yeah, the yaller-head who calls him a 'po-lit-i-cal prisoner!' She's the one. She lives with niggers too. Sleeps with 'em. Tells these black bucks they're as good as white folks, then beds up with 'em just to prove it. Can you imagine a black sonuvabitch gittin' some o' that? I'd like to ketch her in a back alley one o' these nights. I'd fix her."

I walked away to keep from bashing in his head with a chair. One reason I became so angry was that much of what he said was the truth. Addy didn't sleep with Negro men; but, goddam her, she did tell them that they had a right to sleep with white women, and there were at least two Commy women workers in Alabama who did bed up with Negroes to demonstrate what they meant. It was the hardest of all the Red "methods" for a man named Garth to swallow, and the Klan promoters used it to drive other Southern white men wild.

But I had to keep my head and hold to the broad view. I couldn't allow myself to be vexed into madness by the trivial appurtenances of change. I was an educated man. I wanted to be a "liberal." I had to watch the spectacle of "hands desertin' to the Gover'mint," and worlds being inundated, and "Reds beddin' with niggahs," and still remain calm. I had to be able to understand and to look into the future. And through the election of 1936 I was able to maintain this position.

After the election, however, circumstances piled up on me too fast. I began to writhe inside. I could feel my bitterness and my cynicism swelling, and I no longer seemed able to fight them back. I tried to cling to the broad view, but I felt myself concerned more and more with what was happening to "me and my kind of folks." Communism no longer seemed to be an intoxicating

221

bit of marihuana which you watched venturesome people smoke. I began to see it as a loathsome threat to my way of life. As tension increased in the Birmingham industrial district, battle lines were drawn more sharply. Reason disappeared, and emotion supplanted it. I gradually drew away from Harry and Adeline, for I found that I could no longer talk to them calmly. They hardened under the same strain, as war came in earnest to Alabama after the 1936 election.

The fight over the Supreme Court started me on the road to madness. This battle arrayed class against class in Alabama. There was no middle ground; only hot blood and hot words. On one side were the folks who wanted to preserve; on the other side were those who wanted to change at any cost. On one side were those who respected order and due process; on the other side were those who would justify means with ends. On one side were "my kind of folks"; on the other side were the other kind of folks.

I joined my first Committee when the Court fight came. I did more than join the Committee. I gave it my money and time. I urged others to give it money. I went to Washington personally to ask Mistah John and Mistah Will Bankhead to oppose the President. We believed the Bankheads would stand firm. They were "practical politicians," but we knew that at heart they were "our kind of folks," and we knew we could trust them when the chips went down. We wasted no time on the Honorable Hugo Black. He wasn't "our kind of folks." We had plans for him at the next election.

At the conclusion of the Court fight I wrote a letter of appreciation to Senator Wheeler. I told him that if he did nothing else noteworthy in his career, his brilliant and gallant fight against the Court bill had won him a place among the few great men of courage who had sat in the United States Senate.

During the Court fight the Committee for Industrial

222

Organization opened its drive to unionize the ore miners and steel workers. In the first thirty-five days of the drive in the Birmingham District, thirty-five workers' homes were bombed. The procedure was simple and methodical. Each day some worker, prominent as a holdout against CIO, would be marked down for a Treatment. The unionizers had pleaded with him, offered him Salvation on a peaceful basis, but he had refused to be saved. So what-the-hell? The next night a car would speed by the holdout's home, three sticks of dynamite would thud against his front door, and Boom! The holdout could count himself lucky if he and his wife and kids got off with bruises, broken bones, and snaggled teeth. Next morning he limped down to CIO headquarters and signed up. And his neighbors, seeing what had happened to him, were close at his heels.

One morning I stopped at an ore worker's house in the south end of Jefferson County. It was a well-kept farm house with an orchard, a garden, and a chicken yard. I got out and talked to the worker. He was a sturdy fellow of about forty, with an open face. He was an engineman at one of Steel's red ore mines. I told him who I was, talked a few minutes to gain his confidence, and then I asked him: "Have you joined the union yet?"

"Yeah, I joined up last week," he replied. "I got my card 'n' everything."

"I'm a little surprised," I said. "I thought most of you white men with the good jobs belonged to the company Brotherhood."

He nodded. "That's right. That's the way it's been a' being. I been a member o' the Brotherhood for seventeen years. Got no kick a-comin'. The company give me a job three days after I got back from acrost the water, and I been with 'em ever since. But I belong to the union now."

"Why did you join?"

He hesitated. "You aint gonna put nothing in the paper, are yuh?"

"No, no," I assured him. "I just want to know."

He pointed out in his yard to a patch of earth about the circumference of a washtub. Obviously a hole in the grass-covered yard had recently been filled.

"Ya see that," he said. "That aint where my wife's been a-plantin' flowers. That's what halfa' stick of dynamite did. Ya see I live off out here by myself, an' the man who threw that halfa' stick can come back and throw three sticks. He can throw a little harder an' they'll go through the window o' that front room there. An' that's where my two little girls sleep." He sighed heavily. It isn't easy for a strong man to admit he has been bluffed into doing something he might not have done otherwise. Then he went on to add: "They say the reason they can do it an' git away with it is because the Government is fer 'em. So I figger if they got men who'll throw dynamite in yer house while ya're asleep, an' if the authorities'll uphold 'em in it, we better join the union an' join quick. Wouldn't ya a' done the same thing?"

"Yes, suh, I believe I would," I said. He walked out to the car with me, and as I got in the car he said: "Now if you write anything about me just say that I've joined the union—fer good. An' be sho' ya don't say nothin' else."

As I drove away I tried to see both sides of the problem. Change doesn't come easily. The man should have joined the union anyway. Unionism is proper. But in spite of my efforts to reason and to take the Broad View, I felt a bitter, hot anger rising within me.

When the CIO pulled its red ore strike, the leaders knew that they didn't have more than thirty percent of the miners. But the guns-and-dynamite threat closed the mines, the Governor refused to send troopers to protect the homes of the non-strikers. In spite

224

of these advantages, CIO showed signs of losing the strike. A serious back-to-work movement developed. The union lines were breaking.

But there were "organizers" who knew what to do. They calmly selected an Example. The Example was a Negro foreman who was influential among the Negroes and who was advocating back-to-work. He had already violated the strike by doing a day of "maintenance work" for the company.

I saw the Example an hour after they had treated him. He lay across the rows in his potato patch, his overall jumper glued with blood to his body. The sheriff counted eight heavy-rifle bullet holes through his chest and stomach. The coroner emptied his pockets of nine cents, a tooth-marked plug of tobacco, a dirty rag, and a bottle of clapp medicine. In the soft dirt of the potato patch was written a story of unspeakable human cruelty. Unarmed, the Negro had come with his mule and plow at sunup to work his potatoes. In a thicketed ditch at the end of the patch, the assassins representing the workers of the world were waiting for him. Their cigaret butts and rifle shells were there to show where they had waited. Like cats toying with a mouse, they had watched him hitch his mule to the plow and plow one furrow. Then, when he had turned his breast toward them, they had pressed the triggers. He had tried to run from them in the soft dirt, but they poured streams of lead into his back until he lay pawing like a chicken in the sunlight. Then they had sneaked down the ditch and left the Example to be viewed from afar by all those who might have been contemplating going back into the mines before the Big Man off at Washington gave the signal.

The communists and their trusted lieutenants knew how to "cooperate" with the CIO in Alabama. They knew how to stop back-to-work movements.

Nobody likes to pay dues. So you would think that, without the check-off, unions might have difficulty collecting two hundred thousand dollars a month from desultory Southern workers.

But one big union in Alabama employed a collector with a system. He didn't use a typewriter. He didn't use a telephone. He didn't work in the daytime. He used a rifle, and he worked at night. He had once been a sharpshooter in France.

In the soft, Southern moonlight, this collector would stand on a hill overlooking a company village. He would pick out the houses of three delinquent dues-payers. He would fire three quick, well-aimed shots and then fade away. The bullets would whine and tear through the houses. The delinquent would pop up in bed, make a frightened survey to see if any of his family had been hit, and next morning he would be standing at a pawnshop when it opened. Then he would make tracks to headquarters and settle up. Close behind him would be all the other delinquents of that village who had heard the three shots and who knew only too well that they might be next.

Well, what-the-hell? The shots didn't often strike anybody. A union's got to have money, hasn't it? Which is most important? That the unions be able to drive on and win Great Victories for the workers of the world? Or that one nameless Negro woman gets shot in the belly?

I knew the men who threw the dynamite into homes at night. I knew the men who sat in the ditch and laid down their cigarets and murdered the Example to stop a company-inspired back-to-work movement. I knew the collector with the remarkably efficient system. I knew the whole gangster faction which knew how to Get Results for the high-minded Idealists who sat in offices somewhere drawing plans for a world in which workers could be free.

226

I listened to Harry and Addy. "Why, my God, Garth, can't you see that there is no other way? This is war. The chips are down. You have to use Force now. You have to fight fire with fire. In Russia, millions have been killed for the People's sake. There is no place for sentiment now."

Once I looked Harry Lerner squarely in the face and asked him this question: "Harry, would you kill a man in order to win a strike?"

"Of course I would, Garth," he answered.

I knew the other side, too. I knew the private detectives hired by Steel to stop the dynamiters and the assassins. They kidnapped the suspected dynamiters. They beat them. They doped them. They bribed them to expose their fellows. They held them incommunicado for days. They faked enough evidence to wring indictments from reluctant grand juries. They rigged petit juries to get convictions.

I listened to the off-the-record explanations of the public relations chiefs. "What-the-hell else can we do, Lafavor? You gotta fight fire with fire. You know sheriffs and police can't catch these Commy dynamiters. You can't get legitimate witnesses to a dynamiting. We gotta hire these tough boys to go after 'em. You know that as well as I do. If we're wrong, then you tell us how to stop dynamiting."

I looked one of these public relations chiefs in the face and asked him: "Would you send a man to prison on faked evidence in order to stop dynamiting?"

"Of course I would," he answered, "if I was convinced that he was a dynamiter and I couldn't get him any other way."

This willingness on both sides to employ force; this willingness to achieve ends by whatever means necessary, made a deep impression on me. How does a labor leader feel when he sits out under the stars alone after winning a Great Victory? When he looks

227

back down the road and faces the fact that he owes a great victory, not to his own matchless energy and brave dream, but to two men who sat in a ditch and smoked cigarets and waited for the sun to come up so that they could bushwhack a helpless Example and thus halt a back-to-work tide which might have defeated the whole movement. When he faces the fact that some of the dollars which he used in elections came from the pockets of little men who live in fear of a bullet tearing through their matchwood houses in the night? I wondered how representatives of the people feel when they contemplate such Great Victories?

I thought: Do they say to themselves: "Well, the other bunch was doing it to us, so we had to do it to them?" or: "Well, human nature doesn't change. To win victories you've always got to do things that are best forgotten?" Or do they say: "The important thing is leadership. Every leader who wins great victories has to have bastards to do the dirty work?" Or do they say: "Well, the important thing was for the movement to win. For the program to continue. Now that we have won we can do so many Good Works that the method of winning can be charged off?"

I thought: Have we in America, too, subscribed to the theory that ends justify means? Has Due Process become an expression fit only for the mouths of reactionary lawyers?

The blow which finally rendered me incapable of reason and calm judgment was the appointment of Hugo Black to the Supreme Court of the United States.

To understand how this act by the President affected me, you must realize what the Supreme Court meant to "my kind of folks." When I went to Washington to oppose the TVA, I felt that I was in the presence of majesty when I sat in the Hall of Justice. I was cynical

228

about senators and other politicians—even Presidents —but Justice Hughes and Justice Brandeis and the others looked like Justice Personified to me. They were the best we had.

On the other hand, Hugo Black was to me everything that the Supreme Court was not. I knew what has since become an unchallenged public record— that he was saturated with the gaseous odor of the old mumbo-jumbo Klan. I knew that his highest attainment in the law was a police court bench.

Even now I can't figure out why Mr. Roosevelt passed over all the distinguished scholars and jurists in the country to appoint a man like Hugo Black to the Supreme Court.

During the months following the Black appointment I wasn't a rational man. I was motivated by hate. I hated Roosevelt and every organization which supported him. I spent my time with men who hated Roosevelt. Buck Delancey gave me a cartoon of Roosevelt inside a cage, clinging to the bars of the cage and screaming: "Third Term Hell! I'm in here for Life!" I pasted it on my typewriter cover.

The week after the Black appointment I quit *The Press* and started a weekly paper of my own. Steve Leonard tried to persuade me against it.

"Don't be a goddamed fool, Garth," he argued. "You're twenty-four and a damn good newspaperman. Keep your shirt on, and in two or three years you can be editor of a good paper. You can have anything you want."

"Naw, I'm fed up, Steve," I told him. "I'm tired of sittin' on the sidelines describing the battle. I'm disgusted with myself for always tryin' to see both sides of everything. Hell, there's a fight goin' on with no holds barred. My folks have always known where they stood in a fight, so, by God, I'm goin' to get over with my kind of folks where I belong. Where I can find a

229

little peace of mind, and where I can have a part in the victory or the defeat. There's no middle ground in this scrap any more. You just make yourself ridiculous if you try to find one."

"Aw, hell, yuh're talkin' like a goddam preacher," he came back. "Yuh'll be tellin' me yuh got a Mission before long, or that yuh been called to preach. Get smart. Smart guys don't get in fights. They sit on the sidelines and fondle blonde bitches and make money while the Damn Fools fight. Yuh need a week off. Take that new blonde in Happy's office down to New Orleans for a weekend, then come on back and get to work. I'll getcha a five-buck raise."

But I would have none of it. "Naw, Steve, my mind's made up. I'm gonna have me a paper where I can say what I goddam please, and I'm gonna take on some bastards I don't like."

He surrendered. "All right, Lancelot. Go ahead. Break your little sword. Lose your little wad. Make a damn fool out o' yourself. Holler hurrah fer God an' Abe Lincoln. I'll give yuh four weeks. Then come on back here an' I'll accommodate yuh with a boot in the pants an' put yuh back to work."

"Okay, Steve." We shook hands. "You know how it is with you and me," I said. "But I won't be back." I picked up my coat and walked out. I never went back.

2

I always imagined there would have to be a lot of fuss about starting a new publication, but I found it all pretty simple. I had a thousand dollars and borrowed another thousand. I made a deal with a printer. I rented a two-room office. I hired a girl who had never had a job before to keep the books, answer the telephone, and remember where everything was. I hired an amazing young fellow who could double as advertising and circulation manager. We developed an intense cooperative spirit, dreamed big dreams, and decided to call it the *Deep South Defender*. Modesty, it appears, is no virtue for publishers.

I suppose the name *Defender* was no accident, for my purpose was to defend what I thought we had left in Alabama. There was no hope for the world outside America; even the United States was bobsledding toward some alien *ism*, so there was nothing else for me and my kind of folks to do but raise a wall around Alabama and try to preserve the way of life we had known. There was no hope in cooperation; only in isolation. The demagogues of the world were trying to stampede the masses through the orchards of those who worked and accumulated.

Like most Defenders I did little else but attack. I leveled down at the double-headed dragon of communism and corruption and fired both barrels every week. Every time I thought of a new synonym for sonuvabitch I had the guts of a new editorial. It was like shooting fish to attack the New Deal in Alabama, not only because the social worker is a ridiculous figure to the average Alabama mind, but also because all the agencies were being administered by politicians spawned and nurtured under the state's one-party system.

On the home front there was much work for us Defenders-of-Alabama to do. The governor was an amiable old party named Bibb Graves, who believed that "those politicians who help bake the pie should eat the pie," and nothing so well illustrated the Graves theory of government as the appointment of his own wife to fill the Senate seat vacated by Hugo Black. No other governor in American history would have dared do such a thing.

The Bibb Graves formula for success was an old one. He took his pressure groups—the American Legion, which he called the "Heroes Union"; his "ragged-assed labor bastards; them pore boys between the plow handles; and them pore, underpaid school teachers" —and squared off against the selfish "Big Mules and Intrusts." Everybody who supported Graves was "mah loyal friend who's a-heppin' to bake this pie an' he's a-gonna git a slice uv it," and all who opposed were "Big Mules" who were going to get socked with a tax. A Graves administration was a four-year field day for the "pie eaters." Most of the legislators were handed extra sinecures on the state payroll—as were most of the political reporters—and the sixty-seven county machines waxed rich off of job-selling, paroles, back-tax collections, and road work.

I thought the Graves system fitted beautifully into the larger system, so I attacked it every week and stabbed at communists and "labor racketeers" for variety. I mixed satire with sensational serious exposures, so the *Deep South Defender,* if only because of novelty and audacity, became an immediate circulation success.

I didn't kid myself, even then, about where I got most of my support. I could see that the congratulatory letters I received had been dictated to secretaries. I knew that the *Defender* was popular at the country clubs, and that the president of the Rotary Club called attention to it immediately after the singing of "America." When the block subscriptions for employees came in, I knew who paid for them. I also knew that many of the employees, so favored, would consign the *Defender* to the same utilitarian fate as befalls the Sears, Roebuck catalog.

But when you are caught in a battle, you have to fight on one side or the other. In 1937, when I looked at the Battle of America, I saw communists using politicians and pressure groups to try to destroy what I thought was worth saving in America. On the other side, I saw people for some of whom I had no sympathy;

but, taken collectively, I preferred them to the attackers. With all their faults, they were "my kind of folks," and I belonged with them.

To my former friends on the labor and New Deal side, I became "a hired minion of the Big Mules." To the politicians, I became "a slick bastard working the fat side of the fence." To my new Rotarian allies, I became "our boy" and "one of our kind." To Harry and Adeline, I had reverted to the "Fascist whelp" I had been when I arrived at the university out of tobacco-chewing feudalism. But to myself I was sincerely an American and a Democrat trying to save another little island in the world from revolution. I had lost Garth's Island, but perhaps, by fighting hard, we could at least save the State of Alabama.

Something happens to a man when he admits to himself that he no longer trusts the people. When he comes to consider the people as a blind animal to be wooed and cajoled by competing leaders using whatever lures they think will be most effective. When he says that the people should be told This or should not be told That. Or when he hires Publicity Experts to fashion a speech for him out of all the expedient elements at hand. I think this explains why many editors and politicians become totalitarians, and also why so many totalitarians become editors and politicians.

As I see this process in my own experience, it is likely to begin when a man loses his faith in God. If there is no God, if man is not created in the image of a Divine Being, then it soon follows that you have no faith in Man. Man-in-the-mass is the blind animal. But you are not a blind animal. You can see what the animal can't see. You arrogate to yourself the power of wise decision. So, in order for you and your kind to control the animal and lead him in a wise direction, you concede that the lure is a proper means to the end. But when you have come this far, it's goddamed easy to go further and concede that the whip, too, is a proper means to the end if the lure fails.

During my hate-maddened period when I edited the *Defender*, I wasn't a democrat; I was a "fascist" under the modern system of labeling. I baited neither Jews nor Negroes, but I didn't trust the people. I fought to maintain the poll tax and thus restrict the franchise. You can't systematically deprive a large group of the people from voting and still call yourself a democrat. I fought for an anti-sedition bill which would have given the state power to imprison any suspected communist. You can't advocate a "concentration camp" for American citizens and still call yourself a democrat.

While I edited the *Defender*, I was motivated by one principle—to preserve Alabama as it was and to resist "foreign influences."

Some of the established Jews in Alabama were "my kind of people." They thought much the same way I did. They wanted to protect themselves and the Alabama world. I did all I could to help them. They didn't like for New York Jews to come to the University of Alabama. They shared our opinion that Alabama tax money should be used to educate Alabamians and not New Yorkers. So during this period we tried to raise the out-of-state fees at the university in order to force New York Jews to go elsewhere for their education. New York Jews were only "poisoning the Alabama well" for Alabama Jews.

The Alabama Jews didn't like Harry Lerner. He was a Jew and a communist, and some people in Alabama were coming to believe that the two words were synonymous. One old Jewish gentleman, whom I knew very well, frequented a steam bath where I occasionally

234

went. He had come to Birmingham with nothing and had acquired a store and several apartment houses. At the height of the bitterness over the communists in the Scottsboro Case and Harry Lerner in the union movement, some of this old gentleman's tenants began moving out of his apartment houses. He would talk to me every week when we sat in the steam bath. He advocated not only the lynching of the communists but also a military expedition to New York to burn Columbia and New York Universities to the ground.

Because of this experience I can never understand how some people can imagine that there is a "typically Jewish opinion" or a "typically Jewish reaction" in America. I can't speak for other sections of the country, but a solvent Alabama Jew reacts just like a solvent Alabama Irishman.

My hate of Roosevelt and my fear of communism reached a climax in my efforts to support the anti-sedition bill in Alabama. Looking back now I don't know how I ever brought myself to support it. I suppose I was like a fighter who begins slugging wildly after he has been hit in the face. I didn't support the anti-sedition bill without misgivings. I remember the day I arrived in Montgomery to begin lobbying for the bill in the Legislature. It was a cold, dreary, January day. I stood in a hotel room and looked out over the muddy Alabama River. What-the-hell is an anti-sedition law? I thought. Well, it's a law that enables a state to put a man in jail for something he might say. An anti-sedition Law! It's about the most hateful term in the lexicon of freedom. It means a Government, a Mass, a Mob, threatening a man—a dignified human soul—with prison because he doesn't believe what the Mob believes. Anti-Sedition! The very sound of it fills you with loathing and visions of medieval torture chambers or a pompous, perfumed Louis XIV: "I am the State. Say only what I want you to say, scum, or die!" A bloated George III: "You Irish bog-fly, Peter

Garth! Speak against the Throne and be destroyed!"

It's incredible! I thought. I can't support an anti-sedition law. Other men might, but not me. I'm the guy who once fought for Harry Lerner's job on a faculty. I'm the guy who makes speeches about Freedom and Equal Justice. What can I hope for after I admit that an anti-sedition law is proper and necessary in America. But what-the-hell, there is no use torturing myself. This is war. We must face realities. It's either us or our enemies now. The communists are throwing dynamite at the Ark of the Covenant. Opportunists are being put into high places. We have no choice but to suspend Liberty for the duration of the war. To protect the Ark of the Covenant, we have to hide it away in a fortress during the battle, and after the battle, we can bring the Ark back out into the light. Democracy has to be suspended in order to be saved.

Besides, Alabama is my state. My people helped to build it. The dirty Reds are trying to tear it down. They are trying to take over the country. We'll put a wall around Alabama and save one section of America, at least.

I won't recall too many details of the legislative fight over the anti-sedition bill. I had rather forget my part in it.

If it were not dying-time again; if we still lived back in the days when it was fashionable to sneer and debunk, we could get some swell laughs out of the Alabama Legislature. Like all great Democratic Legislatures, it is divided roughly into four sections: the Decent Guys, the Money-Whores, the Job-Whores, and the Business-Whores. The men's toilet in the old Swank Hotel (whatever its local name may be) is officially known as the Bank, for it's the spot where you pay off the Money-Whores. The night before the House vote on the anti-sedition bill, I was standing the Bank with Jack Todd, a wiry, acidic, old lobbyist. We were paying off the Money-Whores. We each wore an overcoat, and in our left pockets we had plain envelopes containing fifty dollars and in our right pockets we had envelopes containing a hundred dollars. The Money-Whore section is subdivided into two groups, the men who are honest up to fifty dollars and the more sincere men who are honest all the way up to a hundred dollars. The smart lobbyist has to know his men so he won't waste any money on the fifty-dollar boys and so he won't insult any of the hundred-dollar class by offering them fifty.

While I was busy influencing one of the hundred-dollar boys, I watched Old Jack out of the tail of my eye. He had button-holed a two-bit shyster from the Black Belt, and in a moment I saw him pass him an envelope, and the shyster disappeared up the stairs. Suddenly Old Jack jumped as if a hornet had stung him.

"Hey, come back heah!" he shouted at the trimmer, and tore up the stairs after him.

"What's the matter with Jack?" I thought. I ran up after him, half expecting to see a murder in the lobby. Jack was tearing through the crowd, chasing the buzzard and cussing. He finally caught him by the arm and began to drag him back toward the Bank. The crowd thought it was a joke, and the shyster was trying to laugh it off. But Jack was serious. When he got him back down the stairs, Jack pinned him against the wall and said: "Now, yuh little bastard, give me that extra fifty dollars I just gave yuh."

"But Jack," the shyster complained, "I ought to have a hundred this time anyway."

Jack shook him. "Like hell you ought to. Business is business, and fifty dollars is your price. I just got careless and gave you a hundred-dollar envelope. Come on, shell out!"

When Jack had squeezed fifty dollars out of this Representative of the People, he turned him loose contemptuously. "Can you imagine me reachin' in the wrong pocket?" he said to me. "Hell, I couldn't a' slept tonight if I had overpaid that little skunk. It aint the money; it's the principle. I bought his old daddy for fifty dollars a throw for years, and I don't want to give this pup any ideas about his importance."

That's a swell story, isn't it? Or it would have been a swell story a year ago. You know: Good Old Democracy, It's Bad, But What-the-Hell, With All Its Faults . . . et cetera.

The Job-Whores are always the Administration stalwarts. They are like women who would scorn a five-buck offer but will put it on the line for a fur coat. They take jobs for themselves and their relatives. The Business-Whores are Pillars of the Community. They hold their noses when they pass a Money-Whore. You buy their votes with New Business. If a Business-Whore is a banker you get an industrialist to shift his account to him. If he is a lawyer you diplomatically provide him fat new clients. Or if he is a sly old duck who wants to play, you get him a smart woman who rapes easy.

What a great novel such stuff would have made ten years ago! A State Senator, looking like Eugene Pallette, comes in and says: "Well, boys, yuh know my motto. 'I'm opposed to all forms of graft I'm not in on.' Haw! Haw! Haw!" Or here's a better one: "Yuh know my old motto, boys. 'I scare 'em; you shake 'em; we split.' " This means that "I" introduce a bill to tax soft drinks to provide "additional revenue for old-age pensions and school teachers." Then "you" run and tell the bottlers you can kill the bill with three thousand. Then we split and forget the damn

238

bill. Only—damn yore hide!—you'll shake 'em for five thousand and tell me you only got two.

That's good bar-stool talk and good stuff for the Debunkers, but it's damn poor fare at dying-time. For the present I think I'll try to remember only those men I have known who stood up in the legislature and voted as they pleased, and whether they voted for you or against you, it was good to know that you belonged to the same race of men they did.

Those men were there. I remember them now. I didn't pay much attention to them in 1937 because they were a tiny minority and I was interested only in "protecting Alabama" by whatever means necessary.

The fight over the anti-sedition bill was brutal. On both sides we went all-out in name-calling and in our appeals to the lowest instincts. We wrote an anti-sit-down strike provision into the bill, and on our side we arrayed all the Big Business interests, the land owners, the "Heroes Union," and all the old Klan elements. We were fighting a new war to "preserve Democracy." Each night our spokesmen shrilled in bass and treble over the radio, calling the new crusade for Americanism. All who were with us were Americans; all who were against us were communists.

A big voice boomed over my desk. "Goddam, I knew you'd see the light some day. Put 'er there, boy, I'm with you." I got up and shook hands with Cartright Newsome, the old Barracks Brigadier at the university.

In Montgomery my telephone tinkled late one night. "Hello, Garth? This is Biff Bargin. How are ya, boy? Great fight, huh? Some of our mutual friends asked me to hang around here with a coupla' boys just in

239

case ya need any help." The private detective from whom I had once hidden a Red "bastard."

What strange bedfellows I was acquiring!

On the other side was the political crowd. The Governor, the labor organizers, the Reds, and some of the newspapers, shrieking the same sort of stuff at us that I had once shrieked. On this side, too, was a large group of ordinary people who refused to believe what we told them about the Reds.

When the firing was hottest and Southern tempers were boiling, I went to see Adeline Reed. By now the Commies had become so bold that they had opened a bookshop in Birmingham where they were selling and giving away literature. Addy spent part of her time in the shop, and on some nights she slept on a couch in the back of the building. It was near midnight when I reached the shop, and we sat on the couch under a light which a curtain hid from the street.

"I've come to tell you, Addy, that you've got to get out of here," I said. "I don't want to see you get hurt."

She took a long draw from her cigaret and blew the smoke slowly through her lips. She wore a mannish brown dressing gown, and she had brushed her hair back behind her ears. She smiled. "You wouldn't want me to leave at the moment of our greatest triumph, would you, Garth? After four years of living in holes, we at last gain the sunlight and you want me to leave! We've won the Scottsboro Case. We've won the Steel fight. We've opened a bookshop, and business is excellent. Any day now I'm expecting to be invited to address the local chapter of the Daughters of the Confederacy."

"Addy, I'm not kiddin' tonight," I insisted. "And let's don't get into any arguments. I've come here to tell you some things straight, and I want you to take my advice."

240

"Oh, how touching!" she mocked. "You think your little bill will pass, and you want me to leave before they put me in jail. You wouldn't want to see me in that nice jail with the whores and hopheads. You want all the other Red bastards and bitches put in jail except me. Why Garth I'm ashamed of you! Here I'm the most dangerous Red rat in Alabama, and you want me to go free and continue gnawing. What a softie you are! You'll have to toughen up before we'll let you join our party."

"Now, cut it out, Addy," I said, irritated. "I'm tired and I'm serious. I'm not concerned about what happens if the bill passes. You Reds will have a field day in the courts for a while, but you'll have to leave us alone. You know that. What worries me is what happens if the bill fails to pass."

She couldn't keep her sarcasm off of me. "That would be a blow to the *Deep South Defender,* wouldn't it? And the young White Hope of Fascism wouldn't get his five-thousand-dollar bonuses. You have got a worry there, haven't you?"

I got up and started to leave. "Let's forget it," I snapped.

"Garth, come here!" she said quickly. "I'm sorry. Come on back and tell me what's wrong. I know what your trouble is. You are like a little boy playing with matches. You have started a big fire, and now you are scared that the fire may burn up the world."

"No, you are wrong, Addy. I didn't start the fire. I'm trying to put the fire out. But let's not quarrel. I came to tell you this. If the bill is beaten, I can take it. But I know some people who may not be able to take it. I was at a meeting tonight where your bookshop was discussed. They are going to put pressure on the insurance company that rented the building to you."

"Let them press. They can't bother us. We've got a good lease."

"Yeah? Well, there's more than that. You can't get people as mad as they are now without somebody getting hurt. When you communists want to stop a back-to-work movement, you kill a man. When you want to break a company union, you throw dynamite into a man's house. You yourself think nothing of telling Negro men that they have a right to sleep with white women. Whatever you do you justify because it's all for the Great Movement. And all the good little Americans who can't conceive of you—they want to protect you from us 'fascists.' But if this bill is beaten, some of these Klan-trained Alabama fascists may decide that the time has come to burn down the Reichstag. They may decide to toss a little dynamite. And that glass out front is not armor plate."

She had at last dropped her sarcasm. "You may be right," she said thoughtfully. "But it's just another risk we have to take. After four years of dealing with Mr. Biff Bargin and his ilk, I guess we can survive a little longer."

Addy Reed had courage, but she had not survived four years as a Party worker in the South by being a damn fool. She usually knew when to get in out of the rain.

"I don't think you should sleep here in this building, Addy," I said. "That front window is too nice a target."

"No, I believe you are wrong, Garth. I know these boys much better than you do. They go great guns with a blackjack in an alley, but their courage fades under a street light. We are only four doors from the hotel. The back's barred, and they'd have to pass the hotel corner after tossing the stuff at us. And you know it's a capital offense in Alabama to dynamite an inhabited building."

"Yes, it is a capital offense, isn't it?" It was my turn to be sarcastic. "I wonder if the people who planned

242

those thirty-five dynamitings for the union knew about that law?"

Adeline gave me a sly smile. "Oh, you mean those yellow company dicks who were trying to discredit the Labor Movement?"

"Yeah, that's who I mean," I mocked.

She laughed. "Let's have some coffee and forget the arguments. Tell me what you've been doing besides baiting Reds. How's Cherry? I hear you are going to become a father."

We talked for more than an hour, and I warned her again not to stay in the bookshop at night. Addy was a remarkable sort of person. There was something about us that drew us to one another, and it was only when we talked politics that we drifted hopelessly apart. Addy could see hope in the communal ownership of property; I could see none. She thought that the American people were being oppressed by the very System that I thought was the finest and freest in the world. She thought that the people ought to organize and march and fight, and I thought that the people ought to preserve what they had. I suppose our trouble was that when we thought of "the people," she thought of one sort of people and I thought of another, and neither of us could see a complete picture of "the people."

The day the anti-sedition bill came up for a final vote in the Senate, the whole State of Alabama went insane. Before dawn, from the more remote sections, banner-waving motorcades started for Montgomery. Headlines screamed For and Against. Radio announcers rode with the motorcades and broadcast running accounts of fist fights, cars being thrown off the road, and state police wrestling with the combatants. One fiery editor, to dramatize his position that every American should be left free to advocate the overthrow

243

of his government, led a hundred men armed with "shillalahs" in a march on the Capitol.

Uniformed American Legionnaires were the backbone of our audible support. Led by a drum-and-bugle corps and displaying giant American flags on their motorcades, they came to pass the Anti-Red Bill and Make Alabama Safe for Democracy. The state which led the union alphabetically would be the first to call a halt to the spread of communism!

The night before, the Governor had gone on the air over a state-wide hook-up and announced that if the bill became a law "every dime of Federal money now pouring into Alabama will be cut off." "Our schools will have to close," he warned. "Our old people will starve for lack of pensions. All Federal projects will stop. The TVA will shut off its power in Alabama. And, worst of all, our farmers—the mud-sills of our society—will have to let their cotton rot in the fields since the Gover'mint will not buy it."

We had countered this propaganda with telegram after telegram from Congressmen assuring the people of Alabama that Federal funds would not only continue but be increased if this action were taken. In Montgomery we had been up all night telephoning our allies in the sixty-seven counties, bringing all possible pressure to bear on the thirty-four men in the State Senate. We knew the holder of every note and mortgage against those thirty-four men. We knew the important clients of the Senators who were lawyers; the important depositors of the bankers; and the important friends and creditors of every one of them. And Senators were being called and wired by men they had to listen to.

The Administration lobby had fought us with both Federal and state jobs. Twenty of the thirty-four Senators had been placed on the payrolls of some state department, and many of them had from one to six relatives on either a state or Federal payroll. The Administration Rumor Mill had spread the report that under the proposed Anti-Sedition Act every church in the state could be closed; every school teacher would be liable to questioning; and no citizen would be safe to express a casual opinion.

We had countered this rumor with the reports of the Dies Committee; and with the report that "every nigger in Alabama" was opposed to the bill; that the communists were opposed to the bill; and that all the "Big Niggah Eastern Papers" were opposed to the bill. Against the rumored threats to cut off Federal money, we yelled "Carpetbagger" and "Fellow Traveler."

The National Guard had been called out to handle the crowds at the Capitol. Jack Todd and I sat in one of the Senate cloakrooms and waited for the vote. We were exhausted. Alternately, we took pulls at a bottle. We had done all we could.

"Howya think it'll go, Garth?" he asked, wearily.

"God knows," I said. "My chart shows nineteen For."

"Mine shows eighteen," he said. "We may both be wrong. Those tramps'll double-cross yuh while yuh're lookin' at 'em."

The oratory finally ended, and the clerk began shouting the roll-call. The Administration lobbyists collared Senators on the floor during roll-call—something we weren't allowed to do. They stood over a Senator and looked at him until he had shouted Aye or Nay.

The vote was sixteen For and seventeen Against. One Senator was stricken with a heart attack during roll-call. We had been beaten. A great shout went up outside as a loudspeaker announced the vote. The papers could tell the People that they had been saved from Fascism.

I was sick and tired and disgusted as I fought through mobs to get back to the hotel. Waiting for me was a message that Cherry had been taken to the hospital suddenly. Peter Garth Lafavor the Second was going to jump the gun by two full weeks. I was about to become

245

a father with a hundred miles of choked highway between Cherry and me. It would take three hours to reach her by car, so I called the airport and arranged to spend the last of the anti-Red slush fund on a chartered plane trip to Birmingham.

As the plane roared along through the gathering darkness, I slumped in the seat beside the pilot, torn between uneasiness for Cherry and disappointment over what had happened. All my nervous energy was gone, and I was exhausted for lack of sleep.

"I'm going to make a resolution," I said to myself. "From now on I'm going to quit worrying about what happens to the State of Alabama or the United States of America. I'm going to have a son now. He'll probably have big black eyes like Cherry. I'm going to devote my efforts to him and to Cherry and to building a comfortable life for us. I know how to get along. I know how to have fun. Good whiskey. Good entertainment. Good food. Good conversation. A Buick automobile. I have everything a man needs to be happy. From now on I'm going to live under my own gourd vine and let somebody else worry about the state of the union and the state of the world. What was it Old Steve always said? 'Smart guys sit on the sidelines and have fun and make money and let all the Groaners and Shouters go to hell.' "

Then I fell asleep, blissfully unaware of the shocks the night held in store for me.

From the airport I went directly to the hospital and found Cherry sleeping under an anesthetic. The baby had been born—dead. The doctor didn't know why. He had not yet told Cherry. I could tell her in the morning.

I went out and sat in the hospital parlor. One feels so helpless at such a time. You are so relieved to learn that the person you know and love is safe that you forget for the moment the person who was yours but whom you never knew. Then you become very sad when you think of all the suffering which has gone for nothing. Suffering which, if it produces a life, is justified; but if it fails to produce a life is only another part of the awful wastage which goes into the human garbage can. Your sadness is mingled with curiosity. You never saw the child. The nurses tell you he had Cherry's black eyes and black hair. You wonder how he would have looked when he was a year old, or six years old, or twelve years old. Then you grasp for the Old Comfort Rail of Lost Humanity which is the conclusion: It was probably for the best.

The doctor assured me Cherry was in no serious danger, so about midnight I went home to clean up and get a drink. I hoped I could sleep. I was in the shower when the maid called me to the telephone. It was urgent and confidential. I recognized the voice of Mr. Biff Bargin lowered to a whisper.

"That you, Garth? Too bad about the Rats licking us today. Yeah. Yuh did a good job, boy. Ought'a put yuh in solid down-town. Yeah. Thought I'd call yuh up and give yuh a little *good* news. Yeah, cheer yuh up. Yuh know our friend the Jew bastard? An' the yaller-headed whore at the bookshop? Yeah, keep yuh shirt on. I think they're gonna have some callers tonight. Yeah. Yuh know there's more'n one way to skin a cat."

Before he had finished I flung down the telephone and tore after some clothes.

"Emma!" I shouted to the maid, "call a cab quick!"

The poor black soul, devoted to Cherry, thought that Cherry was dying and broke into screaming. I had to call the cab myself. I called police headquarters, gave the sergeant the address of the bookshop, and told him to get somebody there quick. I grabbed a gun out of my desk and ran out the door half-dressed.

Had Biff Bargin called me five minutes earlier I might have saved Adeline's life. I reached the bookshop almost at the time the police did. It was a wreck. The heavy dynamite bomb crashing through the window

247

had blown the entire front out of the building. Addy lay on the studio couch, crushed under a heavy case. She had probably been asleep and never knew what happened. I knelt down beside her. One hand had fallen off the couch. Blood was dripping from it onto a pamphlet on the floor. *Join the* CIO *and save the world!* John Lewis' picture.

I'll never forget the scene. The sickening odor of exploded dynamite. The shattered glass. The fallen timbers. The pictures, books, and pamphlets scattered everywhere. Harry Bridges and Joe Stalin and Roosevelt and John Lewis and Tom Mooney and Earl Browder and the Scottsboro Negroes. Every pamphlet bore a picture of the People marching and shouting and brandishing their fists. The clenched fists of hate. The yearning faces of hungry, lost people. Big coppers poked sticks into everything. Reporters shouted and flash bulbs flashed. Firemen's searchlights probed the smoking darkness. While huddled on the couch was the broken and blood-streaked body of a girl who had yearned only to be a part of Something Big Enough and Grand Enough to be worthy of all she had to give. A girl who had laughed and cursed and sneered in college, but who had wanted to be a part of Something Great.

I thought of what she told me one night long ago on the Island. "If I had lived in '49 I would have been in a covered wagon. I'd have deserted all the beauty and security of the Blue Ridge Mountains and gone out where the mountains were bigger and uglier. Maybe I'd have died along the way, and maybe I'd have found the pot of gold. But, by God, I'd have been in the Rush. I want to feel that I am a part of something big and challenging and worthy of my life."

There was no one present who knew her except me, so I gave directions for the removal of her body to a mortuary and turned to my other grim task.

Addy was dead, but "the Jew bastard"—what of him? Biff had said that he, too, was on the calling list. Harry

248

moved so often I wasn't certain where to find him, but I grabbed a cab and headed for the last address he had given me. When I reached the place—it was a basement apartment in a tall, ancient rooming house—three Party workers were yelling and gesticulating. A cyclone had passed through the rooms. Pictures were smashed. Books ripped open. A desk turned over on the floor. It required no sign-reading Boy Scout to deduce what had happened. Harry had been kidnapped, and God help him! I drove away as the cops and reporters arrived. I didn't know what to do. The world had exploded in my face.

But I had to do something. There was a chance the mob wouldn't kill Harry. They'd leave him somewhere, and if he were found soon enough he might live. I stopped at a hotel, gulped down some whiskey, and consulted a city directory for Biff Bargin's home address. I was twenty minutes getting there. A light was burning in the house. Biff was waiting for someone to call him, but he was surprised to see me.

"What-the-hell you doin' out this time'a night, boy?" he asked, puzzled.

"Where'll I find Harry Lerner?" I said abruptly.

"I don't get it," he answered. "Surely you don't give a damn what happens to the Red sons'o'bitches."

"Well I do give a damn. I don't play by these rules. I want you to tell me where I'll find what's left of Lerner—quick."

He darkened. "What'a'ya mean anyhow? Are yuh crazy? Yuh not gonna do any talkin', are yuh?"

"Yes, I'm going to talk, Biff," I gave it to him straight. "The girl's dead. I've seen her."

"So what? The nigger-lovin' whore has stirred up enough trouble, hasn't she?" he barked.

I had an impulse to shoot Biff Bargin where he stood. But I swallowed and said: "Whatever she's done, the man who threw that bomb at her deserves the chair. And I'm going to do what I can to put him there. If

249

you want me to forget that telephone call of yours, yuh better tell me where I'll find Lerner."

Biff Bargin was honestly puzzled. "Well, I'll be goddamed," he said. "I never figgered you this way." Then he began giving in. "I don't know where they took the bastard, but if I was goin' out to look, I'd try the mountain road from Muscoda to Docena. When yuh pass some o' them old mine slopes, yuh might find what yuh're lookin' for. It won't be a very pleasant sight."

I went back to the cab. It was twenty miles to the place. It was two o'clock in the morning. Several square miles of abandoned country would have to be combed. I couldn't do the job alone. I had to tip off the reporters and the sheriff's office. I called Steve Leonard at *The Press* and had him ring me back on a private wire. I gave him the tip. I knew he would send a dozen reporters swarming over the section.

We found Harry shortly after daylight. Naked. Sprawled in a mine slope. Unconscious, bleeding, and beaten, but still alive. I rode in the ambulance with him to the hospital. Even had he been conscious, he could not have spoken through his battered, swollen lips.

When we got back to Birmingham I felt as a man must feel who plunges, completely exhausted, into a snowdrift and waits for sleep. My family had arrived from the valley to comfort Cherry and to bury our still-born son. None of the communist gang knew Adeline's parents, so it was up to me to call her father. I had met him once in Chicago. As I listened to the long-distance operator locate him at his bank, I wondered how a banker must feel to learn suddenly that his militant Red daughter has been blasted to death on the battle line. He took the news calmly, as though he had been expecting it.

"I'll take the next plane to Birmingham," he said, and I told him my brother would meet him.

250

I took a strong sedative and crawled into bed. Addy was right. I had been playing with matches, and now I had set the world on fire.

Somehow I managed to survive the days which followed. Cherry recovered rapidly, but there was a sadness between us. The strange sadness which follows a still-born child. Life looks terribly futile when you realize that you can't successfully reproduce your own kind.

My brother told me the story of the well-tailored, gray-haired banker who came to Birmingham to claim the bomb-broken body of the Southern Secretary of the Committee to Oppose Political Persecution. The banker went to the wrecked, roped-off bookshop where his daughter had met death. He looked at the books and the pamphlets and the pictures and the blood, and he shuddered throughout his tall frame. At the mortuary he found a tattered mass of black and white humanity waiting and hoping to be allowed to pay their respects to one who had been a Joan of Arc to them. But the banker's resentment was too great. He denied them the privilege of looking on his daughter's face, and took her away.

Harry Lerner recovered slowly. I went to see him when he was able to talk. I am tempted to set down his story as he told it, but the time is not right. Until Adolf Hitler is in chains, perhaps it's best for us to think that such human beings as mutilated Harry Lerner exist only among the Gestapo. Harry had calmly accepted the whole turn of events.

"It's all part of the battle, Garth," he said. "We as individuals don't count. What does it matter if a few thousand or a few million people are starved or shot or bombed? The human race has got to be purged before it can adjust itself to this New World. The race has got to vomit. Little episodes like this are what sickens it toward the day when it can vomit."

"Yes, I suppose you are partially right," I said. "After what's happened, I hardly know what I believe. I can agree with you that this revolution has got to be fought through to a finish. The whole world has got to come to some new understanding. There has got to be a readjustment. But there are so many confusing cross-currents. I was taught to believe that I had inherited a grand way of life in America. That I had inherited something to protect, and that I should protect it with my life if necessary. I've wanted to protect and preserve America. I'm caught in the whirl of this change, and I can't see what the result of the change is going to be. I can't see any hope in the way we seem to be heading. I don't think I'd even want to live in a world that didn't allow one man to build and acquire for himself."

"You are wrong, Garth," Harry said, "and you'll soon realize that you are. For men to accumulate property, they must first make profits. And in the world today you can make profits only out of the flesh and blood of other men. The People won't stand for it any more. We are going to build a world where the People work for the People, and where no man is allowed to live off the labor of other men. You can pass laws to put us in jail, and your friends can hire 'private detectives' to beat us and kill us. But, by God, we'll come back stronger every day."

"I guess you will," I said. "I guess that sounds like a beautiful ideal to you, but it sounds like defeat to me. I'd like to see all the people of the world get a higher standard of living. I'd like to see all the energies of the world devoted to giving everybody a healthier and more pleasant way of life. But I've been taught to believe that the American incentive, competing and racing process is the most successful way to help everyone to a better standard of living. I believe that if you'll give a man a chance to lift himself by his own boot-

252

straps, he'll also lift up the general welfare in his striving."

Harry laughed through his bandages. "That sounds like a beautiful ideal, too. But it has been disproved here in America. If you give a man a chance to run a race, he runs off with the prize and leaves the less fortunate to starve and die. You fast-racers are going to have to be broken and hitched to the People's wagon."

I shook my head. "I don't suppose we can ever settle this argument, Harry," I said. "But for the moment we've got to join forces and see if we can convict the brutes who killed Adeline and mangled you."

The fight to bring the murderers of Adeline Reed and the torturers of Harry Lerner to justice was a farce. The Labor Leaders, in order to maintain their false and expedient anti-Red front, shied away from the case. The politicians, who only a few days before had opposed the anti-sedition bill and shouted about "freedom of speech," took to their storm cellars. They had been willing to protect Reds from jail sentences, but to oppose a mob uprising is something that a smart politician just doesn't do. All the high-minded ladies and gentlemen in Washington who had sent telegrams to Alabama against the anti-sedition bill were now on vacation.

The circumstances, it seems, had changed. The anti-sedition fight had been on the "broad principle" of freedom of speech. The Great Americans could oppose anti-sedition bills and still declare themselves opposed to communism. But now two avowed communists, two people who represented the Communist Party, had met grievous mishaps. It was unfortunate, but then what can one do in such cases? It was obvious that the overwhelming majority of the people of Alabama believed that the "nigger-lovin' whore" and the "Red Jew bastard" had gotten no more than they deserved.

253

I, of course, was the most inconsistent sophomore of them all. I was the "Voice of Reaction" in Alabama. I was the "minion of the Big Mules" who had shoveled out the money to try to pass the anti-sedition bill. I was the bitterest Red-hater in the state. Thousands of extra copies of the *Defender* had been printed each week with editorials attacking Reds, Roosevelt, and Revolution, and urging passage of the anti-sedition bill. But now, in the same paper, I dared to print the names of the men who threw the bomb at the "nigger-lovin' whore" and who laid the whips on the "Red Jew bastard."

It was poor journalism and poor strategy on my part. If you are a smart editor or a smart leader, you must never confuse your followers in times of crisis. You must draw your pictures in black or white. Enemy is enemy and friend is friend, and whoever combats the enemy is a friend. So it was "poor policy" for me to crusade for the conviction of a group of men popularly described as "true Americans who had the courage to do something about the Red Menace." Especially since I could see, even then, that by my having helped to stir up the general madness, I was partially responsible for the crimes.

In a book or during an evening before a fire, you can walk tight wires in your reasoning and reach understandable conclusions. You can say: Now here were two communist leaders. I liked them personally, but I regarded them as so dangerous a threat to my conceptions of a proper way of life that I was willing for the state to put them in concentration camps. I knew they were dangerous, because I knew they would use any means to accomplish their ends. I knew they would throw dynamite on people to make them join unions. I knew they would instruct men to wait in a ditch and murder another man to stop a back-to-work movement. I wanted to put them in jail. But, when other Americans became hate-crazed and threw dynamite on these

254

Reds, I thought that these other Americans should be put in prison. I thought that they were as dangerous as the Reds themselves.

You can talk that way in calm conversation when you have all night to talk. But you can't talk that way on the front page of a newspaper and get away with it.

There was no doubt as to the identity of the murderers and torturers. The eight men who had "tended to" Harry Lerner boasted of their guilt. Three special Grand Juries were called in an effort to get an indictment, but not one of the juries would return an indictment. Harry was treated like a criminal in the jury room. I was called by all three of the juries, and when I urged that the guilty men·be indicted, some of the jurors laughed at me.

"What d'ya think ought to be done to these niggerlovin' Reds?" one juror asked me.

"I don't know, sir," I replied. "They should probably be put in jail, but they are not on trial now."

"Well, if you don't know what to do with niggerlovers," the juror retorted, "yuh better let these boys handle 'em who do know what to do."

It was useless to try further.

When it was all over, I was an editor who had run out of something to say. I felt completely defeated. I wanted to think, yet all thinking seemed so futile. I wanted to oppose the socialization process by which Americans seemed to be selling their birthrights for bread, but the whole problem appeared to be so terribly complex. I wanted to believe in such words as Liberty and Justice and Democracy and Equal Opportunity and Due Process, but whose definition of these words would I accept? I wanted to be enthusiastic. And like Harry and Adeline, I wanted to be a part of a Grand and Noble Something that would be worth all I had to give. I wanted to see things in black and white. I wanted to follow the advice Old Mis' Ella gave me

255

when she said: "Get you some things to love and some things to hate, and then love 'em and hate 'em with all your soul." I didn't want to take refuge in cynicism.

For a few weeks I tried to reconcile myself to living just for the hell of it. I told myself that everything would be all right. I could do a little adjusting and compromising and explaining, and everything would be okay. Cherry and I could have fun. We could join the Country Club and play more bridge. I could take up golf. What-the-hell, do you have to believe something and hate something in order to get a bang out of life? What's wrong with just living comfortably, and making money, and listening to great music, and eating good food, and minding your own damn business?

But it was no use. I didn't like the way I was going. I wanted understanding and peace of mind. I wanted to escape from confusion and find something to believe. At twenty-five I couldn't begin living just for the hell of it. At twenty-five you've got to Believe Something and be fighting for something. I decided to fold up the *Defender* and take a trip. There is no use working, I thought, unless you have a purpose, and the simple acquisition of dollars is hardly purpose enough at twenty-five.

I told Cherry I was going away. She didn't understand, and I didn't expect her to. She couldn't understand why I didn't want her to go with me. I didn't understand this either, but I wanted to go alone. I wanted to quit thinking, and live alone for a while until I found some sort of new faith and understanding. Something to give me purpose.

Put into words, it all sounded nonsensical. A man doesn't nonchalantly fold up a good business at twenty-five and wander off into space! Only a crazy man would do such a thing in the uncertain year of 1938. But I quietly folded the *Deep South Defender* and tucked it into a trunk. I amused my friends by posting a notice on the door. It read: "Publication of this jour-

256

nal has been indefinitely suspended until the editor can find something to say."

We closed the apartment and stored the furniture. Cherry tried to be very gay about our "retiring for a year or two," but she cried when the things were moved out. I didn't know where I was going until twelve hours before I left. Cherry and some friends went with me to the train. She was to stay in Birmingham for a while and then visit her mother. Somewhere, soon we would get together again.

I crawled on a night train and headed West.

1939

BUNKER HILLS

THERE IS A Bunker Hill in Boston which symbolizes America: 1776. When you think of it you think of brave young hearts looking up to behold a vision worth all they've got to give. You think of strength and hope and faith and defiance and simple men jerking open homespun shirts to bare their breasts to tyranny. You think of ordinary, potato-digging men who dared to dream of being free rushing with stones in their hands to meet the ordered bayonets of enslaving mercenaries. You think of Arnold Winkelried and Thermopylae and the Marseillaise and Nathan Hale and the whole grand, disdainful process by which men have thrown their lives on the altar for the dream of Liberty. You think of all the warm young heart's blood freely poured into the building of America.

But there is another Bunker Hill, and it symbolized a portion of America: 1941. This other Bunker Hill is not in Boston; it is in Los Angeles. When you think of it your heart aches, for it is the antithesis of the Boston Bunker Hill. It stands for weakness and hopelessness and cynicism and surrender. It is covered with houses for men. Grotesque, misshapen houses, with eight storeys in the back and three storeys in the front,

258

clinging to the steep hillside. And in these misshapen houses, where you climb downward instead of upward from the entrance, live misshapen men and women who have lost faith in God, who have lost respect for Man, who have lost hope for America, and who have lost the will to dream and the power to envision.

To understand what has happened in America in the brief span of seven generations, you must see these two Bunker Hills clearly. One of these Bunker Hills is a birthplace; the other is a grave. One stands for victory; the other for defeat. One is a monument to men who knew what they wanted; the other is a catacomb for the soulless bodies of men who could find nothing they wanted. One was a citadel for men who believed in the divinity of God and the majesty of Man; the other is a concentration camp for men who doubt God and despise Man.

Los Angeles is the Capital of American Despair. It is a sun-warmed magnet with an affinity, not for iron, but for heart-rot and soul-rot. It is an eddy toward which all rudderless Americans gravitate. It is the mecca of a new generation of American tramps. As a colony for those suffering from soul-sickness, it will enthrone any faker who claims a patent remedy for the common disease. And in the center of Los Angeles stands this high hill—Bunker Hill—the densest concentration point for soulless America.

You must not think of these denizens of Bunker Hill as desiccated victims of disease and old age. The physically old don't live on hillsides in California. They live on the sand at Long Beach where even the curbs have been flattened to ease their steps. The denizens of Bunker Hill are physically young. They came of age after 1929. Except for their eyes they have the vitality of healthy youth. Their malady is strictly of the soul. They believe nothing. They hope for nothing. Their longings have perverted even their most natural

259

desires. They live "twenty-four hours at a time"—just for the hell of it.

By May, 1939, I had traveled the whole distance from one Bunker Hill to the other. In May, 1929, I had stood with my fathers in the red earth of the Tennessee Valley which had literally been won on Boston's Bunker Hill. But in May, 1939, I had taken up residence on the other Bunker Hill. Don't misunderstand me. I hadn't "gone to hell." I wasn't the bleary-eyed tramp who staggers against the bar at Singapore and begs for arsenic. Had you met me in an Olive Street bar you might have considered me a successful vacationing reporter with an excellent repertoire of bar stories. I had fallen victim to neither dope nor alcoholism. I didn't consider myself a "sad young man" with the weight of the world's iniquities on his shoulders. I wept no tears into my pillow. My sense of humor was functioning perfectly. I was only another American in search of something to believe.

My whole journey from Alabama to Bunker Hill seemed so damned ironical that I had to laugh when I thought of it. Why had I come to Los Angeles? Why not New York or St. Louis or San Francisco? The answer was clear. The very act of "going to New York" betokens a man who knows what he wants and who is fired with ambition to drive toward a definite goal. But if you are an American who doesn't know what he wants, you automatically go to Los Angeles to lie in the sun and spit in the sand and wonder what-the-hell. The heart-rot magnetism of Los Angeles had worked on me just as on the others. I had joined the parade of tramps to Mecca.

How had I landed on Bunker Hill? Why not in some other section of the town? Well, driftwood drifts toward the eddy.

The misshapen house on Bunker Hill where I hit bottom was called Fremont Place. Wasn't there an explorer or an Indian-fighter by that name? It contained numerous rooms and apartments ranging from the very dark and very cheap rooms far below the street level to the bright, comfortable apartments above the street level. It was managed by a broad-beamed, broad-bosomed woman named Sarah Buckston who had an eye like a gypsy horse trader. Astonished resentment jumped to her face when she realized I was actually offering her my personal check for my first month's rent.

"What the hell d'ya think ya're doing, boy?" she asked as I stood at her desk writing the check.

"Why I'm going to pay my rent. Isn't that customary?"

"Ya mean ya're gonna try to give me a damn check?"

I thought she must be kidding. "Why certainly. Here are my credit cards. How else did you think I would pay you?"

She was on the verge of throwing me out when she decided I didn't know any better. "Lissen, son," she said, "ya're not in Alabamy now. Ya're in L.A. Ya look okay, but 'cha check's no good out here. If ya want to live in this house, ya bring me the money and I'll decide whether it's good or not. I wouldn't take Henry Ford's check if it was certified by J. P. Morgan."

No other Garth would have spent a night in that house, but this, truly, was California and Bunker Hill. I laughed. "That's the trouble with the world today, Mrs. Buckston. We don't trust one another anymore." I gave her the money and, after she examined each bill, she gave me the keys to the apartment. In a few days we became friends in a cold, suspicious sort of way.

For the purest example of persistent effusion in all the world, I nominate a Jewish poet who has been shot in the pants with a buckshot-load of Christian Science. Such a person lived at Fremont Place. He called on me my first night there. I took him for a newsboy when I opened the door, but the papers were only copies of the *Christian Science Monitor* which he distributed regularly to the inmates of Fremont Place. Before I could catch his name he had seated himself and fixed me with sincere brown eyes.

"You are troubled, aren't you," he analyzed quickly. It was not a question. "You are seeking peace. You wake in the night to feel claws tearing at your vitals. You are on a treadmill—running—running—running. The noise is in your ears. You plead wildly for silence and peace. You wish with all your heart that you could be out in the desert—that you could lie in the warm sand and pull it around you like a soft blanket and feel that you were in your mother's arms and all was at peace. You do wish that, don't you?"

"Well, I, ah, what did you say your name was?" He had spoken so rapidly I had not been able to follow him.

"Oh, the name. Sidney Harsh. You know me. I know you. It doesn't matter whether we've met before. I know you. You want salvation from madness. The whole world's gone mad. I know. I spent ten years in hell's darkest dungeons. We have got to have pity. We have got to have kindness. We have got to have love. Everyone who comes here is old. He is dead inside. He is hard, He is groping, struggling, choking with his own blood. You've felt it. I have the answer to it all. I've brought it to you. I'll bring more tomorrow. You must read it all. You must see it . . . feel it . . . live it. It is the only hope of the world. We can replace lust, hate and greed with love, pity and soft understanding. You must read this book and this paper tonight. Tonight, understand! I'll come back in the morning. Lie and rest easily tonight. Quit tearing and shredding yourself inside. I'll be back in the morning. We'll have coffee together."

And Sidney Harsh went bubbling along distributing

262

his papers. I read some of his pamphlets and listened
to his bubblings when I couldn't escape him. He was
a kind fellow. A few years back he had written lyrics
for enough successful songs to provide himself a tiny
income from ASCAP. A Swedish widow up the street
cooked him an occasional decent meal—for a price—
and he hawked a few lyrics in Hollywood. But he
spent most of his time distributing *Monitors* and pamphlets, trying to bring peace to treadmill-worn souls.
His acquaintances studiously avoided him.

I'm afraid I didn't give Sidney a fair chance to lead
me to salvation. I didn't know anything about Christian Science, but an old prejudice against it was buried
deep within me.

Margaret was the girl at Fremont Place who worked
for the bookies. The telephone in her apartment was
connected with the spot where they got the race descriptions, and it was fun to sit with a gang, take a few
drinks, bet on a race every half-hour, and listen to
Margaret relay the crisp story of a running at Tan-
foran or Caliente. I learned about Scratch Sheets and
Dope Sheets and the next-morning pay-off from Margaret. Most all the tenants at Fremont Place were her
customers, and we were classified in her book as to
the regularity of our playing and the promptness of
our paying.

I liked Margaret. She looked something like Mary
Astor, only much younger and more brusque. Her hair
was cut short, and her slacks were like those worn
by the more mannish female perverts who came up
from downstairs, but she was feminine. She had come
from Minnesota and had a kid back there. I think half
the women on Bunker Hill had a kid somewhere back
in the Midwest.

Margaret and I snacked and drank together several
times. She was honest and built like the horses from
which she made her living, but she was hard. She had

bumped into too many rough edges. There was some guy who came to see her very late two or three times a week, and one night I happened to see him as he was leaving her apartment. He was a tough one. Must have been a truck driver or a coal heaver. I was disappointed. I thought Margaret could have done better than that.

Next day I said to her, "I ran into your boy friend in the hall this morning." She read my thoughts. "Surprised at the general appearance, huh?" she asked.

"No, why should I be?"

"You're a liar, of course," she said. "You want to know why I pick a bozo like that to play with? Well, I'll tell you. First he doesn't live on Bunker Hill He doesn't know any better than to work like hell for a living. Second, he's the only man I've found out here whose hands don't feel clammy on my flesh. They feel like Minnesota hands. And next, when he walks into this apartment he knows exactly what he wants, and when he's got it, he is simple enough to feel that he has accomplished something and he's grateful for it. Have you seen any man on this hill you think would feel that way?"

That was Margaret. I suppose she is the type of woman who survives whatever hell happens. But what becomes of her in ten years? And what becomes of her kid back in Minnesota?

I met Chick and Bob in Margaret's place. They liked to place bets, but they were "slow pay" and Margaret never encouraged them to play. Chick was from Syracuse—he had finished at Cornell—and Bob was from South Dakota and the University of Illinois. They shared an apartment. Chick worked intermittently at something-or-other, and he had a girl who worked for Postal Telegraph who gave him money. Bob was an actor-in-waiting. In three years he had been rewarded with two routine movie tests, so his future was as-

264

sured. He had only to wait around and pick up a few bit parts at Pasadena Playhouse. Spencer Tracy couldn't live forever.

Chick was the only person in the house besides old "Salvation Sid" who professed any religion. He was Catholic. When the conversation veered to ideals and purposes, Chick would swell up inside and tell us how valiantly he was struggling to hold onto his religion.

"I've got to keep it," he said. "How the hell can you live in all this rottennness without it? Why should you get up in the morning? How is one day different from the next? What do you do that a dog can't do if you haven't religion? I look at myself in the mirror every day and swear I'll hold onto my religion no matter what happens."

Chick had no more religion than the rest of us. He only felt the need of it more.

Catastrophe struck Bob while I was at Fremont Place. The farm folk in South Dakota cut off his check and wished him well. He had the heart-breaking choice of going back to drive a tractor on the Great Plains or whoring himself for his art. He chose the braver path.

At the world-famous Palm Tree Bar in the Del Rio Hotel, a world-famous Slave Market is held each Saturday at 5 p.m. It is a unique market in that women instead of men do the buying. The men who attend must be well-turned-out, sound-of-wind animals without the price of a bowl of chili in their pockets after they have settled the two-dollar entrance fee. No solvent male would think of attending. The women must have presented some evidence of being desirous of making a purchase and of being able to provide food and lodging for a respectable slave.

The routine is standard. An orchestra plays "I Can't Give You Anything But Love, Baby," while the fugitives from the WPA parade around the floor exuding masculine charm and hungrily watch for a plucked eyebrow to raise among the surrounding palms. There

265

is an air of resigned sadness about it all, for men are more sensitive creatures than women, and the surrender of their self-respect cuts them more poignantly. A woman who sells herself to a man can hope she will be allowed to forget the sale, but a man who sells himself to a woman can entertain no such hope.

As Bob, pride of the old Illinois Phi Delta Omegas, readied himself for the sacrifice, he found he needed my best suit to restore his confidence. He also needed the two dollars to satisfy the man at the door and an extra dollar to buy himself a drink in the event he was not bid off early in the auction. We fixed him up and sent him to the market with our best wishes. Margaret didn't believe he would hit. He was too soft. Chick was doubtful. Mrs. Buckston told him he had better hit or he'd be sleeping on Pershing Square. Sidney hoped he would find a woman with pity and understanding. I marveled at the thought that the whim of some neglected wife could postpone the return of a pioneer's son to the plow.

In two hours Bob was back with a smile, fifty dollars and a tentative deal. It hadn't been bad at all. She wasn't over forty. She lived in Pasadena, and her husband was president of an oil company.

"She's not one of these hard women, is she, Bob?" Sidney inquired anxiously.

"No, Sid," Bob replied, "I really believe she has pity and understanding."

I liked Erik better than anyone else at Fremont Place. He was a Norwegian and a tramp aviator. He had flown in Sweden and Germany and Spain and South America. Now he was in California trying to obtain a permanent passport and a job with one of the big aircraft companies. He told me about his experience in Spain.

"When the war comes I am in Spain trying to teach the crazy Spaniards to fly," he said. "It was one helluva

266

job. The crazy Spaniards they go out and land in a cow pasture, then they call you up and say: 'Hey, I am in a cow pasture. You must come and get the plane.' You say: 'Why the hell you in a cow pasture?' and the crazy Spaniards they say: 'We dunno' and you have to go get the ship. When the war comes I start flying the jaloppies for the Government. We have jaloppies and Franco has beautiful planes. So, I start flying for Franco."

"But how could you do that?" I asked. "Didn't you believe the Government was right? How could you desert to the Fascists?"

"Desert you call it! Listen, Garth, I am not a politician. I am a flyer. I am one little man. How can I know who is right and who is wrong? In such a war there is no right and wrong. I am a flyer. I must have a ship to fly. I must have money so I can have wine and food and love. One little man cannot decide the fate of the world. He can only live his little while and die. So, I fly for Franco."

"How did you feel dropping bombs on those poor, starving kids?"

"I feel like hell. But then I am a flyer. I am not a politician. On either side I must kill poor people who don't know from what the hell. Franco kills children. The Russians kill priests. You Americans help Franco. I am a flyer of ships. Franco has the best ships. He pays me and I can have wine and food and love and music. So, I fly for Franco."

"And now you've come to fly for America for the same reasons, I suppose."

"Sure, America has motor cars. America has the finest ships in all the world. I can fly fine ships and have a little house and a motor car to drive to the airport and plenty of money. That is why I have come to America."

Erik, by his own statements, was an undesirable alien. But his open face, his naive grin, and the precise

267

way he accented each English syllable made me like him. I doubt that I rendered my country any service, but I signed his papers as one of the guarantors against his ever becoming a public charge in America.

The coldest potato at Fremont Place was McKenzie Pruett. He frightened you with every word he said. As you listened to his cynicism ice-picking at your brain, you found it difficult to believe that his fathers had crossed the prairies, the mountains, and the deserts to help build the State of Oregon. Had he really been born on the bank of a great river with great trees towering above his father's house? Had he really worked his way through the University of Oregon, burning with high hope and ambition?

Ken was about thirty now. Five years ago a news-paper had folded, and a good reporter had become a "leg man" for an actors' agency in Hollywood. His belly-knot of cynicism had hardened with the years, so Ken had drifted to Bunker Hill and "simplified" his life. Now he was an agent for women—a procurer—a pimp—the owner and operator of the best damned "date service" on the West Coast. The most expensive apartment at Fremont Place was Ken's home and office. An assistant answered his two telephones, while Ken managed his stable of women and promoted the sale of his wares.

"It took me a while to figure this place out," he told me, "but now that I've got it figured out I do okay. You see, this town's just one big whore house. Every year five thousand new beauty contest winners come to Hollywood. Not one of them can 'go back.' Mary Jones, who got that 'Hollywood contract,' can't go back to Podunk and marry Joe Doakes, the filling station oper-ator. So what happens?

"Well, an agent takes over one of these babes. He sets her down and tells her the facts of life. 'Lissen, babe,' he says, 'ya got a neat pair o' pins an' ya don't need no cotton to make ya sweater stick out in the right places. That's okay. But the pay-off in this town's not on what ya got, but who ya use it on. It aint how much ya work but who ya sleep with that counts. Now we'll have to build up on the small fry, but just remember that the quickest way for you and me to get in the dough is to get you sleepin' with a producer.'

"That's the basic start for most of the women who come to Hollywood. But just one of 'em out 'a five thousand is gonna marry the producer and just ten of 'em are ever gonna get in the dough. That leaves plenty of others who've got to eat, and, brother, this is the toughest place in the world to find a two-bit breakfast in. Then there's two thousand young widows and divorcees who hit this town every year. When ya add 'em all up, they need a lotta agents."

I challenged him. "Yeah but, Ken, surely most of them pull out of it some way and adjust themselves, don't they?"

"Oh, some of them marry doctors and dentists and ordinary honest folks, but most of them never find any anchor. They can't leave here. All of them—even the successful ones—turn to granite. You have to turn to stone to survive here. Nobody in this town would trust his best friend with a dollar, a woman, or an idea. Unless these women can find some man to keep them, they start ringing my telephone and get on my list. My agency is just as legitimate and a damn sight more honest than most of those out on the Strip."

Ken showed me his list. It was a card file of two hundred women ranging from sixteen to thirty-five. These were his "Actives." His "Inactive List" had two thousand names in it. Each card carried a newspaperman's terse description, extent of the wardrobe, education, dancing ability, and general appraisal. The cards were classified as to blondes, brunettes and red-heads; then

269

as to the asking price for the merchandise. They ranged from a large group available at ten dollars for a single evening up to a select few available only at five hundred dollars for a week-end.

"I never realized there was that much difference in the value of the merchandise," I remarked. "What do you get for five hundred you don't get for ten?"

Ken laughed. "It's looks, plus psychology and salesmanship. One woman can make a punk feel like he has conquered the world, while another one leaves him feeling he has been gypped. Then, too, the value of a woman is partially judged by the value of the clothes she takes off."

Ken was the most successful man on Bunker Hill. He considered himself hard, honest, and resourceful. A paper had folded and a pioneer's son had faced defeat. He had turned to the agency business, reduced it to "simple fundamentals," and come bobbing back to the surface. Ken, like his fathers, had proved himself equal to his environment. He was University of Oregon, Class of '30.

There was a girl named Jimmy at Fremont Place. She sang in a church choir for a living. She was the only woman I met on Bunker Hill to whom I made love. She made you feel so damn lonely. Any man would have made love to Jimmy.

Jimmy was twenty-six. Small, well-rounded, like all women named Jimmy, she was part Russian and had the characteristic blonde redness in her hair and cheeks. At eighteen Jimmy had run away from a tank town to marry a big, healthy, what-the-hell bruiser who drove racing cars for cakes, coffee and transportation. For five years they had drifted from race track to race track, getting thown out of respectable rooming houses because of their clamorous wassails and love-making.

"God, that brute could do two things well," Jimmy recalled. "He could drive those cars and make love to me. He lived for nothing else. He used to buy me a new gown every week. He'd make me put it on and parade around before him while we drank hot rum-and-butter. Then he'd pitch in to me and holler and yell until every old maid in the house would start complaining out of sheer envy."

But the brute had straightened out a curve one day and Jimmy was alone. She had drifted to Bunker Hill and a fifteen-dollar-a-week job in a church choir. She had tried to grow a shell to protect her softness.

"I've had three years of hell," Jimmy said, "because I'm looking for a man and I haven't found one. Since the Brute got his, I haven't been able to make enough money to live alone. I've had to share apartments and rooms with other women. And, boy, that's *hell*. I hate women I have to live with. Can you imagine a person like me having to eat with another woman, sleep with her and listen to all her damn ravings and complaints? Other women don't like me and I don't blame them. I'm looking for a *man,* and I've damn near gone nuts trying to find one."

"I'd think that would be very simple for you, Jimmy," I said.

"That's where you're crazy. I don't mean a keeper or a bedmate. I don't want that. I want a man who's nuts about me. A man who belongs to me and a man I can belong to. A man who'll give me four walls and come running home to me because I'm the sweetest, hottest, most adorable wench in all the world. I don't care whether he's a millionaire or a ditch-digger, if he'll only love me and protect me from other women."

Jimmy was the hungriest woman I have ever known. There was something pathetic in the fierce way she clutched at you while tears streamed down her cheeks. She could only partially give herself to a man who wasn't hers and to whom she didn't belong. She seemed to resent the relation, yet was forced by her own great longing to grasp for it. Of all the tragedies

271

on Bunker Hill, Jimmy's was the most poignant to me.

2

Jim Battersea was managing editor of the *Los Angeles Sun*. He was the sort of tub-shaped, frog-faced managing editor who barks, snorts, and growls before deadlines, and then after deadlines he props his feet on the desk, guzzles coffee, and comments broadly on the new rates in Chinese brothels or the newest interpretation of the Einstein Theory. I used to drop in on Old Jim occasionally and sell him a piece for his Sunday supplement, and, naturally, I always hit him just after a deadline when he was feeling charitable and expansive.

Jim gave me some amazing bits of information. In fact, had it not been for Jim I never would have known why birth rates increase after air-raids.

"Yuh know Old Mother Nature is a wonderful thing," he said. "She always provides compensations for everything. We hear about all them thousands o' Chinese the Japs are blastin' to hell. Well, nature's compensatin' for every one of 'em. I got this story straight from our boy in Shanghai. He says every time them Japs start droppin' bombs, it has the goddamdest effect on yuh. He says yuh become painfully desirous of the services of your mistress, and, before yuh know it, you're runnin' like hell to find her. It's the God's truth. He says that's the way it affects him. He says he gives his Chink gal hell every time the planes come over, and every one o' the damn Chinese does the same thing. That's funny as hell, ain't it? Even after all this war, there's gonna be more Chinamen than ever before."

Jim had two reporters he called "The Dook" and "The Lord." "They're my two twenty-five-thousand-dollar bastards," he said.

"You mean you pay them twenty-five-thousand a

272

year?" I asked. "My God, they must be Runyon and Hellinger."

"Naw," he explained, "I pay 'em fifty bucks a week, and it would be grand larceny for either one of 'em to take money from a WPA writers' project. They're both so lazy they wouldn't say 'sooey' if a hog ran over 'em, and they couldn't write a decent church notice for *The Podunk Weekly Aegis.*"

"Why don't you fire 'em?" I said.

"Fire 'em!" he exclaimed with high sarcasm. "How dare you profane the California air with such a harsh term? Haven't you Southerners heard about the New Freedom? Nobody gets fired any more. It'd cost this company twenty-five thousand dollars for me to fire those tramps. When yuh fire a lazy tramp now, it costs yuh twenty-five-thousand to prove why a tramp ought to be fired, and then you have to hire him back anyway. So as long as 'The Dook' and 'The Lord' condescend to come down and punch the clock, I have to put up with 'em."

"It's a helluva note, isn't it?" I said.

"You bet it's a helluva note when the newspaper men of this country let a bunch'a Red rats tie 'em up in a union. I never thought I'd live to see it. I tell ya Lafavor, if we let the goddam punks take over this country, it won't be worth the powder it'd take to blow it into the Pacific Ocean."

I remember the afternoon I walked back up Bunker Hill after that conversation. I thought of American newspaper men—the free men of a free press—huddling together in a rabbit warren of security, whimpering and demanding that ambition and ability be taxed in order to subsidize shiftlessness and mediocrity. I thought of what happened on the *Birmingham Press* when the Newspaper Guild struck and got a closed shop. All the fellows who had anything on the ball got their salaries cut so that a few "punks" could get big raises and job guarantees.

But there must be some reason for this, I thought. I know newspaper men. Some of them are lazy and lousy, but most of them are ambitious fellows who like to do as they damn please. If they, too, are clutching frantically at security, if they are willing to compromise, then something must have happened in America to make security more desirable than Liberty. Maybe we are going to have to rebuild America and substitute security for liberty. Make the Constitution read: Life, security, and the pursuit of happiness."

Not a pleasant prospect for a man who had once rared back and told his college class: "The sons of the men who fought at Bunker Hill will never be content to run their races in the treadmill of collectivism." But perhaps it was an inevitable prospect.

3

There are three places in Los Angeles where it is proper for the crowd to applaud the hero and hiss the villain.

One of these places is in the all-night movie houses along Main Street, where for ten cents you can sit all night and see seven different pictures. Most of the patrons are people who are unable to afford beds, and the ten cents gets them both entertainment and rest. You are expected to boo and hiss when the villain threatens the heroine with a fate worse than death, and you are expected to howl, whistle, and stomp when the cavalry comes charging over the hill to the rescue. The only objectionable feature about these houses is that they are also known as "Groping Operas." They are crawling with prehensile perverts of all varieties, so if you are ticklish it is advisable to be flanked by acquaintances who are non-gropers.

Another place where you hiss and applaud is the Theater Mart. This is a combination bar and theater where a modern version of "The Drunkard" has been running for ten years. You go there and get delight-fully oiled on beer, and spend the evening hissing a double-dyed villain who yanks his mustache and pur-sues a lily-white heroine. The plot, I believe, is some-thing about a mortgage.

But for an evening of real fun, you must go to the third place. It is the temple of Aimee Semple McPher-son, the goddess of the white, form-fitting gown and the scarlet cape. There you can see the New Stream-lined Order of Religion in action. There you can see thousands of What-the-Hellers yelling and hissing in a melodrama of sentimentality.

When you go in you see the goddess on her throne, the red cross splashed on the pure whiteness of her heaving bosom. "Good Lord," you think, "if she only had a mustache and a helmet she'd be the spit'n'image of Old Richard Coeur-de-Lion chasing off to rescue the Tomb." You mustn't think of all the husbands who have provided diversion for the goddess, for goddesses, after all, are goddesses.

The first demonstration of Religion in Action comes when, at the conclusion of a band number, the goddess leaps off the throne, throws up her arms, and yells: "Come on, folks! Make a joyful noise! You're in God's House, so lemme hear a joyful noise!" The crowd breaks into cheers and applause and fifteen rousing rahs for God.

As you sit down you automatically pull out your wallet, for the bargains are already being offered, and you'll want to get into the spirit of things. While the organ booms and the goddess sings her own composi-tions in cracked quatrains, the gentlemen pass among you, and you can purchase for the small price of one dollar a complete, handsomely-bound volume of these melodic gems of worship. The books are going, going, gone, and you'll want to grab one quickly because the postcards are coming out next.

275

These postcards are real bargains. Everybody has a dear old mother somewhere—God bless the mothers of America! Yessir, boys! Amen!—and what would please mother more than a message written on "God's own stationery" and showing her that her wandering boy was spending his time in "God's house." The gentlemen are passing among you, and you can snatch your cards quickly at three for the fourth part of a dollar. Or, if you really want to do right by old Mom, send her the "Master's card" with lace on it for only twenty-five cents.

You grab off a handful of cards, and anxiously anticipate the next round. It comes quickly. The next bargain is a picture of the goddess herself. Specially posed in her own private prayer room. Full size, eight-and-a-half-by-eleven, the very thing you've been wanting to send to Mom or to hang over your own bed. For only one dollar you not only get the picture, but— O Value of Values!—the gentlemen will also take your picture up to the throne and the goddess will autograph it for you.

After you've purchased the picture, complete with autograph, the house goes quiet. Very quiet. The goddess rises from her autographing and explains in measured whispers, "Folks, we've had a jolly half-hour shouting and singing and making joyful noises and buying things for ourselves. We've bought beautiful song books and postcards and pictures to give us pleasure and to give our dear old mothers pleasure. But now it's time to give God something. And certainly we wouldn't dare offer God less than we have spent on ourselves today, would we? This is God's house, this is God's beautiful day, and we are God's Great Army. So let's all get together and let God know how we feel."

If you've taken advantage of all the bargains, you find that you owe "God" quite a little item, and when you've settled, you discover that you've spent five dollars. But you quickly forget this as the show moves on. It's an "Illustrated Sermon." The goddess begins with her favorite gesture. She throws out her arms, and the scarlet cape attached to her wrists accentuates the high-bosomed, satiny figure which still has its points after the rigors of forty-odd winters. She tells about Hell where sinners and unbelievers are confined. The curtain rises behind her, and, sure enough, there is Hell. It's all red and fiery with light bulbs behind red tissue. Old Satan himself parades around in his red underwear, wagging a three-pronged tail with downright immodesty, and poking three or four cringing young sinners with a trident. The crowd boos and hisses, and the louder the boos the more cruelly Old Satan stabs the sinners and smirks.

Going back to Bunker Hill after my visit to the Temple, I found myself muttering softly. I drank two cups of coffee to soften the knot in my belly. Two thousand American people making joyful noises and trying to find soul-sensations! What did it mean? Was it enough to sneer at them as a bunch of poor, dumb bastards who had perverted a spiritual yearning in the same way that the "gropers" in the ten-cent operas had perverted a natural physical desire? Or was it only another symptom of the Modern Disease? Did it mean, perhaps, that the American clock, once wound so tightly, was now running down, and that a great new experience—perhaps a great sacrifice—was needed to wind the clock again and give the American people a new source of energy, a new belief in themselves, and a new sense of nobility?

People can't combat inevitable forces. They must roll with the punches, compromise, build new orders, and gather strength from new understandings. And sometimes people have to lose their lives in order to save their souls.

4

Thousands of people in California do nothing but sit in the parks. It isn't that they can't find jobs; most of them have simply lost the will to strive.

One day I sat down by an old codger and he said to me: "Friend, are you an old man or a young man?"

I thought it was a strange question until I noticed that he was blind. "Well, I suppose, sir, you'd call me a young man," I replied. "I'm twenty-six."

"Twenty-six, huh? I was your age about the time of the Spanish-American War. Why do you sit in the park, son?"

"Oh, I don't know, sir. It's pleasant here in the sunshine, and I can watch all these other people and wonder what they are doing here."

"Do you have a job?"

"No, sir, not at present."

"Could you have a job if you wanted one?"

I started to move away, but he was a lonely old fellow, so I sat back and answered him. "Yessir," I said, "I could find work."

"How many able-bodied men would you judge there are in the park today?" he went on.

"I'd say there are a thousand men in all, and I'd judge that half of them are able-bodied."

He shook his head. "I can't understand it. I just can't understand it. When I was your age I was on a farm back in Ioway. My pap had give me ten acres and I was buyin' twenty more. There just wasn't enough hours in the day for me to work. At night I shucked corn or mended my gear by a lantern in the crib. I was just bustin' to work and git my land paid for and git things for my wife and children. But young men are not that way any more, are they?"

"No, sir. A lot of young men work, but that fierce drive to build and acquire is gone."

"What caused it, son? Have they just gone pleasure crazy?"

"No, I don't think that's quite it," I said. "Most of the young men are pretty serious-minded. They've decided that America has grown old. That there's nothing new and exciting about it any longer. That a man can't get what he wants by working for it. A lot of them can't find jobs, and what's worse, they can't seem to find any meaning to their lives. So they are growing hard and cynical and afraid."

He turned his face toward me, and I felt that he was looking at me. "Is that the way you are, son?" he asked.

I thought for a moment. "No, I try not to be," I said. "I think there is something good left. I think there are still a lot of fellows who'd like to work in the corn cribs at night if we could only give them a reason to. There is still great strength in America if we could only re-direct it and give it purpose. Things were simple when you worked in your corn crib. You knew what you wanted, and how to get it. But big problems have come up now, and the people don't know how to solve them. So they are confused and discouraged."

"I'll tell you how to find what you're lookin' for, son," he said. "Go out and get to work. Forget all this foolishness you hear about leisure. A young man don't need leisure. He needs work. Get yourself a wife and some children and work all the time. Work so hard that you'll fall asleep as soon as you hit the bed at night. Then get up at sunup and go back to work. Then one day you'll see that you've found what you're looking for."

"Did you find it, sir?" I asked him.

He hesitated, then answered slowly. "Yes, I found it. I never did anything but work and go to church on Sunday. I never had much. Me and my wife raised six children and helped them get an education and

279

then helped them get some land. When I went blind four years ago, I had enough for me and my wife to come out here and live. We have fifty dollars a month, and that buys us all we need. We won't ever have to ask the Government for anything. Yes, I guess I found it."

"You were more fortunate than some of the others, sir," I said. "Suppose your savings had been in bank stock and the bank failed. Or suppose dust storms had destroyed the value of your land. You'd be very unhappy now, wouldn't you? You'd be over attending one of the pension meetings and cussing the Government for not giving you Thirty Dollars Every Thursday?"

"Yes, I guess I would have," he admitted. "But I don't see they are ever gonna take the gamble out of life. It's the gamble that makes you go back to the corn crib at night."

I felt better that afternoon, and that night I finished a story which had been lying around for weeks.

But on the afternoons I listened to the pension oratory in Pershing Square, I was always depressed. A speech on any subject from the single tax to trial marriage is in order in Pershing Square, but in the spring of '39 everyone wanted Thirty Dollars Every Thursday. I don't believe that any person of less than middle age can attend a California "pension meeting" without his first impression being that the American Spirit has died somewhere along the road, and that the Man-on-Horseback will soon come riding up to take over the remains. There is something shattering in the sight of Age making a damn fool of itself. Your first impulse is to jump up on the nearest soapbox, propose a new campaign for Forty Dollars Every Friday, and then sneer at them as they desert Thirty Dollars Every Thursday and flock to you.

It takes real effort to beat down your cynicism at a California pension meeting. You want to conclude on the spot that men are little nest-fouling creatures who deserve no more than to become slaves to some sort of totalitarian Government. But if you'll fight for the broad view, you can see that these people are an effect and not a cause. Some of them, it's true, are the effect of their own incompetence and profligacy and laziness, but many of them are the innocent effects of a system which either broke down or else became so efficient that the labor of those past fifty was no longer needed.

One day I sat in the park listening to a pension speech. A chap about my age sat down by me. He wore a crew-neck sweater, his hat was turned up, and he looked hungry, but there was courage in his face.

"You know what's wrong with the world?" he turned to me and said. "Folks are living twenty years too long. When a man got sixty years old, he use to die decently and get out of the way. But now he comes to California, gets a new set of goat glands, and spends twenty years square dancing and howling for a pension."

"Maybe you're right," I said. "Maybe these smart scientists who have prolonged their lives ought to be asked to figure out what to do with these pension howlers."

5

Late in May Cherry came out to California to join me. I remember standing in the big, new, Spanish-style railroad station waiting for her train. We had been separated for five months, and I was more eager to see her than I had ever been. When the train came in, I saw her standing in line in the aisle of the Pullman coach. She had already seen me, so she was smiling and waving and her eyes were wet. She had let her hair grow quite long, and she wore a white hat and a black-and-white linen suit. As she stepped off the train I noticed that she had added a little more of that matured grace which makes a beautiful woman grow more attractive each year between nineteen and thirty-five.

The taxi drove us out Wilshire Boulevard, past the Ambassador Hotel, to the new apartment I had taken. In preparation for Cherry's coming I had moved away from Bunker Hill to a gay, bright little place on Mariposa Street. Cherry didn't belong on Bunker Hill, for she knew exactly what she wanted.

We spent the day doing and saying all the things which two people who belong to each other do and say after their first prolonged separation. Cherry seemed to have forgotten the tragedies of the last dark days in Alabama, and I had no desire to recall them. We both wanted to pick up where we were and make a new start toward the "biggest and best life" which Cherry had always believed we could build together.

The next three months were the happiest of our lives. Cherry could always dispel my loneliness and doubt, for the simple experience of living with her was almost purpose enough for any life. I liked to have breakfast with her in the morning, for she always wore the brightest, crinkliest house coats with a white fluffiness at her throat, and she knew exactly how brown I liked my toast. I liked to watch the graceful, efficient, always-feminine manner in which she moved about the room. I liked to make love to her at five o'clock in the afternoon—the hour at which she contended she was "most easily approached." And I liked the easy, care-free way I slept at night when I slept with Cherry.

We bought an ancient blue Chevrolet coupé for two hundred dollars, loaded our bags into it, and set out to see the West. We drove up through the San Joaquin Valley and stopped at a spotlessly white motor court operated by a sturdy old gentleman and his wife who had come from Oregon. We liked the place so well we stayed a week. It made you feel good to watch the industry of the old people who ran the place.

282

"This is the richest valley in the world," the old gentleman told me proudly. "It grows more food than the valley of the Nile, and it could feed a whole country the size of Italy."

"That's your trouble, isn't it?" I said. "You grow too much."

"Yep. A fellow can't understand it. In one field the Government pays a man not to pick his fruit. In another field the Government pays a fruit picker not to work, and in another field people starve to death for something to eat. But you got to keep working and hoping that we can get it all straightened out."

The old man went with me out to a dry river bed where several trainloads of oranges had been dumped to rot and be washed out to sea when the rains came. At first, hungry people had rushed to the river to get the oranges; then the fruit companies began to spray the oranges with oil so that they couldn't be eaten—so that the "price structure of the fruit market" could be maintained.

"I just want you to explain that sight to me," the old man said.

"It's the most perfect picture of defeat I have ever seen," I told him. "I don't see how any man could look at it without realizing that something new is inevitable in America. I don't know what form it should take, but it'll have to be different from what we have had in the past."

From Fresno Cherry and I drove up to Yosemite, and I remember how terrified we both were when after driving seventy miles, we went through a long tunnel and suddenly emerged on the floor of Yosemite Valley. It was late in the afternoon—almost dark. I stopped the car and we got out. It was several minutes before either of us spoke. The wind was blowing, and we felt so insignificant that we instinctively held to one another.

"Look at it, Cherry," I said. "It's as if Time and

Space both reared up before us in a deliberate gesture to show us how small we are."

I have seen most of the natural wonders of America, but none has ever hit me like Yosemite. At Tahoe and Banff and Yellowstone your eyes have time to become adjusted gradually to Bigness; but at Yosemite you emerge from a tunnel to run against mountains which shoot up a mile into the sky with rivers leaping from their peaks.

We spent a week at the big camp on Yosemite's floor. Our tent was literally staked against a cliff which reared a sheer five thousand feet upward, and we could lie on our cots at night and wait for the moon to peep over the great height. Yosemite is an antidote for cynicism. Lying at the base of a cliff a mile high and watching a great river leap a mile through the moonlight, the little conflicts of one era in the human struggle seem so inconsequential. The river was leaping over the precipice a million years before Christ was born, and it will be leaping a million years after the problems of the twentieth century are forgotten. The Long View comes easily at Yosemite. You can see the one great fact that matters. The fact that somehow, inevitably, and in spite of maddening confusion and heart-breaking defeat, the human phalanx has marched forward out of darkness into light. You can see how human progress must be judged in broad, relative terms and not in terms of the vexing minutiae of the moment. You can see that to find hope, you must find hopeful answers to these questions:

In the century in which I lived, did the human procession move forward or backward? Were there more or fewer men burned at the stake for heresy than during the last century? Were the minority races treated better or worse? Were there more or fewer women and children crushed under chariot wheels? Was there more or less inhumanity of man to man? Was the fight against black reaction stronger or

284

weaker? Did man come to better understand his relation to God and his relation to his fellows? And did the individual man find the life process more thrilling and soul-satisfying?

I think that when a man enters the human struggle, he has an innate longing for significance—a longing to express himself as an individual, to build, to create, to acquire, and to accumulate. I think it is this longing which has given men the energy to build nations and civilizations. And I don't believe any system can endure which denies a man the right to express himself as an individual and to build, create, acquire and accumulate. I don't believe that all men are born equal. I believe that in each generation there are a Positive Few who must be encouraged to build as high as they can build and to create to the limit of their abilities.

But by the summer of 1939 I had come to realize that in America the Positive Few had to negotiate a new compromise agreement with the Many. I didn't turn communist, but I realized that Harry Lerner had come close to the truth when he told me that the "fast runners" in the Great American Race had to be "hitched to the People's wagon." I began to reconcile myself to the idea that in the New America the fast runners would have to be contented on smaller plots of land, would have to build more for the people and less for themselves, and would have to turn their accumulations back to the people at the end of their lives. And I began to try to accept the reality that big and bigger Governments would be necessary.

During the days at Yosemite, Cherry and I hiked and rode horses over the trails. We stood under the big trees and the waterfalls, slept lazily in the sun, fed the animals, and sipped long, cool drinks in the lodges. The day we went upon Glacier Point and looked down into the valley, Cherry said: "You know, Garth, when I see something grand and beautiful like this, I always

285

have two feelings. I'm happy and then I'm sad. I'm happy because I'm looking at something beautiful, and I'm happy because you are with me to see it, too. But then I'm sad when I think of all the people who live and die and never see it."

"But you shouldn't be sad, Cherry," I said. "Not everybody appreciates the same kind of beauty. Only about ten per cent of the people who come into this valley bother to climb up here for the view."

"Then I think they should be required to come up here. Or the Government should build an elevator to bring them up here."

"But you didn't like it when old Professor Barclay tried to make you read Ovid's poetry. Yet some people think it's beautiful."

We both laughed at our recollection of how Cherry had hated Latin, but Cherry insisted that she still wished everybody could go to Yosemite.

We were in Salt Lake City—on our way back to Alabama—on September 1 when the Panzer Divisions rolled into Poland. We were staying at the Utah Hotel, just across from Mormon Square. We had a radio sent up to the room, and we lay in bed and listened to the news which seemed so unreal. It sounded like a re-play of Orson Welles' Martian Invasion.

"There's only one hope now," I told Cherry, "and that's to save the United States. When this is over there'll be nothing but hungry brutes left in the rest of the world. Nothing but hate and hunger and ashes. Unless we stay out and keep the torch burning over here, God help us."

"You don't think we'll get in it, do you, Garth?" Cherry asked.

"Oh, no. Not a chance," I said. "We'll stay in our backyards and mend our fences."

Although I had learned that islands could no longer be isolated, and that states could no longer be isolated,

286

I still thought that nations were large enough units to be isolated.

We liked Salt Lake so well we stayed two weeks. We liked the organ recitals every day at noon in the Mormon Tabernacle. We liked the red and blue flowers in the canyons in the Wasatch Mountains. We liked to watch the water dance in the fountains in the middle of the desert.

So, while Hitler sacked Poland, we lived comfortably in Salt Lake, attending the daily organ recitals, listening to the Moonlight Sonata and Schubert's Ave Maria and sturdy old Mormon marching hymns, watching the water play in the sun, and imagining that the American world could be isolated against a plague which raged both abroad and within our own gates.

1940-1941

TWO GASOLINE CANS

I SUPPOSE IT WAS inevitable that Cherry and I should go back to the Tennessee Valley to make our new start. She had never wanted to live anywhere else, and I found myself giving more and more consideration to what Cherry wanted to do. My own desires were growing simpler. I was selling an occasional piece to the papers and magazines, and I thought I might do a book when and if I learned something to say.

I think, however, that the matter of two gasoline cans was what finally convinced me that we belonged only in the Tennessee Valley. We gave out of gas once in California when we were about a mile from a filling station. I walked to the station and asked the proprietor for a can in which to carry a gallon of gasoline back to the car. He found a battered can, filled it with gas, and then required me to put up a dollar deposit on it.

"If I trusted folks with cans," he snorted, "how long do you think I would stay in business?"

We were back in the Tennessee Valley near Florence, Alabama, when we next gave out of gas. I walked two miles to the station and found the proprietor eating dinner in his combination store and home. He was

288

a gray, heavy old fellow with one leg shorter than the other. He first insisted that I eat dinner with him, and when I declined, he got up from the table, put the gas in a new can with a long, flexible spigot, and told me to pay him for the gallon of gas when I returned to fill up my tank.

"You mean you don't want a deposit on the can?" I asked him.

"Good God, no! Don't 'cha think I trust you?" he laughed.

I was leaving for the two-mile walk when his son wheezed up in a T Model. "Here, son," the old man yelled, "take this fellah down to his car. He's out'a gas."

We filled up our tank at the old man's place, and then bought Coca-Colas and cigarets and candy we didn't really want. As we drove away I said to Cherry: "Yeah, I guess you're right, doll. We'd better settle back here in the valley. The climate's wretched, and there's hookworm and syphilis and pellagra and insanity, but we've still got more of something that's good than any other section of America I've seen."

But for me to go back to the valley to live meant that I had to forget all the old battles of the Roosevelt Revolution and fit myself into the New. I couldn't restore Tara. Garth's Island was gone, and I couldn't bring it back even if I dynamited Wheeler Dam. The old way of life was gone in the valley; the Government had come to stay. The valley was no longer a world of private empires, but a Government world of checkered land plots. Order and Design and Power had replaced *laissez-faire*. The valley now lived on Government dollars with Government management and Government advice. The Government held all the mortgages. The people lived on Government land in Government houses. They bought food and seed with Government loans, planted the seed under Government direction, and stored the fruit of the harvest in Government barns. Government was the agency which provided the biskit for breakfast and the "quatahs" for remedies. Wives conceived at a time advised by Government social workers, and the first face a child saw at birth was that of a Government nurse. The Government was the great giver and receiver, and no man did anything except with the advice and aid of the Government.

What could I do? Install myself on a mountain top and look out on the valley each day and utter mighty curses against the Despoilers and Changers? Go into exile and try to recruit an army to drive out the Government? Or devote my life to yearning and composing sonnets about the injustice of change and the good old days when "the best governed people were the least governed people?"

Of course not. For any man in his right senses could look out on the valley and see that, whatever the means employed, the result of the Government's coming was good. Even if your name was Garth, you had to admit the obvious and accept what had become a reality. When I saw a Government nurse administering pre-natal care at Government expense, any thought I had of increased taxes and socialism was immediately obliterated by the recollection of a night when my mother bore a child without pre-natal care.

If I were to live in the valley, there was nothing for me to do but compromise and fit myself into the new Government Planned Economy. I had to accept the Government as my banker, my director, my adviser, and my employer.

My acceptance and adjustment was gradual during 1940. I wanted to buy a plot of land overlooking the river, and I could buy it only from TVA. So I had to swallow hard and walk back into the same TVA land office where the "filthy Yankee bastards" had once made me sign away the Garth acres. The land agent was the same chap with whom I clashed on that occasion. He couldn't resist the temptation to taunt me.

"I believe we've met before, haven't we, Mr. La-favor?" he said.

"Yes, we have," I replied. "The circumstances were somewhat different. I was selling under duress then, but I want to buy now."

"I'm afraid we'll have to disappoint you," he continued. "You know we only sell five acres to a customer, and I can't imagine your being satisfied with less than three thousand."

I went tense with the old Garth impulse to smack the insolent sonuvabitch into the floor. But I choked it down and said: "Yes, I'm familiar with the Government regulations. If I hadn't been prepared to abide by them, I wouldn't have come back here."

I had to see the land agent two or three times before we completed the transaction by which Cherry and I bought a five-acre plot with the last five hundred dollars we had. The day I got the deed, the agent walked to the door with me and said: "Lafavor, I want to apologize for ribbing you the day you came in. It was an opportunity I couldn't pass up. And I've also got a confession to make to you. You remember you told me that we Yankees might learn something about the 'cement' that holds this world together down here? Well, I've learned a lot about it in the last five years. You people sure love this land, don't you?"

I chuckled. "I guess there's some hope if you 'communists' can say that," I told him. "The land and the river was enough for the Garths for a hundred and fifty years. Now I'll have the land, the Government, and the river."

The plot which Cherry and I selected lay on the Madison County side about a mile down-river from the old submerged Garth world. It fronted on the Hartselle-Huntsville Highway and was ten miles from Huntsville and ten miles from Hartselle. From it we could look down on the great swollen expanse of river and back-water; we could see the graceful arches of the new steel-and-concrete bridge; and across and up the road we could see other Government land plots and Government houses. Down-river from our plot stretched marshy, wooden lands, all owned by TVA.

"Do you think we can build the bigger and better life here?" I asked Cherry when we looked at it.

"It has pine trees and the river," she answered. "We ought to be able to add the rest."

Boys of the Civilian Conservation Corps helped us clear the land under the direction of TVA drainage experts. When we went to borrow money to build the house, the Government offered the best terms, so we made a twenty-year deal with the Federal Housing Administration. The Rural Electrification Administration ran a power line to our land, and the Electric Home Furnishings Administration supplied us electrical appliances from a basement furnace to an attic fan. TVA's privy expert from the Department of Public Health checked our plumbing and septic tanks, and nurses and social workers from the Department of Public Welfare came to instruct us in cleanliness, budgeting, and baby-spacing. The Farm Security Administration advanced us money to pay our poll taxes, subscribe to the county newspaper, and generally rehabilitate ourselves, although an agent from the National Farm Loan Association told us that he should have had the privilege of making this loan. Then the agricultural adjustment administration paid us not to plant cotton on three acres, and we took the Triple-A's money and paid it to the FSA. And to complete my personal cycle, I then went to work for TVA's public relations department at thirty-six hundred dollars a year.

This last step—my decision to become a Government "press agent"—was the most difficult of all. I could borrow money from the Government and live with the Government, but how could I decently live off the Government and promote the Government? I had always held all forms of Government "political employees" in contempt, and I had reserved a special super-charged contempt for Government press agents. Since I left college, I had conducted a one-man crusade to prevent my friends from "desertin' to the Government." Every time I heard of a classmate's considering or trying to get a job with a Government agency, I had called him and asked him why-the-hell he didn't get out and build up something for himself.

I remember a young lawyer named Sam Holman. A brilliant chap who could have had anything he wanted. He was "our kind of folks" from an old South Alabama family. When I heard that Sam was taking a fat job with Home Owners Loan Corporation, I called him on the telephone.

"What-the-hell, Sam," I said, "I hear you're desertin' to the bastards?"

"Yeah, I'm thinking about it," he said.

"You've decided you're not good enough to sit on your own bottom, huh?"

"Now listen, Garth," he argued, "what-the-hell? I'm making a hundred dollars a month over here with this firm. There are three fellows ahead of me who still haven't gotten their names on the door. It'll be a good five years before my name goes on the door and I start making enough money to afford a decent home. Why-the-hell shouldn't I take five thousand a year from HOLC?"

"Yeah, that's right," I sneered, "and why shouldn't your wife do a little whorin' on the side to help out the budget?"

Those were my words in 1937, and here in 1940 I was preparing to accept the most ridiculous type of sinecure.

When I was operating the *Defender*, I heard that Tom Broadwater, another classmate, was resigning a good job with a coal company to go with some Federal commission. I called him and gave him the same treatment.

"Why don't you start a business of your own?" I asked him. "You've got brains and energy and you can get the money."

"Aw, what-the-hell, Garth," he argued. "Why-the-hell should I start a business and spend half my time worrying over strikes and the other half worrying over tax reports? I can make five thousand a year with the Government and work when I damn please and don't have a worry in the world."

"Okay, Comrade," I said, "give my regards to Uncle Joe and all the boys in the Kremlin."

There had been plenty of similar arguments along the trail I had traveled. I had been sincere, too. It really hurt me every time I heard of a talented friend or classmate "desertin' to the Gover'mint." I could see no hope if all the young fellows who should be burning with ambition to start new businesses and new firms were going to crawl on the Government payroll and devote their energies to building bigger Governments. I thought that the inevitable consequence of such a movement would be disaster. A young man has ten years after he leaves college to root out a place for himself in the competitive system. If he spends these ten years drinking complacently at the Government trough, mustn't he automatically become an advocate of bigger Governments in order to safeguard his own position?

For more than a year on the *Press* I handled the daily mountain of press releases which the mail boy dumped on my desk. I had a waste basket big enough for three men to hide in, and every afternoon it was slopping over with neatly mimeographed Government eye-wash and expensive photographs of the New Deal-in-Action. Every time I picked up another armful of the worthless junk and heaved it into the waste basket, I muttered something about a filthy Government that spent a million dollars a week on propaganda. As for the newspapermen who "deserted to the Government," we members of the working press held them in the same high regard as decent, independent women hold the damsel who prefers the perfumed apartment and the periodic, wheezing embrace of some flabby old walrus.

But much water had run over the dams since 1937. Conditions, I reasoned, had changed. I had set my stakes back in the Tennessee Valley. The valley's future was my future, and everything in the valley was interwoven with the Government. I was building a new home and acquiring heavy obligations, and since my income from free lance writing was not sufficient to meet all the obligations, I had to work somewhere within twenty miles of my home. I could work with my father in the lumber business at Hartselle, but the lumber business depended on the Government. Every lumber business in the valley existed by the grace of the FHA and the TVA. I could work on the newspapers at Decatur or Huntsville, but they howled themselves hoarse rooting for more and bigger Government, and they ran every press release TVA put out. Even if I started a paper of my own, I could only sing the Government chorus. For only Government agencies made news now, and every family in the valley was training its sons and daughters to work for the Government.

Whatever I did in the valley, I had to be for more Government and bigger Government and better Government. I had to be for more Government supervision and more Government management. Not only because this was the way it was going to be anyhow, but because this was the way of hope for the valley and its people.

So I became a Government press agent connected with the TVA offices in Huntsville. It was easy to get the job, for we Garths voted many votes in the Congressional district, and our Congressman was anxious to "erase the old scars" and "unify" the district. The day

295

after my appointment was announced I received several letters. One of them was from Sam Holman, who was now well entrenched with HOLC. It said: "Dear Garth: I see you have deserted to the bastards. I suppose Mrs. Lafavor is now picking up extra change around the postoffice on Saturday night." Another one from Tom Broadwater in Washington said: "Why didn't you start a paper of your own? You had brains and energy and you could have gotten the money."

I chuckled. I had it coming to me.

Cherry and I and the Government were building our house while France was falling. At night we stayed at my mother's home, listened to the radio, read newspapers, and talked of the awfulness of war. We said all the things which must have been said around most American firesides during those days. Just wait until the Germans try to pierce the Maginot Line! The French'll pile 'em up so high they can't crawl over their own dead. No Army can advance through modern defensive gunfire. The French have been smart during the last twenty years. They've stayed at home, minded their own business, refused to "Die for Danzig," and have built a great wall around themselves. The French are safe behind a great army and a great wall. Wait until the British attack in force. Just wait, something will happen.

I should have been able to foresee the fall of France, for I had had some experience in the wall-building business. I should have asked myself the question: What if Alabama had been attacked during the anti-sedition fight? And when I got the answer to that one, I should have considered the question: What if Hitler had attacked America during the fight over the Supreme Court issue? We Garths and "our kind of folks" might have preferred Hitler to Roosevelt. But I hadn't come quite far enough in the summer of 1940 to see such parallels.

296

During the daytime Cherry and I forgot France. It was in another world thousands of miles away. We were busy clearing land and planting grass and building a home. I was busy writing stories and doing pieces for the papers. We were finding ourselves. We were building a life together. We had only sympathy for poor deluded France.

The June day on which the German Army marched into Paris, we moved into the new house. You would have liked our house. It was one of those little brick houses painted white and green that look as if they were built to be lived in by people who enjoy living. The Government architects had been generous with us. They had allowed us to veer farther away from the Government plan than was customary, and thus we had gotten in some of the ideas we picked up in California. There was a cathedral living room; not a really big cathedral living room, but it was thirty-six feet long with a stone fireplace and hewed cedar timbers overhead. Two innovations made us appear wasteful to the Garths and all our neighbors. We had built two bathrooms into a house which had only six rooms, and we had insisted on painting the red brick white. What possible use can two people have for two bathrooms, and why should any man in his right mind waste money by painting brick? Paint was still regarded as a luxury in the Tennessee Valley.

The single upstairs room was mine. It had windows on all four sides, and the side which faced the river was almost solid glass. Cherry and I sat down up there late in the afternoon on the day we moved in. It was another significant day in our lives, so we drank some strawberry wine and toasted each other and the future. We felt very proud and happy. The radio was on downstairs, and frantic people were exercising themselves over the fall of Paris and the way refugees were crowding the roads. I went downstairs and shut it off.

"Sometimes I wish there were no radios," I said when

297

I got back to Cherry. "They gather all the sordid waste products of the world and spew them onto your hearthstone."

But after I went to bed that night, I remember I felt uneasy. My heart was swollen. I had never been to Paris, but Paris had always represented something vital to me. A gay, disorderly, human sort of place where everybody wore his opinions like a chip on his shoulder; where beggars cherished their freedom to starve; and where men counted life without liberty as nothing. If booted, hob-nailed Order had to come to all the rest of the world, I thought, why couldn't Paris have been left as the one oasis of delightful disorder?

When I think of a German Army in Paris, I think of an exquisite, intelligent woman writhing in the arms of a clumsy, boorish rapist. I think of an ape hurling stones through blood-red cathedral windows, and a brute guzzling rare wines which should be sipped. The German militarist must know we feel this way about him, for he has always been the boor with the inferiority complex who fights to destroy what he can neither attain nor appreciate.

When we had finished arranging everything in the new house, I went to Birmingham and got the Garth memorabilia out of the bank vault where I had kept them stored since the water came. I framed the Great Deed and hung it over my desk. I shellacked the Conch Shell and put it on the mantel, and I pressed out all the old letters and covered them with cellophane. When I had hung the framed Deed and stepped back to see if it was straight on the wall, I said to Cherry: "It's strange how things happen. At the end of the first American Revolution the Government gave Peter Garth three thousand acres. During the second Revolution the Government took back the three thousand acres, and then built me a house on five acres. I guess the meaning of that is clear enough for anybody."

The only sadness in Cherry's life after the house was

298

built was our apparent inability to produce another life. I didn't think of it much, but I knew it bothered Cherry.

"There's something about a new house," she said, "which suggests that the next step should be a little boy to tear it up."

She betrayed her sadness only on the birthdays of the still-born child when she reminded me that he would have been a year old or two years old, and we got very quiet, and I wiped the tears from her soft black eyes. A few months after we moved into the new house, she went to a doctor and then had me to go, and when he assured her there was nothing wrong with either of us, she felt better.

"The doctor told me we had to keep hoping and trying," she said, "and I told him that I'd do the hoping and you'd do the trying. So don't let me down."

I don't know why some of us What-the-Hellers of the Thirties find the reproduction process so difficult. Maybe our pre- and post-marital adventures with contraception have something to do with it. Maybe our sins are being visited upon us, or maybe the Fates don't want us to reproduce our kind. But it did seem tragic that Cherry and I, who had loved each other so long and so fiercely, built a new house by the river, and then found that we could people it with no one else but ourselves.

By the time the big air raids began on England in September, 1940, I had completely rehabilitated myself back on the banks of the Tennessee. I had a new home among tall pine trees, and the pine needles were beginning to spiral down to protect the new grass and flowers during the winter. I had a boat and on weekends Cherry and our friends and I could ride for miles over the great expanses of Government water. When the boat passed over the submerged Island, I thought of all the old Garths buried down there in the Family cemetery that was never moved. I worked forty hours

299

a week for the Government and made three hundred dollars a month, and I could make as much more out of the pieces I sent to the papers and magazines. I was building a little world for myself, and all I wanted was peace and stability.

2

The complacent little city of Moorestown, Alabama, was a hold-out against the Government and TVA. It had a municipal power plant which it refused to sell to TVA, and thus it refused to buy Government power. The TVA wanted to "crack" Moorestown, and after I became a Government press agent, I was assigned to help "crack" it.

The Battle of Moorestown was the first battle in American history in which a man named Garth fought on the side of expanding Government. And the story of Moorestown and its "cracking" is the story of much that has happened in the United States in the last ten years.

You know how Moorestown looks. It's one of those Southern towns built around a courthouse square, and when you drive through it on a Saturday, you have to creep along blowing your horn to keep from running down overalled farmers and their broods. Old Man Sy Moore's store is on one corner, Old Man Bill Thompson's store is on another corner, and Old Man Jim Sloan's store is on the lot just north of the courthouse. Scattered among these three big stores are the banks, the county paper, the Ford and Chevrolet agencies, and sundry mercantile establishments. A string band is sawin' away on "Somebody Stole My Old Coon Dog" on one side of the courthouse, and a Baptist preacher is a-rasslin' with Satan on the other side.

You'll agree that Moorestown looks prosperous. It's well laid out, the churches and schools are modern, and the streets are paved. There has never been a bank

300

failure in Moorestown. It's solid and solvent. A neat little town of four thousand people, located in the center of a good agricultural county. Not a bad place for a man to settle. A good safe place to invest money.

Maybe you are interested in Moorestown and want to know how it started. Well, it started like most American towns. It started with one man. Old Man Ebenezer Moore, the old daddy of the present Old Man Sy Moore, put up a store at a crossroads. Everybody sorta liked Old Man Eb. He was a workin' piece 'a plunder. He'd give you credit and take a mortgage on your mule, and somehow you'd go back and pay Old Man Eb when you wouldn't pay nobody else. Then Old Man Jack Thompson came along and put up a store, and a little later, Old Man Tom Sloan came in. The three of 'em owned all the land around the place, and when a new building was needed by somebody comin' in to town to open up, one of 'em built it for him and rented it to him.

So Moorestown just grew. The three "old men" were the "city fathers," and they organized most everything and put their names on most everything. They were Builders. They were Pioneers. They were Far-Seeing Americans. They were the kind of men who build towns and empires and worlds. They knew how to keep a tight line, and when they died they passed Moorestown along to sons who also knew the value of a dollar. Even in 1932 and '33 when banks were bustin' all over the country, the three Moorestown banks stood solid as bedrock, for the sons of the "old men" had kept the line tight and never let a farmer get too far behind on his notes and mortgages.

When I drove into Moorestown on a September day in 1940, I wanted to discover why this city was holding out so stubbornly against the New Deal; why it refused to buy the Government's cheap, water-generated power and insisted on generating its own power in a small steam plant. I went in to see Old Man Sy Moore,

301

who had been mayor now for thirty years. He was a powerfully-built man with white hair and heavy jowls. He wore a big black hat, a cheap blue work shirt open at the neck, and a pair o' dollar-ninety-eight cotton britches.

"So yuh're another one o' them Gover'mint men, huh?" he said as he stood behind the counter in his store.

"Yessir," I said. "We'd like to sell Moorestown some good Government electricity."

"Well, yuh can't do it. We've told yuh before we don't want nothin' to do with socialism, and I'm tellin' yuh agin. We make our own power and sell it to ourselves. We don't depend on no big New York corporations, and we don't depend on no Gover'mint. This town's got the best credit in the United States. It pays its bills. It takes care of its people. We just want to be let alone."

"I can understand the way you feel, sir, but how much does it cost you to generate your power in your coal-burning plant?"

"I don't know exactly," he snapped back. "We figger it costs us about four cents a kilowatt, and that's as cheap as anybody on earth can produce it."

"Well, sir, I'm not an engineer, so I don't know anything about production costs. But the TVA will sell Moorestown all the power it can use at a cent-and-a-half a kilowatt. You could save a lot of money in a year. And the TVA will buy your plant at its original cost."

"Yeah, we know what the Gover'mint's tryin' to do. We don't want nothin' to do with yuh. We've still got some idea about how things ought to be run around heah. We'll continue makin' our own power and sellin' it to ourselves. Good day, young fella."

I spent a week in Moorestown and studied all the reasons why Old Man Sy didn't want to have anything

302

to do with the Gover'mint. You can guess most of them.

There were one thousand and three families in Moorestown. The Three families were the Moores, the Thompsons, and the Sloans, and the Thousand families included everybody down to the WPA families who lived in abandoned box cars. The Three families owned the banks and virtually all the business property. The municipal power plant was capitalized at $400,000, and all of these gilt-edged, six per cent bonds were held by the Three families. This gave the Three families a tidy little income of $24,000 every year, and in spite of Old Man Sy's business acumen, he and the city council had neglected to re-finance the power plant at three per cent when the depression made money cheap. They preferred to hold their six per cent bonds, for Six Per Cent is one of the solid old rocks of Americanism.

The municipal power system was operated at a substantial profit to the city every year. This profit was used to help finance the schools and build the streets and pay the police and the firemen. An excellent plan, you might think. Too bad other American cities don't have "good, sound business men" like Old Man Sy to run them. But when you examine the power rate structure, you find the "nigger in the woodpile."

Moorestown had the highest *minimum* power rate in Alabama. The smallest, poorest family had to pay a minimum rate of three dollars a month for lights in a two-room shack. But when a city buys power from TVA, TVA won't allow a higher minimum rate than one dollar a month. So if Moorestown bought power from TVA, Old Man Sy would have to cut the monthly bills of all his poor customers, who couldn't afford appliances, from three dollars a month to one dollar a month. This cut would affect the bills of all the Thousand families, and would mean a saving of thousands of dollars a year to the Thousand families.

303

But there was more to the rate structure. Moorestown had the lowest *industrial* rate in Alabama. The people who paid the minimum rate paid as high as eight cents a kilowatt to burn their lights, but the very few people who could use as much as a thousand kilowatts a month were charged as low as one cent a kilowatt for it. Thus the Widow Lamb, who used only forty kilowatts a month by carefully burning only one small bulb at a time, paid three dollars; while the Moores, the Thompsons, and the Sloans, who used thousands of kilowatts in their stores and gins and filling stations, paid only ten dollars a thousand. But if Moorestown bought power from TVA, the city wouldn't be allowed to make such drastic reductions for quantity use. The Widow Lamb's bill would be cut from three dollars to one dollar, and the Thousand families' bills would be cut proportionately. But the Three families' rate would be raised from ten dollars to twenty dollars a thousand.

I found further that Moorestown had the lowest *ad valorem* city tax rate in Alabama. The city made almost enough out of the sale of its power to pay for the municipal services, so property taxes were ridiculously low. And who paid the low property taxes? Why the Three families, of course, for they owned all the valuable property.

My last interesting discovery concerned the coal which was used to fire the boilers at the city power plant. There was a mine near Moorestown. It was a small "wagon" mine, but it supplied enough coal for Moorestown, and the mine's largest, juiciest contract was with the city power plant. And who owned the mine? The Pioneers had overlooked nothing, for the mine, too, belonged to the Three families.

Thus I had the complete picture before me. The Three families had rigged up an ingenious little system to make the Thousand families pay the freight. I could understand why the Three families considered

304

the sale of power an excellent method for collecting the money to pay for city services. The "city" generated power at a cost of four cents a kilowatt, and much of this "cost" went to pay the Three families $24,000 in interest and a high price for coal. Then the "city" sold the power to the Thousand families at rates ranging up to eight cents a kilowatt, but it sold power to the Three families at a rate of one cent a kilowatt, or much less than the inflated generation "cost." The "city" then took the profits from the power sale and applied them against school and street costs which otherwise would have had to be met with property taxes levied against the Three families.

If Moorestown bought power from TVA, this ingenious little system would be abolished and the process reversed. The city would save the $24,000 interest each year, for TVA would pay off the $400,000 owed to the Three families. The Thousand families would start paying about one-third as much for their electricity, for the city would be required to sell the power under TVA regulations. The Three families would lose their fat coal contract and would also have to start paying twice as much for their "industrial" electricity. And finally, under TVA regulations, the city could make only enough profit on the sale of power to pay distribution costs. Thus the city would have to jump its property taxes many thousands of dollars a year to pay for schools and streets, and most of these taxes would be paid by the Three families.

When I finished gathering all the facts, I went back to see Old Man Sy. I found him out in his mule barn sitting in a trough, with a bunch of his lackeys around him.

"Well, young fella," he said, "We still don't want to buy no Gover'mint power."

"I can understand why you wouldn't," I laughed. "You've got a nice little playhouse rigged up."

He was nettled. "It's better'n anything you socialist

305

boys have got to offer. It's kept this town solid when a lotta others was goin' broke."

"Maybe you're right, sir," I said. "The only trouble is that it's out of date. Before I leave I want to advise you to recognize that you've got to change it. If you don't, it'll have to be changed in spite of you."

He stood up, and I thought for a minute he was going to strike me. I knew how he felt, and I was really sorry for him. I would have liked to have sat down with him and explained to him that the Government had decided that it was no longer proper for communities of men to pay $24,000 a year in interest to one or two or three men. The Government could supply the capital for community projects, and there need be no interest. I would have liked to have explained to him that the day of private worlds was over, and that henceforth communities must be operated for the benefit of the Thousand families and not of the Three. That whereas he and his father had once been Pioneers and Builders, he was now only a Reactionary Boulder in the path of progress. But Old Man Sy would only have boiled over at my explanations and started calling me names.

"We'll fight'cha as long as we got a dollar left," he challenged. "The Gover'mint's got no right to come in here bothering us."

"I'm afraid you'll find that the Government has acquired some new rights you didn't know it had, Mistah Moore," I told him.

We gave Moorestown a Treatment. And during the course of the battle, I had a chance to recognize that Old Orders die very hard and that you can't destroy them by sticking to Marquis of Queensbury rules. For the rules are made by the Old Orders to protect themselves, and during the Battle of Moorestown I found myself conceding for the first time that noble ends sometimes have to be attained by questionable means.

306

We hit Old Man Sy's playhouse with the well-oiled TVA steamroller, and when we had finished, Government electricity was singing through his wires.

Moorestown was the county seat of Webster County. The farmers who filled the stores on Saturday lived out in the county. Until the coming of the TVA most of those farmers had never had any electricity. The few who lived along the main highways were customers of the Alabama Power Company. When the TVA came in, the Alabama Power Company lines were acquired and turned over to the newly-organized Webster County Power Co-operative. Then the REA began lending money to the Co-op to build new lines to carry TVA current to new customers. For five years the Co-op had been growing and building new lines until now there were seventeen hundred Webster County farmers who were members of the Co-op. The TVA substation, which supplied the Co-op, was located just outside the Moorestown city limits.

The Co-ops buy power from TVA on a sliding scale. The more they buy, the cheaper it becomes, so it is to the advantage of every Co-op to get as many customers as it can. This situation gave us all we needed to "crack" Moorestown. Using direct mail and full page newspaper ads and our friends in the other Government farm agencies, we began an education campaign among the farmers of the Webster County Co-op. We told them about Old Man Sy and his set-up. We deliberately precipitated a "class war," an odd thing for a man named Garth to do in America. We told the farmers that Old Man Sy was not a Pioneer or a City Father or a Solid Old Rock in a Storm. We showed them the joker in his kindly paternalism by which he "furnished" them and kept mortgages on their mules and their farms. The Six Per Cent Joker and the Ten Per Cent Joker and the Minimum Rate Joker and the Industrial Rate Joker. And while it all got pretty complicated for farmers to understand, we kept pounding until we showed them the Low Ad Valorem Tax Rate Joker. Then we showed them that while they were now getting TVA current at a low rate, if they could only persuade the Thousand families inside the City of Moorestown to join the Co-op, the rate to everybody would be even further reduced.

The Three families fought as hard as we Garths had fought to save our Island. They fought as hard as "our kind of folks" had fought to pass the anti-sedition bill. They came back at us with the claim that if the "city" lost the revenue from municipal power, the schools would have to close. But we showed the people that the schools wouldn't close, but would be operated on tax money to be paid by the Three families who owned the property in Moorestown. Because the Three families controlled most of the advertising, they were able to cut us out of the only paper in the county, and we had to "waste" Government money on handbills.

Before the New Deal the Three families could have beaten us off, for they would have held mortgages against so many of the farmers that the farmers could not have threatened a boycott. But now the Government agencies held most of the mortgages, and the farmers were free to buy their supplies at other places besides Moorestown. Thus when we finally organized the farmers of the Co-op and showed them how to boycott Moorestown unless Moorestown joined the power Co-op, we had Old Man Sy where the hair was short. He'd either have to give up his municipal power playhouse or stand to lose a great chunk of the farm trade which supported his city.

The Thousand families in the city gained courage from the farmers and began yelling for Government power.

Old Man Sy surrendered when he saw the Government axe over his head. He sent his sons and his attorneys to negotiate with the Government, and the day they came into the TVA office to surrender, I looked at

308

them with some sympathy and understanding. It was an old story to me by then. I had surrendered the Garth World for $220,000. Old Man Sy Moore and his sons came off even better, for the TVA paid them $400,000 for the city steam plant and allowed them to become partners with the Government in the operation of Moorestown.

There is one other little fact that needs to be admitted for the record of the Battle of Moorestown. The TVA paid $400,000 for the city steam plant and power rights in Moorestown, but when we sold the plant to some little town outside the TVA area, we got only $45,000 for it. The Government's profit on power going to Moorestown is very small, and it will be many years before the Government makes back the money spent in "cracking" Moorestown. But the Government must right wrong; it doesn't have to make money.

The Three families got their $400,000 and could begin worrying what to do with it in a world where the Government was drying up the investment pools. They could also worry about their increased property taxes, and where to sell the coal they had been selling to the city. But the Thousand families got lower power rates, more electrical appliances, more Government planning, and a New Deal.

3

In November, 1940, I completed my four-year cycle of change by again voting for Roosevelt. It was hard for me to vote for him. Being a newspaper man and a press agent, I was painfully aware of all the expedient elements in the Roosevelt campaign speeches. I had heard the President "solemnly promising" to reduce Federal expenditures in 1932 while his architects drew plans for big governments and astronomical budgets. I had heard him "solemnly promising" that the "New Deal has been dealt" in 1936, while behind the scenes

309

the Supreme Court fight was being made ready. I could hear him making "solemn promises" to American mothers in 1940 while American seamen were already being sent into waters forbidden by our neutrality laws.

The President's apparent use of subterfuge in his war policy was particularly difficult for me to swallow. By the fall of 1940 I was more war-minded than most Americans, and I approved all the efforts to help Britain; but the President's methods galled me. It seems to me even now that by such methods every man who struggles for sincerity is placed in an impossible dilemma. If you respect such laws as the neutrality law, then you must resent violations. If you approve the actions of the President—and I did—as "necessary in spite of the laws and the people," then you must distrust the judgment of the people. You must admit that the people must have a leader who does, not what the people have ordered done or what he has promised to do, but what is best for the people. Whichever conclusion you choose brings cynicism and despair.

Suppose you decide that this President must be re-elected because he reads the signs in the world aright. He can see that a great war must be fought and that men must die by the millions. But you realize that in order for this President to be re-elected, he must promise the "dear old mothers" that there will be no war for their sons and that their sons will never be sent to foreign soils. What conclusions can you reach —you the man who wants faith? When you are forced to admit that the people cannot be trusted at a crisis, and that noble ends justify ignoble methods?

By November, 1940, I had been forced to concede that desirable ends must be attained through questionable means. Once, when I had passed out money to legislators and written expedient speeches to try to pass an anti-sedition bill, I had suffered violently from my own actions. I had realized how wrong I had been. But now I was using questionable means to

310

"crack" Moorestown. A hired press agent, I was arraying class against class and "wasting Government money" in order to overwhelm the Three Families. Can an injustice only be overthrown by an injustice?

I voted for Roosevelt in 1940 for the further reason that I believed that his defeat would result only in more confusion; and that no good purpose could be served by trying to halt a revolution which was now virtually complete in my part of America.

Since I had "joined the Government" and become a cog in the machine, I was becoming more and more enthusiastic about the New System. You can't be a part of something as vast as the TVA Program and not be impressed with its scope and possibilities. If you have any of the milk of human kindness in you, you can't watch what happens to a Tobacco Road family the first time you turn on the lights in their shack without feeling some emotion. You may doubt the wisdom of bringing the power line to the shack with Government subsidies, but if you are on the spot to see Old Jeeter's eyes pop and his kids dance and clap their hands, you can't doubt that the end has been good. Those young-uns have never brought books home at night because they had only firelight; but now they can bring the free picture books from the consolidated school.

If you live close to Water and Power and Order and Planned Economy, you can't fail to be impressed by your surroundings and by the Great-Good that all-powerful paternalistic government can do. Something happens to the Tobacco Road family after the lights have been turned on; after the government buys the family some land; after the FSA lends it money to pay poll taxes and subscribe to the paper; after the farm agent analyzes the soil and furnishes the correct fertilizer; after the CCC terraces the land to stop erosion; after the Triple-A furnishes money for other crops besides cotton; after the TVA privy expert builds a stream-lined privy with a light in it and brings Old Jeeter

311

and his folks in out of the drafty pine thickets; and after the social workers have taught them how to take sacks and dye the cloth and make red napkins for the table and blue curtains for the windows, and how to knit red-white-and-blue rugs for the floors, and how to dye those flour-sack drawers so that "Angel's Food" and "Grandma's Wonder" no longer shows across the seat. Perhaps Old Jeeter and Maw won't use the napkins, nor will they look at any books under the new lights; but you can hope that the kids will catch on.

Sure, you still recognize all the dangers inherent in this government process. You know where the easy money is coming from. You know that it means a leveling process and that a guy named Lenin called himself "The Great Leveller." You know how Old Jeeter and his folks are going to vote after the FSA pays up the back poll taxes. You can see Old Big Government growing and One Big Party developing. But it all appears so inevitable that you find yourself accepting it as proper. You even find yourself inviting social workers into your new home to drink your whiskey and to rhapsodize over how it is going to be when we've built TVA's all over America and brought New Systems to everybody.

I suppose much depends on where you are sitting when you think about it. If you are in a cocktail bar in New York with solid, successful people, the New Process looks like a lousy process by which some rats are gnawing down the American Structure. But if you are sitting on a rock in a river valley listening to the throbbing of those big, government generators and watching Old Jeeter's kids dance around the lights; and if you are promoting plans for Bigger Governments and Better Worlds, you decide that whatever the cost, materially or otherwise, this is the way it's going to be from now on.

So I voted for Roosevelt in 1940. I'm convinced now that in spite of all the lousy methods and in spite of all his human weaknesses and however painful the process has been to some of us, the President has pointed America in an intelligent and proper direction.

4

Doing pieces for various papers and magazines, I visited most of the Southern Army camps during the months of 1941 when morale was so terribly low, and the only word you thought of when you left a camp was "confusion."

I talked with the Chief Morale Officer of one of the Armies off-the-record over a bottle. "I tell you, Lafavor," he said, "we got to have a propaganda set-up just like Goebbels has. We can't make an army out of these guys we got now unless we can control what they hear and read. Why, goddam, we've got to realize that something has happened to these guys in the last twenty years. These aren't the laughing, cussing, crabbing guys we had in '17. Most of these guys never had a job. Most of 'em come from families that don't own a foot o' land. Plenty of 'em come from WPA and CCC and XYZ. What the hell does America mean to them? And unless we can whip 'em up, how can we ever make fighters out of 'em? We can't do it and let 'em listen to radios and read newspapers. Wheeler and Lindbergh spoutin' off, and what-the-hell and why-the-hell. We've got to have propaganda, so we can tell 'em something and then not let 'em hear anything else. If we don't, we're licked just like the French."

"Maybe we're licked already and just don't know it," I told him. "If we have to resort to damn lies, we may as well call Hitler and tell him to come on over and take charge."

I talked with a major general at one of the camps. "Goddam, Lafavor, there's one thing I can't understand," he said. "We useta build up morale by holding a big review and letting the men parade and the bands play and the flags fly. But what the hell do these guys do now? They gripe like hell every time we take 'em to the parade ground. They call it 'playing Boy Scout for the generals.' They don't give a damn for the flag and music. I can't understand it. You're their age; maybe you can tell me."

"I believe I can," I told him. "The German Army is the best drilled army in the world, isn't it? But were you ever in a theater when they showed a newsreel of the German Army marching and saluting and heiling? What happened? Every young American in the theater laughed like hell. You've got to recognize that you're dealing with fellows who despise armies and regard them as something to be endured. These fellows have been taught to distrust their emotions and to resent appeals to emotion."

I saw the sign in the Louisiana café. "COFFEE—To Decent Folks 5¢; To Soldiers 10¢."

I went inside the café and spoke to the owner. "What'cha got that sign in the window for?" I asked him.

"I gotta protect myself," he replied. "These guys come in the place, muddy up the floor, prop their feet on the chairs, drive customers off, drink one cup o' java, and stay all day. Am I supposed to play nursery to 'em and lose my business?"

"No, I guess not," I said. "But if we lose this war I hope to hell they put you in a concentration camp and make you read that goddam sign a hundred times a day."

A judge told me how he kept his county's volunteer record so high. "Every time a guy gets in jail for anything less than murder," he explained, "we give him a choice of standing trial or enlisting in the army. That kills three birds with one stone. It saves the state money. It provides 'volunteers' for the army. And it fills up our quota so the decent fellows with jobs don't get drafted."

"Yeah," I said, "and most folks down here know you do that, so we can't blame some of them if they lock their doors and refuse to have anything to do with soldiers."

During the summer maneuvers, I ran into a New York outfit the day after the one-vote Congressional decision to extend the term of service. They were a heartsick, disgusted group of men. One sergeant, in particular, had his tail feathers dragging.

"Well, sergeant, where's the war?" I kidded him.

He growled like a bear with sore haunches. "There's gonna be a war all right, buddy. The day my year's up, it's gonna take every goddamed one o' them 204 Congressmen to keep me in here." The sergeant then told me that his sales job, which was paying forty a week when he was called up, was now paying sixty-five. "D'yuh blame me for wantin' to go back?" he asked.

"Why, hell, no," I told him. "But somebody's gonna have to defend the country. We can't all get rich."

"John Lewis's boys are doing all right, aren't they?" he sneered. "And you don't look like you've missed any meals, ridin' around with an officer's car and a chauffeur. Why aren't you doing a little defending?"

"I got a wife to support," I answered.

"Yeah? Well, so have I. And a kid, too. How d'yuh think they're livin' on what's left of my eighty-four bucks after I get robbed on everything from coffee to laundry?"

I drove off. I was sorry for the poor guy.

I ran into one captain who was a state senator before he came to the army. Every night on maneuvers he sent two privates twenty miles in a jeep to get ice for his drinks. After the fellows had marched in the mud all day, they had to spend an hour setting up the captain's "quarters," which included an oversized tent, a mosquito canopy, and an inflated sponge mattress.

315

Then the buckos slept in the mud. A guy like that a captain!

I was at a camp in Georgia the day after Churchill said: "Send us the weapons and we can do the job." That was a bad day in all the camps. "What the hell are we rottin' down here for, if the British need only a few guns? Why aint I workin' in a factory and pulling down some o' that big dough?"

I talked with another morale officer the day after Roosevelt returned from meeting Churchill and assured us that we were no nearer to war. "The A. W. O. L. list went sky-high today," he said. "I don't blame the guys. What the hell, if there aint no war, then what-the-hell they doin' here?"

Several officers confessed to me that they deliberately spread the old Dakar Rumor around the camps. It gave the fellows some reason for sticking it out. They had rather have gone to Dakar or to hell than "rot" in the camps another month.

I remember four disgusted Ohio boys sprawled around a forked stick representing a 105. "When you see the Scoutmaster up the road," one of them yelled, "tell him we're firin' away at the bad old Indians."

I remember the faces of a dozen Wisconsin boys as they stood around the front entrance of a leg show in a two-bit carnival near Camp Shelby. A washed-out wench in faded tights was singing "God Bless America." The fellows were so bored they didn't bother to laugh when she came a cropper on the high notes.

One night I went with a photographer to do a picture story on a bunch of fancy-gowned debutantes going to a camp to dance with the men. I noticed a group of soldiers hanging around outside the hall, neglecting to go in to dance with the Southern beauties.

"Why aren't you guys inside dancing?" I asked them.

"What-the-hell," one of them replied. "Would you like to go to a banquet where they served only appetizers? I'll take a gal who'll get out in the dark with me."

I lounged around a hotel room with a group of flying cadets on a Sunday morning after a violent Saturday night. "Why, hell," a graduate of Colgate University sneered, "even if we went to Europe and licked Hitler, we'd probably have to lick Churchill and his Tories before we could get a decent world."

I listened to Colonel Ben Smithfield explode. He pounded his fist across the table from me and snorted: "The trouble with these fellows is that you damn newspaper guys won't leave them alone. You keep writing a lot of tripe about what we got to fight for. Why, hell, a soldier can't have but one thing to fight for. A soldier fights for something he can see on a map. If you guys'll shut up, we'll give this country something to fight for. We'll whip these guys up just like the Germans are. We'll give them new land and new opportunities to fight for."

"You've shown me one thing we'll *have* to fight for," I told him. "And that'll be to keep you damn professional soldiers from having anything to do with the peace."

I polled a group of twenty-five flying cadets in August, four months before Pearl Harbor. I asked each one of them this question: "If America doesn't enter the war by the time you get your wings, would you like to join the R. A. F.?" The result was a unanimous No. The fellows were willing to fight for America if and when, but not one of them wanted to risk his skin for Britain. And this was after a year of dramatic achievement by the R. A. F. and enlistments by Americans in it; the so few to whom so many owed so much.

Those were terrible months. The Great Storm raged. The lightning split the heavens. The thunder rolled. A Great Voice shouted: "Defend your goal!" And caught in the midst of the storm, we first here and then there, not knowing which goal to defend and lacking

317

the soul-fiber to defend it. In our confusion and despair we could do nothing but attack one another.

5

Driving home from my visits to the Army camps, I always found myself struggling against despair. Because I had been through it all myself; because I had suffered so terribly from cynicism; and because even then I was still confused on many points, I felt that I could understand the poor, bored, disillusioned guys who had been drawn in the draft lottery. The New American soldier was such a tragic figure. The war was catching him with his moral and physical pants down. While we struggled among ourselves to see some sort of vision, the Brute was creeping stealthily up on us. While we fought one another, the black brute of reaction was preparing to spring on us, throw us backward a thousand years and reverse the whole process of human progress.

Less than half of us were physically fit for combat. And those of us who were fit, were they ready to fight for America? Yes, but only if attacked and then with geographical reservations. Were they ready to fight for France and Poland and Britain? Hell, no. They wanted to build another Wall. Did they have any faith, any conviction that poor, stupid, selfish Man was worth saving from the Brute? Very little. Did they have any religion, any burning belief that Man is in the image of God? Some of them. Any cynicism? Yes, the cankerous kind. Any doubts? Yes.

And who did they think the enemy was? Some of them thought Roosevelt was the enemy, just as I had thought in 1937. Hadn't they been told by responsible people that the leader of the Fifth Column in America was the man in the White House? Others pointed to John Lewis as the enemy. Others feared Stalin and the Reds. Wasn't Mr. Dies warning them every week that

318

the Reds were taking over Washington while American soldiers prepared to do battle for democracy? Those who feared Hitler thought of him as a possible future threat who might some day have to be driven from the shores of South America. And what of the Japs? They were contemptible little creatures who wouldn't dare attack us, and if they did, they could be mopped up over a weekend. Weren't American Senators advising the boys that perhaps they needed a week's workout against the contemptible Japs in order to get in shape for the slightly more serious bout with Hitler?

The individual tragedies of the New Army were so real and so close to me. The twenty-five-year-olds who, in another day, would have had homes and children, but who now had known only confusion, the sneer, the what-the-hell, the endless struggle for a new job, and the desperate, frustrated clutches of a girl on the back seat of a second-hand V-8, doubtfully hoping for a square, decent world.

The twenty-three-year-old Harvard graduates who had once taken the Oxford oath, now trying desperately to learn to fly and to feel some thrill of patriotism and to recognize the inevitability of sacrifice.

The twenty-one-year-old WPA-ers from the big Northern cities trying to figure out what there was in America for them to die for.

The twenty-year-old hard-handed, soft-hearted, chauvinistic bumpkins from Old Dixie's eroded acres who, when the flag was unfurled, have an itch to grab a gun, a knife, or a stone, and go hipping-and-hollering and charging up the Ridge.

The twenty-eight-year-old National Guard clerks and salesmen from Pennsylvania and Iowa who had brought their wives with them and now tried to support them on forty bucks a month.

I knew them all—the whole pathetic, confused, feet-out-the-hindgate lot of them—and I felt only despair and sympathy for them. My having come back to the

319

valley; my having built a home; and my having fought for some degree of calm acceptance; all these had helped me to a detached position where I could see the meaning of some of my own experiences and where I thought I could understand the confusion around me. My being close to the New Army saved me from the arrogant over-confidence of many Americans. I could see the disease so plainly. I could watch the victims writhe in pain. I didn't believe that one American soldier was equal to ten Japanese or five Germans, for I could look at an American soldier in bayonet practice and see that there was nothing about his belly to make it more steel-resisting than a German's. I saw a two-hundred-pound Ohio farm boy after a ten-ton tank had passed over him while he was asleep. His magnificent body had crumpled under steel in the same way a Jap's will crumple. I could see that the American soldier had no weapon in his hand, and that his soul-fiber was being attacked by every virus that destroyed France.

Ironically, my being a Southerner saved me from one of the cancerous viruses. I was spared the intense distrust of Britain from which so many Americans suffered. We Southerners remembered that Britain welshed on the war debts and thumbed its nose at Wilson, but, being Southerners, we remembered also that once we fought for a Noble Cause, Britain, using a tactic called "divide and rule," helped us in our war against "some filthy Yankee bastards." It isn't reassuring to admit that at crisis your attitudes can be affected by so remote a circumstance, but apparently this was true in my case. I had great difficulty deciding that America should enter the war, but resentment of the British didn't contribute to my difficulty.

My chief difficulty was my defeatism regarding Europe. Over and over I confronted this hypothesis: Consider poor France. Great, liberty-loving France writhing in the rapacious clutches of the Fascist invader. But suppose today Hitler should withdraw his armies and say to the world: "I am making the grand gesture. I am returning France to her people." What would be the result? Would France then resolve herself into a Great Democracy? I did not know. I had strong doubts.

And what of the rest of Europe?

But when I sat down in the quiet of my own home by the river, I could combat this hopeless line of reasoning by reflecting on what had happened in America. We, too, had fought a terrible Civil War in which all was confusion. The Garths had regarded Appomattox as the end of the world, and Reconstruction as the hell that comes after death. Yet out of all that blood and confusion, something good emerged. It emerged because a man named Abe Lincoln had the guts to fight that war to an end. If he had ever batted an eye; if he had been content to compromise with us Garths; the human march would have stopped and nothing good could have evolved.

Out of all the confusion of the Roosevelt Revolution, I could now see something good evolving. We Garths had had to be kicked around again, and we had had to suffer, but out of it all I could see hope for a revitalized and a better America. Sure, there were still filthy injustices. The Roosevelt Wilsons were still being lynched in Alabama. But wait a minute. The Roosevelt Wilsons had a better chance in Alabama in 1940 than they had had in 1860 or in 1900 or in 1930. And if we could somehow keep ourselves pointed in the same direction we had been going, the Roosevelt Wilsons would have a better chance in Alabama in 1950 than they had in 1941. Confusion didn't matter; fighting among ourselves didn't matter; reshuffling and kicking a few people around didn't matter; if we could only keep the human procession pointed in the right direction.

And the story was the same in Europe. Blood, racialism, wars, intolerance, black, seemingly hopeless confusion. But wait a minute! There were good forces at work in Europe in 1930. There were good forces working in France in 1938. The Jews living in Europe in 1930 were more hopeful than the Jews living in Europe in 1830. Men were working in Europe in 1930 to erase old scars, to bring people of all races together, and to educate the beast out of men.

However cynical you were, you had to recognize that in 1919 there was more hope in the world than there had ever been. There was more reason to believe that Man might some day surmount his confusion and conquer his world and organize it for peace. There was reason to believe in 1919 that wars might some day disappear. Men had conquered plagues; why shouldn't they conquer wars?

In short, in spite of all the confusion, men somehow, perhaps in spite of themselves, were marching forward, slowly but perceptibly, until something happened at some time after 1919. And now there were forces in the world which boasted that they would take whips and set upon the confused human procession and turn it backward and drive it in a single day back over all the blood-soaked ground that had been gained through centuries of heart-crushing, trial-and-error struggle.

If men could somehow stay free to struggle; if they could be allowed a chance to continue fighting to dispel their confusion; then there was hope that the procession could at least take a pain-wracked step forward in the Twentieth Century after Christ. But if men were shackled and denied the right to struggle; if the principle of master-and-slave was re-enthroned; then we free men of the Twentieth Century would be left to face the awful reality that in our lifetimes we not only failed to push the procession forward, but we allowed it to be driven backward.

When Hitler attacked Russia, I was certain the Russian army would collapse in two weeks, and I sup-

322

pose I was momentarily disappointed when it didn't. Then I got lost in a catacomb of reasoning about Russia. I heard Americans say: "Uh-huh, the damn newspapers have been lying to us all these years about Russia. They told us the Russian people didn't like communism and that communism was bad. Well, looks to me like communism's all right. Those people want it, or they wouldn't be putting up such a fight for it." And I heard another American say: "Yeah, they all thought old Stalin was pretty bad when he killed all those folks. But we can see now that he was just weedin' out the damn Fifth Columnists."

I flinched when I heard those statements. I was afraid of Russia. I wanted to see Stalin overthrown. So I joined that group of Americans who read the papers each day and cheered for both Stalin and Hitler, and prayed that they would destroy one another.

Even tonight, when the world is crashing around us and so much seems to depend on the Russian army, I have to admit in honesty that Russian victories give me only a negative thrill. There is something grand about the savage, fatalistic manner in which a Russian dies for his Homeland, but the prospect of a victorious Stalin bestriding Europe and Asia, is not a prospect to inspire hope in the heart of this soldier. Perhaps I should be able to take the Long, Long View and see that something good has come out of Stalinism—that the ends in Russia have been good in spite of the methods—but I'm afraid I can't claim to see that far ahead. For the moment I can only regard Russia as a friend because she is opposing our strongest enemy.

6

The Labor Day week-end was a pleasant one at our house. We had lived in the new house for more than a year, and we had brought order to the little five-acre plot. Raccoon Charley and his wife, Louise, had come to live with Cherry and me. The grass was growing evenly in all the open spots, and the pine trees had been thinned to the proper thickness. Far back of the house was our one agricultural project, a chicken yard where two hundred chickens and fifty turkeys grazed on fresh green rye. On the side of the house overlooking the river we had our garden. There was a furnace and grill which Charley had built; there were rough hickory chairs and benches and stools; and, strung through the pine trees, there were colored lights. There was also a loudspeaker in one tree, connected with the radio and record-player, and at night it was good to sit outside and watch Old Charley's face over the hickory coals as he fried fish or barbecued chicken, and look out over the great expanse of impounded river, and listen to the Moonlight Sonata and Estrellita.

I now had everything in the world a Garth could want, for we Garths are satisfied with what seems so little to many people. All we want is a house by the river, land that is ours, and a glowing fire at night around which we can sit and sing and over which we can toast a fish or barbecue a chicken. Nothing that we want is expensive. We don't want to travel; we want to remain insular and provincial. We don't want fame. We don't want to waste our energies in the hustle of a city street. We don't want to outwit competitors. We don't want wealth, for wealth isn't needed to obtain the things we want. Our women don't want diamonds and mink coats. They want love and order and peace. Land is dirt cheap. The river is full of fish. Chickens are easy to raise. Music can be had for a song. Love is everywhere. And any Garth can make his own whiskey to warm his heart around the fire. The life process, simple and unadorned, is good to us Garths, and every day I spent in my home by the river I realized more how strong is the influence of heredity, and how much like all the other Garths I was becoming.

"Look out there, Bud, and see what you see. The

324

Land and the River. They're all we've got, but they're all we need. For a hundred and fifty years they've been enough for us Garths."

When I sat out under the trees at night, I could hear Old Mis' Ella speaking those words to me. And the Government? Well, the Government had shoved us around and readjusted us, but the Government hadn't really changed us. We had been scattered, but the uncles and aunts and cousins had all managed to get a little plot somewhere within walking distance of the river. Perhaps the Government had only made life easier and more attractive for us. It had given us more money. I now made more money in a year than some of the old Garths had made in a lifetime. The Government had even stocked our river with a new kind of fish that was better than catfish, and anybody who knew how to spit on a hook could catch a dozen in an hour.

The Friday night before Labor Day Cherry and I had no guests, so we sat out in the garden and ate fish with Charley and Louise. I had just returned from Army maneuvers in Louisiana, and for TVA I was helping with the publicity campaign to reduce domestic consumption of power so as to provide more power for the new aluminum plants.

Cherry and I had a policy of never discussing the war after dark. The war belonged with all the terrible things that were happening outside our world, and in our world we wanted only peace and dignity and love and understanding and music and soft, contented laughter. Cherry and I, like all the other Garths before us, wanted only to live and be left alone.

"We-uns 'bout got everything straightened out agin, haven't we, Mistah Garth?" Old Charley commented as he served the toasted croppie. "De Gov'mint kinda shuk us up for a while, but, hell, we Ga'ths know how to git along. Eve'ything allus turns out fo' de best. 'Bout all de Gov'mint did after all was scatter us aroun' and give us them lights an' mo' water an' mo' fish."

"Yeah, Charley, looks like we're doin' all right," I said to him.

We cut off the lights, patriotically, after we had eaten, and Cherry and I sat out in the moonlight for a long time. I always felt so contented and so certain of the eternal goodness of things when I sat with Cherry. Had I really spent two weeks watching confused American boys writhe in confusion and mud, preparing to go somewhere to kill and be killed? Was it true that here in America we were tearing at one another's throats, and somewhere whole races of men were being stood up against walls and shot? I tried to shake off such thoughts, but they seemed to hover over me as though I—just one little confused guy who wanted only a five-acre plot for himself—should attempt to solve all the vexatious problems of the world.

They say only crazy people and preachers "hear voices," but as I sat there by the river it was almost as if I could hear a voice speaking slowly and plainly to me. It said:

"Garth Lafavor, when you first began to think, you thought that America properly belonged to the Garths —to the people who had the git-up-and-git to acquire and build for themselves. And the people who lacked this git-up-and-git were properly dependent on the more fortunate and resourceful. You believed that it was an American's right to build a private domain for himself, and that Government had no right to trespass upon it. This belief, together with the pathetic attachment to the land which you Garths feel, caused you to fight to preserve Garth's Island and the way of life it represented.

"But you can see now that something had happened to make private islands improper in America. The country had become too small and people had become too interdependent. Government had to assume the right to trespass. Government had to assume the right to develop the land and the rivers for the benefit of the

326

Many. Government recognized that the Few are stronger than the Many, so it enlisted on the side of the Many. From now on you Garths will have to be contented with five-acre plots, but you can see that five acres are all a man needs anyhow.

"Then later, in despair, you fought to build a wall around Alabama. To 'defend' Alabama. To 'preserve' Alabama as a state-island in which no man would be allowed to attack private domains. You thought that the way to stop communism was to put communists in jail.

"But you can see now that you were wrong. America has become too small for one state to have a wall around it. Isolation is no longer an intelligent process. Your kind of folks have got to learn to live with and understand New York Jews—and Irish; and New York Jews and Irish have got to learn to live with and understand your kind of folks. Alabama Jews have got to move over and make room for New York Jews, and everybody in the country has to compromise and make concessions and try to understand and try to build a new way of Government-guided life.

"And now look what you are doing. You are making the same mistake in regard to America as you made in regard to Garth's Island and Alabama. America can't build a wall around herself and live apart from the rest of the world. Just as America has become smaller, so has the world become smaller. Before there can be peace and hope in the world, every man and every nation must come forward and restore peace, and then organize the world, not on an island or a state or a national basis, but on a world basis."

And then I'd give the old, universal answer. "But what of me? All I ask is to be let alone. Can I solve the problems of people who live five thousand miles from my door and whose language I can't understand? What is one man in a universe? If the people of France could

327

not solve their own problems, who am I to presume to solve France's problems?"

But the voice came back: "Perhaps the reason the people of France couldn't solve their problems was because they built walls just as you have done. The only hope now lies in the tearing away of all walls and the creating of an ordered world, and this creation can begin only when every little man in every little valley of the world comes forward to establish peace and then to compromise with the mass of men."

"But it will take so long," I contended. "Why can't I live out my little twenty or thirty years in peace? I can't count much in the whole scheme of things?"

"What if it takes a thousand years? Your life will have had purpose if you make your contribution. If you withdraw to your five acres, you will have done no more than a turtle does when he draws up under his shell. Besides, you remember that nigger boy, Roosevelt Wilson? You watched him die, didn't you, while you pretended it was none of your business? But you know now that it was your business, don't you? You might have saved Roosevelt Wilson. But whether Roosevelt Wilson would have been saved or lost wasn't the important thing about that incident. The important thing would have been for you to have *fought* for him. Had you fought for Roosevelt Wilson, you would have gained strength in the fighting, but by pretending you were not concerned, you contributed to your own weakness and cynicism. Men and nations gain strength by fighting for justice and dignity and honor. France would have been saved had Frenchmen been willing to 'die for Danzig;' and you would have saved your own soul from years of cynicism and doubt and despair had you been willing to fight for a nameless black maverick."

I had one more defensive question that I always asked: "But I'm not expected to fight. America has

328

millions of poor chaps who are jobless, or whose scale of living is so low that Army life will be an improvement for them, or who are younger and more adventurous than I am. I support myself and pay taxes and support a wife. If I buy defense stamps and contribute and co-operate and remain calm, surely I will have done my part?"

But there was an answer to that one, too. "In her hour of greatest danger, must America man her battlements only with the poor, confused chaps who have never had a job? Must we send off to die only the farmer lads from the back country who are so uneducated that a drum-beat excites them, and who are so ill-fed and ill-clothed that Army life will be better than they have had at home? Is democracy's battle to be fought by those who have derived the fewest benefits from democracy? If your Army had more men in it who had sacrificed to come there, and who had come there voluntarily for a purpose, your morale problems would be solved."

Saturday and Sunday were gay days for us. Garths, young and old, came to see us, and we rode in the boat and fished and fried fish and swam and sang. Two of my cousins, Wesley and Judson Garth, were leaving for the Army as soon as the crops were gathered, and they had come to talk to me about what kind of outfit to get in. They wanted to know all about the maneuvers and the new weapons and the chances of war, so I talked to them for an hour or so. They were high-school-educated farm boys who had never been outside the valley.

"When do you think we'll get in it, Garth?" Jud asked me.

"I think it'll be about next Spring," I answered.

Every time I was alone that Labor Day week-end, I felt the same oppressive feeling. The "voice" wanted to argue with me some more, and I didn't have any further arguments.

329

Monday morning I got up at sunup, put on a pair of slacks and my fishing hat, and went down to the boathouse. Raccoon Charley was feeding the chickens, and singing at the top of his voice. The old tune *You're As Welcome As The Flowers In May*. I watched him walk around with his face turned up toward the sun, singing in the quiet morning air as though there were no one else in the valley but himself. Charley had no worries. There'd always be a river to fish in, and as long as a Garth lived, Charley would have biskit for breakfast. I cranked the big outboard motor and headed out across the river. I gradually opened the throttle until the cool morning wind was tearing at my shirt front. Across the river on the Morgan County side, I tied up the boat and began walking through the woods and across the fields. When I reached the old cemetery at Gum Springs, I sat down on a rock in the new plot which contained all the old headstones that had been removed from the Island.

Funny, wasn't it, the way we moved those headstones and left the graves behind? And we had the headstones set up just as though the graves were there. The Garths wanted it that way. They wanted to feel that everybody in the family was buried together. I think every Garth wanted to feel that he was buried close to Old Mis' Ella, for she had more strength than any of the rest of us.

I looked at the oldest headstone. Peter Garth. Born December 2, 1747, in County Cork, Ireland. Died January 23, 1825, on Garth's Island, Alabama. For four years with General Marion, at King's Mountain and at Yorktown, he fought gallantly to build a nation where all men can be free.

I looked at another headstone. Capt. Judson Garth. Born June 26, 1840, on Garth's Island, Alabama. Died

September 19, 1863. At the top of the charge at Chickamauga he died gallantly for a Cause he loved.

There were six others who died for that Cause. There was Uncle Sebe. His horse came home all the way from Corinth. And no one was ever allowed to mount that horse again. And there were the others who were with Lee in Virginia. All of them "died gallantly for a Cause he loved." And the Cause was always spelled with a capital "C."

I looked at a third headstone. Pvt. Edward Garth. Born April 13, 1896, on Garth's Island, Alabama. Died October 11, 1918. In the Meuse-Argonne, with Alabama's 167th Infantry, he died gallantly to make the world safe for democracy.

And I looked at a comparatively new headstone. Ella Sparkman Garth. Born August 12, 1838, in Morgan County, Alabama. Died September 12, 1934, on Garth's Island, Alabama. She will live forever in the memories of the Garths who will come after her.

Then I did a very stupid thing for a Phi Beta Kappa and a subscriber to *Esquire* to do in the full light of morning. I wiped the tears out of my eyes. The little yellow men that I meet in the Philippines or the Indies won't have anything on me when it comes to strength derived from ancestor worship. We old-family Southerners derive as much strength from graves as the Japanese do. I tried that morning to figure out how I fitted into the Garth story.

Take Peter Garth, I thought. What did he fight for? He fought for liberty and freedom in the broadest and most literal sense. He fought for freedom to establish a new nation where Garths could be free to own three thousand acres of good land and build a world for themselves. Did he hate anybody? Sure, he hated the British. He hated King George III and he hated the Redcoats and the Hessians. He hated the sight of a king's proclamation nailed to a tree. He hated them all so fiercely and he loved his dream so fiercely that he fought alone. His life meant nothing. Defeat meant nothing. Doubt meant nothing. Hunger and privation meant nothing. He lay behind rocks and killed with hate. And he got what he wanted.

Then take Judson Garth. What did he fight for? What was the Cause he loved so much? Well, in simple words, he didn't like to have filthy Yankee tradesmen try to tell him how to run Garth's Island. He had a way of life that suited the Garths. He didn't want it changed. He wanted to sell his cotton to the British and buy in a free market. He wanted to free his slaves when he got ready to free them. He didn't want a government telling him what he could do and what he couldn't do. So he decided to create a new government to be run by the Garths and "our kind of folks."

But a man named Lincoln had thought that America should be run for the benefit of all Americans rather than for the benefit of the few Garths. So he had sent his millions of tradesmen to kill Judson Garth and sack Garth's Island and burn the houses and steal the gold and the horses. Then Lincoln was shot, and the bastards took over and raped the South. But they couldn't stamp out the Garths, for the Garths are the kind of people who survive. What was it Old Mis' Ella told me? "Don't ever forget you're a Garth, Bud. Whatever they say about us and whatever they do to us, we'll still be livin' and takin' care of our own when all the puny, snivelin' trash of the earth are starvin' to death!"

Yeah, we Garths had a way of surviving. Then take Edward Garth. He had a different angle. He went out to fight for the "world." He died five thousand miles from Garth's Island. He was convinced that he had to go to France to protect Garth's Island. Then after the war, the smart folks proved that he wasn't protecting Garth's Island at all but was protecting the British Empire, so they laughed at him for twenty years for being an ignorant, chauvinistic dope.

332

Now there was another war going on, and I was the Garth who had to make the decision. And it was a tough decision to make, for there were lots of new angles to this war. But there was one thing about the Garths, we always fought and hoped. Peter Garth didn't know what kind of government he would get after he whipped the British, but he had faith that Americans could build a good kind of government and a good kind of country. We Garths had no patience with people who hung on the backing-straps. And we didn't send the Negroes and the pore whites off to do the fighting either. We went ourselves, and the richest and the smartest Garth always led the others into battle. We asked no special favors. We cried when the band played *Dixie,* and we believed that one Garth who knew what he was fighting for was worth ten slaves sent to enslave him.

Well, the other Garths had three thousand acres to fight for. I only have five acres which me-and-the-Government own together. I don't have as much "liberty" or "freedom" as the other Garths had. But I still have the land and the river. I can still say what I please, and when Cherry and I go to bed at night we don't have to worry about a gang of ruffians kicking the door down and pushing us around. I can still work where I please and write what I please. I can still call Roosevelt names if I want to and I can still dislike the appointment of Hugo Black to the Supreme Court. Whatever we've suffered and whatever we fear, America is still free and democratic. Perhaps the terms freedom and democracy will require new definitions, but I can match Peter Garth's faith in believing that we Americans can still build good kind of governments if we have the chance.

I tried to imagine the plight of the epitaph writers if I joined the War of 1942 and died at the top of some charge.

Peter Garth Lafavor. Born November 15, 1913, on

Garth's Island, Alabama. Died March 3, 1942. In the jungles of Java, ten thousand miles from the Tennessee Valley, he died gallantly for . . . well, for a five-acre plot in a government subdivision where he hoped that he and the government could go on trying to bring more light to Jeeter Lester, where he hoped that he and Raccoon Charley could fish again in the river, and he and his wife could sit in the evening under pine trees and listen to the Moonlight Sonata and look out over the river in peace and dignity and safety. He didn't know exactly what form the New World would take, in fact he was badly confused about it, but he fought with the faith that those who came after him would have the strength and the intelligence to build a New America and fit it into a New World in such a way that the folks with the git-up-and-git would be allowed proper recompense, and that the folks without it would at least have biskit-for-breakfast.

I walked back across the fields toward the river. It isn't smart for an intelligent man to admit that he once had to go to a cemetery and conjure up a little emotion in order to help his intelligence make a decision. But when I reached the river that morning I was feeling calm and strong. I opened up the motor and let the boat leap across the Government water, and the wind felt good tearing at my shirt front.

1942

THE NEW YEAR

WELL, IT'S NEARLY MIDNIGHT, and the story is almost finished. One morning last October, a month after my Labor Day visit to the cemetery, I sat on a bench in the Army recruiting office in Birmingham and waited my turn to enlist. Beside me sat my cousins, Judson and Wesley Garth. They had had time to pick most of their cotton, and I had had time to arrange my affairs.

There was no glamour in that recruiting office. Not a flag to be seen. No young debutantes kissing the brave men who were answering the country's call. No *Stars And Stripes Forever* booming out of a juke-box. No smart young officers in well-tailored uniforms clicking heels and saluting. Instead, two old sergeants sat at rough tables, chewed tobacco and spat carelessly at a common cuspidor between them, and methodically interviewed the "men." The "men" were a score of the type of Alabama fellows who enlisted as privates in the Army before Pearl Harbor. They sat on benches around the walls, and there was neither laughter nor enthusiasm.

It wasn't vanity which made me notice that I was the only "college man" in the crowd; that mine was the only white collar; and that all the hands but mine looked as if they had known sharp contact with plow-handles or with CCC or WPA shovels.

I didn't feel heroic as I sat there. To tell you the truth, I was half afraid I was being a damn fool. It was broad daylight then, and I didn't have any emotion to sustain me. I could still hear a voice talking to me, but it was a cold, reasoning voice. It said: "Goddam, if you've got to go through with this rash business, you can at least be smart enough to go on up the hall and get yourself a commission in public relations. This is no place for you. Look around you. This is the place for the poor, untutored fellows who have to do the dirty work. It won't even be patriotic for you to waste your talents digging latrine ditches and wiping grease. Think of all the speeches you can write to stir up the country, and all the fancy propaganda you can turn out for the enlisted men. Think of all the banquets you can attend at Government expense, and the sleek thighs you can contact while you do the samba in the night clubs. Besides, don't kid yourself. You are soft and weak. If you go in this way, you'll die of dysentery or constipation in two months, or pneumonia will get you the first night you sleep on the ground. And you know something about human psychology. You know that the ignorant noncom bastards will try to grind your guts out the minute they suspect that they are inferior to you in any way. And what about your wife and Raccoon Charley and his wife? They could use the money. You are not being smart. You are not being patriotic. You are being a damn fool."

If I hadn't been sitting between my two cousins, I might have walked out that morning and gone on back to the valley. And tonight, instead of celebrating New Year's Eve in this honkytonk, I'd have celebrated it in my home on the river bank in peace and comfort and security. Instead of eating hamburgers, I'd have eaten broiled chicken. And tomorrow, instead of being on

336

my way to a rendezvous with the little yellow men, I'd have continued on my way toward more comfort and security.

I sat there on the bench in the recruiting office for two hours, talking to Jud and Wesley, and the battle that raged inside me then was the toughest one of all. I didn't have anything to help me except those two boys sitting by me and my frail resolution. The battle when I told Cherry goodbye was a hard one, but I had the land and the river around me there. Old Raccoon Charley stood at my side and patted me on the shoulder, and I could look around and see what there was in the world for me to fight for. But sitting there in the recruiting office, I could see nothing but bare walls, and a dirty concrete floor, and poor, ignorant Southern farm boys, and two old sergeants who spat carelessly at a common cuspidor.

When our turn came to be interviewed, the sergeant looked the three of us over and said: "Three brothers, huh?"

"No, suh," I corrected him. "Just cousins."

"Wanna enlist, huh?"

"Yessuh."

"What kinda outfit you wanna get in?"

"We're not too particular," I answered. "Wes here and I want to ride in a jeep and carry tommy guns, and Jud here wants to ride a motorcycle."

He laughed. "Well, that aint askin' too much. Yuh all ready to go today?"

"Yessuh."

"All right," he snapped. "These two boys are farmers, I guess. What are you?"

"I'm a farmer, too," I said.

He shook his head. "You're no farmer. But get in there and get'cha clothes off."

We went in and took off our clothes, and three hours later we were on a bus headed for Louisiana.

There is no need of pretending that my three months in the New Army have been pleasant or helpful or exciting. Or that the prospect of going to the East Indies gives me a thrill of adventure. Or that I am anxious to die for my country. My months in the Army have been lonely and depressing and dirty. All the softening and civilizing influences are taken away from a man when he enters an army, and life seeks its lowest level. You get back close to mud and dirt and dung, and your conversation reflects the retrogression. My heart doesn't leap up when I behold a marching column. There is nothing grand to me about the sight of men who have had to regiment themselves in order to meet an enemy. This war can never be anything but a grim, terrible necessity to me, and I hope that the next generation of Americans will hate armies and will build a world where armies will not be necessary.

I was able to join the New Army eight weeks before Pearl Harbor; I was able to leave my wife and our new home in the valley; I was able to win the battle of the recruiting office; and I have been able to learn how to use a bayonet and a Thompson gun only because I have come to believe from personal experience that men and nations must fight injustice or risk losing their own souls.

I have a selfish reason for being a private in this New Army. There is something I want out of this war, and I want it badly enough to sacrifice for it. I want a new self-respect. When this war is over, I want to know that there is something within me that sets me apart from animals. I want to feel that I am a noble creature, capable of choosing wisely and of making unselfish decisions. I want to feel that an educated man, trained to think, is worthy to be and capable of being master of his own destiny. I want to believe that whenever I am given the choice between complacency and sacrifice, I will never hesitate again.

As I see this war, we Americans who like to believe

338

we are thinking men have a chance to win the world and win our own souls, or else lose the world and lose our own souls. We are standing at the end of an era of debunking. Some of the debunking was good, but we carried it too far. In our efforts to smash false façades, we smashed some of the solid old foundations. We don't really believe that man is a noble creature any more. We are trying to believe it, but there's a long struggle ahead of us. We ourselves have so often turned to selfishness for support that we doubt that any nation or any individual can be motivated by anything else.

Because we distrust ourselves, we distrust everybody else. Because we distrust ourselves, we doubt that man is noble. A man can't believe in democracy unless he respects himself and believes that he can act unselfishly. He can't believe that other men are noble creatures unless he believes that he himself is a noble creature.

I think that we have reached this present crisis in the world because every man and every group and every nation has come to assume that every other man and every other group and every other nation will act only out of selfishness. Hitler has mocked the intelligence of the world and has almost gotten away with it, because he has found people and nations unable to act unselfishly and unable to believe that anyone else can act unselfishly.

Well, how can I begin unraveling all this terrible mass of confusion and finding good and hope in the world again? How can I find calm strength and resolution? As I see it, I have to begin with myself. Before I am fit to fight for decency, I have to do something decent myself. Before I can condemn other persons and other groups for acting selfishly, I have to prove to myself that I can be unselfish. One grand unselfish gesture by a Galilean carpenter was enough to give hope and strength to the world for two thousand years; and it was he who pointed out that the way to save worlds and souls was to be willing to cast them away.

I believe that the immediate future of the world has been laid on the doorstep of the individual American. If the individual American proves equal to the occasion, our century will become one of the glittering centuries of human history.

I believe that Hitler is an effect and not a cause, and I believe that the causes of Hitler can be found within ourselves. This is a war which must be fought within the heart and mind of every man, and within the membership of every pressure group, and within the state houses of every nation, as well as on the battlefields of earth, sea and air. When Hitler and Japan have been defeated, the fighting will only have begun. For this is a war, not only to defeat the immediate enemy who is an effect, but to defeat the causes which lie within our own nation and within our own persons.

I am in this Army because I am searching first within myself for the stuff that will be necessary to build a better nation within a better world. Unless I can find it in myself, I can't hope to find it in others, and I have no right to deplore the selfish actions of other Americans. I have been guilty of most of the sins of my time. Smugness, complacency, provincialism, selfishness, irreligion, sexual casualness, and what-the-hell. And now I am trying to overcome the effect they have had upon me. I am trying to make faith and hope a part of my being. I am coming to believe that in spite of decades of civil wars, there is something great and good and noble in Free China. That in spite of all the bloodiness and blackness of the Stalinist régime, something great and good has been stirring in Russia since 1917. That in spite of all her smug selfishness and all the treaties she has broken, Britain can be a power for good in the New World. That in spite of all the confusion of which I have been a part in America, something good has been emerging. I believe that if I, as an individual

340

American, can prove equal to this challenge, all the forces for good in the world can be marshalled under one banner, and in our own life-times, we can witness a stride forward that will thrill every one of us and make us proud to have belonged to this race of men.

That's why I'm here tonight. That's why I've learned to sleep on the ground and to use a Thompson gun. If we don't win—but, hell, we've got to win. The human phalanx can't have fought its way this far only to be scourged back to a dungeon with whips. Man can't have acquired mastery over the land, the sea, and the air only to allow selfishness and cynicism to canker the soul within him.

I believe we will win. I believe that in spite of all the mud that has been splashed across the stars, the sons of the men who fought at Bunker Hill know that the stars are still there.